The Coach Trip

Morag Clarke

Printed by Createspace, an Amazon.com Company

ISBN – 13: 9781985097315

ISBN – 10: 1985097311

Acknowledgements

Grateful thanks, as always to my lovely writing group friends, Ruth Dugdall, Sophie Green, Liz Ferretti and Jane Bailey, for all their help and inspiration.

Thanks also, to my editor, Doug Watts from JBWB, for his time and effort, and to Margaret Denton for providing the cover design.

Finally, I'd like to thank my family and friends for their patience and encouragement, and to my ever-supportive husband, John Liffen, who helped make this possible.

DEDICATION

To my amazing twin sister, Fiona, without whom I'd only be half the person I am today.

'This one's for you, Sis.'

Chapter One

<u>Before</u>

'It'll be a disaster. You've never got on with Angie and now you're swanning off to France with her. I don't see the point of it, myself.'

'It's only for a week,' Gilly said, struggling to fasten her suitcase. The zip was being stubborn.

In a perfect world Charles would have offered to help her, but he was standing by the window, peering through the blinds.

'Cat's in the flowerbed again. Bloody thing.' He banged on the glass.

Gilly's world was far from perfect. In fact, she could hardly remember a time when it ever had been. She wrenched the recalcitrant zip round the bottom of her case. She couldn't wait to get away.

'Look at it. Staring up as if it owns the place. Clear off!' He flung open the window. 'Go on, clear off.'

'Oh, leave it alone. It's not doing any harm.' She straightened up. She could see the flush of colour creeping up the side of his neck.

'It's digging up the plants, woman. Can't you see?'

She peered reluctantly over his shoulder. Hmm, yes, well that was the trouble with cats. They did like a nicely dug-over flowerbed. Saved them all that hard digging themselves, she supposed. Still, it was a pretty little thing, black and white with a long fluffy tail. She'd always fancied having a cat. Charles, however, had not.

He clapped his hands together loudly.

The cat gave him an imperious stare, before turning and stalking off across the lawn, fluffy tail held erect. Charles attempted to return the stare, but his attempt at glowering like a wildcat only made him look ridiculous.

'I'm going to have a shower,' Gilly said.
She couldn't see why he was getting so worked up. The cat had only dislodged one petunia. It was hardly a disaster. Still, she didn't have much longer to put up with his moods. She'd soon be free of him. Free for a whole, glorious week. It was a delightful and exciting thought.

She lathered her hair under the stream of hot water, feeling the tension ease from her shoulders, to be washed down the plug hole with the foaming suds.

He was right, of course. She'd never been that close to her older sister, but in times of crisis families clung together, and Angie was certainly going through a crisis.

'No one has an affair without good reason,' Charles had said, in his usual pompous tone. 'Simon obviously thought there was something wrong with his marriage.'

'I don't think Angie was at fault.'

'That's a matter of opinion. And why she got you involved, is beyond me. Couldn't she have taken her daughter to France with her?'

'Don't be silly. You know Sarah's pregnant.'

'Conveniently so.'

'Charles! Honestly, you're so insensitive sometimes.'

'Well, don't blame me if it all goes pear-shaped. You were the one that said Angie bossed you about.'

'That was years ago.'

'She hasn't changed. You mark my words. You'll regret this holiday.'

Gilly didn't think she would. In fact, she was rather hoping she'd enjoy herself. It had been years since she'd been abroad. Charles wasn't a fan of foreign travel. Consequently, they'd spent many a rain-swept summer in a cottage in Wales or Yorkshire, or shivering on a blustery Norfolk beach. The chance to tour France and visit the chateaux and gardens of the Loire valley was too good an opportunity to miss.

When Angie had suggested she join her on the coach trip it had come as a bit of a surprise to her. Not least, because her sister was one for sunny beach resorts and lazing by the pool in some exotic location. This sounded more like a cultural trip. Maybe Simon leaving her had changed her outlook on life? Who knows, she thought as she towel-dried her hair. She was just glad of the chance to get away.

'What time's your taxi coming?' Charles said, rapping sharply on the bathroom door.

'In about half an hour. Can you take my case downstairs?'

'I've done it already.'

'Thanks.'

'I presume she's paying for that as well.'

'I hope so,' Gilly lied. She was getting quite good at skirting round the truth. She'd told Charles that Angie was paying for the holiday, reasoning that if he thought it wasn't costing him anything, he'd be happier to let her go. And it had worked. Not that he was happy about it, of course, but he'd grudgingly conceded that she ought to support her sister in her time of need.

6

One thing was for sure, she thought, as she combed through her hair – if she could put up with him for all these years, then she was certain she could put up with Angie for a week.

***

'I still can't believe you're going on holiday with Aunty Gilly,' Sarah said. 'I thought you'd be jetting off to some beach resort with Pauline and Margie as usual.'

'Yes, well, needs must,' Angie said, wandering into the hall, the phone clamped to her ear. Her daughter had rung her just as she was making her final check round to see that all was in order – windows closed and locked, lights on a timer, suitcase by the door, passport, money, credit card and tickets all packed into the pockets of her handbag. 'Apparently, they don't want me to feel like a gooseberry. You know, when their husbands get back from the golf course, and I'm the only one at dinner without a partner.'

Either that, or they felt threatened by her, she thought. Margie said it might be awkward without Simon, but she didn't see how. She didn't mind having a comfy bed to herself whilst they wrestled the sheets from their snoring, probably inebriated and overweight husbands. (She'd been on holiday with Tom and Pete before). And she was quite happy to spend her days lounging on a sunbed with a good book, like they always did. But no – not this year. Possibly not ever again.

'Oh Mum, I'm sure it's not like that.'

'Well, it doesn't matter now. Aunty Gilly is happy to come with me. More than happy, surprisingly.' She didn't add that it had taken very little persuasion on her part, to convince her sister to join her. Gilly had positively leapt at the chance.

'A week in France – oh yes please. That sounds wonderful. I'll go with you.'

She'd never known her sister to show such enthusiasm before – well, not in things that involved her, but she wasn't going to knock it. She would be glad of the company.

'Is Uncle Charles bringing her to your house?'

'No.' Angie gave a small shudder. She couldn't face her brother-in-law first thing in the morning. Or at any other time, really. Not with his all-knowing, sanctimonious smile and his pitying, 'How are you managing, Angie?' when she knew he didn't care one way or the other. 'I'm meeting her at the pick-up point at the bus station. I'm getting a taxi there,' she added, glancing at her watch. The expensive gold watch Simon had bought her for their wedding anniversary. She would have flung it back at him in disgust, if she hadn't liked it so much.

7

She swallowed hard, trying to keep the emotion out of her voice. 'I've left the hotel address on a bit of paper on the hall table. You shouldn't need it,' she added. 'I'll have my phone on me, so you can ring if there's any developments.'

'Mum, I've still got two months to go.'

'I know.'

'And the midwife says everything's fine.'

'Good, good.'

But life could be unpredictable, she thought. Things happened. Things you couldn't possibly anticipate or expect. Like her husband leaving her so soon after their silver wedding celebrations. She wandered back into the lounge, her gaze resting on the framed photograph on the mantelpiece, taken on the day of their anniversary. Simon, in his new suit, stomach tucked in, shoulders back, the faintest hint of a smile on his lips, and her in that dress from Fenwicks that had cost her a small fortune and now, she concluded, made her look fat.

Angie felt her eyes fill with tears. 'I've got to go, darling. The taxi'll be here in a minute.'

'Sorry, yes, I won't keep you, but Mum...'

'What?'

'Try not to fall out with her.'

'With Aunty Gilly? Don't be daft. Why would I do that?'

'Because you always do,' Sarah said, chuckling. 'You know you do, and it's her holiday as well. Just saying.'

'Bye, darling.' Angie swallowed hard and rubbed her eyes with the back of her hand.

How ridiculous. She wasn't going to fall out with her sister. She might find her annoying at times, and a bit of an old fusspot, but that didn't mean to say they couldn't get on, at least for a few days. The way her luck was going, she needed all the friends she could get.

***

Carl Goodman wrestled through the folds of his Dalek duvet cover to get to the alarm clock, his arm flailing wildly as he groped in the dark.

His fingers found the switch, silencing the shrill beeping before it woke the neighbours. Five o'clock – what sort of ungodly hour was that?

He blinked, yawned, and then stretched, before tossing the covers to one side and padding barefoot and naked to the bathroom.

The stark brightness of the fluorescent shaving light above the mirror made him screw his eyes up. He bent his head under the tap and swilled a mouthful of cold water round his teeth, before spitting it

into the plughole, and straightening up. His bleary-eyed reflection stared back at him – remnants of last night's beer and cigarettes were etched into the dark shadows under his eyes. He should never have had that last pint with Jason, let alone the couple of shots for the road. He rubbed his fingers over the growth of stubble on his chin.
The sudden knock on the bathroom door made him jump.

'Do you want a cup of tea, Carl?'

'Yeah, thanks.'

He might have known she would be up first. The old dear had probably been awake half the night. She was so excited about this coach trip and the fact that he was taking her away in the first place. He could hardly believe it himself. Needs must, he thought, bending over to splash water on his face.

'Gran – have you got any aspirin?'

'In the bathroom cupboard,' came the reply.

He swallowed a couple with a mouthful of cold water, straightened up and stared at his reflection again. He'd had his hair cut short to match the photo in his passport. He didn't want anyone questioning his appearance. Not on this trip.

He shaved quickly, splashing aftershave on his chin and wincing as it stung his skin. He'd buy some new stuff in France, something a bit more special.

'You out the bathroom yet, Carl?'

'Yeah – nearly finished.'

He brushed his teeth and swirled his mouth with mouthwash but it still did nothing to improve the foul taste in the back of his throat. It was his own fault. He should have known better than to get drunk, especially when he was going on a ferry crossing.

Frowning, he wrapped a towel round his middle and wandered back into the bedroom. She had left the mug on his bedside table, next to the ashtray of discarded butt ends.
The room hadn't changed much in the twenty-odd years since he'd last stayed with her. It was just how he remembered it – the same blue and green wallpaper, the chipped white melamine wardrobes with the mirrored door; even the same rag rug in front of the dressing table. You'd think she'd have had the place decorated, but he supposed there was no need if no one ever stayed there.

He took a mouthful of tea. It was warm and sweet. He didn't have the stomach for it. Instead, he lit a roll-up and wandered over to the window.

Outside, it was starting to get light. He pulled the curtains and lifted the nets. The street was jammed with parked cars and vans. A lone milk float trundled down the centre of the road. It didn't stop

9

much. He doubted there was much call for doorstep deliveries. Not these days, when it was cheaper to get milk from the shops. It was just old people, like his gran, who kept them in business.

'You want a cooked breakfast, Carl?' she shouted, her voice carrying up the stairs. 'I got bacon.'

'No, thanks.'

'Toast, then?'

'No, nothing.' He opened the window a fraction and tossed the dog-end out.

'You got to eat something.'

'Nah. I don't usually bother. Not first thing.'

His black jeans were draped over a chair beside the bed. He pulled them on and reached for a white T-shirt – a clean one – from the pile in his holdall.

'You sure?'

'Yeah.'

He stuffed his dirty laundry into a plastic bag and tucked it under the bed. Picking up his holdall and suitcase, he headed for the stairs. He needed a coffee – a strong, black one, preferably.

His gran stood by the sink in a faded, pink dressing gown, her feet in fur-edged slippers, and her hair in rollers, clutching a half-drunk mug of tea.

'You look nice,' she said.

He managed to smile, knowing he couldn't quite say the same thing to her. 'Thanks.'

'I've just got me hair and make-up to do,' she said. 'I won't be long.' She giggled as she headed for the stairs. 'Oh, Carl, I can't quite believe it. France – we're going to France!'

'Yep, we certainly are.' He switched the kettle on.

'Look at the time. I've got to get ready. The taxi'll be here in half an hour. Can you bring my case down for me, love? It's all packed and ready to go.'

'Yep.'

He scrolled down the screen of his phone as he spoke. He had one new message. Jason – it had to be. Carl grinned as he read, 'Bon voyage – and happy hunting. Looking forward to seeing some choice souvenirs.'

'You and me both,' Carl texted back. He still couldn't believe he was going ahead with it. He was actually taking his gran on holiday on the basis of a drunken comment at a stag do.

'No one searches the coaches,' Wayne told him. 'I swear to God, they wave them through without a second glance. Why waste time with a load of old pensioners, when they've got illegals and all sorts

10

trying to get through Calais. If you want to bring something back,' he added, 'you get yourself on one of them coach tours. All you need is an excuse to be on one.'

And what better excuse could he have than a holiday with his gran?

'Well?' she said, pirouetting girlishly at the top of the stairs. 'What do you think?'

Carl took in the lurid pink blouse and floral skirt with matching blue sandals in his stride. 'Nice,' he said. 'Very summery.' He was relieved to see she had taken her rollers out, but there was something almost helmet-like about the way she had stiffened her curls with copious amounts of hairspray.

'And I've got me cardi, in case it's chilly on the boat.' She waltzed down the steps as if she was making an entrance at the Oscars. 'So, that's us ready. Just got to wait for the cab now. Oh, and if anything happens,' she added, 'my lottery tickets are under the biscuit tin in the pantry.'

'What do you mean, if anything happens?' he said. 'It's France we're going to, not Outer Mongolia.'

Well, you never know. You can't be too careful.'

Carl dumped his holdall and suitcase next to his gran's, by the front door, and pulled on his leather jacket.

'I've made us some egg sandwiches for the coach. You always liked egg sandwiches when you were little.'

'Yeah, I'm not so keen on them these days.'

'Oh well.' His gran beamed at him. 'We can always feed the seagulls with them. Ooh look, there's the taxi.' She dropped the net curtain she had been peering round and slung her handbag over one shoulder. 'Grab my case, dear. It's time to go.'

Carl checked his pockets one more time – passports, wallet, phone, keys and the envelope containing details of the coach trip and itinerary for the week ahead – the Loire valley and Paris in all its glory. He could hardly wait. His future depended on it.

Chapter Two

The Trip

'It's Bay Fifteen', Gilly said, waving a sheet of paper under her older sister's nose. 'It says so here.'

'I don't care what bay it is,' Angie said. 'I just wish they'd hurry up.'

They were sitting in the cafeteria of the interchange area attached to the motorway services, while their cases were transported to their tour coach.

'I mean, it's not exactly a good start to the holiday. Two hours in a stuffy minibus picking up all and sundry from what seems like every village in East Anglia and then being dumped here while they sort out what coach we're going on. At least at the airport they have shops and things to browse round.'

'There's a newsagents over there,' Gilly said.

'So there is.' Angie studied her perfectly manicured fingernails as she spoke. A newsagents selling *Knitting Weekly*, or *Gardeners' World*, or whatever other magazine would cater for the hordes of pensioners currently wandering round the place. No wonder Pauline and Margie at work had raised their eyebrows when she told them she was going on a coach trip to the south of France. She'd wanted something cheap and simple for her first holiday without Simon. The promise of a home pick-up had swayed it for her. No airport parking, no man-handling of heavy luggage. She could just sit back, relax, and let the tour company take charge of everything.

It wasn't exactly what she had envisaged, she thought, watching an elderly man with a Zimmer frame clump his way past their table.

'I'll get us a couple of magazines,' Gilly said, draining the last of her coffee from the paper cup. 'Watch my stuff.' She plonked her large shoulder bag on the table and took out her purse. 'Won't be a moment.'

Angie looked at her sister's bulging bag with a kind of detached curiosity. Gilly was not a seasoned traveller, but she had apparently packed everything for every eventuality. Sun-cream, umbrella, travel sickness pills, wet wipes, water, a battery-operated fan, boiled sweets, and that was only the things she could see. Goodness knows what she had stashed away in the pockets and zippers. She'd have to have words with her about travelling light. She'd do her back in lugging this thing around with her all day.

'I bought us a travel guide,' Gilly said, coming back and brandishing a pocket-sized booklet at her. 'The Loire valley. It's got everything in it, including a map.'

Angie smiled. 'You're really excited about this, aren't you?'

'Ecstatic. Honestly, sis, you've no idea.' She glanced at her watch. 'It won't be much longer, will it? I mean, I've still got time to go to the loo.'

'Yes, you've got time to go to the loo. They haven't called our number yet.'

The tannoy had announced departures to the Black Forest, Italy and the Isle of Wight and groups of people were making their way to the exit. Angie caught sight of a young man in jeans and a red T-shirt, with a backpack slung over one shoulder and idly wondered if it was too late to change their booking. The Italian Riviera was looking favourable. Then she saw him link arms with a blonde-haired woman in a skimpy floral sundress and she looked away. He was too young anyway. She was after someone interesting and mature, and preferably loaded. She had a certain lifestyle to adhere to – one that her impending divorce would certainly curtail. In the meantime, she was making full use of her joint credit card. An oversight on Simon's part, but she wasn't going to let that trouble her. She deserved a holiday after all he'd put her through and he was jolly well going to pay for it.

'I'll be as quick as I can,' Gilly said, 'unless there's a queue.'

'Go for it,' Angie said, her attention momentarily distracted by the sight of a man in a leather jacket and black jeans. His hair was shaved short and he had a pair of sunglasses tucked into the neck of his top. He was sitting at a table drinking from a can of Coke. Interesting, she thought. Not too young, but not too old either. Maybe in his late thirties or early forties. He was on his own, but there was a large plastic shopping bag on the seat next to him. A black holdall was on the floor at his feet.

Angie put on her glasses and stared at the tag hanging from the strap of his holdall. It was difficult to see, but she was pretty sure – no, certain – that it had the number 15 on it. The very same number as the tag attached to Gilly's shoulder bag.

She made a show of fumbling in her handbag, as she caught him looking in her direction, and hoped he hadn't noticed her staring at him.

'Excuse me, but is this seat taken?'

A wispy haired man in beige pleated shorts and a checked shirt was standing right in front of her, blocking her view. He had a glob of spittle in the corner of his mouth, gold-rimmed glasses, white socks and sandals. Angie took it all in, in one withering glance.

'Yes,' she said.

'Oh.' He looked disappointed. More so, when an old man with a tweed blazer and brown trousers hobbled past him and lowered himself onto Gilly's vacant chair.

'There you are,' the old man said, smiling happily.

'Indeed,' Angie said, deciding he was the lesser of two evils. She smiled back at him as she reached for her mobile phone. It was time she sent Simon a message. She wanted him to know just how much she was enjoying herself, even if she wasn't. And besides, he needed a reminder to feed the cat. Driving across town twice a day would no doubt mess up his rampant social life but, as far as she was concerned, it was the very least he could do.

***

Gilly could hardly contain her excitement as she waited in the queue for the loo. With several coach departures imminent, it was inevitable that there'd be a bit of a delay, but she wasn't going to let a little thing like that spoil her day. She was going on holiday alone – well, without Charles, anyway. Once she was seated on their tour coach she could start to believe it was really going to happen. Lately he'd been getting on her nerves. Well, for months, really, if she was honest. When Angie had suggested she go on holiday with her, she'd jumped at the chance. A break would do them both good. Didn't they say absence made the heart grow fonder? Or was it out of sight, out of mind?

'Typical, isn't it? There's always a bleeding queue,' muttered the elderly woman standing next to her. She had a pronounced London accent.

Gilly glanced sideways and acknowledged her with a shy smile. 'I think everyone's got the same idea.'

'Just hope they don't call our number while we're waiting.' The queue shuffled forwards.

'I hope not.' Gilly hadn't thought of that. Now she could think of nothing else. It would be awful if the coach went without her. What if it wouldn't wait? They had a ferry to catch. Oh God, maybe she didn't need to go to the loo after all. Except that she did. She should never have had that second cup of coffee. She sidestepped round the hand drier. She was nearly at the front now.

'Where are you going?' the woman asked her.

'What? Oh. France - the Loire valley. It's the chateaux and gardens trip.'

'Really?' The woman beamed at her. 'That's where I'm going. Ooh, isn't that funny. We must be on the same coach.'

'Right.' Gilly nodded, suddenly heartened by the fact that she wasn't the only one from their tour stuck in the queue for the toilet. The two of them shuffled forwards.

The woman tilted a conspiratorial head towards her. 'I'm with my grandson, Carl.' She gave a strange high-pitched giggle. 'He's treating me to this holiday.'

'That's kind of him.'

'It is, isn't it? Mind you, I don't know what's come over him. I think he must have had a little flutter on the horses, because he even paid for my passport, and that wasn't cheap. Still, I always tell people he's a good lad at heart, because he is, really, despite everything.' Again, there was this girlish giggle. 'I'm Barbara,' she added.

'Gillian – well, Gilly, really. No one calls me Gillian any more.' She was struggling to keep a straight face. The woman's laugh was infectious. 'Oh – that one's free,' she said, pointing to a newly vacated cubicle. 'Your turn, I think.'

'Thanks, love.'

She popped into the next available cubicle, conscious of the fact that time was ticking by and Angie would be wondering where she had got to. Still, at least there hadn't been any further announcements of coach departures.

She washed her hands quickly and thoroughly under the hot running water. The elderly lady with the funny laugh was either still in the loo, or she had gone. Probably still in the loo, she thought. It would be interesting to see what the rest of the passengers were like, including the woman's grandson, Carl. She had the sneakiest feeling that Angie had been hoping for a younger crowd on the coach. Hence the new haircut, manicure and expensive outfit. She was dressed to impress, whereas Gilly had gone for something more casual – easy-fitting trousers and a nice blouse. It was always better to be comfortable, she thought. Besides, she wasn't out to attract anyone. She still had a husband, though she couldn't help admitting she was looking forward to being shot of him for a few days.

She'd told Charles that Angie was paying for the holiday because he'd never have agreed to let her go if she hadn't. No way was she telling him that it was coming out of her own precious savings – the money she'd steadily accumulated over the years and secreted away into her own private bank account. It was her emergency fund. She'd once read in a magazine that all women should have one and it had seemed like a sensible idea at the time.

The guilt she felt at deceiving him was tempered by the knowledge that she had stocked the freezer with an assortment of pre-cooked and ready-prepared meals for him, and that he was perfectly capable of surviving for a week without being waited on hand and foot. He probably wouldn't use any of them, though. He'd eat out just to spite her.

His loss, she thought, glancing at her reflection in the steamed-up mirror and wondering if she had time to touch up her lipstick.

'There's no loo roll,' Barbara said, coming to stand at the adjacent wash-basin. 'But I had a few tissues in me pocket. Have they called our number yet?'

'No, I don't think so.'

'That's good, then.' She held her hands under the cold tap. 'Would you credit it? No bleeding soap, either.'

'There's some in this one,' Gilly said, moving quickly to one side. She didn't like swearing. It unnerved her. And a woman swearing - particularly an older woman – well, it just didn't sound right, not from a granny, and Barbara had told her she was travelling with her grandson, so she was definitely a granny.

The lipstick would have to wait, she thought. She needed to get back to Angie.

***

In the cafeteria, Carl Goodman drained the can of Coke, wiped his lips with the back of his hand, and burped loudly. He had a hangover and was hoping the caffeine in the Coke might help. Instead, it was making him feel queasy. He belched again. Motorway service stations were not high on his list of places to see. He likened them to a pit stop on the Formula One racing circuit. A place for refuelling and moving on as quickly as possible. They weren't places he wanted to linger in, so having to wait for over an hour at the coach interchange was not the best start to the holiday. It was making him tetchy. But it was a means to an end, he told himself.

He watched with a kind of detached interest, as another coach pulled up and disgorged its stream of elderly passengers. Some clutching bags, others with walking sticks and rucksacks, and all of them with the same distracted and disorientated glaze as they made their way across the concourse to the lounge area. It was like being in a waiting room full of the living dead. And talking of living dead. He drummed his fingers on the table as he waited for his gran to come back from the toilets. Where on earth was she? She'd been gone ages. He was bored waiting and he wanted to slip out for a cigarette, but he didn't fancy carting her raincoat and plastic shopping to bag with him, complete with egg sandwiches that were starting to smell. He crushed the can in his fist, squeezing the middle and then folding the ends in. As he squashed it flat, a sticky pool of brown liquid trickled onto the Formica tabletop. He glanced around, looking for a paper napkin to mop it up with, but couldn't see any. All he could find in the pockets of his leather jacket was an old till receipt, which didn't want to absorb the spilt Coke, no matter how hard he dabbed at it. In the end, he gave up and turned to watch the coaches moving into position in their allotted parking bays. It was like a production line, he thought, the way everyone was shepherded into waiting areas, and then moved on, in a slow walking convoy, to the correct transport for their destination. Hopefully the correct luggage found its way onto the right coach. The men in fluorescent orange jackets seemed to be doing a good job at transporting the cases. He tried to remember if his gran had attached the luggage labels, and when he couldn't recall seeing them, spent the next few minutes scanning the trolleys from the cafeteria for any sign of their suitcases. He'd have to make sure they had the right labels for the return trip. He couldn't take any chances with luggage going astray on the journey home.

Carl dribbled a sachet of sugar into the spilt Coke, and watched it dissolve. He was starting to feel agitated. Where was the old dear? Surely she hadn't taken ill or something just as they were about to get going? That would be about right, knowing his luck.
He eventually caught sight of her making her way, like a blinkered owl, across the crowded foyer. She was with an older woman with snowy white hair.
'Gran – over here,' he called, raising his hand and giving her a wave.
She paused to say something to the woman, then patted her gently on the arm and pointed in his direction.
'Couldn't see you, for a moment,' she said, hurrying over. 'Thought you'd gone. That lady's lost her husband,' she added. She plonked herself down in the adjacent seat, the sleeve of her cardigan resting in the sticky brown mixture on the table. 'I told her he'd be somewhere about. You can't really get lost in a place like this.' She fumbled in her handbag and pulled out a folded piece of paper. 'What Bay does it say we have to go to?' She gave him the letter. 'I haven't got me reading glasses on.'
'Fifteen,'he said, giving it a cursory glance. He stood up. 'I'm going outside for a fag.'

'Wait a minute.' She stuffed the paper back into her handbag. The brown stain smeared the sleeve of her cream cardigan from wrist to elbow. 'I'll come with you.'

'Better wipe that off first,' he said, pointing.

'Oh, heck!' She examined the offending stain with a sigh. 'Now how did that happen?' She dabbed at it with a paper tissue.

Carl picked up his leather jacket and tossed his holdall over one shoulder.

'You could wait.'

'It's too hot, and those sandwiches are starting to smell. What took you so long, anyway?'

'There was a queue.' His gran peered into her plastic shopping bag and sniffed. 'They're all right. Sure you don't want one?'

'Positive. Gran, don't do that here.' Too late, she was happily unwrapping the foil parcels. The pungent aroma of eggs was not helping Carl's hangover. He swallowed hard. 'I'll wait for you outside,' he said.

***

'*Would all passengers for the Loire valley please go to Bay Fifteen,*' came the announcement over the tannoy. '*I repeat, Bay Fifteen for the Loire valley tour.*'

'That's us!' Gilly said breathlessly, as she hurried over to the cafeteria, where Angie was still waiting. 'We need to go,' she added, snatching up her jacket and tossing it over her arm.

She paused for a moment to stare at the old man who had taken her seat while she had been away. He was smiling happily up at her as if she was some long lost relative.

'Hello, dear.'

'Hello.' She glanced quizzically at her sister. 'Who's he?' she mouthed.

Angie shrugged.

'I like your hair, dear,' he said.

He was still beaming at her. Automatically, Gilly's hand went to her chin length bob. 'Thank you,' she said.

She picked up her shoulder bag, which was crammed with the things she thought she might need for the journey but would probably never use.

'Angie,' she said, 'we need to go.'

'Yes. I know. I won't be a minute.'

That was debateable, Gilly thought. Her sister was pre-occupied with her mobile phone and making no effort to move.

The elderly gentleman, however, in his tweed jacket, cream slacks and patterned cravat, was more than ready to go. He struggled to his feet and leaned heavily on his walking stick. 'Could you take my arm, dear?' he said.

'Well, I could,' she said, falteringly, as she glanced round the crowded hall. 'But aren't you with somebody. Angie!' she hissed, from the corner of her mouth. Her sister was being infuriating with her lack of action or interest. 'Help me.'

Angie closed her phone and put it in her bag. 'He's obviously confusing you with someone else,' she said.

'You don't say.'

The man had started to wander towards the door. He seemed to be managing perfectly well on his own, but Gilly wondered if she should follow him. Just as she was considering doing so, she saw a little woman with snow-white hair hurry towards him and take his arm. He gave her the same beaming smile he had given her.

'That must be his wife,' she said.

'Let's hope so.'

'Do you think they're on our coach?'

'Hmm, yes, I think so,' Angie said. Her phone beeped, and she grabbed it from her bag and began scrolling through the message on the screen.

Gilly frowned and looked at her watch. It wasn't that she was anxious or anything – all right, she was, but she wasn't going to admit it to Angie. It's just that she didn't see the point of hanging around and being late. Punctuality was her speciality. She doubted if she'd ever been late for anything in her entire life.

She glanced anxiously at the steady surge of passengers streaming for the exit. The waiting area was looking decidedly empty. A pink-cheeked waitress, her greasy hair scraped back in a pony-tail, was gathering up mountains of discarded napkins, cans, paper cups and wooden spoons, and heaping them together on a plastic tray. Gilly sighed – loudly.

Angie snapped her phone shut and slipped it into the side pocket of her leather designer handbag. 'Honestly, Gilly, I don't know why you're in such a rush.'

'Because they've called our number.'

'Yes, and? They won't go without us. They know we're here.'

'*Ladies and Gentlemen – this is the final call for the Loire Valley tour. Would all passengers please go to Bay Fifteen...?*'

Thank God for that, Gilly thought, as her sister finally stood up.

'Want me to carry your bag?'

19

'No, thanks. I can manage. I'm just going to nip to the loo. The queue will have gone by now.'

'What? What?' Gilly gaped at her in disbelief. 'Do you have to? There'll be a toilet on the coach.'

Angie gave her a condescending smile.

'Oh, for goodness sake! Well, don't be long, will you.' She glanced at the last few stragglers making for the door. 'I'll wait for you outside.'

A damp, misty drizzle stung her cheeks as she hurried towards the coach bay. Most of the passengers were already on board. The suitcases had been loaded. Only a shaven-headed man in a leather jacket stood loitering by the side of the coach, a mobile phone clamped to his ear. He had an angry look about him that made Gilly feel slightly uneasy. She hovered in the background, not wanting to eavesdrop, but he was shouting so loud it was hard not to.

'I'm being serious. I'm going to sort it out. I told you, it's all in hand.'

'Carl. Do you want the window seat?''

Barbara was leaning out of the coach door, trying to catch his attention. So, this was her grandson, Gilly thought. He was waving her away with an irritated flick of his hand. The old woman hesitated, obviously unsure what to do. She glanced up, saw Gilly looking at her, and smiled. 'Oh, hello. Did you want to get past?'

'No, I'm fine. I just need to…er…make a quick phone call, first,' she said. She wasn't sure why she said that, but it seemed to make sense. She'd call Charles – let him know they were safely at the interchange. She had been going to ring him when they got to their hotel in France, but she might as well keep him up to speed with what was happening. He'd only complain about it if she didn't. She found her mobile and pressed home.

'Yes?' came her husband's curt response.

'Oh.' She hadn't expected him to answer so quickly. 'Hello. It's me.'

'I gathered that.'

'We're at the interchange.'

'Uh-Huh – and still speaking to each other?'

'Yes. Yes,' Gilly answered, with a lot more conviction than she actually felt. 'We're getting on fine. We're just about to get on the tour coach now.'

'Coach load of geriatrics, is it?'

'Hmm - probably. I haven't looked.'

She did now, though – scanning the nearest windows. There seemed to be a plethora of grey heads amongst the passengers – most of them female. All of a sudden, she didn't feel quite so dowdy or middle-aged. In fact, she felt positively youthful.

'You could be right,' she said.

'Angie won't like that.'

'Angie's the one who booked it,' she reminded him. 'Anyway, I'd better go.' Out of the corner of her eye, she could see her sister making her way across the forecourt, teetering on heels that were totally unsuitable for walking in. What on earth was she thinking of, wearing those, she wondered? 'I'll call you when we get to the hotel,' she added.

'I wouldn't bother – I'm going out.'

Oh. Well, I'll try tomorrow, then.'

'If you're not too busy.'

'Likewise,' she said crisply. He was sulking. She could tell by his voice. Sulking and feeling threatened – by a coach load of geriatrics, of all things. God give her strength. She switched off the phone and replaced it in her handbag.

'Is this it?' Angie asked, strolling up to her and glancing at the open door.

Gilly nodded, relieved to see that Barbara had resumed her seat and was no longer loitering halfway down the aisle. Her grandson, it seemed, had opted for the window seat. She could see him half slouched against the pane, dark glasses over his eyes.

'Right. Well, what are we waiting for?'

Gilly held her tongue and refrained from saying 'you', as she followed her sister up the steps and onto the coach.

Chapter Three

The coach driver – a man in his forties, Gilly thought, with thinning brown hair and a sun-tanned face, glanced up from perusing the list of names fastened to his clipboard and gave them a welcoming smile. 'You must be Mrs Turner and Mrs Bennett,' he said.

'Actually, it's Ms Turner,' Angie said, and there was something poignant about the way she said it. Gilly knew it wasn't easy for her, coming to terms with the fact that her husband had betrayed her. Despite her outward show of confidence, she knew her sister had been heartbroken, and indeed, still was, though she tried not to show it. Maybe that was why she was wearing such ridiculously high heels and a tight, low-cut blouse. Power dressing, Charles would call it, or 'mutton dressed as lamb', if he was feeling less charitable.

'Ms Turner,' he repeated, scribbling something on his sheet. 'Seats Two A and Two 2 B – the empty ones,' he added, jerking his thumb over his shoulder and grinning at Gilly, who was, by now, blushing profusely.

'Are you a Ms as well?'

'Mrs,' she said, blushing even more. She was patently aware that everyone on the coach was staring at them.

'Mrs Bennett.' He ticked her name off the sheet. 'Right. Well, I'm Dave. I'll give you a moment to stow your stuff in the overhead locker before I do a head count, and then we can get going.'

They were the last ones to board. How embarrassing. Gilly stuffed her jacket in the locker and hurriedly sat down next to the window. She had managed a smile and a nod at the sea of faces staring back at her from the length and breadth of the coach, but that was about all. Not so her sister, who was grinning and uttering cheery 'Good morning' and 'Lovely day, isn't it?' to everyone who caught her eye.

'Isn't this exciting?' Angie said, finally flopping down into the seat next to her. 'They look a nice crowd – a tad elderly, admittedly, but I'm sure we'll have a lot of fun.'

Gilly couldn't trust herself to speak. She was mortified. She hated being the centre of attention – and by being the last ones on the coach, they were the certainly that. She hadn't been mistaken in hearing at least one person mutter, 'There's always someone who's late – always.'

She was saved from any further embarrassment by the driver's announcement that they were now ready to leave.

'It'll take us a couple of hours to get to Dover,' he said. 'Once we're in France I'll run through the first stage of our itinerary. In the meantime, I'd just like to welcome you aboard. My name's Dave Saunders and I shall be your driver for the duration of your holiday. Any questions or problems, please don't hesitate to come and see me. I can't promise to answer everything, but I'll do my best.'

'He seems nice enough,' Angie said, a bit too loudly for Gilly's liking. 'Though I'm surprised he's on his own. I thought we'd have a courier or something.'

'I wouldn't know.'

Gilly fastened her seat belt. She was starting to feel excited. Soon they would be on the ferry to Calais, just her and Angie and a group of fellow travellers, strangers who might become friends. She peered over her shoulder, but only for a moment. It seemed rude to stare. The coach was pulling onto the motorway as she relaxed back into her seat. They were on their way. The holiday had begun.

An hour and a half later, and she was delving into her bag in search of her seasickness pills. She'd never been seasick before – probably because she always took a tablet as a precaution. Charles had always insisted on it. Better safe than sorry being his standard motto. It appeared to have rubbed off on her. 'Want one?' she said, offering the packet to her sister.

Angie screwed up her eyes to read the small print. 'To be taken one hour before sailing. Avoid alcohol.' No thanks,' she said. 'I'd rather have a gin and tonic in the bar. Besides, it looks as calm as a mill-pond out there.'

She pointed to the horizon as the coach headed towards the ferry terminal. Admittedly, the sea did look relatively calm. Blue skies and fluffy white clouds gave quite a beguiling backdrop to the cranes and containers lining the quayside. But looks, Gilly knew, could be deceiving.

'It'll be choppy in the Channel,' Charles had warned her. 'Always is at this time of year.'

And Charles, as always, was right.

The saying 'green at the gills' was a very apt description of the colour Angie had gone as she clung onto the ship's rail twenty minutes after they had sailed from the peaceful sanctuary of the breakwater at Dover, and five minutes after downing her first, and only, gin and tonic.

'Think I'm going to die,' she groaned, clutching a lace-edged handkerchief to her lips. 'Oh God, I feel awful.'

'I told you to take a tablet,' Gilly said, handing her a bottle of exorbitantly priced water. 'Here, sip this. It might work if you swallow one now.'

'Can't.'

'Can't or won't?'

'Can't,' Angie groaned, hanging her head over the rail. Gilly made soft shushing noises as she rubbed her sister's back. Oh dear. This wasn't the best of possible starts. And not with the wind blowing from that direction either.

'Got a problem, ladies?'

It was the coach driver. Dave Saunders – Dave. He was out on deck smoking a sly cigarette but, all credit to him, he put the thing out before striding over to them with a concerned look on his face.

'It's my sister,' Gilly said. 'She's not feeling too good.'

'Oh dear.' He looked genuinely sympathetic. 'That's a shame.'

'I told her to take a seasickness pill, but she wouldn't.'

'They don't always work.'

Gilly felt alarmed. 'They don't?' Was it her imagination, or was she suddenly starting to feel a bit queasy?

'No, but fresh air's the next best thing.'

The air was certainly fresh – fresh to the point of chilly. Gilly shivered.

That, and ginger, of course.' He reached into his jacket pocket and produced a bag of crystallised ginger. 'I swear by it. Friend of mine – a fisherman – told me about it years ago and I've never been seasick yet. Want a bit?'

Gilly wasn't sure. 'Angie? Do you want a bit?'

'Ugh' came the mournful reply.

'Maybe later,' Dave said, pressing the bag into her hand. 'Look, can I get you a cup of tea or something? You look frozen.'

'I am frozen,' Gilly said. She had left her jacket on the coach, thinking that they would be sitting in the warm lounge for the crossing to Calais, or perusing the shelves of perfumes and chocolates in the shops, not perishing to bits on the windy foredeck. A linen blouse, trousers and a thin cardigan weren't much protection from the sea breezes, that was for sure.

'Okay, I'll bring you one out.' He pointed to the opposite side of the deck. 'You might find it's a bit more sheltered round that side. Milk and sugar?'

'Just milk, please.'

'I'll be as quick as I can.'

Okay. Thanks.'

Gilly watched him striding away from them, as she hooked her arm around her sister's waist. She liked him, she decided, and it was kind of him to offer to help. First impressions were usually reliable. She'd read that somewhere. You could usually judge whether you liked someone within the first few minutes of meeting them. Angie had poured scorn on that statement, saying that Gilly tended to like everybody, even con men, given half the chance, and that she was gullible and naive. Not so, she thought. She could recognise genuine kindness when she saw it – and the coach driver had been more than kind.

'It's his job,' Angie muttered, a short while later, as they sat with their backs to the wind, on a seat down the port side of the ship. 'He's no doubt offering tea and sympathy to all his passengers who are chucking up over the side.'

'Don't be so cynical,' Gilly said. 'And give me a bit of that ginger before you eat it all.'

'Thought you'd taken a tablet.'

'Dave said they don't always work.'

'Oh, it's Dave now, is it?'

'That's his name.' Gilly picked up the empty cup and saucer. 'God, I can tell you're feeling better,' she added. 'Do you want anything else?'

'No thanks. Why, where are you going?'

'I'm taking this back to the cafeteria. Then I'm going to the loo. You keep watching the distant horizon like Dave told you to and we'll be in Calais before you know it.'

Apart from Angie's bout of seasickness, the crossing was fairly uneventful. It seemed like hardly any time had passed at all before they received the announcement to return to their vehicles.

'Must we?' Angie groaned. 'The stench of diesel down there will make me puke, I know it will.'

'Well, we could leave it to the last minute,' Gilly said, anxiously watching the rest of the passengers pouring down the stairwells to the car decks. How long they could wait before heading to the bowels of the ship, she wasn't quite sure.

She peered out of the huge picture windows at the front of the ferry. Now that everyone had headed for their vehicles, she was afforded a panoramic view of Calais port and docks and the long sandy beaches that ran alongside the entrance to the harbour. It really was rather exciting. She hadn't been to France since she'd been a small child. Charles didn't believe in foreign holidays. He didn't like foreigners and he was blowed if he was going to give them his hard-earned money. Actually, when she came to think about it, he didn't like people much either. That was part of his problem

25

Gilly raised her hand to her forehead to shelter her eyes from the glare of the sun. It was a good job she'd packed her sunglasses.

'It looks lovely outside,' she said.

'Great. The coach will be hot and stuffy,' Angie muttered, picking up her over-sized designer handbag and slinging it over her shoulder. 'Come on – let's get going.'

With all passengers duly counted and accounted for, the coach driver ran through a brief summary of their itinerary whilst they waited for the stern doors of the ferry to be opened.

'Right, well, as you know, this is the Loire valley tour, but we'll be staying in a hotel on the outskirts of Paris for the first two nights, which will give you a full day to enjoy the sights and sounds of the capital. Then we'll be heading south to Montrichard in the Loire valley for the rest of the week.'

The ship juddered to a halt with a groaning screech of metal. With a loud whirring noise, the huge stern doors began to open.

Gilly saw daylight – blue skies and the odd white cloud.

'To be continued,' Dave said, leaning forwards to switch on the ignition. As the coach engine started, so too did the music, and a rousing rendition of the French national anthem came bursting through the overhead speakers.

Gilly beamed and joined in the round of applause from the rest of the passengers. She was still beaming as the coach bounced down the ramp and drove onto French soil.

She felt excited, liberated, free, and oddly enough, she wasn't missing Charles one single little bit.

The sprawling landscape of warehouses, containers, cranes and lorry parks gave way to huge hypermarkets advertising cheap wines and beers and local delicacies like cheese, honey and pates.

This must be where people came on those booze cruises she'd heard about. Tessa at work said her husband had made several trips in the run-up to Christmas. Why people endured a choppy sea crossing in the depths of winter (to say nothing of the expense of petrol and a ferry ticket), just to buy some cheap alcohol, was quite beyond Gilly. Then again, she wasn't much of a drinker. Red wine tended to give her a headache, and white wine made her feel silly and giggly (which was the whole object of the exercise, according to Angie), so she preferred to remain sober.

Besides, Charles enjoyed his beer, so she had to drive him home if they ever went anywhere that served alcohol. Having a drink herself was never an option. Mind you, it would be different on a coach trip, she thought. There wouldn't be a need to drive anyone anywhere. Perhaps she'd suggest it to Charles when she got home. He might like the idea of being chauffeured round the country with a group of likeminded people. Then again, Gilly thought, as she glanced over her shoulder at the sea of grey heads behind them, maybe not.

From her vantage point high up on the coach, Gilly peered down at the acres of parked cars, and watched people pushing their trolleys laden with crates and boxes towards them. Surely that couldn't all be for personal use? She stared, amazed, as two middle-aged men started loading box after box into the back of a white Transit van. What were they, alcoholics? They'd have to be, to get through that lot.

Her curious gaze then rested on a group of young men loitering by the lorry park, some with backpacks and others with rolled-up sleeping bags. They looked foreign – well, they would be, she thought, inwardly scolding herself for being so stupid – they were in France. But no - no, on second thoughts, they didn't look French. Turkish maybe? Albanian? Romanian? Heck, how would she know – Eastern European, perhaps? Maybe they were the refugees she had read about in the paper, the ones that tried to hide on container lorries heading across the Channel.

Her eyes widened as she saw the young women, swathed in long scarves and shawls, trudging down the side of the road with small children in their arms or toddling in their wake. With huge lorries thundering past. My God! She hardly dared look. For several long minutes, she didn't look, but occupied herself with trying to follow the coach's route on a small, fold-up travel map she had packed in her handbag.

It wasn't long before the uninspiring industrial landscape surrounding the docks gradually gave way to acres of fields and meadows, with traditional French farmhouses, complete with red tiled roofs and whitewashed outbuildings.

This was more like it. Gilly re-folded the map and put it back where she had found it. 'You can tell we're in France just by looking at the scenery,' she said, as she peered eagerly out of the coach window. 'Look at the painted wooden shutters on that house over there.'

'Fascinating,' Angie muttered. She was delving in her handbag for something and hadn't even glanced up.

'That must be corn on the cob – look, over there. Those fields – Angie.'

'Hmm?'

'Corn on the cob.'

'If you say so.'

Gilly glanced at her sister. 'You could at least pretend to be interested,' she sighed. 'Are you still feeling a bit iffy?'

'What do you think?'

'I wouldn't have thought there was anything left inside you,' she said. The memory of her sister throwing up over the guard rail as the ferry had ploughed its way towards Calais was not one she was likely to forget in a hurry. Nor, she recalled, was the kindness she had received from the coach driver, who had not only provided her with a hot drink but had refused to take any payment for it either.

She glanced over at him – it was hard not to, considering they were sitting in the seats directly behind him - and found herself idly studying the tanned nape of his neck and the gold chain that nestled there, half hidden under the crisp white collar of his shirt. He had removed his jacket but not his tie, and she found the sight of his firm and sun-tanned forearms rather attractive. Intrigued, she watched the muscles tighten as he swung the wheel of the coach between his hands. They were nice hands: long, slender fingers and no ring...He wasn't married, then. Or maybe he just didn't wear a ring...

'I said,' came Angie's irritated voice, 'have you got any of that ginger left?'

'What? Oh yes, the ginger.' Gilly hurriedly averted her gaze. 'Here. It's in my bag.'

Goodness, what was the matter with her? She'd been staring at the man as if she was a love-struck teenager. It's a good job Charles wasn't with her. He'd have had a fit.

He wouldn't have been sympathetic with Angie either. She could almost imagine him saying 'Bloody stupid sister of yours. Told her to take a seasickness pill, but no, she'd rather have a gin and tonic. Well, it's her own fault she's ill.'

She handed her sister the bag of ginger and a bottle of water for good measure. 'You might be dehydrated,' she added. 'You ought to drink something.'

'Flat Coke's good for tummy upsets,' said a woman's voice from behind them. Gilly craned her head round and came face to face with an owl. Or at least, that was her initial impression. A woman resembling a retired school mistress peered at her through the gap between the head-rests. She wore round spectacles with thick lenses that made her eyes look like an owl's, and her snow white hair was pulled back into a bun, atop a plump, oval face. Her stare seemed to conceal some sort of ancient wisdom, or at least, traces of it.

'My Cyril swears by flat Coke and pureed apple – isn't that right, Cyril?'

Cyril, who was either stone deaf or fast asleep – Gilly couldn't decide which, since his head was tilted to one side and he didn't respond to his wife's comment - was the old man who had sat with them at the coach interchange.

'Poor love. Is she feeling queasy?'

'Just a bit,' Gilly said.

'There's nothing worse, is there? Not on a coach trip.'

'No.'

Angie darted her sister a look that spoke volumes. 'I am here,' she hissed. 'I'm not invisible.'

'Actually, I think she's feeling a bit better now.'

'Oh, good. Good.'

The elderly speaker withdrew to inform Cyril of this latest development.

'She's feeling better now.'

'Who is?'

'The lady in front.'

'Was she poorly?'

'I told you she was poorly.'

'No, you didn't.'

'Yes, I did. Flat Coke, I said.'

'When was that, then?'

Gilly tried to smother a giggle and was forced to splutter into a tissue.

Even Angie managed a dry smile. 'It can't get any worse,' she said, reaching for the bottle of water and unscrewing the lid.

'I hope not,' Gilly said, laughing. At that moment she caught sight of the coach driver grinning back at her, in the reflection from the mirror above him. As her gaze met his, he gave her a knowing wink. Spontaneously, and totally out of character for her, she winked back.

Chapter Four

Gilly was surprised how long it took them to drive from Calais to their first hotel on the outskirts of Paris. Most of the coach party had dozed off in their seats, including Angie.

Gilly was too excited to sleep. She felt like she was at the start of a great adventure and she didn't want to miss a moment of it. But even so, she felt her eyelids growing heavy by the time the coach pulled off the road and onto a gravelled courtyard in front of a quaint and old-fashioned hotel in the centre of the town square.

'This is it,' she said, nudging her sister. 'Come on, wake up.'

'I'm not asleep,' Angie muttered. 'More's the pity. I feel exhausted. We've been travelling for hours.'

'They'll be serving dinner at half past seven,' Dave said, as they queued at the reception desk to pick up their room keys. 'You've got plenty of time to stretch your legs and perhaps explore the mediaeval ruins of the old church before having a welcome drink in the hotel bar. Dave had reckoned without Angie and her dodgy digestive system.

'What do you mean, you don't feel like it?' Gilly said, as she dumped Angie's suitcase on the bed – it was her second trip of the day - Angie being too weak and feeble (so she said) to manage her suitcase up the stairs from the hotel foyer to their room. 'I was really looking forward to a bit of fresh air.'

She peered suspiciously at her sister. Angie did, she conceded, look slightly pale and sickly. 'Are you okay?'

'No,' she groaned, rubbing her stomach. 'I feel bloody awful. It must have been that gin and tonic on the ferry.' She gave a loud belch.

Gilly sighed. She flicked open the window catch, and pushed up the sash window to let in a warm and welcome breeze. They were on the third floor of the hotel. Below her, she could see Dave unloading the last of the suitcases from the rear of the coach. A couple of men were standing on the gravel drive, puffing away on cigarettes. Some of the women – Barbara included, she noticed - were admiring the pots blooming with pink and scarlet geraniums that edged the footpath.

'He's such a good boy,' Barbara was saying. 'Looks out for me all the time, he does.'

Gilly drew back from the window and pulled the drapes across, before glancing across at her sister, who lay prostrate on one of the beds. 'Can I get you anything?'

'No. I'm just going to lie here and die,' Angie said, stuffing a couple of pillows behind her head.

'Hardly.' Gilly pushed open the adjoining door. 'This must be the bathroom.' The room was small, but had a shower, toilet and a tiny white sink. No room for manoeuvre, though. It looked like it had been fitted into the smallest available alcove. She squeezed through the door and pulled it shut. Her weary reflection gazed back at her from the mirrored tiles above the basin. It had been a long day and it wasn't over yet. She ran her fingers through her hair and rubbed a smear of lip-salve over her dry lips. Maybe she would go for a stroll. If Angie was going to doze off, she'd only get bored sitting watching her. Besides, she needed to phone Charles.

'You don't mind if I go out for a bit, do you?' she said, emerging from the bathroom and reaching for her bag. 'It's such a lovely evening and it seems a shame to spend it cooped up in here.'

'Feel free,' came the feeble reply. 'I'm not shifting.'

Gilly glanced at her watch. 'All right – but I won't be long.' She toyed with the idea of taking her jacket with her, but the air felt wonderfully warm and balmy, so she reasoned that a cardigan would suffice. Besides, she didn't intend to go far.

She took the stairs, rather than the lift – she had a thing about lifts, ever since she'd been stuck in one in Debenhams for half an hour with a harassed mother and an inconsolable toddler – and anyway, she didn't mind the exercise.

The warm evening sunshine filtered through the cover of trees that edged the driveway. Gilly headed for the garden, where she could see a couple of wooden benches and a patio area. She would take a seat and try to ring Charles on her mobile. It was almost seven o'clock, she thought, and probably a good time to get hold of him.
It wasn't.

'I've just sat down to eat,' he complained, in response to her cheery 'Bonsoir'.

'Oh. Sorry.'

'What did you want, anyway?'

'Just to let you know that we're at our hotel,' she said. 'We'll be here for two nights, and then we go to Montrichard. You know how I've always wanted to visit Paris, Charles, and guess what - tomorrow we're going on a cruise down the Seine.'

'I'm in the middle of dinner, Gilly. Do you think you could tell me about it some other time?'

'What? Oh...well, yes, I suppose,' she faltered, deflated. 'What are you having?'

'I'm with a business colleague,' came the brusque reply. 'Look, I'll ring you later.'

'Yes, but Charles, I'll be going to dinner myself, shortly, and I just thought...'

She paused, listening. The line had gone dead. 'Charles?' She stared in disbelief at the screen on her mobile. He'd cut her off. No two ways about it. He'd cut her off.

'Problems?'

'Huh?' She jerked her head up to see Dave standing on the path, smoking a cigarette, and watching her.

'Reception problems?' he said, pointing at her mobile phone.

'Oh – er, yes,' she said.

'It's always a bit hit and miss round here. You'll probably find if you walk up to the church you'll get a better signal from there.'

'Thanks.' She slid her phone back into her handbag. 'I'll do that.'

'I'm going up there myself,' he added, tossing his butt onto the ground and grinding it into the gravel with the toe of his shoe. 'I can show you the way.'

Gilly couldn't think of an excuse to say no, so she didn't. She picked up her bag, positioned it over her shoulder, and stood up.

It was almost as if he sensed her hesitation. 'We can wait for your sister,' he said, glancing back at the hotel entrance. 'I don't mind. There's no rush.'

'Oh, she won't be coming with me. She's not feeling very well.'

'Really?' He sounded surprised. 'I thought she would have been over her seasickness by now.'

'So did I,' Gilly said. 'But she still feels queasy.'

'Do you think she needs to see a doctor?'

'I don't think so.' God, she hoped not. That would be just typical. And knowing Angie, she wouldn't have proper medical cover either. 'I'm sure she'll be fine after a lie- down.'

'Well, if you're sure.'

'I'm sure.'

'Right,' he said. 'Well, follow me.'

Dave told her it was a short ten-minute stroll to the church – what was left of it, anyway, which, according to the guide-book, was nothing more than a few ruined walls and a handful of round pillars, surrounded by chain-link fencing. But the view from the top of the hill was worth viewing. That much Gilly did know. She'd had time to read up about it on the coach.

At any other time, and on such a pleasant evening, the leisurely walk away from the hotel would have been relaxing, but Gilly was feeling far from relaxed. Distant memories of not going anywhere with strange men had been drummed into her from a young age by an over anxious mother. No matter how hard she tried to tell herself that this was different – that Dave wasn't a stranger; he was their coach driver, and she wasn't exactly going off with him, he was only taking her to where she could get a decent phone signal – a small pinprick of doubt was making her feel uneasy. Whatever way she thought about it, the facts remained. She didn't know him and she was in a foreign country, letting him take her goodness only knows where.

She risked a cautious sideways glance at him as they waited to cross the street. He looked normal enough – reasonably attractive, she supposed. She guessed he was in his late forties, maybe a bit older. His hair was thinning on top, but was neatly cut. He wasn't overweight or unshaven and with his suntanned face, he looked quite handsome. He certainly didn't look dangerous. Nevertheless, the newspaper headlines had already formed a distinct picture inside her head. *'Middle-aged tourist found dead in lonely churchyard.'*

The image of her mother sobbing from her nursing home was pretty vivid too. 'I told her not to go off with anyone she didn't know. I've always warned her about strangers.'

And Angie would be distraught. 'The holiday was my idea. It's all my fault...'

'Mrs Bennett'

'Uh, what? Oh.' The touch of Dave's hand on her arm jerked her out of her daydream and almost sent her into a panic.

'We can cross now,' he said, looking slightly bemused. He indicated, with a sweep of his hand, the now empty road.

'Oh, right. Sorry.' Blushing furiously, Gilly stepped forwards.

'It's always best to be sure,' he said. 'You've no idea how many tourists are knocked down because they look the wrong way when they're crossing the road.'

'I can imagine,' she said, trying hard not to appear embarrassed. It was good that he had assumed her hesitance was caused by confusion over the traffic. That was a bit of a relief.

'Is this your first visit to France?'

'Er...yes.'

'Good. I'm sure you'll like it.'

He paused at the entrance to a narrow, tree-shaded avenue. 'This way, I think.'

Gilly peered up the quiet, gloomy-looking street.

He was already walking ahead of her. 'The church is at the top of the hill. It's not far now,' he added.

Oh God! She hesitated, and then looked back over her shoulder, wondering if anyone had noticed them heading this way together. What should she do? What would Angie do? Forget that – she knew exactly what Angie would do.

Dave had stopped and was watching her expectantly – waiting for her to catch up with him.

'Got a stone in my shoe,' she said, quickly crouching down and fiddling with her sandal. 'I won't be a moment.'

'There's no rush.'

Now be sensible, she told herself sternly, as she made a show of removing her shoe and shaking it about a bit before slipping it back on her foot. He's not going to do anything. He's in charge of the coach tour.

She straightened up, smiling. 'Got it.'

As she hurried to join him, she inwardly scolded herself for having such a vivid imagination. Here was a man, trying to be helpful, and she was acting as if he was an axe murderer or something.

With a smile planted firmly on her face, she pushed the thought that the avenue was shaded and deserted and that she was on her own with him, to the back of her mind. Then she did what she always did when she was nervous. She started to gabble. Stupid small talk – inane comments about the weather, the scenery and God knows what else. She even told him about the struggle she had to keep her fuchsia plants alive over the winter, what with that sudden and unexpected early frost.

He must have thought she was mad.

To his credit, he showed a polite interest in everything she said, but even as the words left her mouth, she was cringing at her inability to keep quiet.

'It's because you're shy,' Angie had told her. 'That's why you do it.'

'If I was shy, you'd think I'd shut up.'

'Not necessarily. You're nervous, so you don't listen, and you keep talking to avoid answering questions. It's really quite simple. I see it all the time in school.'

'What do I do about it?'

'God knows.'

'Thanks.'

'Well, you could try listening. Count to ten or something before you open your mouth. It's not that hard.'

With that thought in mind, Gilly found herself making a conscious effort to actually listen to what Dave was saying as they reached the top of the rise. He was telling her something about a French nobleman, whose name, of course, had escaped her.

'They say his remains were buried here, but there's no sign of a gravestone. We could have a wander round, if you like. Try and find the headstone.'

34

Seeing as how she didn't have a clue who he was talking about, she gave a hurried shake of her head. 'I need to phone Charles.'

'Your husband?'

She nodded.

'Okay. Well, you should get a good signal from here. I'll leave you to it. I'm going grave-hunting.'

Gilly gave him a grateful smile and perched herself on a pile of stones, the remains of some sort of ruined crypt, she thought, and fumbled through her bag for her mobile phone.

She thought it best that she did try to contact Charles again, just in case she had accidentally cut him off in mid-sentence earlier.

She held the phone to her ear and listened to the precise tones of his voicemail messaging service. He had switched his phone off. How could he? And what was she supposed to do if she needed him in an emergency?

Dave was watching her intently.

'Darling!' she said, at the top of her voice. 'Yes, we're at the hotel now. Yes, it's lovely. We haven't had dinner yet. Angie's gone for a lie-down.'

She tilted her head. The recorded message was ending with a '... so leave your name and number and I'll get back to you.'

She paused momentarily to make it look as if she was listening to his reply, then said 'You can look it up on the internet if you like. I left all the details in the top drawer of the bureau. Talk to you later, darling. I'll ring again soon. Yes. You too. Bye, dear.'

She kept the smile pinned to her face as she slipped the phone back into her handbag.

'You got through, then?' Dave said, strolling back towards her.

'Yes, no problem,' she lied. 'What about you? Did you find the grave?'

'No, but that doesn't mean he's not here. A lot of those headstones are so worn or ruined, it's hard to read what's on them.' He glanced at his watch. 'We'd better get going. It'll soon be time for dinner.'

The walk back to the hotel was infinitely more pleasant than the one to the church. Now that Gilly realised Dave had no ulterior motives for accompanying her, she let herself relax a little. Not only did she listen to what he was saying, she actually found herself enjoying his company. He had an observant sense of humour that made her laugh, as he told her about incidents from previous coach trips - of pensioners trapped in the loo and passengers left behind or getting on the wrong coach at Dover.

'One guy got halfway to Bruges before he realised he should have been going to the Dutch bulb fields,' he said. 'We arranged to get him transferred, but by then he'd made friends on the coach and didn't want to leave them.'

'Oh. What did you do, then?'

We let him stay. It wasn't a full trip,' he added, 'and it meant he'd be back the next year.'

'Why?'

'To see the bulb fields, of course.'

Gilly laughed.

He smiled as he glanced sideways at her. 'What about you?' he said. 'What made you decide to come on a coach tour?'

'My sister suggested it,' she said. 'She's on her own since her husband moved out and she didn't want to travel by herself.'

'And you decided to come with her.'

'Yes – well, I wasn't keen at first,' she added. 'My husband didn't like the idea of me going off without him.'

'I don't blame him.'

'What?' She glanced sharply across at him.

'Well, an attractive woman like you and a coach-load of pensioners.' He shook his head sternly. 'Risky. Who knows what you might get up to?'

He was grinning as he spoke.

Gilly found herself smiling. His humour was infectious. 'Do you think he was right to be worried?'

'Absolutely.'

'I'll bear that in mind,' she said.

They had reached the end of the avenue. A light breeze ruffled the leaves on the overhanging branches. Sunlight glimmered through the dappled shadows. It was a beautiful evening, and Gilly was feeling pleasantly relaxed and happy. Not least by the fact that he had called her an attractive woman. It had been years – no, decades - since she'd thought of herself as attractive and even though she knew he was just saying it as a figure of speech, she still rather liked the thought. It gave her a nice, warm feeling inside.

'It must be lovely to be able to travel all the time,' she said dreamily. 'Seeing lots of different places and staying in nice hotels.'

'There are certain benefits to this job,' he said, 'but it's not all fun.'

'No.' She looked thoughtfully across at him. It suddenly occurred to her that he must live a nomadic sort of lifestyle. He had already told her that he spent the best part of the year driving coach tours across the continent. In which case, he wouldn't have time for much of a family life – that's if he had a family.

She was just about to ask him, when her mobile started to ring. Damn. She blinked in disbelief as Charles' name and number flashed up on her screen. She stared at it for a few more seconds. Trust him to ring back at this time.

'Aren't you going to answer that?'

'Um...' She paused. 'Actually, no, I'm not.' She switched it off and put it away in her bag. 'Work,' she added, dismissively.

'Don't they know you're on holiday?'

'Yes, so it's probably not important.'

'No rest for the wicked, eh,' he said lightly.

They had reached the corner of the street. To her dismay, Gilly could see several of the coach party standing around outside the hotel foyer or wandering about in the gardens. What made it worse was that most, if not all of them, were watching their approach. How bad must that look?

'Think I'll go and have a quick shower,' she said.

'Good idea. You've got time. They won't start serving for another half hour.'

'Fine.'

'Unless you want a drink first?'

'I don't.' Her cheeks were burning. She could feel everyone staring at her – staring at him -adding two and two together. Oh dear. This was how rumours started. Even Barbara was grinning like a Cheshire cat – and there was no way she wanted to explain things to her. She gave a hurried wave as she walked past - one that the older woman returned with equal fervour, seeing as how she was on her own again. Gilly couldn't help thinking it was odd that her grandson never seemed to want to stay with her.

'Okay. Well, no doubt I'll see you at dinner,' Dave said, adding, 'I hope your sister is feeling better.'

'So do I,' she said, as she headed for the lobby. Because if she wasn't, she didn't know what she would do.

Chapter Five

The restorative effects of a glass of wine on her sister never failed to amaze Gilly.

In spite of spending the best part of the afternoon declaring she was at death's door, Angie was currently slathering butter on a large piece of crusty bread to accompany her duck pate, whilst partaking liberally of a large carafe of house red.

Gilly would have taken a more cautionary approach and gone for a few dry crackers and water at dinner, if it had been her.

'You made a quick recovery,' she said.

'Thank goodness. Oh, but I did feel poorly.' Angie ground some black pepper over her lettuce leaves. 'Did you get through to Charles?'

'Yes, but he was busy.'

'Sulking?'

'Probably.' Gilly finished her soup and pushed the bowl to one side. 'I had a lovely walk, though.'

'So I heard.' Angie topped up her glass. 'That funny little woman – the one that's with her grandson - she was telling that elderly couple behind us about you and Dave going off together.'

'What?' Gilly felt herself blush and glanced quickly around the crowded dining room. 'Oh God, what did she say?' She was mortified. She knew this would happen. 'I wasn't with him. We just – he was showing me where to get a good phone signal.'

That's novel.'

'Angie!'

'I'm only teasing, darling. I know what you're like. Mind you,' she added, 'he's not bad looking. And you must be one of the youngest ones on this coach trip. I'd say the average age is about seventy.' She scanned the room as she spoke. 'He probably thought his luck was in.'

'He did not,' Gilly squealed, but she was blushing profusely as she spoke. Angie was right – apart from Carl and another couple who had seats at the back of the coach, they did appear to be the youngest passengers on board. 'He was just being helpful.'

'Course he was.' She popped the last morsel of bread into her mouth and patted her lips with the serviette. 'Yum. That pate was lovely. You know, I hadn't realised quite how hungry I was.'

They were seated at a table for two halfway down the dining room. Angie had her back to the wall, which gave her a clear view of the rest of the room. Gilly was thankful that she didn't have to look at anybody apart from her sister, disliking the thought that she was being talked about by the other passengers. It was embarrassing.

Angie, however, had no such qualms, and was giving her a running commentary on all their fellow diners.

'It's mostly elderly couples. There's a weird looking guy on his own – he's reading a book at the table. He's the one that tried to sit next to me at the interchange,' she added, 'and there's a woman with a hearing aid who she keeps fiddling with it. I think she's with a friend. And that shaven-headed guy, he looks interesting.'

'He's the one that's travelling with his grandmother. That Barbara I was telling you about.'

'Hmm.' Angie perused him with interest.

'Will you stop staring,' Gilly hissed.

'I'm not staring, I'm observing. We've got a week with these people. I'm trying to decide who we should get to know and who we need to avoid. Oh, hang on a minute.' She bent over to retrieve her phone from her handbag. 'It's Simon,' she added, glancing at the screen. 'He keeps sending me messages.' She popped her glasses on and peered at the text. A slow smile spread across her face. 'He doesn't like the idea that I'm on holiday and enjoying myself.'

'Why? What does he say?'

'Nothing. Well, nothing important, anyway.' She switched the phone off and dropped it back into her handbag.

'Aren't you going to answer him?'

'No. What I do is none of his business. He lost that right when he went off with that woman. Now then, I think I'll have the grilled trout. What are you having?'

By the time they had finished dinner, it was getting dark outside – too dark for a stroll around the gardens. Gilly was anxious to get back to their room to sort out her stuff anyway. They had a seven o'clock start in the morning and a packed itinerary to look forward to.

'I want an early night,' she told Angie. 'And you should get one too.'

'But it's the first night of our holiday.'

'Yes, and it's been a long day.'

'You sound like mother,' she grumbled. 'All right, but only because we're going to Paris tomorrow and I want to make the most of it.'

So did Gilly. She'd never been to France before, let alone Paris, but she'd read enough about it to know that it was a buzzing and vibrant city, bursting with culture, fashion, beautiful architecture and, of course, romance. Well, possibly not romance, she conceded, not for her, but she was looking forward to it, just the same.

***

'Lunch in Paris,' she sighed, gazing out of the coach window the next morning as they headed towards their first scheduled stop. 'Doesn't that sound wonderful? There was that film,' she added. 'You know, the one with Meg Ryan in it...oh, what was it called? It had that man in it, the one with the funny moustache.

'I don't know,' Angie said.

'You were with me when we went to see it. At the Odeon, remember?'

'No, I don't remember. Anyway, what does it matter?'

'It was set in Paris.'

'Oh.'

Gilly settled back in her seat to flick through the handy, pocket-sized guide to the nation's capital city that she had brought with her on the coach. She rather fancied the boat trip along the Seine. Dave had told them he would be parking the coach alongside the departure point, and they would have time for a leisurely ride along the river, where they would be able to see all the sights. A tour guide would be on hand to give them a running commentary. It sounded fabulous.

Angie, however, did not share her enthusiasm.

'Stuff that,' she muttered, as Dave gave his passengers a glowing account of the highlights they would see from the deck of the pleasure cruiser.

Gilly peered at her over the top of her reading glasses.

'Oh, come on,' her sister added. 'You surely don't think I want to go on another boat trip, not after the hell I've just gone through on the last one.'

'That was the English Channel,' Gilly said. 'This is a river. It'll be flat calm. I promise you.'

'You go then. But I'm staying on dry land.'

'I can't go without you.'

'Why not?'

Gilly thought for a moment. Why not? Why not indeed? It was her holiday just as much as it was Angie's. There was no law to say they had to be joined at the hip, and she really did want to go on the cruise along the Seine.

'I would like to go,' she admitted.

'Well go, then.'

'You're sure you don't mind?'

'Not in the slightest.'

'Oh.' Gilly removed her reading glasses and popped them back in their case. She hadn't expected her sister to be so gracious. 'Thanks,' she said. She glanced sideways at her. 'What will you do instead?'

40

'I don't know.' Angie shrugged. 'Shop, eat, stroll along the riverbank.' Her gaze rested momentarily on the back of the coach driver's head. 'I won't be the only one not going on the cruise. I'm sure there'll be something I can do to pass the time.'

It was all sorted. By the time they reached the dropping-off point on the banks of the Seine more than two thirds of the coach party had decided to go on the escorted riverboat tour.

Gilly was delighted to be going, a delight that was tempered by the fact that the elderly lady she had been trying to avoid since their encounter in the public lavatories at Dover was also going.

'Carl won't come with me,' Barbara complained, as she shuffled behind her in the queue for tickets at the quayside. 'He said he wanted to go for a walk and stretch his legs. But I can sit with you, can't I? That's if you don't mind.'

'No, no,' Gilly lied, frantically looking for someone else she could link up with.

'Only you looked like you were on your own.'

'Well, I'm not really...'

'And it's nice to have someone to chat to. Carl's not much of a talker. Bit like his father in that respect. I always used to say I did the talking for all of them.'

Gilly could well believe it. She slid a handful of coins at the bald man in the ticket booth and smiled as he handed her a ticket with a cheery '*Merci bien.*'

'What was that he said about mercy?' Barbara said, fumbling in her purse for coins and staring at them suspiciously before placing them on the polished wood of the counter.

'It's French,' Gilly explained.

'Well you'd think he'd talk English. One ticket,' she said loudly. 'One.'

The man stared blankly back at her.

Barbara held up her finger to emphasise her point.

Gilly blushed profusely. She really wished she wasn't with this woman with the tight corkscrew perm and the cardigan with the suspicious brown stain on the sleeve.

'*Un Billet, s'il vous plait,*' she said, smiling helpfully at the man. He handed her another ticket, which she gave to Barbara.

'Oh, thanks, love.'

Gilly wondered if it would be deemed rude if she left her and went to join the rest of the party waiting to board the riverboat.

Dave, the coach driver, was waiting by the boarding ramp, ready to help his passengers, most of whom were elderly, to step on board.

He really was quite chivalrous, Gilly thought, as she watched him deftly supporting an outstretched arm or an unsteady hand with a 'Steady now,' or 'Hold tight,' or 'Mind how you go.'

She half wondered if he was going to be joining them on the trip, and rather hoped that he was. She needed something to distract her from Barbara, who was, even now, making a beeline straight towards her.

'When do we need to get back on the coach, Dave?' asked Cyril's wife, who was hanging onto her husband's arm. Gilly thought it was probably to stop him from wandering off. He had that look about him.

'Three o'clock, so you've plenty of time to get something to eat when you've finished the cruise.'

He pointed towards the lower deck of the boat. 'You might find it a bit breezy on the upper deck, so I suggest you sit indoors. Enjoy the trip.'

Gilly stepped forwards and smiled as Dave turned back to face her, his arm automatically extended in readiness.

'I think I can manage, thanks,' she said.

'Nevertheless, it's my duty, and my pleasure, to assist you.' He caught hold of her hand.

Was it her imagination, she wondered, or was he actually squeezing her fingers? She glanced up at him as she stepped onto the gangplank and immediately felt the swaying motion beneath her. Her fingers automatically tightened around his.

'Steady,' he murmured, giving her a knowing smile.

Gilly gripped the rail as she made her way onto the deck. 'Thanks.'

'No problem.'

He released her almost as quickly as he had caught hold of her, and turned his attention towards Barbara, who was following behind, her large plastic shopping bag dangling over one arm.

'Oh, I say – it's a bit bleeding wobbly, isn't it?'

Gilly was tempted to go up the stairs to the top deck, reasoning that the view would be panoramic from the upper level and that Barbara would be unlikely to join her there. Then she felt mean and guilty for even considering it.

It was only for an hour or so. Surely she could put up with her for that long.

She made herself comfortable – or as comfortable as she could be, on one of the hard white plastic seats that ran in rows along the breadth of the deck.

Barbara sat beside her and immediately started delving into her bag for a scarf to tie round her head.

'Expect it'll be windy up here and I've just had me hair done.'

Gilly's attention wandered to the river bank and the groups of people strolling along the banks of the Seine.

'Ooh, look, there's my grandson Carl. Cooeee! Carl!'

Barbara started to wave.

'Oh, he hasn't seen me,' she said, disappointed, as she watched him hurrying up a flight of concrete steps away from the river.

Gilly suspected he might have heard her, though. Along with half of Paris, it seemed. She tried to suppress a giggle.

'And look, there's your friend. Oh, that's nice. They're having a chat together.'

And so they were. Gilly watched, appalled, as she saw Angie standing at the top of the flight of steps, apparently having an animated conversation with the man she had previously decided was rather unsavoury and unpleasant.

What made it worse was the fact that they were walking away together. She craned her neck round. The pleasure boat was moving away from its mooring and she couldn't quite see where Angie was going.

'She seems nice, your friend,' Barbara was saying.

'She's my sister.'

'What's that, dear?'

'My sister,' Gilly shouted, more because of the noise of the engines and the crackling of the microphone than anything else.

'Oh. Well, she seems nice.'

'She is nice,' Gilly said. And vulnerable, and on the rebound. That was what was worrying her.

Chapter Six

The thought of a leisurely boat trip along the Seine with his gran and a coach-load of pensioners was about as appealing to Carl as having his teeth pulled, with or without the raging toothache.

He fiddled with the earpieces of his MP3 player. By turning up the volume, he could more or less drown out his grandmother's constant and inane chatter, which usually began with an, "Ooh, Carl, look at that," or a "Carl, Carl, you've got to see this."

He had perfected the art of the occasional nod and sympathetic smile, and it seemed to keep her satisfied. The old bat was just glad of his company – though God knows why. She hardly brought out the best in him.

He tapped his fingers rhythmically on his knee, inwardly giving thanks to whoever had invented this portable music device that was making his journey infinitely more bearable.

'We're here.'

His gran was nudging his elbow and jabbing a finger at the quayside, as the coach drew alongside a row of other tour buses, and the driver reversed it into the allocated parking bay.

'Are you sure you don't want to come? You'll like it, Carl – all them famous buildings and stuff – Notre Dame, the Eiffel Tower...'

'Seen them.' He removed his earphones and wound the cord round them, before stuffing them into his jacket pocket alongside his MP3 player. 'Came here with a mate, a few years back,' he added.

'You never said.'

He shrugged. 'Why would I?'

'Who was it, then?'

'Who?'

'This mate that you came to Paris with?'

'Just a mate,' he said. 'No one you'd know.' He was hardly likely to tell her about his drunk and debauched weekend in Paris with a crowd from the building site he'd been working on at the time. Not that he could remember much of it anyway, apart from Robbie chucking up outside the Moulin Rouge. Some stag party that had been. All that glitz and glamour, and he'd been too pissed to make the most of it. It was a wonder they'd managed to get back to the airport on time.

He stood up. 'Anyway, I need to stretch my legs. You'll be all right on your own. There's loads of them going,' he added, pointing to the group of passengers assembling on the quayside.

His gran didn't look convinced. He half wondered if she was going to change her mind and insist on coming with him. He didn't think he could cope with that – not with what he had planned.

'You go with them, and I'll meet up with you later,' he said. 'You know how you always liked those boat trips down the Thames – well this'll be the same, but better.'

'Oh, I don't know, Carl.'

'Trust me – you'll love it,' he said, and before she could say anything, he had risen from his seat and was heading for the door. 'See ya,' he said, as he jumped down from the coach.

In ten strides he had crossed the plaza and was climbing the flight of concrete steps that took him away from the river, and towards the Champ-de-Mars and the Eiffel Tower.

'Excuse me. I said, excuse me. You're from our coach, aren't you?'

Carl hesitated at the sound of the woman's voice. Now what, he thought, glancing back over his shoulder, half-expecting to be admonished for leaving his gran behind.

The woman following him up the steps was blonde, buxom, and on her own. He vaguely recognised her from the café at the interchange. She'd been with someone then – another woman, if he recalled correctly, though he hadn't paid much attention, other than to register that they were two of the younger women on the trip. Not that that was saying a lot, seeing as how the average age had to be about seventy.

'I don't suppose you could take a photo for me, could you?' she said, holding out a camera to him and smiling somewhat expectantly. 'Only I thought this would make a good picture.' She positioned herself at the turn in the steps. 'If you could take it from above looking down at the river.'

'I'm not much good with cameras,' he said.

'This one's easy. You just point and click.'

She wasn't leaving him any room for argument. Carl took the offered camera and squinted down at the dials.

'I'm Angie,' she added, smiling and posing. 'You're with your grandmother, aren't you?'

'Yep.' He raised the camera to eye level and looked into the viewfinder. She was wearing a black lacy bra, which was clearly visible through her pink blouse. A chunky gold locket nestled between her breasts. Voluptuous was the word that sprang to mind. Carl clicked the button.

'Could you take another one?' she added, changing her pose. 'Or maybe two or three. Sorry, I don't know your name?'

'It's Carl,' he said.

'Carl – right – thanks.' She postured again. 'I can delete the ones that don't come out. It's easy with a digital camera. My ex-husband gave it to me,' she said. 'I never thought I'd get the hang of it, but it's like everything, isn't it – practice makes perfect.' She turned sideways, giving him a new profile to look at. 'I didn't fancy the river cruise, did you?'

'Nope.' He pressed the button again.

'Not after that ferry crossing. Christ, I couldn't think of anything worse.'

Carl smiled. He was beginning to feel like a professional photographer, perched up high on the balustrade, clicking down at this middle-aged woman. In the background he could see the large pleasure cruiser drifting away from the mooring.
'Want me to take one of the boat?'

'Oh, yes please. My sister Gilly's on it. That's her on the top deck – next to the woman in the headscarf.'

'That's my grandmother.'

'Oh.' Angie gave him a quizzical look, perhaps hearing the note of derision in his voice.

'Okay, I'll admit it - this coach holiday probably wasn't one of my better ideas, but she was on her own, so I thought, why not? I'll give the old dear a treat. Trouble is, I'm not sure it's going to be much fun for me.'

'In that case, it's kind of you to take her.'

'So she keeps telling me.'

'And it's a good enough reason to skip the pleasure cruise.' Angie slipped her camera back into her handbag, and secured the straps tightly. She smiled back at him. 'Fancy a drink?'

Carl stared back at her, somewhat bemused. Bloody hell, she wasn't shy about coming forwards. His gaze rested momentarily on her large breasts that were threatening to spill out of the top of her blouse. She looked all right for her age. He could do worse.
The raucous shriek from his gran drifted over the still calm waters of the Seine.

'Cooeee! Carl! Oh, Carl!'

'You know something,' he said, 'I think I do.'

Angie hadn't expected him to say yes. She had mentally prepared herself to be dismissive and casual, with a, 'Oh well, it was just a thought.' The words were poised on the tip of her tongue, ready to be delivered. She fully expected to be spending the next few hours trailing the streets of Paris on her own.

The thought that she might now be spending them in the company of this young man (and he was young, she decided – probably in his late thirties or early forties) had left her feeling somewhat flustered.

'Oh, right. Good,' she said. 'Well, we could get something to eat.'

'We could,' he agreed.

'Just a snack – something light.' She didn't think she could face a large meal, although she was feeling a bit peckish. 'I expect we'll be having a proper dinner later at the hotel.'

'I'll go with that,' he said, glancing at his mobile phone, which had suddenly started to beep.

His brow furrowed as he stared at the screen.

'Problems?' Angie asked.

He looked up at her sharply. 'No.' He pocketed the phone. 'Come on – let's get going. I need a beer.'

Angie rather hoped that somebody from the coach tour would see them strolling the streets of Paris together. If so, she'd ask them to take a photograph – for posterity. She hurried to keep alongside Carl's lengthy stride. It wasn't easy in her high-heeled shoes. She should have thought to wear something more sensible on her feet but had reasoned that a day spent travelling did not require sensible walking shoes. Not that she possessed such a thing, anyway. Her one pair of trainers was reserved for sunny afternoons at the tennis club. At her age, she had decided to go for style, rather than comfort. 'Every little helps' being her new motto, and the extra height a pair of heels afforded her made her feel less dumpy-looking, slimmer even. She sucked in her stomach as she tottered after Carl, inwardly giving thanks to the bout of seasickness that had flattened her middle-aged spread, albeit temporarily.

He had no such problems walking. In fact, he seemed to be marching like a man on a mission. Every so often he would pause and glance at a map he had produced from one of his pockets, a creased and stained diagram drawn on a piece of paper. Angie wondered if he knew where he was going. She was about to ask him when he suddenly stopped and pointed down a narrow side street.

'That's what I'm looking for,' he said, jerking his head at a small bistro, which had tables and chairs on the pavement outside, where a couple of men were sitting drinking beer. 'Marcel's'.

'Marcel's,' Angie echoed. 'You've been here before then?'

'No. A friend recommended it to me.' He was rolling a cigarette as he spoke. Angie wondered if he'd be allowed to smoke it. She thought the laws about smoking in public were as strict in France as they were in England. Carl, however, seemed unperturbed. He put the roll-up between his teeth, lit it and inhaled deeply.

'All right, it might not look much,' he added, 'but the food's supposed to be good.'

'I'll take your word for it,' Angie said, as she followed him down the narrow street. Outward appearances left a lot to be desired. The café looked tired and run down and the locals didn't seem particularly welcoming. The two men sitting outside the bistro positively scowled at her as she plonked her bag on one of the wrought-iron chairs beside them.

'Bonjour,' she said, smiling pleasantly.

Their expressions did not change.

Neither did Angie's. She peered at the faded and weather-worn menu pinned to the wall with a couple of rusty nails and pretended to be engrossed in the contents. She glanced at Carl, but he was so busy texting on his mobile phone, that he appeared to be oblivious to the hostility of their immediate neighbours.

'Pigs trotters and onion soup', she read, mentally translating the menu and wondering if there was anything slightly more appealing on it. 'Moules mariniere' was always a tasty dish – she could probably stomach that, especially if it came with some of that delicious French bread, as long as they weren't too garlicky. She sniffed the air, wrinkling her nose. There was a definite smell of overpowering garlic in the vicinity, but she suspected it came from one of the swarthy-looking men sitting opposite them.

She glanced at Carl, wondering who on earth this friend was who had recommended the place to him, and whether, indeed, he was a friend. 'What do you want to drink?' she asked.

'Huh?' He looked up from his phone. 'Oh, beer, thanks. I won't be a moment. Just got to send this.'

He seemed distracted. Angie sat down at the table and felt in her bag for her purse. She supposed she might as well order for them. The waiter, a sallow-looking man with a stained yellow apron, was hovering in the doorway, watching and waiting like a predatory vulture.

'*Deux bieres, s'il vous plait,*' she said, in her best, textbook French.

The waiter nodded and disappeared.

It was at this point that Angie rather wished she still smoked, which was ridiculous, since she had given up years ago. She fiddled with the straps of her over-sized handbag. Then she decided that a touch of lipstick might be needed. Carl was so engrossed in sending messages on his mobile phone that she doubted whether he would notice if she excused herself to the ladies room – if there was a ladies room. Judging by the look of the clientele, this was a male-dominated establishment.

She stood up. A young girl in skin-tight black jeans and a black T-shirt was wiping down one of the adjacent tables.

'*Ou sont les toilettes, s'il vous plait?*' Angie asked her.

The girl gave her a curious stare.

'Les toilettes?' Angie repeated.

'Think she's probably foreign,' Carl muttered, glancing up from his phone. 'Albanian, probably. They usually are.' He pointed at the door to the bistro and then to Angie. 'She wants the toilet,' he said, rather too slow and loud for her liking. Goodness, she didn't want the whole street to know.

'The toilet!'

'Ah!' The girl's face brightened and she nodded visibly. 'Yes.' She wagged a finger towards the flapping net curtains that were supposedly to stop flies and insects getting inside the small café. 'Toilet.' She held out her small and delicately formed hand expectantly.

'You need to give her a tip.'

'What on earth for?' Angie muttered, delving into her purse.

'It's expected.'

So was good service, and she'd seen precious little of that. Angie slapped a couple of coins into the girl's outstretched hand before sweeping aside the net curtains and stepping over the threshold. She found herself in a shady, stuffy room that smelled of old wood and alcohol. The bar was covered in dirty glasses and half-drunk bottles of beer. A couple of old men sat at a corner table, playing cards, and a fat ginger cat lay curled up on one of the chairs next to a door marked WC. A unisex loo, she thought. Brilliant. Just bloody brilliant.

Angie hurried past the two men, ignoring their faintly curious and yet hostile stares. The scent of unwashed bodies, old leather and stale urine wafted past her nostrils. God, this place was revolting. The toilets weren't much better. They were much as she had anticipated – a urinal and a cubicle alongside each other, thus catering for both sexes, At least she was afforded a certain degree of privacy once inside the cubicle, but the seat-less toilet, with it's chipped white porcelain bowl and a precariously balanced overhead cistern with a long rusted chain left a lot to be desired. Still, at least the water was hot and she could wash her hands thoroughly. Drying them was another problem. She dismissed with a shudder, the grey-looking stained towel hanging from a hook on the wall. Flapping her hands like a demented chicken ensured that most of the droplets were shaken loose, and she was sure that she had a packet of tissues in the bottom of her handbag to mop up the rest.

49

Suitably relieved, Angie smeared a fresh coat of lipstick onto her lips and pouted suggestively into the cracked mirror. Not bad. Not bad at all. She fastened her bag securely – no point in taking unnecessary chances (this place looked a haven for pickpockets and muggers) and headed back the way she had come.

Emerging from the gloom of the bar, she was momentarily surprised to see Carl sitting talking earnestly with a shifty-looking foreigner – another Albanian, presumably – and even more surprised to see him peering into a brown, padded envelope that the man had slid across the table to him.

She hovered in the doorway, wondering if she should nip back to the loo – then decided she couldn't face the stench, and coughed to clear her throat and announce her presence.

Carl glanced up at her and quickly folded down the top of the envelope. '*Merci*,' he said.

The man smirked and stood up. He smirked again as he brushed past Angie and she caught the unmistakeable scent of spices and tobacco on him.

'Friend of yours?' she said.

'Street pedlar,' Carl said, taking the envelope and placing it on the seat behind him. 'You get them everywhere in Paris. Sometimes you get a good deal.'

'What do you mean, a good deal?'

'Something worth having,' he said. 'Most of the stuff they try and sell is cheap tat – but you get the odd bargain. My gran will be pleased with it, anyway.'

Since it was obvious he wasn't going to elaborate further, Angie made a show of peering at the menu again, though she was dying to know what was in the brown package. If it was such a good deal maybe she should have tried to buy something from the street trader as well. She'd never been one to resist a bargain.
The arrival of the waiter with their drinks saved any further awkwardness. Carl took a long draught of his beer and wiped his lips with the back of his hand. 'Shall we eat here?'

'I don't mind.'

'Might as well,' he said, picking up the menu.

Angie hoped the food was better than the beer, which was lukewarm and tasted suspiciously oily – though that could have been the glass it came in, she thought. It had a definite greasy feel to it. Still, the place must have something going for it – if it had been recommended to him.

'Think I'll have the mussels,' she said.

Carl waved the waiter over. He ordered a steak for himself – medium rare – and a bottle of red wine to go with it.

By the time their meal was served, Angie had started to relax a little and was trying to enjoy the ambience of the place – a rustic back-street bistro in the heart of downtown Paris. She had to admit, it had a certain charm when she thought of it like that. The reality wasn't quite up to expectations, but nevertheless, she was on holiday, and she was prepared to make the most of it.

'So, Carl,' she said, leaning forwards and dipping a chunk of bread into the garlic and cream sauce that smothered her mussels. 'What do you do when you're not on holiday with your mother?'

'Labouring, mostly,' he said. 'Got a few friends in the building trade. I can turn my hand to most things – carpentry, bricklaying, bit of plumbing.'

That would explain his muscles and strong forearms, Angie thought. He had the appearance of a man who did physical work.

'Sounds like you're a useful person to know,' she said. 'My ex-husband couldn't do anything round the house. He was hopeless at DIY.'

'He must have been good at something.'

'Accounts, mainly,' she said. (Which would explain why he had totted up the sum total of their proposed divorce to the last penny.) 'Have you ever been married?'

'Briefly.' Carl topped up their wine glasses and grinned. 'Thought it was a good idea at the time. Mind you, I was only twenty-three and Susie was pregnant, so I guess it was the right thing to do. Didn't last, though.'

'You're a father, then?'

'Allegedly.'

'What do you mean, allegedly?'

'Well, she said he was mine, but I wasn't convinced.'

'Goodness.' Angie gulped back a mouthful of red wine and nearly choked on it. What was she expected to say to that? It was like something from *The Jerry Springer Show*.

'We lasted about five years, till Jake went to school. Then she took off with one of the dads she'd met in the playground, and that was that really. I don't see much of him now. He must be...' He paused. '...fifteen – no, sixteen.'

Angie did some mental arithmetic. Carl must be thirty- nine – thirty-nine! A positive toy-boy. She gulped back another mouthful of red wine.

'What about you? You got kids?'

'Two. They don't live with me,' she added quickly. 'They've both left home now.'

'So you're on your own.'

She nodded.

'It can't be easy.'

'No,' she said. 'It isn't.' And that was all she wanted to say on the matter. Just thinking about Simon made her feel angry and hurt and humiliated all over again.

But she would show him. She'd plaster pictures all over Facebook of her on holiday, having a good time and enjoying herself. He'd rue the day he left her for a younger woman.

She mopped up the last of her cream sauce. The mussels had been quite delicious – surprisingly.

'How was your steak?'

'Good.'

Angie dabbed at her lips with her serviette. The girl in the tight black jeans came to clear away their plates. As she did so, she gave Carl a little sideways smirk. Angie felt peeved, though she wasn't quite sure why. She looked at her watch. 'We'd better make tracks,' she said. 'The cruise should be over by now.' She reached in her bag for her purse, half wondering if he might offer to pay, and when he didn't, wondering if she should pay.

'We'll just split it in half, shall we?' she suggested.

'Yeah, fine.'

He slapped a handful of euros onto the silver platter left by the waitress. 'It was cheap enough,' he said, picking up the brown package. He paused and glanced at her for a moment. 'I don't suppose you could put this in your bag, could you?' he said. 'Just till we get back to the coach. It's not heavy,' he added.

'Course I can.' Angie held out her hand. 'What did you say it was again?'

'I didn't.' He smiled. 'It's just some stuff I bought for my gran.'

'Stuff?'

'Chinese medicine,' he said, tapping the side of his nose. 'Probably not strictly legal, but she swears by it for her stomach problems. I expect it's made from tiger's teeth or something stupid like that. You know what these alternative practitioners are like. I usually get them off the internet, but a mate told me I could get them from street traders at half the price. I didn't believe him until now. What a bargain,' he added, grinning.

Angie wasn't sure if she believed him or not, but she took the package anyway, and placed it in her bag. It wasn't heavy at all. In fact, it felt light as a feather. She hoped his 'not strictly legal' was just a joke, and she wasn't carrying something highly illegal.

'Don't look so worried,' he said, laughing. 'What do you think I am? Come on – we'd better get going.'

It took them a while to make their way back to the coach, purely because of the heat of the day and the fact that Angie's feet were killing her. Feeling decidedly tipsy, didn't help either. She kept bumping into Carl and at one point felt the need to steady herself on his arm, as she tripped over the kerb.

'Are you all right?' he asked.

'Fine.'

He grinned down at her. 'I'm glad we paired up. It's been fun.'

Angie beamed. 'Yes, I wasn't looking forward to wandering about on my own.'

'Maybe we'll do it again.'

'Yes, maybe,' she said.

Then again, maybe not. Judging by the stony-eyed glare Gilly was giving them as they meandered across the coach park, she didn't think her sister approved of her current choice of companion.

'You're late,' Gilly snapped. 'You should have been back fifteen minutes ago. Everyone else was here on time.'

So they were. Angie peered up at the sea of faces staring down at them from the windows of the coach. 'Shorry.'

'And you're drunk.'

'Pleasantly pissed,' Angie agreed, swaying slightly.

'For God's sake!' Gilly caught hold of her arm and positively glared at Carl. 'Hurry up and get on the coach.'

'In a minute.' She reached for the flaps of her handbag. 'Just got to give this...'

'Later.' Carl caught hold of her arm and winked at her. 'I'll get it later, okay.'

'Oh.' Angie smiled. 'Okay.'

Later, hmmm – now that sounded interesting. She patted her bag shut and her gaze followed him as he stepped up onto the coach, taking in the neat fit of his black jeans and the firm broadness of his shoulders. He really was quite an interesting young man.

'Angie!' Gilly snapped. 'Hurry up.'

'Yes, yes, okay,' she said, reaching for the rail to follow him. She settled herself into her seat for the next leg of the coach journey, hoping that her cheery greetings had soothed the frayed tempers of some of her fellow passengers (though judging by the irritated glares, possibly not all of them), and tried to ignore the bloated and full feeling in her stomach. She swallowed and tasted garlic at the back of her throat.

'Have you got any of that ginger left?' she asked. 'Either that or a mint?'

'You're not feeling queasy again, are you?' Gilly looked exasperated.

'Um, no, not really,' she lied. 'Just fancied a peppermint or something.'

'I've got some Extra Strong Mints. Will they do?'

'They'll have to,' she said – and fervently hoped that they would.

Chapter Seven

The afternoon city tour of Paris by coach more than lived up to its expectations.

 A French tour guide called Jules came aboard to give them a running commentary. To say he was a bit of a character was an understatement. His crumpled corduroy trousers, jacket and navy beret gave him the appearance of a country farmer. His skin was the texture of gnarled leather and he stunk of brandy and cigars, but, on the plus side, he was entertaining and informative. Gilly was enthralled, though mildly embarrassed that Angie had decided to doze off just as Dave was suggesting a collection for the guide, at the end of his talk.

'Trust you,' she muttered, delving into her bag to find some Euros for the tip. 'I hope you're not going to sleep through the visit to Versailles.'

Angie wasn't sleeping. She was merely, as she put it, resting her eyes. She was, however, feeling decidedly bilious. A stroll through the palace gardens would be just the thing to shake off her nausea.

Gilly hoped she was right. Her sister was looking quite pale as they clambered from the coach in front of the magnificent chateau of Versailles.

'I should never have eaten those mussels,' she said.

'Mussels?' Gilly spluttered. 'You ate mussels in a back street café.'

'They tasted all right at the time. Besides,' she added, looking pitiful, 'there wasn't anything else on the menu that I fancied.'

'Yes, well, serves you right if you get food poisoning. Although, judging by the amount of wine you've consumed, I would expect the alcohol to kill off any toxins.'

She gave Carl a pointed glare as she spoke. He was sitting on a wall by the Bassin de Neptune, engrossed in texting on his mobile phone. She blamed him for leading her sister astray – not that she would have needed much persuading, but that was beside the point. He didn't appear to notice, though, which was probably just as well. Gilly didn't like confrontations, and even if she felt like giving him a piece of her mind, she knew she wouldn't say anything.

'Don't go on,' Angie groaned. She sat on a seat beside the ornamental lake, apparently oblivious to the wonderful statues and breath-taking scenery that had the rest of the coach trip in raptures. 'And stop staring at Carl. I don't want him coming over and seeing me like this. I must look a sight. How long till we go back to the hotel?'

Gilly looked at her watch. 'Dave said five o'clock on the coach, so not long now. Do you want to walk back that way?'

'Think I need to visit the toilets first.'

Thankfully, and even with the rush hour Paris traffic, they were only half an hour's drive from the hotel, and Angie survived the journey without having to make use of the coach's facilities. She did, however, retreat to the bathroom the moment they got back to their room.

Delightful, Gilly thought, plonking her bag and jacket on the bed. She wondered if she had packed enough stomach medicine to cover the entire trip. No doubt Angie wouldn't have brought anything with her.

'Are you going to be okay if I just pop down to reception for a moment? I want to pick up some of those leaflets from the stand. I meant to get some when we came in, but you were in such a hurry to get back to the room that I forgot.'

'I suppose so,' came the feeble reply.

'I won't be long.'

She let herself out of the bedroom and quietly closed the door behind her.

'Oh, hello, dear.'

The woman's voice made her jump, and she turned around quickly to see the elderly couple who had sat behind them on the coach standing in the corridor beside the lift.

'We were going down to dinner but Cyril forgot to take his tablet. We must be in the next room to you.'

'Oh. Right.'

Cyril was grinning rather amiably at her, though he had a distracted look about him. Gilly didn't like to ask what the tablet was for.

'Is your sister feeling better?' the woman asked.

'No, not really. She's having a lie-down.'

'Oh, that's a shame. It's a shame, that – isn't it, Cyril?' Her voice had risen audibly.

'What is?' came the vague reply from her elderly companion.

'She's not any better.'

'Who isn't?'

'This lady's sister.'

'Do we know her?'

'She was on the coach.'

At this point, Gilly decided it was time to leave. 'If you'll excuse me,' she said, backing away. 'I... er... need to...' She waved her hand in the direction of the lift. 'I need to make a phone call.'

'What's that she said?' Cyril looked confused.

'She's going to make a phone call.'

'A what?'

'A phone call.'

'Who to?'

'Well, I don't know, darling. She didn't say...'

The lift doors closed mercifully on Gilly. She breathed in deeply and pressed the button for the ground floor, steadying herself against the brass rail as the lift began its descent.

The hotel boasted a small bar and lounge area, which was already crowded with passengers from the coach tour. Gilly felt horribly self-conscious as she made her way across the foyer. The meaningful glances she was sure she was attracting didn't exactly make her feel better either. She was sure she could read their thoughts.

'She's the one who went off with Dave last night.'

'They were gone for ages.'

'She looked a bit flushed when they got back.'

'And she's wearing a ring. She's obviously married.'

'The married ones are the worst kind.'

With her cheeks burning she headed to the rack of tourist leaflets and began selecting the ones that interested her, whilst trying to ignore everyone around her. She planned to make a scrapbook of all the places they had visited. She had bought a large notebook just for that purpose, and would stick in leaflets, tickets, brochures and postcards. Angie would probably ridicule her for being childish, but she didn't care. She wanted to remember this holiday. She might not get another one like it.

As she turned to head back to the lift, she saw Dave leaning on the counter talking to the hotel receptionist and for one brief moment, she felt a flutter of what could only be described, bizarrely, as jealousy. Gilly marvelled at the girl, so slim and chic and so utterly French. Her glossy dark hair was pinned back with a silver clasp and she looked very stylish in her smart white blouse and tailored jacket. If she didn't know different, she could have sworn the girl was flirting with him. That enticing smile, those glistening eyes – the blatant eye contact. Transfixed, Gilly watched them, and then froze as Dave suddenly looked sideways and caught her staring at them.

He smiled. 'Ah, Gilly,' he said, 'I was looking for you.'

'You were?' Her heart sank. He was turning towards her, grinning. The people in the foyer were staring at her. Everyone was listening. At least, that's what it seemed like to her.

'There's a message for you.'

'For me?'

Dave was busy thanking the receptionist. He glanced up again and waved the sheet of paper at Gilly. 'It's from your husband,' he added.

Oh no. What now? She hurried forwards, glad that the other passengers would hear she was married.

'He wants you to call him on this number.'
Dave handed her the piece of paper with a smile.

'Oh, right.' Gilly looked at the paper. It wasn't Charles' work number, nor his mobile number. Maybe he'd got a new phone? Which was odd, she thought. Why would he get a new phone? Unless he'd lost his old one. And why wasn't he at home?
She could feel her cheeks burning. Everyone was watching her, including Dave.

'Thanks,' she said, folding up the sheet of paper. 'I'll call him now.'

As she scuttled from the foyer, one elderly gentleman touched her kindly on the arm.

'Not bad news, I hope?'

'No.' She shook her head.

'Only, you looked a bit upset.'

'No, I'm fine. Really.' She carried on walking.

Her sister was lying groaning on her bed as Gilly burst through the door.

'Where've you been,' Angie said. 'I've been so ill.'

'You have?'

'Sick as a dog,' she croaked. 'It must have been those mussels.'

'Or the wine,' Gilly reminded her. 'You were a bit drunk.'
She sat down on the edge of the bed and patted her sister's hand.
Angie was looking very pale.
'Can I get you anything?'

'A drink of water.' Angie flopped back on the pillows. 'I feel awful.'

Gilly refrained from giving her a lecture about self-imposed illness. She'd talk about that later, when she was feeling better. 'It'll have to be bottled,' she said, delving into the holdall she had taken as hand luggage on the coach. 'You can't risk drinking the tap water here.'

'We're in France, not Africa,' Angie muttered, but she accepted the bottle graciously, just the same. She took a few sips, and burped uncomfortably. 'Think I'll skip dinner,' she said.

'It's paid for.'

'Christ, you sound just like Charles. It's paid for so you'd better eat it.'

'Oh, please,' Gilly groaned. 'And talking of Charles, I suppose I'd better ring him.'

'Why?'

'Well, because I should, that's why. He left a message at reception.'

'Saying what?'

'That I should ring him. He's left a new number.' She showed her the piece of paper. 'It's not his work. Mind you, he wouldn't be working at this time, would he?'

'No, but he should be at home.'

'Unless he was out for dinner.'

'Just like you are,' Angie said. 'Honestly, that man. He doesn't give you a moment to yourself, does he? Go on, send him a text. Tell him you're busy.'

'Charles doesn't like text messages. He can never read them without his glasses on.'

Angie gave a snort of derision. 'That's what glasses were invented for. Don't let him rule you when you're on holiday, Gilly. You're here to enjoy yourself, not pamper to his whims. Have a night off, for once. Go for another evening stroll with Dave if you want – I won't say anything. He is quite charismatic,' she added, giving her a knowing wink.

'Angie!' Gilly was incensed. 'I'm married.'

'Oh, yes. So you are. To Charles.'

'Who I'm going to ring right now.'

'Why? Because you're feeling guilty?'

'I am not feeling guilty.'

'Aren't you?' Angie looked surprised. 'Well, good for you.'

'I'm not feeling guilty, because there's nothing to feel guilty about.' She sighed. 'Honestly, you have no idea.'

'You'd be surprised.'

'Anyway, you're a fine one to talk,' Gilly said, affronted now. 'Cavorting round Paris with a bloke who's young enough to be your son.'

'Hardly.'

'And he's rough looking.'

'Really?' Angie considered this for a moment. 'I thought he was rather tasty - in a rugged sort of way.'

'Oh, please!' Gilly groaned.

'Well, what does it matter? I'm not the one who's married.'

'Yes, but you're not divorced either. Think what Simon and the kids would say.'

'Oh, stop being so bloody stuffy. We only went for a meal together. I very much doubt we'll be doing it again.' She groaned and rubbed her stomach. 'Certainly not the way I'm feeling. I thought you were going to phone Charles.'

'I am.' Gilly glanced at her watch. She had about twenty minutes left before dinner and she wanted to have a shower and get changed. She felt hot and sticky and tired from all the travelling.

'Send him my love,' Angie said, smirking. The sarcasm was all too evident in her tone. She had never got on with Charles. Even when Gilly had first married him, she'd said he was overbearing and pompous and she didn't like him.

Gilly flipped open the cover of her phone. Never one to mince her words was Angie. She started to press the keys.

'Blimey. You're not sending him a text message, are you?' Angie sounded incredulous.

'Well, I haven't got time to chat. We'll be going to dinner shortly.'

'You rebel.'

'Shut up and let me concentrate.'

Angie smiled. 'Hope he can find his reading glasses.'

'You and me both,' she said ending her message with an x. There – she'd done it and if he didn't like it there was nothing she could do about it. She pressed the 'send' button and popped her phone back in her handbag. 'Right – a quick shower and then dinner.'

'Count me out,' Angie groaned.

'Oh.' Gilly paused halfway to the bathroom and glanced back at her. 'Won't you come down to the dining room with me? You don't have to eat anything. I don't really want to go on my own.'

'Darling, I'd heave at the sight of food. It's not a good look.'

'Yes, but...'

'You'll be fine,' Angie assured her. 'They won't leave you on your own. They'll sit you with someone else. Failing that,' she added, giving her a wicked grin, 'you can always sit with Dave.'

Gilly stood under the steady stream of warm water, and lathered herself liberally with the complementary shower gel that had been provided for them. It smelt of magnolia and roses and was actually quite pleasant.

The same could not be said for the plastic shower cap, which looked like a freezer bag and wasn't particularly efficient at keeping her hair dry.

She rubbed a clear space in the steamy mirror with the back of her hand and peered at her bedraggled reflection. It was a good job she'd packed her hair-dryer.

'Are you sure you won't join me?' she asked Angie, teasing the last few tangles from her hair. She had changed into a long, linen skirt and a crinkled white blouse that the sales person had assured her was ideal for travelling since it didn't require ironing. Gilly thought that a quick run-over with a steam iron might have improved the look, but who was she to judge. Besides, Angie said it looked fine.

'It's more me, than you,' she said, 'but it suits you.'

'You're sure it's not too see-through?'

'So what if it is? It's not,' Angie added, quickly. 'And no, I won't be joining you for dinner. I'm sorry, Gilly, but I just don't feel up to it.'

'Maybe I could order room service?'

'Oh, and you think watching you eat will make me feel better?' Angie shook her head. 'Now don't be such a wimp. Off you go and let me suffer in silence.'

'That'll be a first,' Gilly said, picking up her handbag. She didn't want to go on her own, but she was feeling hungry – starving, in fact. She'd had nothing apart from a coffee and a delicious lemon crepe after they got off the riverboat in Paris. The handful of ginger and some travel sweets on the coach weren't enough to fill her up. There was nothing else for it, but to make her way downstairs and hope that she could find a like-minded person to share a table with. It was only for one night, after all. Angie, she decided, would be right as rain by the morning.

Chapter Eight

'Carl? Coo-ee! Carl, are you ready yet?'

His gran's frantic tap tap tapping on the door sounded like a demented woodpecker overdosing on speed.

Carl stood in front of the mirror, slowly fastening the buttons of his black shirt. 'Give me five minutes.'

The knocking stopped. 'Aren't you going to let me in?' The door handle began to jiggle up and down.

'I'm getting dressed.' He tucked the shirt into the waistband of his jeans and then buckled his belt.

'I don't mind.'

No, but I do, he thought, adding, 'I won't be long.'

The jiggling stopped. 'I'll go downstairs, shall I?'

'Yes.' He put some aftershave on his hands and rubbed it onto his jaw and neck. 'Good idea.'

'You won't be long, will you, Carl?'

'No.'

'Only they're all going down for dinner.'

'I'll be there in a minute.'

He slipped his wallet into the back pocket of his jeans and then stood listening by the door to make sure she'd gone. The old dear still thought of him as a little boy. "Can I come in?" He smiled to himself. She hadn't seen him in the all together since primary school. He'd always been a private person, and that was just how it was going to stay – or at least, it was as far as his gran was concerned. With other people, there was always room for negotiation

He cocked his head to one side. He could hear the soft whirr of machinery as the lift made its descent. Satisfied that his grandmother was on her way downstairs, he eased open the door and peered along the passageway. His room was on the second floor, thankfully far enough removed from his gran, who had secured a room adjacent to the lift on account of her dodgy hip.

Angie and her sister were on the third floor – almost directly above him, he reckoned. It was time he found out. He needed to get that package back.

Tempting though it was to let them take it through customs for him (and he had considered that idea) he knew he couldn't run the risk of Angie opening the envelope.

He took the stairs, two at a time, and eased the door open in time to see the younger of the two sisters stepping into the lift. Gilly was on her own, which was a stroke of luck. It meant Angie must be in the bedroom.

He watched discreetly, waiting for the lift doors to close. She had a nice figure, he thought – in fact, very tasty – trim and toned. Her top was virtually see-through. It didn't leave a lot to the imagination – and he had a very vivid imagination.

The thoughts of a threesome flitted briefly across his mind – an interesting idea – but probably unlikely. Still, one could always live in hope. People often lost their inhibitions when they were on holiday. He could vouch for that.

The lift doors closed with a loud swish. Carl stepped onto the landing. At the far end of the corridor, an elderly couple were fumbling with their key card. They spotted him before he could duck back out of sight.

'Oh, I say – young man?'

Carl cursed under his breath. He forced a smile onto his face.

'Could you help us?'

They were making futile attempts to insert the card into the lock, jabbing it up and down in a frenzy that was doing nothing for the inner workings of the electronic mechanism.

'I don't know why they couldn't give us a key,' the woman said, bewildered. 'This thing doesn't seem to work at all.'

'Do it slowly,' Carl said, taking the card from them and inserting it into the lock. 'Really slowly.' (His thoughts were still playing with the idea of a cosy threesome.) 'See? Slow and gentle.' He ran his tongue over his lips. 'Then leave it a few seconds and bingo - the green light comes on.' He pressed open the handle and the door swung open.

'Oh, you're so kind.' The woman was in raptures. 'Isn't he kind, Cyril?'

'So kind,' repeated the old man.

Carl got the distinct impression that the man was away with the fairies. He was pressing the handle down and swinging the door backwards and forwards as if he couldn't quite believe what he was seeing.

'You're welcome,' Carl said. 'Now, if you'll excuse me.'

He tried to make out he was a man in a hurry – which indeed, he was.

'Oh yes, sorry. And thanks again.' The woman ushered her husband through the open bedroom door, with a 'let's just see if we can find where you put your pills, dear.'

Carl didn't hang about. He made his way back along the softly carpeted corridor. Judging by the direction that Gilly had come from,

Angie's room must be one of the front-facing ones and there weren't that many to choose from.

He tilted his head towards one of the closed doors and gently jiggled the handle, on the off chance that it might be open. It wasn't. He gave a light rap on the door. 'Angie?'

Silence.

'Angie,' he hissed again. 'You in there?'

He knocked again – louder this time. He was sure he could hear something. It sounded like the creaking of bedsprings.

'It's me,' he said, and then added, in case she'd forgotten, 'It's Carl.'

Carl? Angie sat bolt upright on the bed and immediately wished that she hadn't. The room swam dizzily around her and a fresh cramp gripped her intestines. Oh God, she couldn't let him see her like this. She eased herself off the bed and groped her way along the wall towards the toilet. Perhaps if she kept quiet he would think she wasn't there, and would go away.She squeezed into the small cubicle and pushed the door shut.

'Angie?'

She froze as she heard him trying the door handle.

Carl pressed his head closer to the bedroom door. Someone was moving about in there. It had to be Angie. Who else could it be?

'Look, I won't keep you,' he said. 'You obviously want to be left alone. I just need to collect my gran's medicine.'

The medicine? Of course – the stuff he'd bought from the street pedlar in Paris.

Angie perched herself on the seat of the toilet and pressed her stomach with her hands in an effort to ease the cramps.

It was no good. She couldn't open the door to him – not when she was feeling like this. The last thing she wanted was to frighten off the only young and half-decent man on the coach. Not before she'd managed to take a selfie with him to put on Facebook, anyway. She wanted Simon to see how much she was enjoying herself, even if she wasn't.

'I'm in the bathroom,' she said, trying to keep her voice light and airy. As a stroke of genius, she quickly turned on the shower.

Carl swore under his breath as he heard the splishing and splashing of water. 'How long are you going to be?'

'Ages,' came the cheery reply.

Carl sighed. 'Right. I'd better wait downstairs for you, then'

What else could he say? He didn't exactly have a lot of choice in the matter. 'You won't forget to bring the package with you?' he added. 'Only gran's been having a spot of trouble with her ulcer and this rich foreign food won't be doing her any good at all. You know what these old folk are like.'

'Yes, okay. I won't forget.'

Angie tried to keep her voice steady as she was gripped by another agonising cramp. Crikey – this was worse than being in labour. One thing was for sure: she wouldn't touch another mussel for as long as she lived – if she lived.

Carl was left with two choices. He could either hang about in the corridor and hope that Angie was quicker than she said she was going to be, or he could give it up as a lost cause, and go and join his grandmother.

In the end, the decision was made for him by the untimely arrival of the coach driver, who was shepherding the last stragglers towards the dining room, where the French hosts were eager to get the first coach-load through dinner, so they could set the tables for their other, more lucrative, 'a la carte' guests.

'Ah, there you are,' Dave said, stepping out of the lift with a clipboard in his hand and ticking his name off the list. 'If you could make your way downstairs, Mr Goodman, they're ready for us now. Mrs Turner?' He rapped on Angie's door. 'Mrs Turner.'

'She's in the shower,' Carl said, as he brushed past him.

'Will she be joining us for dinner?'

He shrugged. 'Your guess is as good as mine.'

The dining room was full to overflowing, with seats squeezed around every available surface in an effort to accommodate all the passengers in one sitting. It was not conducive to a relaxing and intimate atmosphere.

Carl found himself positioned between his gran and a middle-aged man from Luton, a librarian, apparently, called Geoffrey with a G, who informed them that he was on his own because none of his friends could be persuaded to go with him. The highlights of European architecture, he said, were not everyone's cup of tea, and this trip had much to recommend it in the way of cultural heritage.

Carl hacked a piece of bread from a French stick and smothered it in butter. He had lost interest in the conversation somewhere in the middle of Geoffrey's account of Gustave Eiffel's engineering contribution to mark the centenary of the French Revolution.

Who gave a shit about the Eiffel Tower, anyway? From his experience, it was a haven for tourists, pickpockets and over-priced souvenir sellers. He reached for the carafe of red wine. As he did so, he was conscious of being watched. Glancing up, he found his gaze drawn to Angie's sister. She was seated almost opposite him, and staring at him with a look of blatant curiosity on her face. He poured himself a generous amount of wine, and then smiled as he raised the glass to her.

Looking flustered, she dropped her gaze.

'You going to pour me a glass of that?' His gran gave him an unwelcome dig in the side with her elbow.

'Thought you didn't drink.'

'Well, I'm on me hols, aren't I? One glass won't hurt.'

'You won't like it.'

He dribbled a small amount into her wine glass.

Beaming, she raised it into the air and grinned at her fellow diners. 'Cheers everyone.'

Carl cringed. 'Cheers,' he muttered, taking a large mouthful.

All around him, his fellow diners were exchanging pleasantries and trying to engage him in conversation – helped, no doubt, by the generous amounts of gut-wrenching wine that was free and therefore had to be drunk in vast quantities.

As the meal progressed, he saw several florid cheeks and sweat-beaded foreheads, all belonging to those who were presumably unaccustomed to consuming alcohol except maybe the odd dry sherry at Christmas or on special occasions, but who, like his gran, felt obliged to indulge the moment they were on holiday, especially if it was included in the price of the meal.

Carl felt like the proverbial fish out of water. What the hell was he doing here with this motley assortment of people? The retired clerks and shop workers, the group from an old people's block of flats in Salford, and bloody Geoffrey with a G, who he was tempted to throttle should he utter one more sentence beginning with, 'And I don't suppose you know, but...'

There had to be easier ways of earning a quick buck. He'd swing for that idiot Wayne, who'd been so full of 'oh, join a coach-load of pensioners; it'll be a cinch, man, and you get a holiday into the bargain.' Well some bloody holiday this was turning out to be. Christ, he'd had more fun at Butlins as a kid when he'd come down with mumps, and that was saying something.

'And I don't suppose you know, but the Chateau at Versailles...'

Carl was rapidly losing the will to live.

His gran, however, was in her element, happily telling complete strangers about her wonderful grandson and how kind it was that he had offered to take her on this holiday – to foreign climes, no less.

'Think you've had enough of that wine, gran,' Carl muttered, taking the carafe out of her hands. 'It's pretty heady stuff.'

'Rubbish – I'm on me hols.'

'Yeah, and we've got a long drive tomorrow. You don't want a hangover.'

'Personally, I've never touched alcohol,' Geoffrey said, taking a sip of mineral water.

Somehow, Carl wasn't in the least bit surprised.

'I don't know if you know this,' he continued, 'but alcohol is actually a poison.'

'Indeed.' Carl fiddled with his steak knife, idly wondering just how sharp it was, and whether it was worth risking a life sentence to sever the man's jugular.

'Oh yes. It's rather toxic.'

'It's also bloody liberating.' Carl drained his glass and reached for a top-up. 'People speak the truth once they've had a drink. No inhibitions – nothing. Just the plain truth.'

'Carl.' His gran rested a warning hand on his forearm.

The moment passed. He had to stay calm; he knew that. Drawing attention to himself was not part of the plan. Yet this annoying prick was doing his head in. He stabbed his knife into the plump and juicy steak, and watched the blood trickle in rivulets into the heap of green beans and sautéed potatoes.

'The food's nice, isn't it?'

Carl glanced up, surprised, since the comment seemed to be directed at him. It was.

Gilly gave him a shy smile from her seat across the table. 'I don't usually like steak,' she added, 'but this is very good.'

'Yeah, it's not bad.'

He chewed slowly, giving her a considered look as he did so.

'Where's Angie?' he asked. 'Isn't she joining you for dinner?'

He had already noticed that the seats either side of Gilly had been taken. He would have expected her to keep at least one of them free for her sister. The fact that she hadn't suggested that she wasn't going to be eating with them. Which again posed the problem of when he was going to get that blinking package from her.

'She's not feeling very well.'

'Really?' This was news to him. She'd been fine at lunchtime.

'It'll be the water,' Geoffrey with a G, said, speaking with the firm assurance of a man who knows these things. 'I always drink bottled when I'm abroad.'

'So do I,' Gilly said, sounding almost gleeful that she had discovered a kindred spirit. 'I told Angie that as well, but she said it didn't matter when we were in Europe.'

'Nonsense. It's better to be safe than sorry. I'll tell you something else, as well. Now you might not know this, but...'

'Mussels,' Carl said, spearing his last bit of steak onto the end of his fork and waving it in Geoffrey's face. 'It would be the mussels she ate at lunchtime. Invariably dodgy,' he added, 'but I expect you know that.'

'Well, yes.' Geoffrey said, sounding a trifle peeved that his speech had been stopped in mid stride. 'Yes, actually.' He drew in a breath, paused a moment to seemingly re-gather his thoughts, and then continued with: 'Shellfish are renowned for...'

'Causing food poisoning.' Carl reached for the carafe of wine. 'Yes, I think we all know that.' Christ, he'd had enough of this idiot. He glanced at Gilly. 'Is that what's wrong with her?'

'Um, well, she's been sick.'

'Oh please!' An elderly woman with a face like a boiled prune scowled at them from the end of the table. 'Do we need to have this conversation? We are trying to eat, you know?'

'Sorry.' Gilly blushed.

Carl was incensed. 'Don't apologise to her. You'd think she'd have a bit more sympathy.' He glared at the woman. 'Her sister's ill,' he announced loudly. 'She's got food poisoning. And she's supposed to be enjoying the first day of her holiday.'

'It could be the water,' Geoffrey muttered, but no one was listening to him. An awkward hush had descended on the dining room, broken only by the clatter of cutlery and the odd subdued whisper here and there.

'Is there a problem, here?' Dave said, rising from his seat. He was watching Gilly as he spoke.

'No.' She shook her head.

'Yes, there is. Her sister's bleeding ill,' Barbara said, adding her opinion to the conversation. 'I thought she looked a bit peaky on the coach.'

'Yes, well, she'd been ill on the ferry,' Dave said. 'Sometimes it takes a while to get over a bout of seasickness.'

'Oh, for goodness sake!' The exasperated sigh came from the prune-faced woman.

Dave ignored her. He glanced back at Gilly. 'You should have told me she was still poorly. What's your room number, and I'll go and check on her?'

'Twenty three.'

'Right – have you got your key card?'

'Yes, but I think I'd better come with you. She won't appreciate it if you just walk in.'

Carl saw his chance. Never one to miss an opportunity, he scraped back his chair. 'I'll come with you,' he said.

'You?' Dave and Gilly chorused together.

'Well, I was with her when she ate the mussels. It's the least I can do. Besides,' he added. 'I've finished here.'

'But you ain't had your pudding, Carl. You know how you always liked your puddings.' Barbara looked disappointed. 'I think it's some sort of fancy gateau.' She was peering at one of the nearby tables as she spoke. 'Shall I keep you one?'

'Yes, all right.'

'There's no need for all of us to go.' Gilly was protesting feebly. 'I'm sure Angie will be fine.'

'I'd like to see her for myself,' Dave said, ushering her forwards. 'She might need medical help.'

Carl followed with what he hoped was a look of sympathetic concern on his face. With any luck, he'd get a chance to retrieve the package while they were fussing over the invalid – and by being helpful he was showing himself in a good light, which wouldn't do any harm. My God, he could win an Oscar at this rate.

Standing in the lift together gave him a chance to study Gilly at close quarters – discreetly of course, seeing as how the coach driver seemed to be doing the same thing, but with an altogether more protective stance.

His reassuring pat on her shoulder as he did so was giving Carl the clear signal that he fancied her – loud and clear. Mind you, not that he could blame him. Of the two sisters, she was certainly the more attractive, and with a tidy looking body on her as well.

The lift doors opened and he followed the pair of them onto the landing.

'I think I should go in first,' Gilly said. 'She might be in bed. Angie?' She knocked sharply on the door. 'Angie, Dave and Carl are with me. We just want to check you're okay.'

The tinkle of laughter startled all three of them.

Gilly glanced up at Dave, puzzled.

He shrugged. 'Go on. Open it.'

Carl had a sudden horrible sinking feeling in the pit of his stomach. Oh God – she couldn't have. Could she?

'Angie?' Gilly pushed open the door. 'Are you all right?'

Oh God! She had. Carl's heart sank.

Angie lay sprawled in a position of gay abandon on the bed. She was draped in a flimsy sheet like a latter day Marilyn Monroe, her brightly painted toenails peeping out from beneath the covers. The clothes she had been wearing were scattered on the floor. A plump and tanned thigh showed revealingly in a gap between the sheets.

'Darlings!' she said, flopping her head back against the plumped-up pillows. Her eyes were glazed and she had a stupid grin on her face. 'I'm absolutely fine.'

No, she bloody wasn't. She was stoned – off her head and high as a kite. Somebody was going to have some explaining to do, and Carl had the uncomfortable feeling that it was going to be him.

Chapter Nine

'I don't know what you were thinking,' Gilly muttered, as she stuffed her sisters' negligee and folded-up towelling travel slippers into her suitcase. 'Stomach medicine indeed.'

'Carl said they were good for ulcers,' Angie moaned. 'He said his grandmother swore by them.'

She was perched on the end of the bed, peering at her sallow-faced reflection in the mirror. She was feeling a bit like death warmed up, and looking like it too, if she was honest with herself. She raised a tentative hand to her forehead and wondered if she dared to take a painkiller to ease the throbbing in her temples.

'Anyway,' she said. 'They made me feel better at the time.'

'They could have killed you.' Gilly slammed the suitcase shut and yanked at the zip. 'Unregulated Chinese medicine. I ask you. And bought from a street trader as well.' The scorn was evident in her tone. Angie's half-hearted confession - that she had opened the envelope and taken a couple of the tablets Carl had bought for his gran's stomach problems - was not going down well. Perhaps it might have been better if she'd just pretended to be drunk. They'd assumed that much, anyway.

'Oh, don't go on.'

'Well.' Gilly sniffed. 'I would have expected better from you. You're the one that's always telling me how naïve I am. How gullible.'

'All right, all right – I made a mistake.'

'Not just you. That Carl wasn't so clever either. Just imagine what would have happened if he had given them to his gran?'

'I don't want to think about it.' Angie dabbed blusher onto her cheeks with a soft sable brush. She felt like she had the hangover from hell, coupled with a raging thirst that had her downing two of Gilly's bottles of water in rapid succession. Oddly enough, she had felt perfectly fine the night before. So much so that she'd actually wanted to stay up and party, long after her sister had insisted she go to bed and stay there, in the tone of voice that had left no room for argument.

She had vague memories of Dave wanting to call a doctor, and Carl protesting loudly, saying she was obviously drunk and no French doctor would appreciate being called out at this time of night. He'd been most insistent – saying it was his fault. He'd even offered to sit with her while they went back to finish their dinner.

Angie knew that Gilly wouldn't have contemplated leaving her, the state she was in, but it was kind of him to offer, just the same.

She folded down the top of the envelope containing the tablets – the ones she had innocently assumed would do her some good and settle her stomach - and tucked them into her handbag. She wondered if Carl would still want them, when she told him what had happened. She ought to tell him what she'd done, if only to protect his gran from any harm.

'You should flush those down the loo,' Gilly said, exasperated.

'I can't do that. He paid good money for them.'

'From an itinerant street pedlar – oh, do me a favour.' Gilly pummelled and puffed up the pillows on the bed as she spoke. 'If it was up to me I'd be calling the local gendarmes. That stuff could be dangerous.'

'I'm still here, aren't I?'

'Yes, but you didn't see the state you were in last night.'

'Well, I felt all right,' Angie recalled. 'They stopped me feeling sick. In fact, they made me feel better.'

'Oh, please!' Gilly groaned, pulling up the covers and straightening the beds as she spoke.

'All I'm saying is, I'll give them back to Carl and he can decide what to do with them.' She watched her sister tidying around the bedroom and added, 'I don't know why you bother. The cleaners are only going to come in and change all the sheets.'

'It makes the place look better.'

Angie pouted into the mirror and patted her rose-red lips with a piece of tissue from the complimentary box on the dressing table. 'Who cares?'

'I do,' Gilly said, a trifle tersely. 'And if you cared about appearances, you'd get a move on. We're due down for breakfast and you know how I hate to be late.'

One liberally buttered croissant, two pieces of fresh crusty bread smothered in jam, and a decent pot of coffee later, and Angie was beginning to feel a whole lot better. Embarrassed, obviously, and rather more subdued than usual (even Gilly commented on that one), but ready to face the human race again or, in this case, the rest of the coach party.

'How's the hangover?' Dave asked, pausing to stop at their table on his way out of the dining room. He had a knowing smile on his face.

'I've had worse,' Angie sighed, reaching for the jug of orange juice. 'Sorry.'

'Don't worry about it. As long as you're feeling better.'

'I am, thanks.'

He nodded. 'Well, as long as it doesn't spoil your day. We've got a long drive ahead of us this morning.' He straightened up and glanced at his watch. 'About twenty minutes, folks,' he said, letting his gaze circle the crowded dining room. 'I'll just check the last of the cases have been brought down by the porters and then we'll make a move. Twenty minutes,' he added loudly, for those who were hard of hearing.

That would be most of them, Angie thought, as she downed yet another glass of fruit juice. She'd never felt so thirsty in ages. Presumably the sickness had left her seriously dehydrated.

'See.' Gilly dug her in the ribs with her elbow. 'I told you it would be all right.' She glanced round the room. 'There's no sign of that Carl, though. He must have come in earlier.'

'Good.' At this precise moment in time, Angie didn't think she was up to facing him – not after Gilly had given her such a graphic description of how she had behaved the previous evening. Apparently (and her sister wasn't prone to exaggeration), she had even patted the bed and suggested he join her – and in front of Dave as well. Oh, and high as a kite, too. That was it! Angie suddenly had a moment of clarity. What if they weren't stomach tablets? What if they were something else? Oh God! She glanced down at her handbag, nestling at her feet. What if they were something illegal? One corner of the brown envelope was on show, and she hurriedly leaned over and tucked it out of sight.

'No sign of Barbara either, thank goodness,' Gilly said, topping up her cup with a watery brew that was supposed to be tea. 'Do you want some? It's a bit weak but the coffee was far too strong for me.'

'No.' Angie drained her glass. She was feeling quite sick and it wasn't to do with anything she had eaten or drunk.

Carl wouldn't have known, of course. She was sure of it. He'd bought the tablets in good faith for his grandmother. That was the trouble with buying from an un-licensed source. She'd read about things like this in the papers, of people buying vitamins and medicines – particularly Chinese medicines - from the internet and ending up being really poorly. Good grief, the tablets could have been anything. She was sure she'd read somewhere that illegal traders mixed them with chalk and salt and all sorts of stuff.

She reached for the jug of fruit juice and topped up her glass again. This unquenchable thirst was unlike anything she'd ever had before and it could only be due to one thing: the tablets. How could she have been so stupid? The trouble was she'd been feeling so horribly sick she would have taken anything to settle her stomach, and the tablets had, supposedly, been for stomach problems. It had seemed like the perfect solution at the time. Thank goodness she'd only taken a couple of them.

'Excellent. Plenty of fluids – that's the trick.'

Angie stared upwards at the thin, weedy-looking man with the small chin and wispy hair who had made a point of stopping right in front of their table and was nodding solicitously at her.

'Oh, er, Angie, this is Geoffrey,' Gilly said.

'Geoffrey?'

'We met last night.'

'Oh.'

'When you were ill.'

'Yes, I know. Don't remind me.' She managed a weak smile. 'Hello, Geoffrey.'

'He's from Luton,' Gilly added.

Angie resisted the urge to say, 'So?' and merely nodded agreeably. She didn't feel like making small talk with anyone – least of all this man, who couldn't have been more unappealing if he had tried. Her quick appraisal of him had taken in the rumpled shirt, creased trousers and shabby sandals (with socks) and found him wanting.

Geoffrey, however, had no such reticence. To Angie's horror, he immediately pulled out a chair that had been newly vacated directly opposite her and plonked himself down on it.

'It's not unusual to fall ill when travelling,' he said. 'I've had years of experience. Oh yes. I like to think of myself as a seasoned traveller. You have to be so careful with the water and the food – and basic hygiene, of course. Re-hydration – that's the secret. I don't suppose you know this, but...'

Angie kicked Gilly quite sharply under the table, and shot her a look that spoke volumes.

'Goodness!' Gilly choked, giving her a pained glare. 'Is that the time?' She scraped back her chair with an apologetic, 'Geoffrey, we need to go. The coach will be leaving shortly and we're not quite ready yet.'

'Oh,' he said. He looked disappointed. He'd obviously been getting into his stride. Another one to avoid, Angie thought, giving him a practised smile.

'Maybe we could chat later.'

'Maybe,' she lied. Not if she could help it. She swallowed the last mouthful of juice, snatched up her bag, and headed after her sister.

Gilly was standing by the lift, jabbing at the button.

'Where did you find him?'

Her sister glared at her. 'I'll have you know it wasn't very nice having to go down to dinner on my own. At least he was friendly and took the time to talk to me.'

'Well, you didn't have to talk back. Anyway, I couldn't help it. I was ill.'

'Drunk, more like.'

The lift doors opened. Angie stepped to one side to let the people come out. It was probably just as well that her sister thought she was drunk. She was so bloody moral that if she thought she'd been taking – to say nothing of carrying – illegal drugs, she'd be on to the police like a shot, and being banged up in a French jail wasn't exactly an appealing thought. Oh God, how could she have been so stupid? She tucked her bag under her armpit. The thought of what it contained was making her feel distinctly nervous. As soon as she got back to their room she intended to flush the whole lot down the loo.

She was so intent on getting into the lift that she failed to pay attention to who was coming out of it. Which is how she found herself practically face to face with Carl Goodman and his grandmother Barbara, who chose that precise moment to step out into the foyer.

'Oh, there you are. Carl was wondering how you were feeling.' The older woman beamed knowingly at her. ' "Too much of the French vino", that's what he said.' She tapped the side of her nose. 'Mind you, I'll admit to feeling a bit iffy myself, this morning.'

Angie managed a weak smile. 'I'm fine, thanks.'

The look Carl gave her showed that he wasn't convinced. 'We need to talk,' he said, abruptly side-stepping in front of her, so that her way was blocked.

Angie saw that Gilly was already in the lift and several people had crammed in beside her.

'It's not really convenient...'

'Now.' He didn't move. Nor did Barbara, who was continuing to chatter away, oblivious to the fact that her comments were being totally ignored by the pair of them.

Angie caught sight of Gilly's worried look as the lift doors closed on her. 'I need to go back to my room,' she said.

'I'll come with you.' Carl lowered his head closer to hers, so close that she caught the heady scent of his aftershave. 'What were you thinking of?'

'Me!' Angie was affronted. 'What were you thinking of?'

'I'll just go hand these key cards in, shall I, Carl?' Barbara waggled a finger in the direction of the reception desk. 'There's a bit of a queue.'

'Yeah, okay.' He straightened up. 'I'm just going to help Angie with her bags.'

Like hell you are, Angie thought. With a defiant toss of her head, she turned and headed for the stairs.

Carl was right behind her.

'I should be touched you're so concerned,' she said.

'Of course I'm concerned. You were off your head last night.'

'Yes, on your grandmother's bloody tablets.'

He sighed and shook his head. 'You shouldn't have taken them, Angie. They weren't prescribed for you.'

'Or your grandmother either, actually,' she snapped. 'What on earth possessed you to buy them for her? They could have been anything. Don't you know about the dangers of unlicensed medicine?' She paused to let an elderly couple that had obviously tired of waiting for the lift make their slow and laborious way down the stairs.

'Angie, I had no idea. She's had them before.'

'From here?'

'From the internet. I've ordered them online but it's expensive. A guy I worked with told me about these traders – told me where I could get them really cheap. I only did it for her,' he added.

Angie remembered the way he had walked the streets of Paris like a man on a mission after they had left the others on the pleasure cruiser. The way he had seemed to know where to go and why he had headed for the rundown bistro instead of one of the more trendy cafes. It all started to make sense now – and it all seemed perfectly plausible.

'Yes, well, it's a jolly good job you didn't give her any. I only took a couple of tablets and look how they affected me.'

'Yes, I know, and I'm so sorry. I had no idea. Honestly, I didn't.' He leaned against the oak banisters and sucked in a deep breath. 'Where are they now?'

'What?'

'The rest of the tablets.'

They had reached the landing, and she pushed open the fire doors. 'I threw them away.'

'You did what?' he choked, the colour draining from his face. 'Angie, you can't have...' He stopped in mid-sentence as they both stepped to one side to let a porter with two cases struggle past them. 'Seriously – you haven't chucked them out, have you?'

'I have, actually,' she said, reaching in her pocket for the key card to her door. She wasn't sure why she was lying to him – not that it mattered, as she had every intention of throwing them away - but she was quite surprised at his reaction.

'Where are they? Did you put them in the bin?'

76

He had caught hold of her arm and his grip was so tight that it was starting to hurt her.

'Of course not,' she said. 'I flushed them down the toilet. Why? Did you hope to get a refund?'

She slid the card into the door and breathed out a sigh of relief as the green light flashed and she could turn the handle.

'Jesus, Angie! You don't know what you've done.'

'Likewise,' she said, pulling her arm free. Her gaze met his, and held. 'See you on the coach, Carl.'

She slipped into the bedroom, closed the door and leaned with her back on it, listening to the sound of his footsteps heading away from her.

'Is that you, Ange?' came Gilly's voice from the vicinity of the tiny en-suite bathroom.

'Yes.'

'I'll be out in a minute.'

'There's no hurry.'

Angie felt as if her legs were made of jelly. She needed to sit down. She also needed the toilet. Drinking copious amounts of liquid before a long coach journey was probably not one of her better ideas.

Gilly stepped out of the tiny bathroom, a foaming toothbrush poking out of the corner of her mouth. 'At last,' she said. 'Well, did you get it sorted?'

'Naturally.' Angie plonked her handbag on the bed and nodded her head.

'Did you give him the tablets back?'

'No. I told him I'd thrown them away.'

'Quite right too.' Gilly ducked back into the bathroom to swill her mouth out with water from the bottle she kept by the basin. 'I expect he was quite relieved,' she added.

'Possibly,' Angie said, though she wasn't quite sure how she would have described Carl's reaction. Probably not 'relieved'.

She reached into the bottom of her bag and pulled out the brown envelope. The packet contained about a hundred tablets – ninety-eight, perhaps, as she had taken two. She had no idea what they were or what they contained and she didn't want to know. But she had a good idea what they were used for.

She folded down the top of the envelope and squashed the packet into as small a parcel as she could make. Then she placed it into the zippered pocket of her handbag. She'd think about it later, she told herself, firmly. She had far more pressing things to think about first – getting ready to board the coach in less than fifteen minutes being one of them.

Chapter Ten

'Montrichard.' Gilly jabbed at the pocket map with her index finger. 'There it is, in the Loire valley. That's where we're staying.'

Angie tried to feign interest, even going so far as to glance at the itinerary, but the delights of the French countryside were furthest from her thoughts.

She was uncomfortably aware of the hostile vibes coming from several rows behind them on the coach, where Carl was seated with his grandmother. Real or imagined, the result was the same. It didn't make for a pleasant journey.

Angie peered at her reflection in the polished glass of the window. Her eyes looked puffy and bloodshot. She groped in her handbag for her sunglasses. So far, she had managed to avoid speaking to him. A short comfort stop at a motorway service station had seen her scuttling to the ladies room without a backward glance, and loitering there until it was time to get back on the coach.

Not even Gilly's offer of a tempting iced coffee would lure her from the sanctuary of the cubicles.

'There's a loo on the coach,' her sister had reminded her. 'You don't have to stay in here.'

'Believe me, I do. Now leave me alone.'

No way was she going to give Carl the opportunity to confront her over the tablets. Not since she still had them in her handbag. Consequently, she'd spent the best part of half an hour pretending to touch up her makeup, whilst making amiable comments to all the passengers that streamed past her, including Barbara, who was never short of a word or two.

'Ooh, there you are, duck.' The older woman peered at her over the top of her spectacles, whilst liberally rinsing her hands under the tap. 'How are you feeling now?'

'Fabulous.'

'That's good. At least it hasn't spoilt your holiday.'

'No.'

Angie reapplied her lipstick for the zillionth time. She was conscious that Barbara was standing alongside, patiently watching her. 'Don't wait for me,' she added. 'I'll be ages.'

The last thing she wanted was Carl's gran escorting her back to the coach, tempting though it might be to have a chat about the restorative merits of stomach medicine.

Stomach medicine my foot!

Goodness, she'd been such a fool. And Carl wasn't as innocent as he made out to be, either. He must have known what the tablets were. You didn't buy drugs from a dodgy dealer and assume they were legit. He knew full well what they were – and got her to carry them for him into the bargain. The conniving, lying toad.

The trouble was, she was still carrying them. Short of flushing them down the loo – and it was a tempting option, if she could be convinced that they would flush away, and not sit in the bottom of the pan – what else could she do? Her sense of moral righteousness refused to let her just dump them in the bin. What if a child found them – or a tramp searching for something edible? No, she would just have to hang on to them until another, more suitable option presented itself to her, though what that would be, she wasn't quite sure. Perhaps she could stick them through the letterbox of a local pharmacy – anonymously, of course – should they ever get near to one.

She flicked a comb through her hair. It was time to head back to the coach. Hopefully Barbara and Carl would have resumed their places and she wouldn't have to face them – at least, not until they stopped for lunch, when a protracted stay in the toilets was probably out of the question.

'Are you sure you're all right?' Gilly whispered, as she followed her on to the coach. 'I was starting to get worried.'

'Yes, I'm fine.' Angie fastened her seat belt. 'Honestly - I'm fine.' As she glanced across at her sister, she also managed a surreptitious glance down the length of the coach. She could see Barbara's plastic shopping bag bulging out from the side of her seat, which meant that Carl was safely tucked away by the window seat. That was good. At least he wouldn't be able to glare at her for the rest of the journey.

'What were you doing that took you so long?'

Angie looked back at her sister and sighed. 'I phoned Simon.'

'You what?'

'I phoned Simon,' she repeated. It wasn't a lie. She had, in fact, rung her soon-to-be – ex-husband's number on her mobile, knowing full well that he wouldn't be able to answer it. He never did when he was at work. But it had been somewhat reassuring to hear the familiar tone of his voice on the answering machine.

'Hello, Simon Turner here. Sorry I can't take your call at the moment but leave me your number and I'll get back to you.'

If he had answered, she wasn't sure what she would have done – pretended she'd got a wrong number, or called him by mistake, she supposed. She wouldn't have known what to say. The thing is, she remembered fondly, he'd always been good in a crisis. And he'd always been extremely attentive and concerned when she'd been ill. Like that time when they'd been on a cruise ship in the Med, and a particularly debilitating tummy bug had left her with such severe disorientation and dehydration that he had insisted on staying with her in the sick bay, even though the doctors warned him that he could come down with it too. He'd held her hand the whole time, without a thought for his own health, and he'd been fine, not even a twinge of nausea. He must have loved her then, she mused. But it had been a long time ago. Years before his midlife crisis had led him into the arms of another woman – a much younger woman, she thought bitterly.

'But why did you ring him?' Gilly gasped.

Angie shrugged. 'I don't know. I think I just wanted to hear his voice.'

'But you're in the middle of divorcing him.'

'I know.'

'For adultery.'

'Yes, I know. Don't rub it in.'

'So?' Gilly looked perplexed. 'You're not having second thoughts, are you?'

Angie wasn't sure. Was she? Or wasn't she?

No. She didn't want to stay married to a man who couldn't keep his trousers on. It was the ultimate betrayal. And all right, they hadn't been having much sex at the time, but the menopause had a lot to do with that. She couldn't be expected to be all loving and attentive when she was awake half the night with pouring sweats and raging hormones. It was worse than being a teenager. Simon should have understood that. He'd always understood her so well before.

'You said this holiday was a new start.' Gilly was looking worried. 'You said it was just the break you needed – your chance to get away and have some fun.'

'Well, I'm having bucket-loads of that.'

What with seasickness, food poisoning and drug induced hallucinations, what else did she need?

'You're just feeling a bit low,' Gilly said, which was a blatant understatement. 'You'll be fine once we get to our hotel. Look, it's by the river, and I think they have a spa pool and relaxation centre.' She wagged the brochure at her. 'You could have a massage, or some treatments. You're always telling me to have a treatment, a facial or something.'

'You've changed your tune,' Angie said, managing to smile. 'You told me that Charles thought it was a waste of money and only for the likes of the mega-rich or those with aspirations above their station to have any kind of spa treatment.'

'Yes, well, that was Charles talking. I don't have to agree with everything he says.'

'No.' Angie grinned. 'And lately you've been agreeing with him less and less. Odd, that.'

Gilly pulled a face at her. 'Anyway, you've got a few weeks before the decree absolute is final, so you can always drop the proceedings against Simon. It's not too late.'

'Darling, I don't want to talk about it. Now shut up and let me try and catch up on some sleep.'

The coach headed southwards, away from Paris, eating up the kilometres. It was after one o'clock before they pulled off the motorway and into the market square of a pretty little village, which boasted a patisserie, a couple of small restaurants, and a variety of shops.

Dave told them the name of the place, but Angie wasn't paying attention. She had far more important things to think about, primarily divorce and drugs; the two subjects she had been mulling over during the long hours of coach travel, when she'd tried to sleep and failed miserably.

'You've got plenty of time to have some lunch and stretch your legs,' he told them, 'but I want you all back here by three o'clock. That's three o'clock,' he repeated loudly, for the benefit of those who were hard of hearing.

That would be several, judging by the number of people who asked him, 'What time do we have to get back here?' as he helped them down from the coach.

'Some people just don't listen,' Angie muttered, reaching into her bag for her lipstick. As she pushed the brown paper envelope to one side, to delve deeper, she was suddenly and horribly conscious that she was being watched. Gilly had stood up to get her jacket down from the overhead locker, causing a stop to the steady stream of people working their way towards the door of the coach.

Angie glanced up to see Carl standing directly behind her, staring intently at her open bag. The look on his face said it all. Angie flushed pink and hurriedly shut her bag, but the damage had been done. He had seen the envelope.

A slow, steady and horribly supercilious smile spread across his face. He leaned his arm across the head-rest.

'After you, ladies,' he said.

'Oh no, we're fine,' Gilly said, squeezing in to let him pass. 'You go. I'm just sorting out which jacket to take.'

81

'That's all right. I'm not in any hurry.' His lingering gaze was causing Angie to positively squirm in her seat.

'Oh, come on, Gilly,' she snapped, clutching her bag to her chest as she rose to her feet. 'Just take your raincoat and let's get going.'

'But I might get too hot.'

Angie sighed. 'Don't wear it then – just carry it.'

'Oh. Okay.'

The warmth of the pleasant afternoon sunshine hit them like a cosy blanket after the cool air conditioning on the coach.

Gilly had barely time to comment on how nice it was, when she was yanked forwards by an ever more anxious Angie.

'Come on!' she snapped. 'We've only got two hours to explore.'

'You want to explore?'

'Yes, of course. Look, we'll go with what's-his-name – over there.'

'Geoffrey?' Gilly sounded puzzled.

'Yes, Geoffrey.Yoohoo!' Angie called, causing the man in question to stop and gaze, like a bewildered owl, around the assembled crowd. 'Well, he's on his own,' she added quietly, then shouted, 'Do you fancy joining us for lunch?'

'Me?'

The recipient of the request sounded as puzzled as Gilly looked.

'Well, why not?' Angie said, with a gaiety she was far from feeling. The looming shadow of Carl Goodman was drawing ever closer. 'I think it's time we all got to know each other a bit better, don't you? I mean, you must feel a bit awkward, being on your own.'

'Well, no, actually...'

'I mean,' she linked her arm through his and gave him the benefit of her most charming and flirtatious smiles, 'I think holidays like this are all about making new friends.' She risked a furtive glance at Carl, who was staring at her quite blatantly, with an expression on his face that she couldn't quite fathom.

'Angie?' Gilly hissed. 'What on earth are you doing?'

'Making new friends.' She beamed at Geoffrey. 'Lunch, then. What do you fancy? A quick snack or something more substantial. I could do with a glass of wine,' she added.

'I don't drink.'

'No? Oh, that's a shame, Maybe a tonic, then?' She was steering him away from the main square and towards a tree-lined avenue scattered with roadside cafes and pubs. Gilly was following hurriedly in their wake.

Angie was in freefall. Conversation flowed in a gabble of words, interspersed with anxious looks over her shoulder that had Gilly asking if she had developed a nervous twitch.

'Of course not,' she said, as they took their seats at a pavement café, leaving Geoffrey to go for the drinks. 'I'm keeping an eye out for Carl, that's all.'

'Why?'

'Why what?'

'Why are you keeping an eye out for Carl?' Gilly's eyes widened as slow realisation dawned. 'Oh Angie, tell me you got rid of the tablets.' She paused and frowned. 'You didn't, did you?'

'No, but I meant to.'

'Oh God! Where are they?'

Angie cast her eyes towards her handbag, as Geoffrey came ambling out of the café carrying a tray with glasses of fizzy water and a carafe of chilled white wine.

'Does Carl know you've still got them?'

'Yes. He saw them when we were getting off the coach.'

'Shit!'

It was Angie's turn to look shocked. Her sister rarely swore. Next to never if she was honest.

'Oh Geoffrey, you're a star,' Angie said cheerfully. 'I don't suppose you could get us a menu as well, could you?'

Gilly waited until he had obligingly gone back inside the café, before continuing. 'I told you he looked suspicious.'

'Who, Geoffrey?'

'No. Carl. I told you, but you wouldn't listen. I expect he's a drug dealer or something. Well, that's it. You'll probably be found dead in an alleyway. He won't take kindly to being crossed.'

'And this is making me feel better, how?'

'Oh God, Angie, I'm scared. Do you think we should go to the police? He could be dangerous.'

'Thanks.'

'Well, he might be.' Gilly glanced around, looking to all intents and purposes as if she had developed the same nervous twitch as her sister. 'What are we going to do?'

Angie reached for the carafe of wine and poured out two generous glassfuls. 'We,' she said, 'are going to have lunch with Geoffrey – in fact with anyone who wants to join us and keep us company.' She smiled and waved at two elderly women who were from the trip and standing across the street looking over at them – Shirley and Linda, if she recalled correctly. 'Oh yes, do please join us,' she called, motioning them to two empty seats. 'Geoffrey has gone to get the menu. He won't be a moment.' She dropped her voice but retained her smile. 'And until I can get shot of these pills, we are going to be the life and soul of the party. Understand? We are going to be everybody's friend.'

Gilly nodded, though she looked somewhat ashen. 'But you promise to get rid of them.'

'Yes, as soon as I can. Soon as I see a pharmacy, they're gone, darling. I promise you.'

'And you'll tell him.'

'Yes.

Gilly paused. 'What if he doesn't believe you?'

'Well, he'll have to.'

'But he might not...'

'Darling – thank you. You're so kind.' Angie's voice had raised an octave as she welcomed Geoffrey back into the fold. 'You've met Shirley and Linda, haven't you? Yes, I thought so. We thought they could join us as well. Geoffrey's a librarian,' she added, glancing back at the new arrivals. Shirley and Linda had come armed with paperback novels, so she reasoned they would have something in common. The more the merrier, as far as she was concerned.

Across the road, Carl and his mother were peering into the window of a small patisserie. It looked like they were opting for a takeaway lunch. Good.

Cyril and his wife were sitting at a pavement café further down the tree-lined boulevard with a group of other passengers. Dave was heading back to the coach park, carrying a brown paper bag and a folded-up newspaper.

A loud guffaw of laughter brought Angie's attention back to the table, where Geoffrey had obviously said something amusing – in his opinion, anyway.

Shirley, the older of the two women, with the most startling head of white hair Angie had ever seen, was smiling politely back at him, but Linda, her friend, looked like she hadn't heard a word he had said. (A furtive fiddle with her hearing aid implied that she probably hadn't.)

'Of course, it could just be a publicity stunt,' Geoffrey was saying, 'I expect we'll never know for sure.'

'No.' Angie nodded agreeably, whilst trying to give the impression that she knew what he was talking about.

She glanced at Gilly, who was slurping back her wine as if it were water. Her sister's anxious eyes were peering over the rim of the glass like those of a frightened mouse.

Angie patted her reassuringly on the knee. 'Let's eat,' she said. 'Have you looked at the menu?'

'I'm not hungry.'

'You've got to eat – maybe a baguette or an omelette or something.'

'Salade Nicoise,' Geoffrey said, jabbing a finger at the menu. 'Tuna, salad, anchovies and green beans – oh, and there's an egg as well. That'll do nicely. That'll tide you over till dinner.'

Gilly looked like she was going to burst into tears. She leaned forwards to fumble in her bag, which was on the ground next to her chair.

'What you looking for?' Angie said.

'My hanky.'

'Don't worry. I've got some tissues.'

Gilly straightened up as Angie bobbed her head down to reach into her large designer handbag that was also placed beside her chair. The opportunity was there, and it presented itself to her. In a flash of what she later thought of as genius, she took the envelope containing the tablets from her bag, and tucked them inside her sister's handbag.

'There you are,' she said, handing her a somewhat crumpled pack of paper tissues. 'I knew I had some somewhere.'

'Thanks.' Gilly dabbed at her eyes and blew her nose.

'Hay fever,' Angie lied, catching sight of Geoffrey's concerned stare. It was all she could think of to explain Gilly's tears. 'She's had it since she was a child. I expect she forgot to take one of her tablets.'

'Oh, my youngest had that,' Shirley said. 'Right bad, it was. Couldn't leave the house in the summer without her eyes swelling up and her nose streaming. We thought it was an allergy to the cat at first. But no, the doctor said it was hay fever. Mind you, she's been better since she got married.'

Geoffrey looked puzzled. For once, he seemed stuck for a reply.

He was saved by the appearance of the waiter, a tall, distinguished-looking man with blue-black hair and a crisp white apron tied round his waist.

Why did French men always appear so ridiculously handsome? Angie was suitably impressed, more so, after she caught a whiff of expensive aftershave. It even managed to disguise the faint aroma of garlic.

'I think I'll go with what you suggested, Geoffrey,' she said. 'I'll have the tuna salad. What about you, Gilly?'

'Hmm, what? Oh yes, yes, whatever.' She was still looking distracted.

'Deux thon – avec du pain?' The waiter was scribbling on a small pad of paper.

'Yes, please.' Angie nodded.

'I'll have the same.' Geoffrey handed the menu to Shirley.

'Oh, my God!' Gilly started to splutter over her drink.

'What?' Angie jumped as she felt her sister's nails dig into the plump part of her leg, just above her knee.

'He's coming over,' she hissed. 'Oh, my God, he is!'

Angie followed the line of her gaze and sure enough, there was Carl and his grandmother, waiting to cross the road. They were standing directly opposite them.

'Relax,' she murmured. 'It'll be fine.'

'Will it?'

'Yes. Just act normal. He can't do anything.'

Gilly took a large gulp of her wine. Her face had drained of colour, apart from two bright pink spots on her cheeks.

Angie gave her a reassuring smile as she poured herself half a glass from the chilled carafe. One of them would have to keep a clear head, she reasoned, and this time, it better be her.

Chapter Eleven

To an interested observer, the lunchtime coach party were having a convivial time, enjoying good food and conversation at a pretty, pavement café.

Several of the tables were full, their ubiquitous red checked tablecloths laden with a tempting array of food, bread, wines and salads. Laughter and chatter were the order of the day.

But all was not as relaxed and jolly as it would first seem.

Angie couldn't help noticing that Gilly was picking at her salad and moving it aimlessly round her plate like an anorexic teenager. She'd been like that ever since Carl and his grandmother had sat down at a nearby table.

She, however, had no such reservations about eating. She was starving and the food was delicious. She was, however, a tad concerned at the way Carl kept glancing over at her. It was almost as if he was sizing her up and trying to calculate his next move.

The fact that his grandmother was talking continuously didn't appear to disturb him. Barbara seemed oblivious to the fact that he was ignoring her and that his whole and undivided attention was centred on the two sisters.

Surreptitiously, Angie edged her chair closer to Geoffrey. 'You see, it's based on fact, but marketed as fiction,' he was saying. 'Very clever, really. You can't get sued if it's sold as fiction.'

Angie didn't know what he was talking about, but Shirley seemed engrossed in his tale. Linda less so, but she did keep tweaking her hearing aid, judging by the odd high-pitched whistle that kept emitting from it.

'I don't read much,' Angie said. 'Magazines, mostly – or biographies. I like reading about people.'

Geoffrey sighed. 'The curse of celebrity fiction. It's all to do with reality television, you know. Goodness knows why it became so popular. Footballers, wags, pop-stars and wannabes.'

'It's called escapism.'

'Ah yes, but you can't beat a good plot. Now you might not know this, but…'

'I need the loo.' Gilly nudged Angie's elbow. Her voice contained a hint of desperation.

'Well go, then.'

'I can't. Not with *him* there.'

'Don't be so ridiculous.'

'Angie, I'm scared.'

'For God's sake!'

Angie leaned forwards on the pretext of reaching for the salad dressing. Carl was slicing his way through a large pizza and seemed pre-occupied with his meal. Barbara was still talking to him.

'Just go. It's not you he's after.'

'You'll come after me if he follows, won't you?'

'Yes, now go on. Honestly, Gilly, don't be so wet.'

She watched her sister scurry inside the restaurant like a frightened rabbit, her handbag clutched tightly to her chest. It was with some relief to see that Carl hadn't noticed her leave. Maybe they were over-reacting, reading things into the situation that weren't there. Maybe he hadn't seen the tablets in her bag, though she had the sneaking suspicion that he had.

Angie dabbed the last of her crusty bread into the deliciously flavoured dressing on her plate and popped it into her mouth.

Geoffrey had decided to digress and was now talking about his favourite topic: architecture; old buildings, mainly, and he'd seen quite a few.

She smiled agreeably, and took a sip of her wine. She supposed he could be quite entertaining, in his own way. He was a knowledgeable man, and full of interesting anecdotes. The sort of man who would be a useful guest at a dinner party. There'd be no awkward silences with a man like Geoffrey around.

Simon had been a good after-dinner speaker, she recalled fondly, and then scolded herself for doing so. Simon was past history, she told herself. She wasn't going to forgive him for betraying her. Why should she? He'd made a fool out of her and everybody knew about it – their friends, neighbours, family – everybody. Mid-life crisis, indeed. It was a feeble excuse – his feeble excuse. No, she was much better off on her own. He didn't think she would manage, but she would. She would show him. A hefty divorce settlement would just be the start of it.

Distracted by her own thoughts, she failed to notice that Carl had left his seat. It was only when Geoffrey happily pointed out an elaborately beamed and ancient building opposite, that she noticed he had gone.

Glancing idly in that direction, following the line of Geoffrey's finger, she caught sight of Barbara looking over at her, and saw that Barbara was on her own.

Swinging her gaze back she caught sight of Carl going through the restaurant doors – and Gilly was still in there. Crikey!

Angie snatched up her bag. 'Won't be a moment,' she gasped. 'Just going to check that my sister's okay.'

'Oh.' Geoffrey looked disappointed. Once again, he'd been stopped in mid flow. 'She has been gone rather a long time,' he added.

Angie's thoughts precisely. She burst through the door of the restaurant at the very same moment that Carl, having presumably placed another order at the bar, was heading back to his table. They collided head-on and Angie's bag went flying, the contents tumbling over the polished wooden floor.

Angie wasn't sure who had received the bigger shock. His hands caught her on each arm as she fell against his chest.

'Steady!'

For a moment he held her.

'Carl!' she choked, recovering enough to shake herself free.

'Angie!'

His gaze lingered for just a second, before he glanced down at the floor, and at the scattered contents of her handbag.

Angie was on her knees in a millisecond, scooping up lipsticks, brushes, her purse, umbrella, make-up and keeping a firm grip on her bag as she knelt on the floor in front of him.

He crouched down. 'Let me help you.'

'It's okay, I can manage,' she said.

'I'm sure you can.' He caught hold of her arm and held it firmly 'But I insist.' His voice sounded stern and hard. He was trying to manoeuvre her out of the way. She could see the look in his eyes as he tried to grab hold of her bag.

Angie clung onto it for all she was worth.

A helpful waitress was retrieving coins and a pen that had rolled into the middle of the floor. People were watching them. He couldn't do anything.

It was at this point that Gilly emerged from the ladies toilet.

Angie would never forget that precise moment. It was, as she later described it, a classic case of perfect timing.

Her sister's hysterical screeching was enough to attract everyone's attention, even those of the party who were hard of hearing.

'Thief! Thief!' Gilly screamed, flapping her arms in the direction of Carl, who had risen to his feet with a look of sheer incredulity on his face. 'He's trying to steal her bag! Stop him!'

'What?' He gave a weary shake of his head. 'You stupid woman. I'm trying to help her.'

'Call the police! Help!'

'Gilly, it's okay.' Angie struggled to her feet, still clutching her bag as tightly as she could under one arm. Her sister was quite hysterical. 'It's okay,' she repeated.

Gilly looked wary, but at least she had stopped screaming. A crowd of people had gathered in the doorway, all intent on seeing what was going on. Geoffrey was first in the queue, a worried frown furrowing his brow.

'Are you all right?' he said, casting a suspicious glance at Carl. 'Is this man bothering you?'

Angie thought it was a very chivalrous thing for Geoffrey to do. He was only a little man, with thinning hair and glasses, whereas Carl had the muscular build of a physically active man, plus he was years younger than him. But for all intents and purposes, Geoffrey was prepared to take him on. She felt her heart warm towards him instinctively.

'It was a misunderstanding,' she said. 'I dropped my bag and he was,' she paused and glanced up at Carl, 'he was trying to help me.'

'Thank you,' Carl said, somewhat curtly.

She managed a feeble smile.

He lowered his head slightly. 'I know you've still got them, Angie,' he hissed, his breath warm against her ear. 'I want them back.'

He straightened up, a practised smile on his face.

Gilly was sniffing loudly into a paper tissue. Shirley was resting a comforting arm around her waist and saying, 'Well, it would have been the shock. Gave me a rare fright too, so I can see why you were upset. You do hear of all this bag pinching going on. Dave warned us, didn't he? Especially in Paris, he said, but I suppose you have to be careful wherever you go.'

'I wasn't trying to pinch it,' Carl said, brushing past them. 'Okay?'

Too right he wasn't. Angie hugged the bag to her bosom and tried to stifle a smile. It was a good job he hadn't succeeded either, or he would have been really disappointed.

'Come on, Gilly,' she said, giving her sister a reassuring pat on the arm. 'Let's go finish that carafe of wine.'

Carl rolled a cigarette, lit it and inhaled deeply. He was not in the best frame of mind. Even the generous measure of brandy delivered by a buxom waitress had done little to lift his mood.

He swilled the potent amber liquid round his mouth and swallowed hard. He needed to get those pills back. They'd cost him enough. Why Angie was still hanging onto them was beyond him. But the fact that she had them made him even more determined to get them back.

He drained his glass and watched her as she rejoined the group from the coach. Seeing as how she had surrounded herself with every misfit on the trip, the chances of him getting her alone seemed pretty remote, but he would work on it. He would just have to be patient.

'Ooh, that was lovely. A real treat. Did you enjoy your meal, Carl?' His grandmother brushed away the crumbs from the table with her linen serviette as she spoke.

'Yeah, it was okay.'

'Do you want anything else?'

'No.' He inhaled on his cigarette and blew a cloud of smoke over the table. Barbara waved it away from her face with an exasperated glare.

'I don't know if you should be doing that. I don't think it's allowed.'

'We're sitting outside,' he said. 'What's the problem?' He didn't see one, but obviously his grandmother did, judging by the expression on her face. 'Okay, fine.' He stood up. 'I'll do it elsewhere.'

Barbara's face fell. 'Oh. No, I didn't mean you had to go... Carl, we haven't paid yet... Carl!'

He opened his wallet and handed her a couple of notes. 'I'll see you at the coach.'

'Why can't you just wait,' she said, sounding flustered. 'You know I don't understand this funny money.'

'You'll get used to it. Better do, really,' he added. 'We're here for a week.'

With that, he turned and crossed the road, before heading down the tree-lined boulevard that led away from the café. He needed to speak to Jason, see if he could come up with any other ideas. He had to have a contingency plan, should Angie fail to deliver, and he had the sneaking suspicion that she was going to be awkward. It was his own fault for giving her the tablets in the first place, but it had seemed like a clever idea at the time. He didn't want to be caught with a stash of illegal uppers or downers, or whatever it was he had bought, and to be frank, he didn't have a clue what they were. He was a total novice when it came to that sort of thing. All he was interested in was the idea of making easy money, except it wasn't turning out to be that easy. Carl headed down a side street of small shops and boutiques. He wanted to make sure he was well out of earshot of any interested parties. He held the mobile to his ear, waiting for the call to be connected.

'Jason? Hi. Yeah, it's me. Got a bit of a problem with the stuff I bought. I'm not sure I'll be able to bring it back – long story,' he added. 'Got any other suggestions? 'He listened carefully, his eyes narrowing. ' Yep, thanks for that, mate.' He shook his head. 'I'll see what I can do.'

Well, that was a waste of time, he thought, pocketing his mobile. Jason's suggestion of buying porcelain souvenirs of the Eiffel Tower and stashing them with cocaine was about as far-fetched as it could get. Like he'd be doing that anytime soon. What planet was Jason on? And who did he think he was? I mean, seriously. He glanced at his watch. Nah, he'd have to try and get those pills back. Either that, or try and get some more. In the meantime, it was time to head back to the coach. Time to meet up with his gran and pretend he was enjoying himself, which he might do, if she'd only stop embarrassing him. He couldn't believe she'd told people all his personal details – how his marriage had broken down and how his girlfriend had kicked him out. It made him sound like a right loser. Debbie and him were having some time apart, that was true, but if he could clear their debts and make some cash, she'd have him back. He'd told her he would get it sorted, and with the threat of court action hanging over him, plus a potential visit from the bailiffs, he couldn't afford not to.

Dave was standing by the front of the coach, smoking a cigarette as he approached. A few people were already in their seats. Others were ambling across the coach park in groups of twos and threes.

'All right, mate?' Carl said, pausing to stand alongside him. 'Got a light?'

'Yeah, sure.' Dave flicked open his lighter and handed it to him.

Carl lit a cigarette and inhaled deeply. 'Thanks. I bought one of them disposable ones on the ferry, but it seems to have packed in. Reckon you and I are the only smokers on this trip.'

'We're a dying breed,' he said, smiling ruefully. 'Probably quite literally.'

'Yeah, but it must be stressful doing your job. It's a big responsibility. And you're driving on the wrong side of the road. I couldn't do it.' He took another puff on his cigarette. All the while he was scanning the coach, looking for Angie and her sister, but they weren't back yet. 'You ever left a passenger behind on one of these trips?'

'Not personally.' Dave ground his butt into the tarmac, then picked it up and tossed it into a nearby litter bin. 'But it does happen. People forget the time, but they also forget that my driving hours are limited, so when I say we have to leave, there's usually a good reason for it. Did you manage to explore the town?'

'Yeah – had a bit of a wander.' He let his gaze run the length of the coach as he talked. His gran wasn't back either. He hoped she wasn't going to be late. Be just typical if she was the one they had to leave behind. 'We're heading to Montrichard now, right?'

'Yes. It'll take us about three hours.' Dave smiled and nodded an acknowledgement at an elderly couple who had reached the door of the coach. 'You can never really tell with the traffic.' He assisted the woman up the first high step, then glanced back at Carl. 'How's Angie, by the way? Did you see her on your travels?'

Not as much as he'd have liked to, he thought. 'Yeah, I think she's okay. She was having lunch with her sister. I didn't join them. I was with my gran.'

'Oh, right.' Dave nodded. 'Well, she can't be feeling that bad. Mind you, she must have drunk a few last night, considering the state she was in.'

'Tell me about it,' Carl said, smiling. 'The things some people do on holiday.'

In the distance, he could see a gaggle of passengers making their way towards them like homing pigeons returning to the roost. Angie was walking with her sister and the weedy bloke from the café. His gran and two older women were wandering slowly behind them. He actually felt quite relieved to see her, but the feeling didn't last.

'Ooh, there he is. Carl! Yoohooo!'

Christ. Did she have to be so loud? He swore inwardly as he managed a cursory wave. He dreaded to think what she'd been telling her new friends this time. By the way they were all beaming at him, it had to be something juicy. He planted a welcoming smile on his face, inwardly wondering if his performance was worthy of an Oscar. Maybe an acting career wouldn't be such a bad thing after all.

As Angie and her sister approached the coach, he could have sworn he saw Gilly sway a little. Yes, she was definitely a bit unsteady on her feet. Which might account for the way she was clinging on to her sister's arm – and she looked a bit glassy-eyed.

'Ladies,' he murmured, stepping to one side to let them pass. 'I take it you had a good lunch.'

93

'Lovely, thanks,' Angie replied. Gilly said nothing, but stared blankly ahead, her gaze transfixed on the steps of the coach. She looked petrified.

'Oh Carl, you should have waited,' Barbara scolded him. 'I got in ever such a muddle. Shirley had to sort it out, didn't you, Shirl?'

Her companion with the snow-white hair nodded.

Great. His gran had found another geriatric friend to keep her company. Excellent. Carl tossed his cigarette butt on the ground and stood on it. He was looking forward to a scintillating dinner later – not.

'Where'd you get to, anyway?' she said.

'Nowhere special. I just had a look around, that's all.' He glanced up to see that Angie and Gilly had taken their seats. Gilly was by the window and looking decidedly pale and washed out. Angie had tucked her bag under her seat and was sitting with her hands resting in her lap. She looked worried, but not as anxious as her sister.
'Come on,' He rested his arm under his grandmother's elbow. 'Get on the coach.'

Chapter Thirteen

'Okay, folks, I hope you all had a good lunch and managed to see a bit of the town.'

Dave was talking into his microphone as he steered the coach away from the parking area. 'It's about a three-hour drive to our hotel in the Loire valley. I'll be passing a menu round for this evening's meal. If you could make your choices, I'll let the hotel know. Dinner will be at seven thirty.'

He glanced over his shoulder and handed a clipboard to Gilly. 'Can you fill this in and pass it round, thanks.'

Gilly gazed blankly back at him, apparently oblivious to what he had just said.

'Here, I'll take it,' Angie said, giving her sister an irritated look. 'It's okay,' she added, in response to Dave's concerned expression. 'She's just a bit tired – all this travelling, you know. She's not used to it.'

'Yeah. Well, this is the longest day. The rest of the week will be better.'

Angie blooming well hoped so. She took the menu from him and gave it a cursory glance: beef, pork, fish – the usual safe choices – ah, but with a tarte Tatin for dessert. That might be rather nice.

She leaned sideways as Dave expertly swung the steering wheel round. It was impressive how he managed to negotiate some of the narrower streets in the village. Angie wouldn't have attempted it in her car, let alone a huge touring coach – and on the wrong side of the street as well.

'Pull yourself together,' she said, giving Gilly a dig in the ribs with her elbow. 'You look like you're in a trance.'

'I wish I was at home.'

'Oh, rubbish. Here, choose what you want for dinner.'

'I'm not hungry.'

'No, but you will be later.'

Gilly sighed. 'I shouldn't have come with you. Charles was right. He said I shouldn't have come. He said it would end in disaster.'

'Charles was not bloody right.' Angie ticked the fish and the beef and reasoned that they could sort out who ate what later. She passed the clipboard over her shoulder to Cyril and his wife. 'And I don't know why you're so anxious. There's nothing to be worried about.'

'No? No?' Gilly's voice was rising sharply.

'No.' Angie insisted, resting a warning hand on her knee. She didn't want her saying anything else, not when people might overhear them. But, judging by the conversation behind them, she doubted if they would. Cyril and his wife were having trouble over the menu choices.

'It's fish.'

'What is?'

'For dinner. You like fish.'

'Do I?'

'Yes, dear, you've always liked fish.'

'I don't think I've had it before.'

'Cyril, you have, dear.'

'Have I?'

Angie lowered her tone. 'I got rid of them.'

'What?'

'The tablets – I got rid of them.'

Gilly glanced sideways at her. 'Really?'

'Yes. When we were at the café.'

'Oh, thank God for that.'

Gilly looked so relieved that Angie didn't have the heart to tell her she'd hidden them in her bag instead. Her sister had had far too many histrionics for one day. Skirting the truth was the most sensible option. Besides, she was sure she'd find a way to safely dispose of the drugs eventually and her sister need not be any the wiser.

'So, what about Carl?'

'We don't need to worry about him. Anyway, what can he do on a coach trip, for goodness' sake?'

Her explanation seemed to appease Gilly. It wasn't long before she'd resorted to what she did best, ploughing through the maps and leaflets she had brought with her to discover where they were headed and what they were going to do when they got there.

Angie leaned back against the headrest and closed her eyes. A short nap might be beneficial, she decided.

The swaying of the coach and the steady drumming of the wheels had a soporific effect. Many of the passengers were starting to doze off in their seats, the hum of background chattering punctuated by the odd snore here and there.

The fact that Angie didn't sleep but spent the time day-dreaming about Simon instead, troubled her a bit. Why did she keep thinking about him? And why was she only remembering the good times – the happy times – and not the way he'd betrayed her with that blasted woman. He'd always been there for her in a crisis, she recalled, always been the big protective hero figure, taking charge when it mattered, and backing down when he saw she could handle herself, like with that irritating little gardener man, who'd demanded an extortionate amount of money for pruning the leylandii, and then dumped the trimmings round the back of the shed. She'd soon sorted him out, even if it had taken her several trips to cart the waste to his front door, where she'd left it in a ceremonial pile on his brick weave. It was the school teacher in her that made her act the way she did, outwardly confident and inwardly shaking. You couldn't let your cover slip in the classroom, not for one moment, or the little blighters would have you. It was how she planned to deal with Carl Goodman – confidently and with self-assurance. Or at least, that was what she tried to convince herself. It would be much easier if Simon was here, she thought. Mind you, if Simon was here with her, she wouldn't have got herself into this situation in the first place.

She closed her eyes. What was he doing now, she wondered? Enjoying life in the small flat he had rented after she threw him out. Or was he lonely? Was he missing her? Maybe that's why he kept sending her so many text messages? He'd sent her three that day already. Or was it because he was bored? The children had told her he wasn't seeing his fancy woman any more, that he spent his days working late, and his evenings having dinner with clients, or ordering a takeaway.

Maybe she'd ask him round for a meal once she got back from holiday. He'd always complimented her on her cooking – she could do a nice cordon bleu meal from that book he'd given her. She didn't have to eat it herself. She was fully aware of the fact that she needed to lose a few pounds. There was buxom, and then there was obese and she was borderline towards the latter. Maybe she had let herself go a bit. But this menopause thing wasn't always easy to deal with. Her expanding waistline had been a result of comfort eating and a sedentary lifestyle. She'd felt so tired all the time. Perhaps she ought to see about joining that new health and fitness club when she got back from holiday. Simon could do with losing a few pounds too. She toyed with thinking about asking him to join her, then realised how ridiculous that sounded.

With her thoughts coming and going, Angie dozed off, lulled into sleep by the rhythmic rocking and swaying of the coach as it ploughed down the motorway.

It seemed like only a few seconds later that she was rudely awakened by Gilly shaking her arm.

'Wake up. Come on, Angie, we're nearly there.'

'Uh, what? Where?'

'The hotel. Oh look, look, isn't it pretty, right on the banks of the river? Oh, and see that stone bridge – my goodness, it must be ancient – oh, and the flowers…'

Gilly was extolling every virtue. Angie could barely open her eyes. She blinked, yawned and tried to stretch in her seat.

'What time is it?' she murmured sleepily.

'Quarter to seven.'

'Good grief – I must have been asleep for hours.'

'You and half the coach,' Gilly told her. 'But don't worry. I stayed awake.' She said it as if she had been assigned to sentry duty. 'He didn't move,' she added, jerking her head back over her shoulder. 'I kept my eye on him.'

'Great,' Angie said. Not that she'd expected Carl to do anything anyway.

'Right then, folks.' Dave's cheerful voice came over the tannoy. 'I want you to stay on the coach until I've had a word with reception. The porters will sort out your luggage and take it to your rooms, and I'll get someone to bring you your keys. All right, ladies,' he added, glancing down at Angie and Gilly as he stood up from his seat.

'Fine, thanks,' Gilly said. 'The hotel looks beautiful. I can't believe it's so close to the river. The view from those upstairs rooms must be amazing.'

Dave smiled. 'I don't think you'll be disappointed. It's a favourite with many of our regulars.'

'Oh, well that sounds promising, doesn't it, Angie?'

'Yes, I suppose so.'

She was peering at her weary-eyed reflection in the mirror of her compact and attempting to smear some lipstick on her lips. Good grief, she felt exhausted, and looked it too. Tilting the mirror upwards, she caught a brief glimpse of Carl Goodman, standing up to remove his leather jacket from the overhead locker a few rows behind them. Lean, mean and dangerous. The thought flitted momentarily through her head. She snapped her compact shut.

'Come on,' she said, unclipping her seat belt. 'Let's get off this coach.'

'Oh, but we have to wait for Dave to come back.' Gilly looked worried. 'He told us to stay in our seats.'

'Fine, fine.' Angie flopped backwards in her seat. 'I forgot this was a school outing. I only wanted a breath of fresh air,' she added, seeing her sister's crestfallen expression.' But I suppose I can wait.'

It was a good job she did, she thought, as seconds later, Carl strode past them, hurried down the steps and jumped off the coach. Shortly afterwards, a thin wisp of tobacco smoke drifted upwards through the open door.

His departure was the signal other passengers had apparently been waiting for, and so began a sudden lemming-like surge towards the exit.

There was safety in numbers, Angie decided, snatching up her bag. She certainly didn't intend to be the last one left on the coach.

'Gilly, just carry your jacket – you don't have to put it on.'

'But it leaves my hands free.'

'Oh, give it here.'

She took it from her and draped it over one arm.

The group of passengers were heading for the hotel foyer and Angie was eager to join them.

An exasperated Dave was trying to shepherd the group into some semblance of order. 'Can we have the Miltons and the Browns and anyone else who asked for ground floor rooms? Yes, over here, please.' He was brandishing his clip-board as he spoke. 'If you follow Pierre, he'll show you the way. The rest of you,' he turned back to the assembled crowd, 'wait here and the reception staff will sort out your keys.'

He gave a half-hearted shrug at the harassed looking girl behind the counter. 'I told them to stay on the coach – what more can I say?'

The chaos reminded Angie of the last school excursion she had taken with a group of hormonally charged adolescents to a youth hostel in South Wales. Suffice to say, never again - but they, too, had stormed reception like a band of soldiers on a mission, demanding to know which room, and who was sharing with whom and when was dinner.

'I told you we should have waited,' Gilly said.

'Yes, well, we're all pack animals at heart – it only takes one person to make a move, and everyone else follows.'

'Like sheep.'

'Exactly.' Angie took a step closer to the reception desk. The queue was getting smaller. The receptionist had stopped cowering against the onslaught and was handing out forms and keys like a true professional, even managing the occasional *bonsoir* now that she had calmed down.

'Ms Turner and Mrs Bennett,' Angie said.

'Ah, *oui*. Sign here, please.'

'Thank you.' She glanced over her shoulder as she picked up the key. The coast was clear – no sign of Carl or his grandmother, thank goodness.

'Madame?' The receptionist slid the paper towards Gilly.

'You need to sign the form,' Angie said, nudging her sister.

99

'Yes, I know. I was looking for a pen.' She was fumbling in her bag. Her fingers had closed on the brown envelope.

Angie's heart sank.

'What's this?' she said, jerking her head up.

'It's nothing. Just sign the form.'

'Oh, my God!' Gilly's eyes widened. 'Oh, my God!'

'Look, I'll explain later,' Angie said, gripping her arm. 'Come on, there's people waiting – and I mean, *people*.'

She jerked her head in the direction of the doorway. It had the desired effect. Gilly scrawled her signature and hurriedly moved away from the desk.

'I can't believe it,' she hissed. 'You put them in my bag.'

'Yes, well, needs must.'

Gilly appeared to be on the verge of tears. The sooner Angie could get her to their room, the better.

'How could you?' she sniffed. 'You, of all people.'

'Look, I had my reasons. Now stop fussing or people will start wondering what the matter is. Smile – you're on holiday.'

'I wish I wasn't.'

'You and me both,' Angie muttered. 'Now come on.' She hoisted her designer bag over one shoulder. 'We're on the second floor. I suggest we find the lift.'

The bedroom was small, but comfortable, boasting two single beds with pretty rustic quilts and a large en-suite complete with bath, toilet and matching bidet in shades of peach and cream.

'Very nice,' Angie said, plonking her bag on the ornate oak dressing table and lifting the net curtains to peer outside at the view. 'We're overlooking the river.'

Gilly, however, was neither concerned about the room, nor the view.

'How could you?' she shrieked, brandishing the brown envelope that she had retrieved from the bottom of her handbag in one hand, and then throwing it at her.

'Oh, for goodness', sake.'

'You said you'd got rid of them.'

'Well, I had – technically.' Angie sighed and picked up the package. 'Look, I'm sorry.' She frowned. 'This is ridiculous.'

'You're telling me,' Gilly sniffed.

'Which is why I'm going to do what I should have done in the first place,' she said. 'I'm going to give them back to him.'

'What?' Gilly looked mortified.

'Well, maybe not these, exactly,' she said, emptying the contents of the package onto the bedroom floor. 'What do you think - paracetamol maybe?'

The small pile of white tablets looked strangely harmless – innocent, even. They could pass as normal, everyday painkillers, if it wasn't for the grotesque smiley face on each one. Angie knelt on the carpet and started to count them.

'I don't understand,' Gilly said. 'What are you doing?'

'Sorting things out.' Angie straightened up. 'Where's your first aid kit – I know you've got one.'

'It's in my suitcase.'

'Damn.'

The cases hadn't been brought up to their room yet. With the whole coach to empty, and only one overworked porter and Dave to do it, Angie reckoned it would be some time before they were reunited with their luggage

'Haven't you got anything in your handbag?'

'Like what?'

'Like these!' she snapped, waggling a finger at the offending drugs.

'Oh!' Gilly snatched up her bag. It looked like the penny had finally dropped. 'Oh, I see what you mean. Well, I've got all sorts of things.' She paused and looked at the heap of tablets on the carpet. 'Maybe not enough of the same, though. There's antacid tablets – you know, for all that rich foreign food – Charles' suggestion.' She waved a small packet at her. 'Aspirin, travel sickness...' She rummaged deeper. 'Oh, and yes, I've got paracetamol. How many do you need?'

'Anything white and round will do. Carl hasn't actually seen what was in the package.'

Gilly's expression changed. 'You're right!' She looked instantly animated. 'You're absolutely right. He doesn't know what was in that envelope, so as long as we give him something that looks like a tablet, we should be all right.'

Angie's thought exactly.

Within a short space of time, they had two corresponding heaps of drugs, medicinal and otherwise, on the bedroom floor, and not a lot of difference to show between them.

Angie gathered up the pile of assorted medicines and dropped them into the brown envelope. The rest she scooped up and hid in the bottom drawer of the dressing table, under a leather-bound bible and a telephone directory.

'I'll get rid of them later. There's got to be a local pharmacy in the town.'

101

'Can't we just flush them down the toilet?'

'And risk poisoning half the fish in the river.' Angie jerked her head towards the window. 'Who knows how the sewerage system works over here?'

Gilly nodded, her expression serious. 'You're right. I didn't think.'

'We can't be too careful – you know that, don't you?'

The thunderous rapping on the door made both sisters jump. Gilly's hand shot to her mouth in dismay.

Oh no!'

Angie regained her control much more quickly. 'Who is it?' she called.

There was no answer. She stepped closer to the door and listened carefully. All she could hear was the distant creak of squeaky wheels. She closed her fingers round the door handle.

'Oh, Angie, don't open it,' Gilly begged. 'It might be him.'

It wasn't. Angie pushed the door open wide. 'Your suitcase, madam,' she said, with a mock flourish. The two cases stood side by side in the corridor, their luggage labels clearly marked with the sisters' names and room number. 'Shame the porter didn't hang about,' she added, dragging the cases into their room. 'I would have given him a tip. Now, where's your first aid kit?'

'What do you need that for?' Gilly said. 'I thought we'd got enough tablets.'

'We have, but we need somewhere to hide the drugs.'

Gilly looked appalled. 'You're going to put them in my first aid kit?'

'Can you think of a better place? It's only till we can dispose of them properly,' Angie added, motioning her to open the suitcase. Gilly didn't look convinced, but she opened it just the same. The green, zipped-up bag contained enough drugs to stock a pharmacy, plus enough bandages and elastoplasts to treat the whole coach, should the need arise.

'Blimey, you came prepared,' Angie said, selecting a plastic aspirin bottle. 'This will do.' She emptied the contents and carefully replaced them with the tablets she had stashed in the drawer.

'What about the aspirin?'

Angie shrugged. 'We'll give them to Carl.'

'But what if we need them?'

'That's the least of my worries.'

With the deed done, all they had to do now was return the envelope to its rightful owner. And dinner, Angie decided, would give them the perfect opportunity to do just that.

Chapter Fourteen

The pre-dinner drinks party was intended as a relaxed introduction to the hotel and an opportunity to discuss optional excursions and activities with the coach driver.

Since Gilly wasn't intending to pay for anything that wasn't already included in the cost of the holiday, she hadn't planned on going to the meeting.

'I'm going to phone Charles,' she said.

'That'll be nice for you.' Angie powdered her face and applied a liberal squirt of perfume to both wrists and down her cleavage.

Gilly pulled a face. 'You and him never got on, did you?'

'Darling, it was pretty mutual. He never liked me and I guess he'll like me even less now I've led you astray.' She patted an errant strand of hair into place with her fingertips. 'Admit it, he likes you at home, where he can keep an eye on you.'

'Well, yes, but that's because we're married.'

'Oh, rubbish, it's because he's a control freak. He's got you well and truly under his thumb, and you know it.'

'No. No, I disagree,' Gilly said, but inside, she knew her sister was right. Charles liked to be the one in charge. In the early years of their marriage, she had been more than happy to let him make all the decisions. It had been quite flattering, really, and anyway, he had seemed so strong and manly – decisive. She'd never been good at making decisions.

'You dither around like a headless chicken,' he'd once told her. 'Procrastination could be your middle name. I know what's best for you, my dear – you know I do.'

And she'd believed him. They went where he wanted to go, visited friends that he liked, and went on holidays that he organised.

Which was why this coach trip with Angie was so out of the ordinary for her. In fact, she had to pinch herself once or twice to remind herself that it was real – nightmarish at times, but certainly real.

What made it more surprising was the fact that she'd wanted to go – not just agreed because she thought her sister needed her, but actually wanted to go – on her own, without Charles.

She toyed with her mobile phone. She really should ring him. But it was almost time for dinner, pre-drinks party or not. What if he kept her talking and she was late for the starter? She'd hate to have to walk in late and have everyone staring at her.

'Oh, for goodness' sake, stop wasting time and just ring him,' Angie said, getting up from her seat in front of the dressing table and reaching for her bag. 'You know you want to. I'll go down to the bar and try to find Carl,' she added. 'That'll give you a bit of privacy to murmur sweet nothings to each other.'

'I wasn't going to...'

'I know.' Angie gave her a sad half smile. 'I know you weren't.'

'Don't you want me to come with you?' Gilly said, fingering her phone almost absent-mindedly. 'You know, as moral support, or something.'

'I think I can manage.'

'Aren't you frightened?'

'Do me a favour,' Angie said. 'It'll take more than someone like Carl Goodman to worry me. Besides,' she added, 'I'm rather looking forward to getting one over on him.' She slipped the brown envelope into her bag and zipped it shut. 'See you later, darling.'

Gilly waited a moment, gathering her thoughts together. That was the difference between her and Angie. Her sister was confident, outspoken and self-assured. She was like a timid mouse in comparison, with no confidence and precious little self-esteem. Was that because of Charles? she wondered. Had he made her that way? And did she really want to speak to him?

She sat in front of the mirror, staring at her reflection. She wasn't bad looking – not for her age. She had nice hair – thick and glossy – no grey, due to an expensive colour rinse at the hairdressers before she left. Her crow's feet weren't that obvious, either. But she looked anxious and that was ageing. She forced a smile onto her face. Better. She grinned wider, remembering a magazine article she had once read that said if you smiled, it automatically lifted your mood. The grin became a grimace as she wondered how long she had to keep the same expression before she began to feel better.

Her phone rang just as she was trying to decide if an open-mouthed smile was better than a closed grin.

'Charles! I was just about to call you.'

'Then, why didn't you?' came the curt reply.

'Well, because I...'

'Two hours. That's how long I've been waiting. You said you'd call before dinner.'

'Yes, and this is before dinner.'

'Not in this country, it isn't.'

'Oh.' She glanced at her watch. 'Oh, I forgot, there's a time difference, isn't there?'

'Yes, of course there is.'

He spoke as if he was dealing with an irritating and silly child. Maybe that's how he saw her, she thought. Maybe that's exactly how he saw her.

'So, how are you?' he added. 'Been up to much?'

'No, not much.' She was tempted to say, 'Only drug smuggling and drunken flirtations with a librarian from Luton and a very dishy coach driver,' but she didn't. She said, 'We're at Montrichard. The Hotel Belle Vue. It's very nice.'

'How's your sister behaving?'

'Who, Angie?'

His sigh was loud and audible.

Gilly tried to smother a giggle. 'She's fine. She's gone down to join the pre-dinner drinks party.'

'Now why does that not surprise me?'

'I should be with her, but I wanted to phone you first.'

'Shame I had to be the one to make the call, then,' he said. 'Do you realise how much it costs to ring a mobile from home. Especially one in France.'

'No, but it can't be that much.'

'It's bloody extortionate,' he said.

Gilly tried to remain calm, though his attitude was starting to annoy her. 'I better not keep you talking, then.'

'No, you go and enjoy yourself with your sister. Don't worry about me.'

If only he meant it, she thought, but he wasn't even trying to disguise the sarcasm in his tone.

'I won't,' she said lightly. 'Bye, darling.'

She switched off her phone. Prat!

Turning back to the mirror, she delivered herself a beaming and surprisingly mood-enhancing smile.

Now then, where were her high-heeled shoes? It was time she joined the party.

The small bar and lounge of the hotel was on the ground floor and had panoramic views of the river and ancient stone-arched bridge.

Gilly scanned the room as she stood in the doorway. It was crowded and noisy, and she couldn't see Angie anywhere. Nor Carl, for that matter.

She glanced over at the bar, where waiters were busy pouring out glasses of wine for the guests. Chairs had been set out in rows. It looked as if they were preparing for a seminar or a lecture, and she began to wonder if she had gone to the wrong room, until she saw Geoffrey over by the window, talking to Shirley. A few other familiar faces convinced her that she was in the right place. Cyril and his wife had plumped for front row seats, and Barbara was in the process of joining them. She wondered if she should do likewise.

'You look a bit lost. Can I help you?'

Gilly smiled as Dave came to stand beside her.

'Thanks. I was just wondering if I was in the right place. This all looks a bit formal to me.'

He grinned. 'Believe me, it's the best way. I like to keep things organised. Then I can be sure of their undivided attention.'

He gestured to one of the seats by the window. 'Here, you sit down and I'll get you a drink. White wine, okay?'

'Yes, please.'

She couldn't help wondering if he was so attentive to all his passengers. Not that she was complaining, but it wasn't as if this was the first time he had singled her out. That walk up to the churchyard, for instance – she hadn't noticed him taking anyone else for an evening stroll. She toyed with a stray lock of hair, curling it endlessly round her finger as she watched him chatting to the bar staff. Maybe Angie was right – maybe he did fancy her.

The thought caused her a momentary flutter of panic, quickly followed by a sense of wonder and, if she was brutally honest with herself, a twinge of excitement. Was she desirable – at her age? Could she still be considered attractive? Charles had never said as much. He'd always treated her with a vague sense of contempt and irritation if she so much as broached the question of 'Do I look all right in this?' Consequently, her sense of fashion and style had deserted her over the years, and she had gone with what was considered safe and middle of the road – nothing too risqué or daring.

Angie had tried to change her outlook, treating her to expensive hair cuts and trips to the beauty salon, but she'd never been that keen on having a stranger do her make-up, or pummel and massage her aching limbs, and as for the waxing session – well, she'd never forgiven her for that bikini wax and her promise of 'It won't hurt.' She had lied.

Perhaps she didn't need all that. Perhaps she could attract a man by just being herself. And maybe – just maybe - she had attracted Dave Saunders. She risked a casual glance in his direction, admiring the broad set of his shoulders beneath the white crispness of his shirt. Broad shoulders, slim hips – not bad, for a man of his age – a man with a sedentary job, as well. She wondered if he worked out to keep fit. He'd need to do something – hotel food and driving for a living weren't conducive to good health and fitness, were they? Perhaps he used the hotel gym facilities when he was off duty. She registered a mental note to do the same.

He turned and looked at her, then raised his eyes to the roof in a gesture of helplessness. The bar staff were taking their time. Well, they did have a lot of people to serve. But she couldn't help wishing he would hurry up. She felt a bit like Billy No-mates, sitting there on her own. If he didn't get a move on, it would be time for him to make his speech, or whatever it was he planned to do.

She smiled back at him and as she did so, became suddenly conscious of someone standing behind her. She glanced over her shoulder. Oh no, it was Carl. She jerked her head round, but it was too late.

'I'm presuming this seat isn't taken,' he said, deftly sliding onto the chair alongside hers.

'Well, actually...'

His leg pressed quite forcefully against her thigh. It wasn't accidental. It was deliberate. Gilly stared up at him – at the firm, chiselled set to his jaw, and the steely glint in his dark eyes. Words failed her.

He leaned his head closer. 'Where's your sister?'

The heady smell of tobacco, beer and aftershave assailed her nostrils.

'I've checked her room. She's not there,' he added.

Gilly gaped at him. How did he know where their room was? Had he been following them? And then she realised that it was obvious – he must have followed the porter when the suitcases were delivered to their door. 'She went to look for you,' she said, trying to ease her leg away from the firmness of his touch.

'Oh, really.' He gave a dismissive shrug. 'So, where is she?' His voice had become colder and more sarcastic in its tone. 'I can't see her. Being elusive, is she? Playing hard to get?'

'Don't flatter yourself.'

Carl looked as surprised as Gilly suddenly felt. Goodness, what had over her? Why on earth had she said that? This man could be dangerous; he was a drug dealer – well, allegedly - and she was being flippant with him.

'She did go to look for you,' she said. 'Honestly. I don't know where she's gone. Are you sure you haven't seen her?'

Carl gave her a stony stare.

'No. Well, obviously you haven't, or you wouldn't have asked me where she was. Oh dear. I don't know what to say. Maybe she went for a walk – you know, to get some fresh air.'

107

'In that case,' his fingers tightened around her elbow and practically levered her to her feet, 'maybe we should go and find her.'

Gilly didn't think this was a good idea at all. No, no – it was far better that they stayed right where they were. Her imagination – vivid at the best of times – had cranked itself up a gear. She had the nightmarish vision of Carl doing away with Angie to keep her quiet, and now turning his attention to her.

She looked frantically at Dave's shoulders, willing him to turn away from the bar and his animated conversation with the wine waiter. If he could see what was happening, surely he would do something.

Carl's grip had tightened further on her arm. 'Coming?'

Salvation came in the unlikely form of Carl's grandmother, who had been keeping a seat for him in the front row, and was clearly starting to wonder where her grandson had gone. An anxious glance behind her, and she suddenly spotted him.

'Carl!' she called, rising to her feet and beckoning. 'Over here! I've kept a place for you.'

At this point, Dave turned his attention away from the bar, and met Gilly's panicked expression with a quizzical frown. He straightened up.

'Um, ladies and gentlemen,' he said. 'If I could have your attention a moment.' His gaze didn't waver from her frightened face. 'If you could all take your seats. Quickly, now.'

Gilly shook herself free from Carl's grasp and sat down hurriedly on her chair. Barbara was still waving and gesticulating at her grandson.

'Sir – if you wouldn't mind. There's a seat in the front row.' Dave beckoned him forward.

Gilly hardly dared breathe. Her shoulders shook as she watched Carl stroll to the front of the room and take his place beside his grandmother.

Dave picked up the glass of wine and brought it over to her. 'Are you all right?' he said, his eyes narrowing. 'What did he want?'

'Nothing.' She shook her head. 'He was looking for Angie.'

'It didn't seem like that to me.' He straightened up and stared at the back of Carl's head, his lips set in a stern frown. 'Are you sure you're okay?'

'Yes. Honestly, I'm fine. Well, I am now.' She gave him a weak smile. 'Go on, your audience is getting impatient.'

He grinned, and she felt her stomach give a sudden lurch. Why did he have to be so helpful, so genuine, and so nice? She watched longingly as he strolled to the front of the room and clapped his hands to get everyone's attention.

All of a sudden, her eyes began to fill with tears.

She gulped back a mouthful of the chilled wine and tried to take deep, slow breaths in order to calm herself, but only succeeded in making herself feel dizzy. Carl had frightened her. She was scared of being in the same room as him. She had to get out of there.

Dave had started to speak – something about the various chateaux of the Loire valley – but it may as well have been in Japanese. She couldn't concentrate on a word he was saying. All she could think about was Angie. Where was she, and why wasn't she here? Something must have happened to her and it must be something to do with Carl, which meant it was probably bad. Oh God, what should she do? What could she do?

Gilly downed the rest of her wine in one and placed the empty glass under her seat. Picking up her bag, and as discreetly as she could manage, squeezed past the passengers who had sat alongside her and headed for the exit.

The foyer was empty, save for the dark-haired girl behind the reception desk, who seemed engrossed in her computer screen.

'Excuse me.' Gilly leaned on the polished wooden counter and tried to attract her attention. 'Excuse me?'

'One moment, please.' The girl continued to type something into her keyboard, her eyes not shifting from the monitor in front of her.

Gilly felt her cheeks flushing. She glanced back at the closed door behind her. She was half expecting Carl to follow her out. She couldn't hang about here. She turned back to the receptionist, just in time to see her pick up the phone.

'Oh wait, I just need to ask you…'

'One moment,' the girl repeated, waving a silencing finger at her, before launching into an animated conversation with whoever was on the receiving end.

Gilly sighed. This could take forever. She turned and headed for the front door. She wasn't sure what she was going to do, but a breath of fresh air seemed like a good option, whilst she tried to sort out the jumble of thoughts whirling about in her head. She was trying to still the rising feeling of panic. How was she going to explain Angie's disappearance to her family? Who would she contact first? Should she tell Dave or should she confront Carl? Maybe she should just go to the police?

She glanced at her watch. How stupid – Angie had only been gone about twenty minutes. She was being ridiculous – again. She sucked in a deep breath of balmy, evening air.

The road outside the hotel was quiet. The river meandered slowly past, trickling against the sides of the concrete walkway. Gilly crossed the road and stood at the water's edge, staring down at the ripples and eddies, at the occasional flash of silvery fish and dark green reeds, twisting and waving in the clear water.

'Oh, there you are! I wondered where you'd swanned off to.'

Angie!' Gilly croaked, jerking her head round, to see her sister hurrying towards her from the door of the hotel. 'Where the hell have you been?'

'Me?' Angie looked perplexed. 'Hey, what's wrong? Darling, what's the matter?'

Gilly's sudden flood of tears took them both by surprise.

'Don't cry. Oh, come on.' Angie gave her a hug. 'What is it, what's wrong?'

'Oh God.' Gilly wiped her face with the back of her hand. 'I'm such an idiot. I thought he, you know, that Carl, I thought he'd done away with you.'

'What?'

'Well, you weren't downstairs.'

'No, I was on the phone to Simon.'

'And he wanted the pills. He came and sat next to me. I was so scared…' She paused, as her sister's words suddenly registered. 'Simon?' she said, glancing curiously sideways at her. 'You rang Simon?'

'No, he rang me.' Angie handed her a tissue.

'Why?' Gilly dabbed her eyes and frowned at the sight of black mascara streaks on the white paper. She probably looked like a panda now.

'I expect he saw some of the photos I'd put on Facebook and thought I was enjoying myself a bit too much. He's keeping tabs on me, that's all. Anyway, what do you mean, you thought Carl had done away with me? That's a bit dramatic, even for you. What were you doing? Looking for my body in the river?'

'It's not funny. He's a drug dealer,' she hissed.

'Allegedly. Anyway, he's got his drugs back – well, our drugs,' Angie said, with a short laugh. 'I gave them to his gran.'

'You what?'

'I gave them to Barbara.' She linked her arm through her sister's and gave her a reassuring smile. 'I left you in the bedroom and came downstairs. Barbara was in the reception area, on her own,' she added, 'so I gave her the envelope and told her to give them to Carl.'

'Oh,' Gilly said. 'I wonder how he's going to explain that to his gran.'

'Who cares? That's not our problem.'

Gilly had the uncomfortable feeling that it might be, but she didn't say anything. She had seen how menacing Carl could be and it had frightened her. And yes, admittedly, she did have an overactive imagination, but her sister's flippant attitude was probably not sensible either. They didn't know what they were dealing with here.

'Come on,' Angie said. 'Let's go in. We're missing the party.'

'Some party,' Gilly said scornfully. 'I'd rather hear what Simon said to you, first. Does he want to come home?'

'Yes, of course he wants me to come home,' she said. 'He says I'm adorable, the love of his life, and he misses me desperately.' She linked arms with Gilly and smiled thoughtfully at her. 'The question is, do I want him back, or do I want to have some fun on my own?'

Chapter Fifteen

'You never said you were feeling poorly.'

His grandmother's concern was both touching and irritating, in equal measures. Carl shrugged his shoulders dismissively. 'I'm fine.'

'I had aspirin in my bag – you only had to ask.'

'I told you, I'm fine. Now stop going on about it.' He tried to stuff the envelope into the pocket of his jeans. He couldn't believe Angie had given them to his gran. On the other hand, why shouldn't she, if she believed it to be an innocent mistake on his part? Or did she? He wasn't quite sure.

'Here, I'll put them in my handbag till we've had dinner,' Barbara said, seeing his struggle to conceal them.

'Yeah, okay.' He reluctantly handed the package to his gran. He had no alternative. His jeans were too tight, and to try and hide them in his pocket would make them more obvious.

The coach driver was summing up his talk and Carl was anxious to be out of there. Sitting in the front row was bad enough but sitting in the front row under the watchful eye of Dave Saunders, who had obviously witnessed the tension between him and Gilly earlier, was not good.

'If you'd like to make your way to the dining room, the staff are waiting to serve you. If you can't remember what choice you made for dinner, I've got a list here to remind you.'

Carl scraped back his chair. He was in dire need of a cigarette. Ignoring his grandmother's worried look, he headed for the foyer and pushed open the front door.

His timing could not have been more perfect. As he stepped outside, he came face to face with the two sisters, who were just about to enter the hotel lobby.

Who received the greater surprise was debateable. Gilly looked worried, glancing sideways at her sister, whereas Angie looked more relaxed.

'Carl,' she said, nodding slowly. 'Did you get the tablets?'

'I did.'

Gilly's cheeks turned pink.

Carl couldn't help but notice. He smiled. 'I've left them with my gran.'

'You're not going to let her take them, are you?' Angie said.

'No.' He shook his head. 'She thinks they're for me. She also thinks you're a very kind person for showing me such concern.'

'She does?'

'Apparently so.' He lit a cigarette and inhaled deeply on it. 'You weren't really going to keep them, were you?'

'No, of course not.'

She was going to throw them away,' Gilly said.

'It might have been for the best.' Carl breathed out a stream of smoke, which had Gilly turning her head away in disgust.

'What are you going to do with them?' Angie said.

He inhaled on his cigarette again. 'Oh, I'll get rid of them. Don't you worry about that.' He jerked his head in the direction of the dining room. 'They're going into dinner now. Shall we join them?'

'I'd rather go to my room,' Gilly said, glancing meaningfully at her sister. 'I'd like to freshen up,' she added.

'My thoughts exactly,' Angie agreed.

Carl smiled and tossed his cigarette butt into the river. 'Maybe we could meet up for a drink later.'

'Maybe.'

He held the door open for them. As Angie walked past him he caught the scent of her heady and exotic smelling perfume. Interesting, he thought. His eyes met hers and held for a moment. 'I'll look forward to it, he said.

'No, no, no, this is silly. Stupid. I can't believe you're even thinking about it,' Gilly raged. 'After everything he's put us through. What is the matter with you? Are you mad?'

'No, darling, I'm on holiday.' Angie fluffed her fingers through her hair as she peered at her reflection in the dressing table mirror.

'He's a drug dealer.'

'Oh, piffle. It could have been a genuine mistake, and let's face it, he's got a certain, intriguing charm about him.'

'So had Hannibal Lecter, by all accounts.'

'Yes, well he's a darned sight more interesting than your librarian chap – what's his name?'

'Geoffrey.'

'That's right, Geoffrey.' Angie applied another generous squirt of perfume to her cleavage as she spoke. 'Honestly, Gilly, you certainly know how to pick them.'

'I did not pick him!' Gilly was almost beside herself with rage. 'He merely sat with me when you weren't available and we all know why that was, don't we?'

'Oh, here we go...'

'You were drunk.'

'Yes, yes, drunk and incapable. I know, I've heard it all before.'

'It was embarrassing, degrading, even.'

'Oh, get off your high horse. You weren't so morally righteous when you were swooning all over that coach driver.'

Gilly's face had turned scarlet. 'I was not, repeat not, swooning over Dave Saunders.'

'Whatever.' Angie dabbed her cheeks with blusher.

'You know, I really do dislike you at times,' Gilly snapped, as she picked up her handbag and flounced towards the bedroom door. 'Do whatever you want. I'm going down to dinner.'

She slammed the door behind her with a very satisfying thud. But once in the hallway, she felt a shade less confident. She didn't really want to go downstairs on her own. Angie could be infuriating at times and unbearable at others, but at the end of the day, she was her sister, and they should stick together, especially in a foreign country.

She strolled the length of the carpeted corridor, pausing to admire the many pictures that hung on the walls, in the hope that Angie would hurry up and come out of their room, and that they could go down to dinner together with at least the pretence that all was well between them.

After ten minutes of concerted loitering, she decided that enough was enough. She would go back and apologise, for what she wasn't quite sure, but it was silly to fall out, especially after all they'd been through together. She marched back to the bedroom but just as she was about to open the door, she heard Angie talking. She tilted her head and leaned closer. Yes, she was talking, but to whom? She hadn't seen anyone go into the room. She was probably on the phone. She leaned closer but couldn't make out what her sister was saying. Torn between the desire to go in and find out, and the fear that she might cause more offence by disturbing her, she stayed just where she was.

It was where Dave Saunders found her, as he emerged from the stairwell at the far end of the landing.

'Gilly? Are you all right? Have you lost your key?'

'What? Oh, no...no, I ...' Her cheeks flushed. 'Sorry, I was about to go downstairs. I was just...' Her words faltered as she met his quizzical gaze. He really did look quite concerned.

'Is it your sister? Is she ill again?'

'Um, no.'

'Something else, then?'

'What?'

'That's worrying you.' He gave a short laugh.' Honestly, you look like you've seen a ghost. I'm here to help, you know.'

Gilly sighed, and shook her head.' Yes, I know. I'm sorry, this is silly. We had a row,' she said.

'What? You and your sister?'

'Yes.'

'Well, these things happen. She'll get over it, whatever "it" was,' he added. 'In the meantime, I suggest you leave her to her own devices, and come downstairs. You'll feel better once you're in the company of others.'

Gilly didn't think that she would. She wasn't really in the mood for small talk with a load of strangers, and apart from Geoffrey, Linda and Shirley, she hadn't really got to know anybody on the coach. She certainly didn't want to sit with Barbara and Carl.

'You can sit with me,' Dave said, as if he had read her thoughts. She glanced up at him. He was still wearing his coach uniform, but he had obviously showered as his hair was damp, and she could detect the faint hint of aftershave. It was rather nice.

'Is that allowed?' she said.

'Why shouldn't it be?' Dave grinned. 'Come on. We'll save a place for Angie, if you think you need a chaperone.'

Gilly blushed, feeling awkward and embarrassed in equal measures. Oh dear, she hadn't meant it to sound like that.
'I just thought, you know, as the coach driver, you had to be more, um...' She faltered.

'Discreet?' he suggested.

'No!' Oh goodness, this was getting worse. She felt the heat rush to her cheeks.

He looked down at her with an amused half smile tugging at his lips. 'That's a shame. I can do discreet.'

Gilly blinked up at him, suddenly realising how tall he was and how close he was and how deliciously intoxicating his aftershave was. The moment was broken by the sudden abrupt opening of the door behind them, and a rather harassed looking Angie stepping into the corridor.

'Oh, there you are,' she said, 'I thought you'd wait.'

'I wasn't going to,' Gilly said. She didn't know whether to feel relieved or disappointed. She risked a shy glance at Dave and thought she could see a resigned expression on his face. Had he resented the intrusion, she wondered, or was she imagining it?

'I can't believe Simon,' Angie said, jiggling the key in the lock. She was apparently oblivious to the undercurrents passing between them. 'He's now saying he wants us to have counselling. Imagine me, having counselling, I ask you. Oh, hello.' She straightened up, acknowledging Dave for the first time. 'Sorry, are we late?'

'Possibly.' Dave smiled as he stepped to one side and ushered them forwards. 'I expect everyone else has already started.'

His hand rested briefly on the small of Gilly's back as she passed. The sensation was electric, but when she glanced up to see if he had felt it too, he didn't show any sign of having been similarly affected. He did, however, give her a wink and a knowing smile, and she hugged that thought to herself as they headed for the stairs.

The dining room was packed, and the only available place where they could sit together was at the table reserved for Dave. Otherwise, they'd be sitting on different tables, which, come to think of it, might not be such a bad idea, Gilly thought, considering how her sister had been behaving recently, and how awkward the situation might become with Dave. She peered slowly round the dining room. She could see a spare place on Linda and Shirley's table.

Dave, however, pre-empted her. He pulled out a chair. 'Ladies?'

'Oh, that's so kind. Thank you.' Angie graciously accepted a place at the table. 'Gilly, sit here.' She patted the adjacent seat.

'Thanks,' she said, trying to appear indifferent to the fact that she would now be sitting directly opposite the man who was making her feel like a giddy teenager. There, she'd admitted it. There was no point in denying it. She would put it down to a touch of menopausal madness. The symptoms, she recalled, were not unlike those of adolescence, with all the highs and lows of hormone-fuelled fantasies.

'So, tell me about Simon,' she said, turning pointedly towards her sister, though she had about as much interest in talking about Simon as she did of having her teeth filled. 'You said he called you?'

'He did.' Angie smeared butter over a large piece of French bread as she spoke. 'He says he misses me. That's why he wants us to have counselling.' She paused to chew on a mouthful of buttered bread, then added, 'I'm not sure about that part, but I suppose it's quite sweet of him really.'

'Yes, but do you miss him?'

'Darling,' her voice lowered as she leaned her head towards her, 'I've never stopped missing him.'

Gilly found this hard to accept. For weeks her sister had been gleefully extolling the virtues of her new and busy single life, doing what she wanted, when she wanted. She'd been full of it. And now she was saying she missed her husband and that she'd always missed him.

'I think about him every day,' she added.

'You never said.'

'Why would I?'

Gilly's mouth had formed into a silent 'oh'. She was surprised, no, shocked, by this revelation. What made it more surprising was the fact that she didn't think about Charles at all and she was the one who was, supposedly, happily married. In fact, she barely gave him a second thought unless he rang her, which he was tending to do more often now, seeing as how she kept forgetting to call him.

'Taste the soup,' Angie said. 'It's delicious.'

The aroma of tomato and garlic and freshly cut bread was making Gilly's mouth water. She hadn't realised quite how hungry she was. Perhaps having something to eat would distract her from the turmoil she was feeling. It wasn't easy having Angie sitting on one side, confessing to missing her husband and thinking of him all the time, and Dave sitting opposite, smouldering away like some latent force that was trying to attract her attention, and succeeding, if she was brutally honest with herself.

She supped up a spoonful of soup and caught herself meeting him eye to eye across the linen tablecloth. The look of longing probably mirrored hers, she thought, hurriedly glancing away on the pretext of reaching for the pot of black pepper. Interesting thought, though. Immediately, she scolded herself. This was ridiculous. She was married. She was also, she thought guiltily, on her own.

If someone had asked her what dinner had been like, Gilly would have been at odds to find the right words. She could barely remember what she had eaten or drunk. It had all passed in a haze of polite conversation and awkwardness, mainly on her part. Even passing the water had caused her to brush fingers with Dave and make her jerk the jug away so that the contents splashed over the tablecloth.

On one occasion she had stretched out her leg and found it connecting with his under the table. The bemused smile he had given her almost made her choke. She had tucked her feet firmly under her chair, determined not to do that again. He must have thought she'd done it on purpose, and she hadn't, she really hadn't.

'Well, I think we should have a nightcap at the bar,' Angie said, patting her lips with her serviette. The waitresses were busy clearing away the last of the dishes and were handing round cups of tea and coffee, which she declined with a polite shake of her head. 'What about you, Dave?'

'I'd like to,' he said, eyeing Gilly as he spoke. 'Maybe later. I've got a few things to sort out first. We've got an early start in the morning.'

'How early?' Angie groaned.

'We need to leave by eight. It's the full-day tour of the chateaux.' He stood up and clapped his hands to get everyone's attention. 'Right, folks. I hope you enjoyed your dinner. Breakfast will be at seven, and I need you all on the coach and ready to depart by eight. Any questions?'

Several people started to speak, or wave their hands in his direction.

'Time to go,' Angie said, giving Gilly a nudge. 'Come on, if we move now we'll beat the queue at the bar.'

Gilly wasn't bothered about having another drink. She just wanted to get out of there. She was feeling flustered and self-conscious. It was becoming increasingly apparent that Dave was attracted to her and she wasn't quite sure how to deal with the situation. She wasn't used to having male attention. It was quite flattering, really, and she wanted to have a quiet word with Angie, if only to gauge how to handle the matter. She didn't know whether to be dismissive, or casual and pretend she hadn't noticed, or friendly and flirtatious. What was best? she wondered. And did she want to encourage him? And shockingly, a tiny, guilty part of her, said yes, she did.

'I fancy a gin and tonic.' Angie was fumbling in her bag for her purse. 'What about you?'

'Hmm? Oh, yes, okay.' Distracted, she found herself agreeing to a drink that she didn't really want or need. They'd drunk sufficient wine at the table. She would have preferred to go for a gentle evening stroll. It was still light outside and the air was mild and balmy for the time of night. Her gaze lingered on the footpath bordering the river, and then on Carl Goodman, who was standing outside, talking into his mobile phone. He was always talking to someone, she thought. Which was a bit odd, considering the cost of using a mobile abroad. Maybe he'd rung his ex-girlfriend, the one Barbara said had thrown him out?

'Here.' Angie handed her a glass that seemed to contain more ice and lemon than liquid. 'We'll sit by the window. Oh look, there's Carl.'

'I know, I just spotted him. Who do you think he's talking to?'

'I don't know and I don't care, but it'll cost him a fortune if he's calling home.'

'He doesn't seem to spend much time with his grandmother.'

'Can you blame him?' Angie said, laughing.

'Yes, I know, but she seems to dote on him. She's always saying how good he is for taking her on this holiday. She'd never been abroad, before. In fact, she hasn't had a holiday for years.'

'Which makes you wonder why he's taking her now.' Angie tapped the side of her head in a knowing gesture. 'Things aren't always what they seem.'

Gilly took a mouthful of her drink. It was so cold it made her head hurt. 'I think Dave fancies me,' she said quietly. She glanced round nervously, hoping no one else had overheard.

'You mean, you've only just noticed.'

Gilly gaped at her. 'Is it that obvious?'

'I could see it a mile off. Right from that first day on the ferry crossing, remember?'

'He was just being friendly.'

'He fancied you.'

'Shush!' She took another nervous sip of her drink.

'You like him as well, don't you?' Angie gave her a conspiratorial smile.

'I never said that.'

'You didn't have to, darling.'

'Oh, God!' Gilly groaned.

'Look, you're on holiday. Where's the harm in enjoying a bit of male company. He's on his own and so are you.'

'But I'm not on my own. I'm married.'

'And he might be married. You don't know. Just enjoy the moment,' she added. 'I'm not saying you have to leap into bed with him...'

'Which I wouldn't.'

'Wouldn't you? Oh, no. No, you wouldn't.' Angie said, shaking her head. 'But there's no reason why you shouldn't have a bit of fun together. I mean, I'm going to have a drink with Carl, later.'

'Are you?'

'Hmm. If he gets off his phone for long enough to get to the bar. He's an interesting man,' she added, running her finger round the rim of her glass and then licking it. 'And let's face it, there's not a lot of them on this trip.'

'He seems a bit shifty to me and he might be dangerous, especially if he is involved with drugs. You just don't know. And anyway,' she protested, 'you said you missed Simon.'

Angie's smile dropped a fraction. 'Yes, I do.'

'Well, maybe you'll get back together with him.'

'Maybe. But in the meantime,' she added, 'there's no harm in keeping one's options open and Carl is certainly an intriguing option.' She stood up and waved to him. 'And just for the record,' she added. 'I'm quite sure he's not a drug dealer. If he is, he's a pretty hopeless one. No, I think he made a genuine mistake.'

Gilly wasn't convinced. 'Don't say I didn't warn you,' she muttered. 'You must be mad.'

'Possibly.' Angie smiled as she pulled up another chair. 'Yes, quite possibly. But at least I'm enjoying myself. I'd advise you to do the same.'

Chapter Sixteen

Gilly had slept rather well, which surprised her. It must have been the effects of that large gin and tonic in the bar, she decided, as she glanced bleary-eyed at the slumbering shape of her sister in the bed beside her.

The soft bleeping from her travel alarm clock was increasing to a piercing ring. She reached over to silence it.

'What time is it?' Angie groaned, stretching and yawning noisily.

'Six thirty.'

'Ugh. Middle of the night.' She pulled the sheet over her head.

'Yes, but we've got to have breakfast and be ready for the coach at eight.' Gilly tossed back the covers. 'Dave says we need to make an early start.'

Angie groaned, but made no attempt to get up.

'I'll have the first shower, then,' she added, lifting the edge of the curtain and peering outside. A pale, misty fog was drifting above the river. The sky was still dark, but she thought it was going to be a nice day.

The previous evening had been unexpectedly jovial. Most of the coach party had been in the bar with them, and Geoffrey had regaled them with tales of his travels, which had turned out to be quite entertaining. He was, he had admitted, a regular speaker for various groups including the Women's Institute, though usually he had the benefits of an accompanying slide show to accompany his talk.

It had been a good night, Gilly thought. Even Carl had seemed slightly less threatening, probably because he'd got his tablets back, or thought he had.

She rubbed herself down with one of the soft white towels provided and stepped out of the shower. The trouble was, they still had the problem of getting rid of them. She glanced back at the toilet. It was tempting to just tip them into the pan, but knowing her luck they wouldn't dissolve or flush away and they'd sit in the bowl waiting for the cleaner to find them. Or, like Angie had said, they'd flow into the river and kill the fish. Or, even worse, a local fisherman might catch a fish that had swallowed a tablet, and then he'd take it home to cook it for his family...

A gentle snore interrupted her spiralling and irrational thoughts. Angie had fallen asleep again. Her lips were trembling and parting with every soft exhalation of breath.

'Wake up.' Gilly flicked the damp towel at her. 'Come on, get up.'

'Why?' came the pained reply. 'Honestly,' she added, pushing the covers to one side and stumbling towards the bathroom. 'Sometimes I think you're worse than Simon.'

Breakfast was in the smaller dining room, off the main lounge. A meagre affair, according to Angie, who, for some reason had anticipated a full English fry up instead of the French offering of croissants, bread, and jam that had been laid out, buffet-style on a table by the window.

'At least the coffee is strong and black,' she said, stirring a heaped spoonful of sugar into her cup. 'Bread and jam, I ask you. And at these prices as well.'

'Oh, stop moaning. It's a continental breakfast. It's what they have in France. You can have a yoghurt or fruit if you'd prefer.' Gilly had already selected a bowl of muesli and a croissant from what she thought was a plentiful and tempting display of food. 'It's probably a lot healthier for you, anyway.'

'Stuff that. I'm on holiday. I want to enjoy myself.' Angie spread a large amount of butter and an even larger dollop of apricot jam onto her chunk of crusty bread. 'But if this baguette breaks my teeth, I tell you, I won't be very happy.'

Breakfast over, or endured, according to Angie, the sisters headed back to their room to pack a few essentials for their day out. In Angie's case, this consisted of lipstick, face cream, dark glasses, a sun hat, and a bottle of water for the coach.

Gilly, however, liked to be prepared for whatever the day threw at them. In a large shoulder bag, she packed sun cream, a waterproof jacket in case of showers, an umbrella, ditto, and a large straw hat. In a smaller bag, she packed travel sickness pills (they would be spending a long time on the coach), insect repellent (because of all the lakes and trees around the chateau), antihistamine cream (in case the repellent didn't work), indigestion tablets (all that rich food) a box of plasters (in case of blisters), and painkillers.

She held the bottle of so-called 'aspirin' in one hand. 'Shall I take these with us? Just in case we get a chance to dispose of them.'

'Why not? You've packed just about everything else.'

'Oh, ha ha, very funny.'

Angie shrugged. 'I'm just saying - you're the one who's got to carry it all.'

'I don't mind.'

'Good.'

'Good. Right.' She slipped the bottle of pills into the front flap of her handbag. 'I'm ready.'

By eight o'clock sharp, everyone was on board the coach as planned, even the late- night stragglers, who had propped up the bar until well after midnight. (Angie and Gilly had not included themselves in this small and select group, being much too tired and inebriated at the time.) Angie had a grudging admiration as to how late some of these pensioners (Stanley had confessed to being over seventy and Bill was well on the way to that) could party. 'It's probably because they don't go to work,' she said.

'Yes, but even Geoffrey was in his element, and he still works.'

'He doesn't drink, though.'

'Ah! Good point.' Gilly clipped on her seatbelt and settled back in her seat. Dave was wandering down the length of the bus, counting heads. She had tried to avoid eye contact with him ever since the previous night, when Angie had said that yes, he probably did fancy her, and she should make the most of it. For some reason, she had been haunted by guilt ever since. Even though she hadn't done anything and wouldn't do anything, no, of course she wouldn't. She really wouldn't, she told herself firmly. But the thought was still there, lurking, lingering, in the back of her mind, that he was rather nice, and if she hadn't been married and if he wasn't married – and she didn't know if he was or he wasn't - then maybe, just maybe...

The shrill and piercing ringing of a mobile phone interrupted her thoughts like a claxon going off at the start of a race.

'Well, answer it,' Angie said, nudging her sharply with her elbow.

'It won't be mine.'

'I think you'll find that it is.'

'Oh God, you're right - it is,' Gilly said, frantically fumbling in her bag. The ringing was getting louder, and she couldn't remember which pocket contained her phone. The bag had so many handy zips and compartments in it. Not that one. No, not the side zip.

Angie gave her an exasperated glare. 'Just answer it.'

'I'm trying to,' she snapped, flipping open the front flap of her bag in an embarrassed panic. The bottle of 'aspirin' fell out as she did so, and before she could catch it, had rolled down her leg, over her knee and tumbled to the floor. The child-friendly lid proved less than up to the job and clicked open on impact, cascading the tablets down the floor of the coach at the precise moment that Dave had put his foot on the accelerator and the bus had zoomed forwards.

'Hello, hello,' Gilly said, having found her phone and flipped it open. She couldn't see who the caller was (she hadn't had time to put on her reading glasses) and she had no idea who would be ringing her at such an early hour. As she spoke, she was making manic eye gestures at Angie, jerking her head in the direction of the small white pills that were scattering down the central aisle of the bus and which were, even now, being diligently collected by several of the elderly passengers.

'You took your time answering the phone.'

'Charles,' Gilly croaked.

'Well, who did you think it was?'

'I didn't know, I...' She paused as Angie attempted to scramble over her knee from her position by the window. 'Just a minute.' She swung her legs to one side.

'What's going on? Gilly? Gilly!'

Even with the phone held away from her ear, she could hear the indignation in her husband's tone. He hated being kept waiting, or ignored, or both.

'Hang on a minute,' she said. She gesticulated wildly at the floor and realisation suddenly dawned on Angie's face. 'Oh Christ!' she muttered.

'Are you going to talk to me or not!' Charles sounded cross, very cross.

Gilly took in a deep breath, steadied herself, and said, 'Charles, it's really not a good time. We're on the coach and we've just set off to go the chateau at Chenonceaux. You know, that one in the brochure I showed you.'

'For God's sake, woman,' he snapped. 'I don't need a step-by-step description. That's not what I phoned you for.'

Gilly's bottom lip quivered. 'Oh.'

'I need to know where you put that invoice from Jennings.'

'What invoice?'

She could hear his exasperated groan on the end of the phone. 'The one that came from Jennings the other day, and I told you to put it in a safe place as I'd have to pay it by the end of the week.'

Gilly tried to conjure up a mental image of her kitchen. She could remember him getting the letter, if only because it had prompted one of his usual rants. ('How much? The man's having a bloody laugh, isn't he? It was only a stop-cock. I could have replaced it myself if I'd had the time.')

'Have you tried the bureau?' she suggested.

'Of course, I've tried the bureau. That was the first place I looked.'

'Letter rack?'

'Yes.' She could hear the barely suppressed irritation in his tone.

'How about the drawer in the kitchen?'

'What drawer?'

She could hear the sound of cupboards and drawers being yanked open as she spoke.

'You know, the one with all the odds and ends in it.'

'Oh, that bloody drawer. Oh yes. Such an obvious place to leave an important invoice.'

By the rustling noise, she gathered he had found what he was looking for. She didn't know why he was making such a fuss, though. It wasn't due till the end of the month.

She glanced with relief at her sister, who had retrieved the empty tablet bottle, and was now collecting all the tablets from the passengers, who had helpfully searched under their seats for the wayward pills. 'Just aspirin,' she was saying. 'Yes, thanks, thank you, thank you, yes, they do look a bit different but they're just aspirin. Supermarket brand.'

Thank God, Gilly thought. She breathed in deeply. 'Charles? Did you find it? Was it there?'

'Yes, no thanks to you. I mean, honest to God, Gilly, who else would think of putting such an important document in such a stupid place. What on earth were you thinking of?'

'My holiday, probably,' she muttered.

'What?'

'I need to go, Charles. Angie's waiting.'

'What?'

'Goodbye Charles.' She switched off her phone. She'd forgotten just how tiresome and annoying her husband could be at times and she really couldn't deal with him right this moment. She raised an anxious gaze towards her sister, who was making her way back down the aisle towards her. 'Did you get them all?'

'Yes, I think so.'

'Good.' Gilly smiled.

As Angie clambered back over her knees and into her seat by the window, her shoe crunched down, unnoticed, on the one remaining tablet she had not managed to find in her casual scrutiny of the coach. As a fine white powder, it would remain undiscovered and unseen for some considerable time.

Chapter Eighteen

'Good morning ladies and gentlemen,' Dave said over the coach's microphone and speaker system. 'I hope you all had a good night's sleep.'

Several people replied in the affirmative. Somebody said no, it had been too hot, but before they could elaborate, Dave had started to summarise the day's itinerary, and they were shushed into silence. (Gilly had a sneaking suspicion it had been Geoffrey who had done the shushing, but she couldn't be too sure.)

'Today's visit will be to the *Chateau de Chenonceau*,' Dave was saying. 'One of the most elegant and romantic Renaissance chateaux in the Loire valley. We'll also pass a few others that I can point out to you on the way. This area is renowned,' he added, 'for both its chateaux and its wine, but more of that later, Thursday, to be exact, when we visit a local vineyard and wine cellar.'

'Oh, good,' Angie said. 'I'll look forward to that.'

Gilly delved into her bag and pulled out the map. She did like to follow the route. It made the journey so much more interesting – and besides, it kept her eyes from wandering to the sight of Dave's broad shoulders and those firm, tanned forearms that she found so irresistibly attractive.

'Have you spoken to Dave this morning?' Angie asked, following the line of her gaze.

'No. Why?'

'Oh, no reason,' she said airily.

Gilly frowned as she offered her the bag of boiled sweets. 'I'm not like you, Angie. I wish I was, but I'm not. And even if Dave does like me,' she added, lowering her voice so that there was no danger he could hear, 'I'm not going to do anything about it. I'm married.'

'Ah yes, which reminds me, what did Charles want? I presume it was him on the phone.'

'It was.' Gilly sighed. 'You know, I'm not missing him, not at all. He'd lost an invoice, a very important invoice, that I, stupid woman,' she made a good imitation of his tone, 'had hidden in the kitchen drawer, deliberately, of course, so that he couldn't find it.'

'Cheek. Did you tell him where it was?'

'I did.'

'I'd have told him where to stuff it,' Angie said.

Gilly smiled. 'You know, I'd forgotten what a despot he could be at times.'

'I've been telling you that for years, darling.'

'Hmm.'

'I mean, for all his faults, Simon would never tell me what to do.'

'He probably wouldn't dare.'

Angie looked affronted. 'That's not true. He might suggest things and we'd talk about them. We'd make mutual decisions. Charles belittles you and you let him get away with it. In fact, it's a wonder he let you come on this holiday. I'm not sure how you got away with that so easily.'

'I told him you were paying for it.'

Angie's look of surprise said it all. 'You mean you lied to him?'

'Well, it worked, didn't it? And I did have a bit of cash put to one side.'

'Good girl. Every woman should have an emergency escape fund.'

'It's not an emergency escape fund.'

'Ah,' Angie tapped the side of her head and smiled knowingly, 'but it could be.'

'Oh rubbish. Gilly flipped open the map and peered at it. 'Now then, I think we must be about...here.'

The route to the chateau took them through a winding landscape of lush, fertile fields and wooded valleys. It was a picturesque route, dotted with rustic farmhouses and pretty villages.

'It's all so typically French,' Gilly enthused. 'I think it's the shutters that do it. Mind you, the houses must be ever so dark inside. I wonder how much they pay for electricity? It must be cheap, don't you think?'

'I can honestly say,' Angie said, 'I hadn't given it a thought.'

'I'm just going to pull over here for a photo stop,' Dave said, parking the coach in a lay-by at the side of the road. In front of them, and just over a narrow stone bridge, perched a spectacular and many turreted, white castle. A chorus of oohs and aahs resonated down the coach. 'The Chateau d'Usse,' he told them. 'Legend has it that Charles Perrault found the inspiration for his fairy tale, the Sleeping Beauty, from this chateau,' he said. 'The best view is from over the bridge. Five minutes, folks, that's all.'

'Oh, it's beautiful,' Gilly sighed. 'I've got to take a picture of it.' Several of the passengers were queuing to get off the coach, and she was anxious to join them. Carl had been one of the first to alight, not to take a photograph, it turned out, but to have his usual cigarette break. The acrid smell of tobacco wafted in through the open door.

'I can't be bothered to move,' Angie said.

'Oh.' Gilly sat down again, disappointed.

'But you go. Honestly, Gilly, you don't need me with you to take a photo. You're not with Charles now, you know. Do something on your own for once. Go on. You've only got five minutes. Shirley and Linda are over there and Barbara too.'

The castle was straight out of a children's book of fairy tales, all dark grey slate turrets and dazzling white stone, perched high on the hillside overlooking the river. Gilly had never seen anything more beautiful. She took picture after picture, each one zooming in on different arches, or towers or windows. Charles would have poured scorn on her, but she didn't care. For once she didn't have to listen to him being overbearing and critical. She could take as many photos as she wanted and she could delete any she didn't like later.

'Oh, it's lovely, isn't it,' Barbara said, coming to stand beside her, still clutching the large plastic holdall she had started the journey with. 'I wanted Carl to come over the bridge and take a closer look, but he wouldn't. He's been a bit moody this morning. I don't know why and he's not likely to tell me. But men don't see things the same way as we do, do they?'

'No.' Gilly lowered her camera. 'No, they don't.'
She looked back at the coach. Dave was standing by the open door, talking to Cyril and his wife. Carl was leaning against the parapet of the bridge, talking into his mobile phone. He looked agitated. She raised the camera and took several snaps in quick succession. Why not, she thought? They were all part of the holiday experience.

'Do you want me to take one of you?' Barbara said. 'I'm not sure how these things work, but if you tell me which button to press....'

'No, that's fine, thank you,' Gilly said. 'I'm not very photogenic.'

'Oh, me neither.'

'And we need to get back.'

'Ooh, yes. We don't want to be late. Can't keep the driver waiting, can we?' Barbara gave one of her high-pitched giggles, which had Gilly understanding why Carl was so keen to put some distance between himself and his gran. Mind you, she thought, as they walked past him to get to the front of the coach, he did look a bit distracted. He had ended his phone call with a muttered expletive and had slammed his fist against the stone wall of the bridge so hard it must have hurt. Stupid man. Gilly kept her gaze averted from him as she walked past.

Back on the coach, Angie was engrossed in writing what appeared to be a long and detailed text message on her phone.

'That'll cost you,' Gilly said, as she sat back in her seat and reached for her safety belt.

'Hmm? Oh, it doesn't matter.'

Obviously not. Gilly took the opportunity to view the pictures she had taken on her camera. The castle ones were stunning, but she flicked through them quickly, until she reached the final few shots – Dave with Cyril, Dave on his own, Dave glancing in her direction. She pressed the enlarge button. Her cheeks felt hot as his face suddenly zoomed into view. He was staring straight at her. No doubt about it. She could feel herself blushing. She went on to the next picture of Carl, looking moody and talking into his phone. She peered closer. Now that was strange. He actually looked a bit scared.

'Did you get some good shots?' Angie asked.

'Yes, loads.'

'Show me.'

'Oh, later. I've switched it off now,' she said, stuffing her camera into her handbag. 'Who were you sending messages to, anyway?'

'Simon, but he sent one to me first. Apparently,' she added, 'he's unbearably lonely.'

'Did he say that?'

'Not in so many words.' Angie smiled. 'But I know him. He doesn't like to think of me having a good time without him. It was fine when I was hurt and miserable at home, but the fact that I'm on holiday and having fun, well, he can't handle that idea.'

'Yes, but it's his fault you're on your own.'

'Exactly.'

'And now he wants you back.'

'It's starting to look that way.'

'Oh.' Gilly shrugged. 'Well, I don't know what to say.'

'Me neither, darling.' Angie reached for her seat belt and fastened it with a loud click. 'Me neither!'

***

'You ain't got one of them headaches again, have you, Carl?' His gran was patting his arm reassuringly as she spoke. 'You're looking a bit peaky. Let me look in me bag, see if I've got any paracetamol.'

'I don't need paracetamol,' Carl snapped, brushing her hand away. 'I'm fine.'

'You don't look fine. What's the matter?'

What's the matter? What wasn't the matter, more like? Carl didn't know where to start. He should never have watched that late night news bulletin on the television. Nor the replay on the morning's breakfast television news. If he hadn't watched it he would have been none the wiser. But he had watched it and now he was scared, really scared.

An Albanian drug dealer had been shot dead on the streets of Paris. Grainy CCTV footage from a Paris side street had shown images of himself and Angie sitting at a pavement café, both with their backs to the camera, admittedly, but at the very same table where, just a few hours later, the drug dealer had been blasted to death. Oh, and there was a zoomed-in close-up of the blood-splattered metal table and chairs, and as a bonus, a close up of his leather jacket with the distinctive dragon pattern on it. Now, his French may not be very good, but he could understand a lot just by looking at the pictures.

'Oh look, Carl, I got aspirin. That'll do, won't it?'

'I doubt it,' he muttered. He took them anyway, if only to keep his gran happy, swallowing them with a mouthful of bottled water. It made him feel like he was twelve years old again. If only, he wished. Jason had been a fat load of good. He'd tried talking to him on the phone, but all he'd been concerned about was the fact that he still hadn't got much stuff to bring home.

'I'm relying on you, man. I got people waiting.'

'The man is dead, Jay!'

'Yeah, and it wasn't your fault.'

'But I was seen with him.' Blurred pictures, maybe, grainy images, definitely, but people could do stuff with pictures like that. He'd seen a programme about it once. 'I don't do French, but even I can figure out they're trying to trace his last contacts. They've got pictures of my jacket in close-up plastered all over the television news.'

'So, ditch the jacket. Wear glasses, colour your hair. Think out of the box, man, and think of the money.'

The money – the hopeful promise of enough cash to clear his debts and give him something for a fresh start, a new start. But was this really the way to do it? Carl took another swig from the water bottle. A tablet was stuck halfway down his throat. He coughed.

'Want me to pat you on the back?' his gran asked.

He shook his head and coughed again.

'I think I ought to,' she said, thumping and rubbing between his shoulder blades.

Carl found the rhythmic pummelling comforting. He swallowed hard, clearing his throat. Maybe he'd just stay at home and let his gran look after him. She wouldn't mind. She liked the company. She'd look out for him.

'Better?' she asked.

'A bit.'

'Them pills are always a bit tricky to get down. Have another drink. Your mouth will be dry with all that coughing.'

Dry with dread, more like, he thought, taking another mouthful of water and wishing he'd never listened to Wayne and his, 'It's so easy' spiel. He'd never liked that Jason in the first place. Wayne had reckoned he was the one with all the contacts. Well, the first one he'd met had been murdered, so things weren't looking great on that front. And now he was going to have to ditch his leather jacket, and it had cost him a bomb. It was stuffed in a plastic bag between his feet on the floor of the coach. He was hoping he'd get a chance to dump it somewhere when they were out. It was too distinctive, too recognisable.

'There, I said you'd be all right.' His grandmother smiled reassuringly at him.

'Yeah. Thanks Gran.' He returned her smile. All was right in her world, which was good. She was on holiday and she was enjoying herself. At least he'd managed to do something right.

He turned and gazed broodingly out of the coach window. It wouldn't do for both of them to be unhappy.

***

The visit to the chateau at Chenonceaux was memorable, not for its stunning, raised arches spanning the river and the beautiful, landscaped gardens and park, but as the place they lost Cyril.
He'd been threatening to wander off for some time but had been kept in check by the beady eye of his wife, Edith, a retired school teacher. In fairness to Edith, she had been good at this task, but when nature called it might have been wise for her to have enlisted backup. Instead, she thought she could trust him to sit happily with a slice of gateau in the restaurant, while she popped to the loo. She would only be a moment or two, and he seemed quite content. Indeed, he was almost always content, but she put that down to his tablets.

However, in keeping with most tourist destinations that catered for coach parties, and usually several of those at a time, there was a queue for the ladies toilets. Edith was, she said later, aware of time passing, but she was also aware of the urgency of her own needs. Cyril would be fine, she told herself. He had coffee and cake and a nice view from the window. He'd be fine.

'How can you lose an eighty-one-year-old man?' Angie sighed. They were running an hour late for their departure time already, and some of the group were starting to get restless.

'He's got dementia,' Gilly said. 'He forgets where he is. Edith says he's like a child at times.'

'Well, I've been on loads of school trips with children, and I've never managed to lose one. Why didn't she ask someone to keep an eye on him?'

'I don't suppose it occurred to her,' Gilly said. She was trying to place herself in the same situation. If Charles had dementia, as opposed to just plain forgetfulness, how would she cope with him? Perhaps, like Edith, she would pretend that everything was normal, even when it wasn't. Then again, wasn't that what she was doing now, pretending everything was normal, pretending that she had a loving, caring husband, instead of a bullying, self-righteous pig.

She was still annoyed at the way he had spoken to her that morning. He hadn't shown the slightest interest in her or asked how she was enjoying her trip. In fact, he probably didn't care whether she was enjoying it or not. The inconvenience of upsetting his routine was what was concerning him, that and the fact she had misplaced an important letter. Maybe she was getting to be like Cyril too, she thought, though she suspected she was a little bit young for even early onset dementia. How would Charles cope with her? With indifference, she decided. Yes, that would be his answer. He'd ignore the problem and hope it went away. Which was pretty much what Edith had done, bless her.

'Right, well, I think we need to widen the search,' Dave said. 'It might be better if we split up. How many of you have mobile phones?'

There was a show of hands. Not that many, Gilly thought, as she peered down the length of the coach.

'Okay. Right. Now I suggest that you, Geoffrey, go to the restaurant. Maybe take the Braithwaites with you.' (This to an elderly couple seated just behind Geoffrey.) 'Angie, can you head back to the toilet block?'

'He's hardly likely to be in the ladies loo.'

'Well, take a man with you. Carl, can you go with Angie?'

'I suppose so,' Carl muttered. By the look on his face it was apparent that searching for senile pensioners had not been on his agenda.

Dave continued to peer down the coach, allocating various search areas to those who possessed mobile phones. Those without phones, and those who were just too plain exhausted, would remain on the coach. Dave obviously didn't want to risk losing anyone else. 'You've all got my number, so we can keep in touch. Right, I think that's all of you. Ah, Gilly,' he added, almost as an afterthought. He glanced down at her. 'You'd better come with me.'

132

'Oh,' she said, momentarily surprised. 'Okay.' She wasn't sure why he had said that, but she wasn't going to protest.

Barbara, Shirley and Linda were left to console an increasingly agitated Edith.

'I only left him for a few minutes,' she sobbed. 'He's usually very good at waiting.'

'I just hope he's not fallen in the water,' Angie said, as they got off the coach again.

'Oh no. That would be awful.' Gilly had horrific visions of Cyril's lifeless body floating down the river between the white stone arches of the chateau.

'I'm sure he'll be fine,' Dave assured her. 'He's got lost, that's all. This is a big place. These things happen,' he added. 'Don't worry. The staff are aware he's missing and have put an alert out for him. I'm sure he'll be found safe and well.'

He sounded very confident, which Gilly found comforting. She was worried sick. Cyril wasn't only forgetful and confused, but he was in a foreign country as well. How would he cope? Could he even speak French? Would he be able to make himself understood? Poor, dear Cyril.

'Come on, we'll head up to the information desk,' Dave said.

'Angie, you know where you're going?'

'The toilet block, when Carl gets his act together.'

The man in question was making what seemed like a rather reluctant saunter down the length of the coach, egged on by his over-eager grandmother.

'Oh, good lad, Carl. Now you make sure you find him. Poor Edith is getting all wound up and anxious.' Barbara turned her attentions back to the worried wife. 'He'll find him, my Carl. He was always so good at hide-and-seek when he was a boy.'

'Like that matters,' Angie muttered. 'Come on, hurry up. We've wasted enough time as it is.'

Gilly fell into step beside Dave as they strode towards the information desk.

'Does this happen often?'

'You mean, do I make a habit of losing my passengers?' He glanced sideways at her.

'Oh no, I didn't mean it like that,' she said, flustered.

'I know.' He grinned. 'And no, it doesn't happen very often.' He felt in his pocket for his phone. 'Is your mobile switched on?'

'Yes.'

'Good.'

'Although I'm not sure why I need it when you've got yours,' she added.

'I don't.'

'Oh.' She wanted to say more, but they had reached the ticket office and she had to wait patiently as he held what seemed like a long and protracted discussion, in French, with the woman behind the counter.

He was making elaborate hand gestures as he talked. She liked that. She liked watching him. He was confident and self- assured, not overbearing like Charles.

'*Ah, oui! Merci.*'

Polite too, she mused.

'No, they haven't found Cyril,' he said, turning back to her. 'But all the staff have been alerted and they've got extra security doing a tour of the gardens.'

'That's good. I'm sure he won't have gone too far.'

'Not at his age,' Dave said, 'but you never know. These older pensioners can be quite sprightly when they put their minds to it. Come on, let's head for the river.'

'Oh dear. You don't think...' Her voice tailed away. It was too awful to contemplate. 'You're worried, aren't you?'

Dave gave her a reassuring smile. 'He'll be fine. I promise.'

She only wished she shared his confidence. But the place was milling with people and trying to find one pensioner amongst all the hundreds seemed a pretty hopeless task.

They made their way along one of the elevated terraces overlooking the river. It was fast flowing, turbulent, dark and dangerous.

She shielded her eyes from the sun. The reflection, glinting on water, made her wish she had kept her sunglasses on, but she had left them behind on the coach,

'I can see something,' she gasped. Look! Look over there.' She pointed her finger at a clump of reeds and vegetation. Something was in the water, half submerged, caught up in the weeds. It looked like clothing. It looked like Cyril's cream shirt.

'What is it? Where?'

Dave came to stand behind her, resting his hand on her shoulder as he followed the line of her gaze.

She was shaking so much she could barely speak. The firm touch of his fingers was reassuring but she was feeling sick and giddy. Her imagination had already galloped away, out of control. Cyril was dead, drowned. This was his lifeless body, all cold and tangled up in the reeds. She'd never seen a dead body before. She didn't want to see one now.

'Oh, Dave, do something.' She clutched at his arm, panicking. The sun was in her eyes, making them water. She blinked rapidly.

'It's okay. I don't think it's him.'

'Are you sure?' She felt a slight glimmer of hope.

'No.' Dave vaulted over the terrace wall and dropped onto the bank below. Without a second thought, he had kicked off his shoes and was wading into the swiftly flowing shallows, striding his way through the current towards the bobbing shape that had Gilly convinced it was Cyril's corpse.

'Help! Help!' she shrieked, waving her hands around her head in the vague hope of catching someone's attention, but succeeding only in getting a few curious stares from a couple of passers-by. 'Oh help, he's in the river,' she sobbed. 'Please help.' What was wrong with these people? They all seemed to be trying to avoid her. Some of them had turned away and were walking in the other direction. Quite blatantly as well. Didn't they understand? Didn't anyone speak English?

Dave, meanwhile, was almost thigh deep in the water and looked in danger of losing his footing if he wasn't careful. The river was flowing fast, even though he was in the shallows.

'Oh, Dave, do be careful,' she said, wondering if she should climb down to the riverbank, or whether it was more prudent to stay on the terrace and try to get some help.

'It's okay. I think I can reach him.'

He was leaning forwards, half hidden in the reeds. Gilly gnawed nervously on a fingernail as she watched, and nearly jumped in to join him when the shrill ring tone of her phone suddenly broke the moment.

'Angie. Oh, thank God,' she sobbed. 'You've got to get help. We've found him. He's in the river.'

'No, he's not.'

'He is. Dave's trying to reach him now.'

'Cyril's in the coach park,' Angie continued, in what sounded like a mildly irritated tone. 'He's been there all the time.'

'What?' Gilly looked at Dave, who was trying to pull something from the reeds. 'But he can't be.' If Cyril was in the coach park, then who was in the river? Her heart sank like a stone. Not another body, surely.

'Dave. Dave, it's not him,' she said. 'Cyril's been found.' Whether it was because she shouted and startled him, or whether he lost his balance anyway, she wasn't quite sure. Either way, Dave splashed full length into the water and came up coughing and spluttering and clutching what now looked like a large plastic bag.

'Dave, oh God.' She sat on the edge of the terrace, ready to jump to his assistance.

'It's okay.' He waved her back. 'I'm all right.' He straightened up, frowning. The white cotton of his shirt clung to every rippling muscle on his chest and arms. A green strand of weed hung round his neck and shoulder like a casually draped scarf. He looked... he looked gorgeous. Gilly felt her cheeks flush at the sudden and totally absurd thought. He was like a modern-day Mr Darcy, all wet, and moody, but deliciously handsome.

'They've found Cyril.'

'I gathered,' he said, wading back towards the river's edge. He tossed the large bag onto the terrace.

A small group of people had assembled and were watching the scene with interest. Some were even taking pictures. They were joined, belatedly, by a couple of chateau staff, who were gesticulating rather expressively. One was talking into a walkie-talkie.

'*Monsieur,* it is forbidden to go in the water. Very dangerous.'

'You don't say.'

Dave vaulted up onto the terrace and brushed his hands down the length of his wet trousers. 'I wasn't doing it for fun.'

'*Monsieur?*'

'We thought we saw a body in the river,' Gilly explained.' We thought it was Cyril.'

'Ah, Cyril. Your pensioner has been found, I think.'

'Apparently so.'

'Good. And this?' The security man prodded the sodden bag with the toe of his highly polished black shoe.

'It's a jacket,' Dave said. 'A leather one.'

The man tipped the contents of the sodden carrier bag onto the gravel path and stared at it with interest.

As did Gilly. Black leather, with a dragon motif – it looked a bit like the one Carl had been wearing the other day in Paris. She'd noticed it because it had been warm that day, too warm for a leather jacket. She'd decided it was a fashion statement. He'd bought it, so he would wear it. How strange that there should be two jackets the same.

'Come on,' Dave said. 'Let's go. We've wasted enough time as it is.'

'Yes, and you need to get out of those wet clothes,' Gilly said. 'You're soaked.'

'Like I hadn't noticed.' He gave her a rueful smile.

She felt her limbs go weak and shivery. Oh goodness, what was the matter with her? She needed to get a grip of herself. It must be the shock, she decided. But she'd be fine. She just needed to think calming thoughts. Cyril had been found and he was safe and well.

He was also, it seemed, something of a minor celebrity.

'He was happily posing with a group of Japanese tourists,' Angie explained. 'They all wanted his photograph. He'd been asleep in their coach for hours. It turns out that when he had found himself abandoned by Edith in the cafe, he made his own way back to the parking area and found his seat on the coach. Unfortunately,' she added, 'it was on a coach reserved for a visiting party from Japan. He didn't know that, of course. He just sat in what he thought was his seat. Apparently, Edith had written the number down on a slip of paper in his wallet,' she said. 'He was tired from all the walking, so he had a little nap while waiting for the rest of the group. Of course, when all the tourists got back on the coach, Cyril was head and shoulders above the rest of them. That's when the driver realised he'd got an extra passenger.'

'I suppose he is quite tall, compared to the Japanese,' Gilly said. 'Poor Cyril. He must have been very confused.'

'Not at all. He was in his element. I think he liked being the centre of attention, and Edith was so pleased to see him she didn't have the heart to tell him off for wandering away.'

'Well at least he's safe, that's the main thing.'

Angie grinned as she clipped on her seat belt and settled back in her chair. 'No darling, that's not the main thing.'

Gilly gave her a puzzled sideways glance as she fastened her own seat belt. 'What?'

'It's you. You and him,' Angie said, tilting her head in the direction of Dave. 'You're the "main thing". So, do tell, darling – I'm waiting, and I'm all ears.'

Chapter Nineteen

'There's nothing to say,' Gilly said, fastening her seat belt.

'Oh please.' Angie smiled knowingly at her. 'You're blushing.'

'I am not,' she said, knowing that her cheeks were turning crimson. 'And shush, I don't want anyone to hear you.'

'You mean you don't want Dave to hear.'

'Well he's not likely to, is he?' she said, glancing back over her shoulder. 'He's in the loo, getting changed out of his wet clothes.'

'Your hero,' Angie teased.

The passengers were waiting patiently on the coach for Dave to emerge from the cramped confines of the on-board toilet. All apart from Sidney, one of the Salford group, who was tapping furtively on the cubicle door.

'Dave? Will you be long?'

'I'll be out in a second.'

Sidney was obviously getting desperate. A lot of the old boys seemed to want the loo a lot. Gilly was relieved she wasn't the only one who had frequent urges to go.

A few moments later, and there was a faint ripple of applause as Dave stepped out of the cubicle, wearing clean trousers and a dry white shirt.

'Mrs Bennett said you were ever such a hero, jumping in like that,' Edith said, fondly patting his arm as he passed. 'I told Cyril, didn't I, Cyril?'

'Told me what?'

'About the coach driver going into the water.'

'Why would he do that?' Cyril said.

'To look for you.'

'But I wasn't in the water.'

'I know, dear. But you could have been.'

Dave smiled. 'It's fine,' he said. 'Honestly.' He made his way to the front of the coach and took his seat, reaching for the microphone as he did so.

'Right, folks, time to head back to the hotel for dinner. Did you enjoy your visit to the chateau?'

There was a loud chorus of approval.

'Good.' He switched on the engine. 'Tomorrow you've got a free day in Montrichard to relax at your own pace. After the excitement of today,' he added,' you might all appreciate that.'

As the coach headed back to the hotel, several of the passengers fell asleep, judging by the amount of snoring that was going on. Gilly looked behind her and saw Edith asleep on Cyril's shoulder, which was rather sweet, and Geoffrey lolling with his head back and his mouth open, which wasn't.

Angie was flicking through the photos on Gilly's camera. 'I can't believe you were taking pictures of Dave,' she whispered.

'I wasn't doing it deliberately.' Gilly shrugged. 'He just happened to be in my line of view.'

'Of course, he was.' Angie peered closer. 'Mind you, he's rather photogenic. I think he's looking at you.'

'No, he's not.' Gilly snatched the camera back. 'Honestly, Angie, sometimes you see things that just aren't there.'

'You wish.'

'Oh, stop it.'

'And now you're blushing.' Angie gave her a smug and knowing smile.

'Well, what about you and that, that drug dealer?' Gilly fanned herself with the book about the chateau that she had bought in the gift shop. 'You went waltzing off with him.'

'Only because Dave told me to and anyway, we don't really know if he's a drug dealer. It's all supposition at the moment.'

'You said...'

'I know what I said.' She lowered her voice. 'But Carl seems a decent bloke when you get to know him.'

'Angie, for goodness sake.'

'Oh, stop being so self- righteous.'

'Well, it's true. I don't think you should be associating with him. And,' she added, speaking more softly, 'we've still got the problem of those pills to get rid of.' Gilly glanced nervously over her shoulder, but most of their travelling companions seemed to be in a state of stupor and no one appeared to be listening.

'There's bound to be a pharmacy in Montrichard. We can hand them in there,' Angie said.

'I'm not handing them over the counter,' Gilly hissed. 'We might get arrested.'

'For what? We can say we found them.'

'Oh, I don't know. It sounds a bit risky to me.'

'So does posting them through the letterbox in the dead of night.'

'It wouldn't be the dead of night,' Gilly muttered, flicking through the pictures on her camera again. She was wondering if she should delete some of them. Not the ones with Dave in, well, at least, not until she got home, but maybe some of the others. A couple were a bit blurred, and some of the chateau pictures were a bit dark. She should have changed the settings, but she wasn't sure how.

'Oh,' she said. 'That's odd.'

'What is?' Angie glanced sideways at her.

'Carl, in this picture here.' She held the camera for her sister to see. 'He's carrying a large bag.'

'Call the press. Breaking news, Carl Goodman is carrying a large bag,' Angie laughed.

'No, you don't understand.' Gilly pressed the zoom button. 'See? I'm sure that's the bag Dave fished out of the river. And come to think of it, it had a black leather jacket in it.'

'So?'

'It had a red dragon motif on it.' Gilly looked through the gap in the seats, but most of the passengers were sleeping. She couldn't see Carl or his grandmother, but they were way down the coach anyway.

'What are you trying to tell me?' Angie said. 'That Carl threw his jacket into the river? Big deal. Maybe he got fed up carrying it.'

'Don't you think it's a bit strange?'

'Darling,' Angie gave her a condescending smile. 'I think this afternoon's events have unnerved you more than you care to think about. Stop trying to act like Miss Marple and let me get forty winks before we reach the hotel.' She wriggled down in her seat and pointedly closed her eyes.

Gilly stared at the picture again and frowned. It was the same bag. She was sure of it and it was Carl's jacket. So why would he do something like that unless he had something to hide?

The answer, which only confirmed her suspicions that Carl was a thoroughly bad lot, came later that evening in their hotel room, when she was amusing herself flicking through the television channels whilst Angie hogged the shower.

'Hurry up,' she said. 'I want to wash my hair before dinner.'

'Five minutes, darling,' came her sister's muffled reply.

Gilly switched over from a gloomy black and white film to the evening's news headlines and there it was: grainy footage of Carl and Angie in Paris.

'Angie,' she shrieked. 'Come here, quick.'

The blood-splattered pavement zoomed into view and the newsreader was saying something about all known contacts. That much she could decipher and then there was another view of a jacket similar to the one Dave had pulled out of the river.

'What? What?' Angie burst out of the shower, towel wrapped turban-style around her head.

'I think he's killed someone.'

'Who?'

'Carl,' she sobbed, wagging her finger at the television screen. The picture had changed to a woman talking about the weather. 'He was on there with his jacket, and there was blood, and you were with him,' she gabbled.

'Darling, I don't have a clue what you're talking about. Now calm down and tell me what's going on.'

'We need to get a newspaper,' she said. 'It'll be in the papers.'

'What will?'

Gilly sucked in a deep breath and swallowed hard. 'Some drug dealer has been murdered, in Paris, and the footage shows you and Carl at some seedy looking bistro, just before the murder. Then they showed a close-up of Carl's jacket. The same jacket that Dave fished out of the river, thinking it was Cyril's body. Carl's trying to destroy the evidence. He's a murderer, Angie.'

'Don't be so stupid. How can he be a murderer? He was with me that day.'

Gilly narrowed her eyes suspiciously.

'Oh, for God's sake,' Angie flopped onto the edge of the bed beside her. A pool of water dripped down her legs and seeped into the carpet. 'We went for a meal and a drink, which, if you remember, made me rather tipsy. Carl was with me the whole time. You saw us come back to the coach together.'

'I know, but...'

'And if the police have looked at CCTV footage, they probably just want to talk to anyone who was there, which will probably include me,' she added, looking thoughtful. 'Not that I can tell them much. To be honest, it's all a bit of a blur.' She shook her hair free from the towel, scattering droplets all over the bed.

'Exactly. You might not have noticed if you were drunk.'

'Gilly, I think I might have noticed if he'd killed someone.' She raked her fingers through her hair.

'So why did he get rid of his jacket?'

'It might not have been his jacket.'

Gilly frowned. That much was true. They didn't know for sure, and Angie was making it sound perfectly plausible. But she had a bad feeling about this.

'Go and have a shower – go on,' Angie said, nudging her off the bed. 'And stop worrying about it. Honestly, Gilly, you let your imagination run away with you sometimes.'

'But aren't you worried?'

Angie shrugged. 'He's not a murderer, Gilly. I can promise you that.'

'I don't know how you can be so sure,' she sighed. 'You don't know anything about him, and I don't think we should be seen with him.'

'Bit difficult, seeing as how we're on a coach trip together.'

'You know what I mean.'

'I do. Now hurry up and get ready. I'm starving and it's almost time for dinner.'

Chapter Twenty

'He's not here.'

'Who?' Angie asked, as she followed Gilly into the dining room.

'Carl,' she said.

The room was crowded, but she could see an empty table for two by the window, with panoramic views of the river and the old arched stone bridge.

'We can sit here,' she said, hurrying over to secure their place before anyone else took it. For once, she wanted them to be able to sit together without having to make small talk with anyone else.

'He might be running late.'

Gilly draped her cardigan over the back of her chair and glanced once more round the crowded room. 'His grandmother's here. She's sitting with Shirley.'

'So?'

'You'd think she'd save him a seat. She usually does.'

Angie gave her an exasperated look. 'Are you going to be like this all night?'

'Like what?'

'Agitated,' she hissed. She smiled pleasantly as the wine waiter came to take their order. 'What are we having - red, or white?'

Gilly shrugged.

'We'll have red, please.' Angie tapped the menu with her finger. 'That one.' She folded it and passed it back to the waiter. *'Merci bien.'*

'I was just making the point that he's not here, and it doesn't look like he's going to be joining his grandmother either.'

'Maybe he's not hungry.'

'Ha-ha.' Gilly started to butter a chunk of crusty bread. Her gaze flitted to Dave, standing at the door talking to one of the receptionists. He had changed into casual clothes, dark jeans and a shirt, and he carried a light jacket in one hand. It didn't look as if he would be joining them either. He pecked the girl on both cheeks and then turned and walked away.

'Don't you know it's rude to stare,' Angie said drily   .

'I wasn't.'

'Not much.' She smiled. 'You never did tell me how you got on when you went for that romantic stroll together.'

'We were looking for Cyril.'

'I know – and?' She gave Gilly a meaningful look.

'And nothing.' She chewed on a mouthful of bread and tried to ignore her sister's questioning stare. 'Oh, I don't know,' she added. 'He's very nice.'

'Nice?'

'Kind, considerate, thoughtful.'

'All the things that Charles isn't, then,' Angie remarked lightly. 'Don't worry, darling. Your secret's safe with me.' She sipped wine from the proffered glass and nodded at the waiter. 'Lovely, thanks.'

Gilly waited till her glass had been filled and took a large mouthful. Her thoughts were in turmoil, and she didn't know if it was because of Carl, or Dave, or because she was having doubts about the state of her marriage. The more she was away from her husband, the more she could see how much he had controlled her. Bullied her, really, dismissing her ideas and thoughts and making her feel inadequate. It was so lovely to have this time on her own, to be her own person. She could wear what she liked, do what she liked, make choices and follow them through. And Angie was the best person to do that with. Angie understood her like no one else could.

'I'm just, I don't know, confused, I suppose,' she said. 'I've spent my whole life doing what I thought was best, and now I'm not so sure that it was the best.'

'That's because you're suddenly seeing there's another world out there. I've been trying to tell you that for years,' Angie said. 'Charles moulded you into the person he wanted you to be. Not the person you wanted to be.'

'It wasn't like that.'

'No?'

But inside, she knew that it was. She'd been a dutiful wife and a dutiful mother. She'd loved it when the children were at home, but now that they had moved out, she wasn't sure what she should be. She just knew that she wanted a different life, but she didn't know what that was yet.

She took a spoonful of soup. It was warm and thick and bursting with flavours of garlic and onion. 'This is lovely,' she said, surprised at how delicious it tasted.

'French onion soup, you can't beat it,' Angie agreed. 'Probably got a million calories, all that cream and caramelised onion, but who cares. We're on holiday. We can enjoy ourselves.'

Gilly smiled. 'We can, can't we?' She took another mouthful of wine. 'We should go for a walk, later, maybe explore the town a bit?'

'If you like.'

'Or we could stay in the bar,' she added, seeing the less than enthusiastic expression on Angie's face.

'No, no, an after-dinner stroll will do us good, as long as I get out of these shoes,' she added. 'They're killing me.'

It was after nine by the time they had finished their meal and polished off the rather heady bottle of red wine. Carl Goodman had not made an appearance. A fact that Gilly found troubling, but Angie less so.

'He's probably having a burger and chips somewhere,' she said. 'I get the impression that fine dining isn't his thing.'

'Shouldn't we ask his gran if he's okay?'

'No, why would we?'

'I don't know.'

'Exactly. Now grab your jacket and I'll change my shoes, and we can go for that evening stroll you wanted.'

The air outside was pleasantly balmy and still. A path ran down the side of the hotel to a narrow street filled with small boutiques, a patisserie and a couple of gift shops, all closed now, but each with individual and attractive displays.

'We could come here tomorrow,' Gilly said, peering into a window stuffed with ornaments and local pottery. 'I need to get a few postcards.'

'I don't bother with them,' Angie said. 'I don't think people do, these days.'

'Well I do. I want to send one to the kids anyway.'

'You'll be home before they get there. Send them a text instead. Tell them you're having a wonderful holiday with Aunty Angie.'

She laughed. 'They won't believe me.'

'Oi!'

Gilly linked arms with her sister. 'We are having a good time, though, aren't we? I mean, despite everything that's happened, it has been fun.'

'Yes, darling. And we're only half way through the week. Who knows what might happen next?'

The road through the village rose steeply towards a castle, perched on the hill overlooking the river.

'We won't go up there now,' Angie said. 'That's something we can do tomorrow, if you like.'

Gilly nodded. As they turned to head back towards the hotel, she suddenly stopped and pointed. 'Angie, look. It's a pharmacy.'

The illuminated green sign hung over a small shop on the opposite side of the road. 'And it's got a letterbox,' she added.

'Have you got the tablets on you?'

'They're in my bag.' Gilly glanced up and down the street. A couple of people were window shopping like them, but otherwise, the town was quiet.

'Go on, then,' Angie said.

Gilly's hands were shaking as she crossed the road and fumbled in her bag for the bottle of tablets. She didn't know why. Guilt, maybe? Fear, quite probably. The bottle was almost as wide as the letterbox. She wasn't sure if it would fit through. She glanced back over her shoulder. 'I think it's stuck,' she said.

'Give it a whack.' Angie hurried to join her. 'Go on, push it.'

Gilly twisted and wiggled the bottle. It seemed to have got wedged half way. 'It won't go through.'

'Try harder. No, stop, there's someone coming.' Angie turned to face the street, her ample shape blocking the doorway. Gilly made a point of pretending to peer into the window, though with the blinds drawn, there wasn't much to see.

'It's the Braithwaites,' Angie said. 'Hello, lovely evening,' she added, as the elderly couple strolled towards them.

'Oh, hello. Are you heading back to the hotel?'

'Yes – yes, we've just been exploring,' Angie said.

'It's lovely, isn't it?'

'Very nice.'

Mrs Braithwaite was giving Gilly a puzzled look.

Gilly didn't blame her. She turned around. 'Just wondered when they were open,' she said.

'There's a sign on the door,' Mr Braithwaite said, helpfully pointing towards it. 'Do you want me to translate it for you?'

'No, we're fine, thanks.' Angie took a step sideways to block the letterbox, from which the lid of the bottle was still protruding. 'Have you had a look at the castle? We've just come from there. It's at the top of the next road.'

'Oh, we did wonder how to get to it,' Mrs Braithwaite said. 'We could have a walk up there now, couldn't we, dear?'

'It's only a short stroll,' Angie added. 'It won't take you long.'

Gilly managed a weak smile, which she kept firmly cemented to her lips until the couple had walked around the corner and out of sight.

'That was close,' she muttered, turning back to the problem of the wedged pill bottle. 'What's the matter with it? Why won't it go through? Oh, hang on.' She crouched down and groped through the letterbox with her fingers. 'There's some sort of brush cover. I can feel it.'

146

'For goodness sake, here, let me do it.' Angie nudged her to one side and gave an almighty whack on the bottle with the heel of her hand.

It fell, with a clatter, onto what sounded like a tiled floor. 'Right, that's done it,' she said. 'Now let's get back to the hotel before anyone else sees us.'

Gilly exhaled loudly. She had been holding her breath for so long she was beginning to feel quite dizzy.

'I could do with a nightcap,' Angie said cheerfully.

'You and me both,' Gilly sighed.

As she turned to walk away she noticed, with a sickening feeling of impending doom, the security camera, blinking inconspicuously at them from the right-hand corner above the pharmacy door.

'It doesn't matter,' Angie said, trying hard to console her sister with a large gin and tonic from the hotel bar. 'It probably doesn't even have a film in it. Lots of these places put them up for show. They act as a deterrent.'

'Well, it didn't deter us,' Gilly sniffed. 'Oh, Angie, why didn't we look first? How could we have been so stupid? It's a pharmacy. We should have known it would have security cameras.'

'Exactly. Which is why we have nothing to worry about. I mean, come on, we returned the drugs and if anyone asks us, which I'm quite sure they won't, we'll say we found the tablets in the street and we put them through the letterbox because the pharmacy was closed. It's a simple explanation.'

Gilly stirred the slice of lemon and trio of ice cubes round her glass with the tip of her finger. 'And you're sure it'll be all right?'

'Yes, of course. Darling, you really must stop worrying.'

'Like that will ever happen,' she said. She took a long, cool drink from her glass. Her gin tasted remarkably strong, and she suspected Angie of ordering her a double measure, which probably wasn't wise, on top of the wine she had consumed at dinner. But for once, she didn't care.

The bar was crowded with people from the coach party, and all seemed to be having a jolly evening. She could hear various snippets of conversation, interspersed every so often with a loud shriek from Barbara, who was perhaps having more than her fair share of sparkling wine.

'It's local wine,' she heard her say, as if that was a good enough excuse to indulge herself. 'Dave says there's caves in the hills where they store it.'

147

'I wonder where he's gone,' Gilly mused.

'Who?' Angie said, draining her glass.

'Dave.' She glanced idly out of the window, but it was dark outside and she could only see her reflection staring back at her. 'I mean, it must be a lonely life for him, don't you think? We're all here enjoying ourselves, and he's on his own, out there somewhere.'

'He's probably in his room, watching a film.'

'Do you think?'

'I don't know.' Angie sounded vaguely irritated. 'Maybe he's having a lads' night out with Carl.'

'I don't think they like each other very much.'

'I was being sarcastic,' Angie said. 'Come on, I think it's time you went to bed. You look like you've had enough for one night.' Gilly gripped onto the arm of her chair and levered herself to an upright position. Oh dear, she was feeling a bit light-headed. She struggled to hoist her handbag over one shoulder. It didn't seem to want to stay there, though. It kept slipping, rather annoyingly into the crook of her elbow. She sat down heavily again, blinking at it.

'Give it here,' Angie muttered. 'And give me your arm.' In the bedroom, the sensation of dizziness was even worse. Gilly lay flat on the bed, one eye open, trying to focus on the impressive chandelier that graced the centre of the ceiling and the intricate plaster rose that surrounded it.

Angie was in the bathroom. She could hear her brushing her teeth. She must remember to do that before she fell asleep, she told herself, as she made a half-hearted effort to kick off her shoes. One of them thumped to the floor; the other balanced precariously on the end of the bed. Gilly nudged it with her toe and it toppled onto the carpet. Satisfied, she turned her attention to getting undressed, though for some reason she was having problems with the buttons of her blouse.

It wasn't the best moment for Charles to ring. It was only when she heard the shrill tone of her mobile going off in her handbag that she remembered she hadn't given him his expected nightly call. So here he was, checking up on her. She stared bleary-eyed at the blurred display on her phone. She didn't think she could talk to him.

'Aren't you going to answer that?' Angie said, poking her head around the corner of the bathroom door.

'No.'

The ring tone was getting louder. Gilly stared at the phone, her eyes filling with tears, her finger trembling as she pressed the off button.

'Darling, what's wrong?' Angie came to sit on the edge of the bed. She put a comforting arm around her shoulders. 'What is it? You're shaking like a leaf.'

148

'I don't love him.' She sniffed and stared tearfully back at her sister. 'Most of the time I don't even like him. Oh, Angie.' She gave a loud, hiccupping sob. 'What am I going to do?'

Chapter Twenty-one

The tourist guide leaflet referred to Montrichard as a picturesque town of timber-framed buildings clustered beneath the remnants of its ancient chateau. The artificial caves and quarries on the north side of the River Cher were used for growing mushrooms and maturing the region's sparkling wines and goat's cheese.

It was hardly a mecca for drug dealers, Carl thought, as he flicked through the pamphlet he had picked up at the hotel's reception desk. But every place had its dark side. He just had to find it.

The bar he had chosen was half way down a gloomy side-street. Some might have called it quaint, but to him it looked shabby and run down – not the usual haunt of tourists. He sat at a corner table, nursing a glass of cold beer. The clientele was much as he had expected: working men on their way home, labourers by the look of their dusty clothes, a couple of youths, and definitely no women – a typical working man's pub. Still, they seemed friendly enough and a couple of older men had given him a nod and a smile.

He read the leaflet again, not because he was interested, but because it gave him something to do. Jason had told him to visit the local pubs, so here he was, visiting them. He took a long draught of beer. It was strong and bitter, and left a sour taste in the back of his throat. He should have had something to eat first, but sitting in the dining room with his gran and her geriatric buddies did not appeal to him, not after the day he'd had.

Ditching the leather jacket had been bad enough. He was regretting it now, considering how much it had cost him. But having to trawl local pubs on the off-chance that he might spot a drug dealer, should he know what one looked like, seemed ridiculous. This wasn't his scene. He'd be better off trying to find a nightclub or something. He drained his glass and stood up. He needed a piss.

The toilets were at the end of a dark, wood-panelled corridor. He groped along the walls for a light switch but failed to find one. At least he could see the urinal, courtesy of a small frosted window in the corner of the dim room, which was letting in a few rays from the street lamps outside.

As he relieved himself, he caught sight of his reflection in the grimy mirror. He should have had a shave, he thought, rubbing his chin with the back of his hand. He looked rough as anything. This holiday was ageing him. He flexed his muscles. Still looking good, though. Nothing a quick workout wouldn't fix.

'*Monsieur?*'

It was then that Carl realized he was not alone. The youth was lounging against the door frame of one of the cubicles, watching him with interest. Carl didn't like the way he was looking at him, eyeing him up. Blimey, he thought, with a sudden sick feeling in the pit of his stomach. He really was eyeing him up. He jerked his zip up. 'Sod off!'

As he hurried back to the bar, he suddenly saw what he had failed to notice earlier. The men standing in the corner were holding hands. Another had his arm draped loosely over the shoulders of one of the workmen and the barman with the handlebar moustache was giving him a very suggestive smile.

Carl flung open the door and stumbled out onto the pavement. He fumbled for a cigarette, lit it and inhaled deeply. Great, just great. Out of all the bars in this sodding foreign backwater, where should he end up? Well, it didn't surprise him. Not the way his luck was going. All of a sudden, he had the urge to hear a familiar and comforting voice.

Debbie, however, was anything but comforting.

'What do you mean, you're in France?' she shrieked. 'You've got no money.'

'I know. But I'm getting some.'

'How, Carl? No, don't tell me. I don't want to know. In fact, I don't want to hear any of your hare-brained schemes.'

'Debbie, just hear me out.'

'Sort yourself out, Carl. And don't call me again until you do.'

He swallowed hard. This couldn't be happening. If she'd only listen to him he could explain things. He was sorting things out. He was going to get the money and then they'd make things work. 'Debbie... '
The line went dead. He stood for a moment, leaning back against the wall, staring at the phone in disbelief. What the hell? He tried her number again, but it went straight to voicemail. For f..ck's sake! He coughed and cleared his throat. Right, it was time to step things up a gear. He'd show her. He'd show all of them, though how he was going to do it, he wasn't quite sure.

He crossed the street and headed back in the direction of the hotel. He was hungry, tired and lonely. His life was a mess and the one chance he had of putting things straight seemed to be getting further out of reach. Maybe he should just give up on the whole drugs idea and go for cigarettes and spirits? He could cram quite a few cartons in his case – his gran's too, come to that. It wasn't as lucrative, but it had to be easier than what he was trying to do now. Then again, he did need the money – and easy money was a temptation he was finding hard to resist.

151

He had reached the footpath by the river. The road arched over the old stone bridge ahead of him, but he turned right, towards the hotel. Through the window he could see the passengers from the coach trip enjoying their after-dinner drinks. Gilly and Angie had a table by the window. He paused outside, smoking yet another cigarette, as he watched the two sisters. Angie was wearing a low-cut blouse. The thick gold chain around her neck kept dipping into her cleavage every time she moved. He found the sight of it quite erotic. Not that he'd ever fancied an older woman before, but she had something about her that he found attractive. Maybe it was time for a change, he thought, as he tossed his cigarette onto the path and ground it into the gravel with the sole of his shoe. Forget the skinny bimbos and go for someone solid and sensible and reliable.

He watched her raise her glass to her lips and noticed the chunky gold bracelet on her wrist and the assortment of diamond and gold rings on her fingers. Someone with money too, now that would make a change.

In that brief moment, he suddenly saw another solution to his problems, one that wasn't illegal either. It was time, he decided, to turn on the charm.

***

Gilly was sound asleep. Either that, or she had passed out. One minute she had been in full flow, and the next she had yawned loudly and sprawled sideways across the bed. Now she wasn't moving, though she did give the occasional hiccupping sob. Angie leaned closer to make sure she was breathing properly, before gently moving the crumpled and sodden piece of tissue from her sister's hand.

Well, this was a pickle and a half. She hadn't seen that coming. In fact, she'd hardly ever heard her sister complain about Charles before. But to say that she didn't love him, let alone like him, well, that was something else.

'Are you all right, darling?' she said.

'Hmm.' Gilly sighed and rolled onto her side. 'I'm so tired,' she murmured.

'Yes, you need to sleep.'

'Shleep,' she echoed.

Angie pulled the duvet over her sister and sat on the end of the bed. She waited a few moments until she heard a soft snore emitting from her parted lips. Maybe she should phone Simon to see what he made of it. Although her estranged husband had never been close with his brother-in-law, they did play the occasional round of golf together.

He might have some insight into what was going on. Maybe Charles had spoken to him over a beer in the clubhouse.

She reached for her phone, but there was no signal, not even by the window. She would have to go downstairs. Angie glanced at her watch. It was only half past ten. She might be able to get some reception in the foyer, or outside.

'I'm just going to ring Simon,' she said, draping a jacket round her shoulders. 'I won't be long.'

Her sister looked out for the count. Peaceful too. Oh well, she would only be a minute. Angie pulled the door softly shut behind her and headed down the main staircase. She could hear the buzz of conversation from the bar. In the dining room opposite, she could see the waitresses laying the tables for breakfast. She rang Simon's number as she reached the foot of the stairs. Annoyingly, it went straight to voicemail.

'I need to speak to you,' she said. 'Can you ring me in the next half hour or so? Otherwise I'll call you tomorrow.'

She slipped her phone into the pocket of her jacket. She wasn't sure what to do next. She didn't want to go back to the bedroom until she'd spoken to Simon, and she was fairly certain that he would call her back. He'd spent most of the day sending her text messages, saying how much he missed her, so she supposed she had better give him the benefit of the doubt. He only ever switched his phone off when he was driving, so she was pretty sure he'd get her message. She strolled over to the rack of leaflets by the reception desk. She might as well have a browse while she was waiting, to see if there was any information on places to visit the next day.

And that was where Carl found her – alone and at a loose end, exactly as he wanted her.

Chapter Twenty-two

Carl took a moment to straighten his shoulders and compose his thoughts before casually strolling over.

'Looking for something?' he said.

'Oh.' Angie turned. 'No, not really.'

'Where's your sister?' He glanced around the foyer as he spoke.

'She was tired.' Angie stuffed a couple of pamphlets into her handbag. 'She wanted an early night.'

'That's a shame. I was thinking of having a drink at the bar. You're welcome to join me, if you like.' He could see the look of indecision flickering across her face. 'Just one drink,' he added, grinning. 'After the day we had traipsing after that old boy at the chateau, I'm pretty knackered myself.'

Angie smiled. 'Oh, all right.'

She followed him into the lounge bar. It was fairly crowded, but he found them a table with two wing chairs by the fireplace. 'You sit down and I'll order. What will you have?'

'Red wine, please.' Angie draped her jacket over the back of the chair as she spoke. Her blouse was cream and silky, and the first few buttons had been left undone. He caught a glimpse of plunging cleavage and hurriedly looked away.

'Ooh, Carl, there you are,' came the raucous shriek from his gran, who was being helped to her feet by an equally unsteady Shirley. 'You missed a lovely dinner. Didn't he, Shirl?'

'Lovely,' repeated her new-found friend.

'Right.' Carl managed a thin smile. He turned back to the barman. 'Beer, please, and a glass of red wine – a large one.'

'I'm going up now,' his gran said, in a somewhat slurred voice that had Carl wincing. 'I've had such a good evening. Did you have a nice night?'

'Excellent,' he lied, trying not to think about the seedy pub, nor how hungry he was. He took a handful of mixed nuts from the bowl on the bar.

'Oh, that's good. I was a bit worried, you know, when you said you didn't want to come to dinner. I know this holiday isn't your kind of thing. But I want you to know how much I appreesh....appreciate...' She pronounced the word carefully, accentuating all syllables.

'I know – you've told me before,' Carl sighed picking up the glasses. Why didn't she just leave him alone? Couldn't she see he was with someone?

She patted him fondly on the arm, making him slosh his beer over the toe of his shoe. 'Goodnight, dear. He's ever such a good lad,' she added. This, to Shirley, who was still hovering beside them. 'Ever such a good lad.'

Carl gritted his teeth in the semblance of a smile. 'Goodnight, Gran. I'll see you at breakfast.'

He headed back to Angie, patently aware that he was being watched by the two old biddies. If he wasn't careful, they'd be offering to join them and he didn't want that happening. He placed the drinks on the table and, as an afterthought, returned to pick up the bowl of nuts at the bar.

'Want some?' he said, sliding the bowl towards her.

Angie shook her head. 'No, thanks. The wine's enough for me.' She took a small sip. 'You didn't fancy dinner in the restaurant, then?'

'Nah.'

'It was very good.'

'I heard,' he muttered. 'No, I wasn't hungry and I fancied some time out on my own.' He jerked his head in the direction of his grandmother, who was ambling her way towards the lift. 'She's harmless really, but she does my head in at times.'

Angie smiled. 'It's good of you to take her on holiday.'

'Yeah, well, it keeps her happy.' He took a mouthful of beer. He wondered if he was overplaying the doting grandson role. He couldn't quite fathom out what Angie was thinking. She seemed thoughtful and a bit pre-occupied. 'So, what about you?' he added, anxious to keep the conversation going. 'Why did you come on holiday with your sister?'

'Because I didn't want to be on my own,' Angie said. 'It's a long story and I won't bore you with the details.'

'Try me,' he said. 'I'm a good listener.'

This wasn't entirely true. In fact, Debbie complained that he hardly listened to a word she said. She was a bit of an airhead, so that wasn't surprising. Anyway, she was past history. It was Angie who intrigued him now She was single and wealthy, judging by the designer clothes and handbags. She was also sexy, in a mature way. Which meant he was perfectly happy to listen to everything she said. It was, he conceded, in his best interests to be charming and attentive.

By the time they had finished their drinks, and he had persuaded her to let him buy another round, he was feeling much more relaxed. He was sure that their previous misunderstanding about the drugs was behind them. She was on holiday and seemed to be enjoying his company. It was all looking good, so far.

'I must just nip to the loo,' Angie said, picking up her bag. 'I won't be a minute.'

'I'll get the drinks,' Carl said. 'Same again?'

'Oh, just a small wine for me.' She giggled. 'I think I've probably had more than enough.'

You and me both, Carl thought, only his was on an empty stomach. He emptied the bowl of nuts and brought a new one back to the table with his beer.

He could hear a phone ringing and it took him a moment or two to realise that it must be Angie's. The shrill and ever ascending ring tone was coming from the jacket she had draped over the back of the chair. He glanced around the room. People were looking at him. They were starting to tut. The phone was getting louder and louder. Oh, what the heck. He supposed he'd better answer it. It might be important. Phone calls at this time of night invariably were. He fumbled in her pocket and found her mobile.
'Hello.'

Nobody spoke.

'Hello,' he repeated.

'Who's that?' the caller wanted to know, his tone none too friendly, Carl thought.

'This is Angie's phone,' he said. 'Can I take a message?'

'No, you bloody well can't. Where is she and why isn't she answering her phone?'

'She's er...' He didn't like to say she was on the toilet. 'She's not available at the moment.'

'Why? What's she doing? And who the hell are you?'

Sod it. Carl switched off the phone and slipped it back into the pocket of Angie's jacket. He didn't need this right now. He glanced up and smiled as he saw her making her way across the room. He caught the scent of her freshly applied perfume and noticed that her was looking newly brushed, all promising signs. He waited until she had sat down again, before raising his glass to her. 'So,' he said, 'you were telling me about your sister.'

'Oh God, yes, and I've been ages. I shouldn't have left her alone for so long.'

'I'm sure she'll be fine.'

'I know, but I really ought to get back.'

She looked as if she was going to stand up again. Carl smiled and slid her wine glass towards her. 'We'll call it a night after this one. Come on, let's make the most of it. We're on holiday. You deserve this.'

All in all, he thought later, the evening had gone rather well. They'd chatted till almost midnight and though he wasn't prepared to push his luck, he had escorted her back to her room, on the pretext of checking that her sister was all right. It turned out that Gilly was still sound asleep, so no harm done there.

'Thanks for listening,' she had said.

Excellent. She was grateful to him as well.

Carl lay back on the pillows and folded his arms above his head. It had been a long day, an eventful day, but things were going in his favour now. It was all looking good.

***

'I'm sure I didn't switch my phone off,' Angie said, peering at the blank display on her mobile. It was a little after eight in the morning and she had woken to the sound of Gilly's alarm clock.

Gilly groaned and rolled over in bed. 'Ugh, my head hurts.'

'I was waiting for Simon to ring. Why would I have turned it off?' She pressed the buttons.

'Maybe you wanted to save the battery.'

'Maybe.' Angie searched her brain. 'I don't know. I can't remember.' She padded through to the bathroom and turned on the shower. Her head was thumping more than she cared to mention. Perhaps she had switched it off, though she had no recollection of doing so. Then again, she had had a lot to drink. With Carl! Oh God, what was she like? She wouldn't mention that bit to Gilly. She might not be very happy if she'd known she'd left her all that time.

As she lathered up her hair, she wondered if Simon had tried to call her. Well, it was too late now. She'd need to find a discrete moment when Gilly wasn't around to ask him about Charles.

She stayed in the shower for ages, letting the warm water wash over her. It was a good job they had a free day today, she thought, wrapping a towel around her head, what with both of them being a bit the worse for drink.

'Never again,' Gilly groaned, swallowing the first of a couple of painkillers. 'I shouldn't have had that last drink in the bar.'

'Me neither,' Angie agreed, though hers had been a lot later than her sister's.

'I can't even remember going to bed.'

'Oh well, there's no harm done. It's all part of the holiday experience.'

Gilly gulped the last of her bottled water. 'And I didn't speak to Charles. He'll never forgive me for cutting him off.'

'He will, you daft thing.'

'You don't know what he's like,' she said, pulling a face.

'I think I'm starting to find out.' Angie tugged a comb through her wet hair as she spoke. 'Did you mean what you said last night?'

'Why? What did I say last night?'

157

'About not loving him anymore.'

'Oh.' Gilly looked anxious. 'I don't know. Sometimes I can't stand the man, and at other times I think, well, maybe he's all right.'

'Think I'd be wanting more than just "all right",' Angie said. 'Anyway, enough about him. Why don't you have a shower? It might make you feel better. We don't have to go down to breakfast. We can find a little café or one of those nice patisseries in the town.'

'But breakfast is included.'

'Yes, I know.' Angie sighed. Gilly was being true to form.

'Unless you don't want to go?'

Angie peered at her reflection in the mirror. Her eyes were blood-shot and had dark circles beneath them. It wasn't her best look. Besides which, she was feeling a bit queasy. 'I'm not very hungry right now,' she said.

'Oh, okay.'

'You're sure you don't mind?'

'No, of course I don't.' Gilly fluffed up the pillows and straightened the duvet as she spoke.

It was settled, then. They would skip breakfast, and take a leisurely stroll into the town later, when they were both feeling a bit brighter.

That was the plan, anyway, but of course, things never seemed to go entirely to plan.

Charles phoned first, irate and in a typically foul mood, as Gilly had predicted. Angie didn't know what he said, but whatever it was reduced her sister to tears. Angie could hear her sobbing through the closed bathroom door.

The man was a bully, she thought. It was time she spoke to Simon. Failing to get any response from his mobile phone – it went straight to voicemail again – she decided to call him at work. Except, he wasn't there.

'Mr Turner has taken the rest of the week off,' his secretary, Josie Bradford, told her, in an imperious and irritated tone. Angie had never liked her. In fact, she'd first suspected Simon of having an affair with her, seeing as how the woman knew more about his business than she did at times.

'What do you mean he's taken the rest of the week off?' she said.

'A family crisis, I'm afraid.'

'What family?' Angie was shocked. Had his mother suddenly died or something? Maybe it was one of the kids. Maybe there'd been an accident. 'What's happened, Josie?'

'I'm afraid I can't tell you, Mrs Turner.'

'What do you mean you can't tell me,' she snapped, realising she was beginning to sound a bit like a parrot. 'What's going on?'

'I'm afraid I don't know,' came the apologetic and apparently sincere reply. Angie guessed this was the truth. The woman sounded quite disgruntled not to have been told all the gory details. 'He left me a message last night saying he wouldn't be in for the rest of the week. That there'd been a crisis in the family that had to be dealt with.'

'Oh,' Angie said. 'Oh, well, thank you. Goodbye.'

She immediately phoned her eldest daughter, Sarah, who didn't seem to know anything of a family crisis, or indeed, where her father might have gone.

'So, you don't think it's about Granny?' Angie asked.

'No, and I spoke to her yesterday. She was complaining because the council hadn't emptied her bin, but I told her it was probably because of the bank holiday. That's not a crisis, is it?'

'Well, it would be in Margaret's eyes,' Angie said wryly, 'but no, I don't think that would be why your father has taken time off work.'

'Want me to ring her and find out?'

'Would you? Oh, thank you, darling, and call me when you've spoken to her.'

Angie was worried. She thought about trying to get hold of her son, Martin, but decided against it. He'd be at work and they didn't like him taking personal calls in the office. Anyway, if anything had happened to him, Sarah would have known about it. They were very close. So, what now, she wondered?

The sobbing was becoming muted behind the bathroom door. Angie wondered if she should intervene. She'd give that Charles a piece of her mind, making Gilly cry like that. She knocked tentatively on the door. 'Are you okay in there?'

'Yes, I'm fine.'

'No, you're not. I heard you crying.'

'I'm fine,' Gilly said, opening the door. 'It wasn't me making all that noise.' She pointed to the open window. 'It was one of the cleaners. She's had a row with her boyfriend. I think he's one of the waiters. Well, I presume that was the gist of it. You know my French isn't as good as yours.'

Angie peered through the thin slats of the shutter and saw the young woman in the courtyard beneath them, sobbing into a crumpled piece of tissue paper. An older woman with dark hair had a consoling arm around her shoulders.

'So, Charles didn't upset you?'

'No, well, not like that,' Gilly admitted. 'He made me cross. I told him I didn't want to speak to him at all, if he was going to moan at me.'

'You didn't!' Angie was shocked. This was so unlike her sister. 'What did he say?'

'I don't know. I switched my phone off.' Gilly gave her a wicked grin. 'See, I'm not such a pushover, am I?'

'You're getting better,' Angie conceded. 'Anyway, I appear to have a bit of a problem now.' She sat down in front of the dressing table mirror and glanced at her reflection. The colour was returning to her cheeks and her eyes looked slightly less blood shot. 'I can't get hold of Simon.'

'Why would you want to?'

'I need to speak to him – it doesn't matter why,' she added hastily. 'The thing is, his secretary says he's taken leave from work over a family crisis.'

'What family crisis?'

'I have no idea,' she sighed. 'I've spoken to Sarah. Oh, hang on that's her now,' she said, snatching up her phone which had suddenly started to jangle. 'Hello darling, did you speak to Granny?'

'Yes, and she's absolutely fine,' her daughter replied. 'And I got hold of Martin, but he has no idea what dad's doing either. He reckons he just told his partners there was a family problem because he fancied a few days off. That friend of his, George, was flying to Portugal to play golf and Dad had mentioned going with him.'

George Addison – Angie knew him well – snooty being the word that sprang to mind whenever she thought of him. He'd been an accountant in the same firm as Simon before opting for early retirement, funded by his wife's generous inheritance following the death of her father.

'And you think he's gone to Portugal?'

'It's a possibility, yes.'

'Okay, well thanks, darling. If I hear any different I'll let you know.'

Angie popped the phone back into her handbag. Typical. Men could be such liars and Simon had lied more than most. She should have known better than to let herself get all worked up over nothing.

'I don't know why I bother,' she muttered.

'Is everything all right?' Gilly asked.

'Apparently.' Angie applied another dab of powder as she spoke. 'But if it isn't, I expect I'll be the last to know.'

Chapter Twenty-three

Fortified by strong black coffee and a chocolate croissant from the town's famous patisserie (or so it said in Gilly's tourist guide), the sisters made their way towards the ruins of the chateau which perched on the hill overlooking the river. They were not the first of the coach party to have made the trip.

Geoffrey was sitting on the ground by the ancient drawbridge - 'From the eleventh century, you know,'- sketching the ruins of the archers' tower on a large pad balanced on his knees.

'That's really rather good,' Angie said, peering over his shoulder to get a better look.

'Have you studied art at college?' Gilly asked.

'Oh, no.' Geoffrey looked bashful, but pleased. 'No, it's just a hobby of mine. I like architecture, you see, and I like to keep a record of the places I've seen.'

His pencil darted over the paper, shading and highlighting, as his head kept bobbing up and down, studying the stones and the rugged grandeur of the ruins.

'Most people would just take a photo and have done with it,' Angie muttered as they carried on walking towards the keep and the small museum. 'Let's take a look in here.'

She froze at the entrance and turned abruptly away. 'Actually, maybe not.' Carl and his grandmother were standing just inside the doorway. She felt heat rising in her cheeks. 'Let's look at the chapel instead.'

'Why? What?' Bewildered, Gilly turned and followed her along the uneven path.

'Carl's in there,' Angie hissed.

'Oh.' Gilly risked a furtive glance over her shoulder. 'Did you notice what he was wearing?'

'What?'

'Was he wearing his leather jacket?'

'I don't know. I didn't look that close.' Angie turned to face her. 'Why? You're not still thinking he's a murderer, are you?'

Gilly shrugged, non-committal, but the expression on her face said it all.

'Oh, for goodness' sake,' Angie said. 'He's a young man on holiday with his grandmother. If he was going to murder someone it wouldn't be on a coach trip.'

'It might if he was a drug dealer.'

'He's not a drug dealer. That was a genuine mistake and one he readily admitted to. It was all a misunderstanding. He told me so last night.'

'Last night?' Gilly raised a questioning eyebrow at her.

'Or whenever. I can't remember.'

'You saw him last night,' Gilly said accusingly. 'When I was asleep?'

'Yes, well, only briefly,' Angie said. There seemed no point in lying. 'I couldn't get a phone signal in our room, so I went downstairs. We got talking,' she added. 'He bought me a drink.'

'Well excuse me, but your phone worked pretty well in the bedroom this morning. Honestly, Angie, I can't believe you would go off drinking with him when I was so...so...'

'Pissed,' she snapped. 'Yes, all right and I'm sorry. But I wasn't gone long and if you must know, he was good company, seeing as how you'd passed out on me.'

'I was upset!' Gilly looked like she was going to burst into tears.

'Yes, I know, darling.' Angie gave her a hug. 'I know. Look, just forget it. I had good reason for leaving you at the time. I wanted to speak to Simon about Charles,' she said. 'I got waylaid, and I'm sorry. It won't happen again.'

'You wanted to talk about Charles?' Gilly said. 'With Simon? But why?'

'Because I was worried about you, you twit,' she sighed. 'Anyway, come on, I don't want Carl seeing us here.'

She hurried down the rough stone steps and through the narrow gate onto the pavement. She couldn't explain why she didn't want to see Carl – only that she felt a bit embarrassed. She had vague memories of being grateful to him, and for thanking him for his help, although she couldn't quite recall what that help had been. It was enough to know that she felt awkward and wanted to avoid him at this precise moment in time.

'Let's go look at the souvenir shops,' she said. 'You wanted to buy some postcards for the kids, didn't you?'

'Yes, but I don't have to get them right now. I thought you wanted to look at the church.'

'I'd rather go shopping,' Angie said. She'd already made a mental note to visit a smart looking boutique they had passed the night before. It was on the road running parallel to the river, somewhere near the pharmacy, she thought, and it had a bag in the window with her name on it – soft sable-coloured leather with a gold clasp.

162

'We can't go down there,' Gilly said, when realised where Angie was going. 'We'll need to take a detour.'

'Don't be so ridiculous.'

'I'm not being ridiculous. I'm being sensible.'

A woman in a white overall was brushing the pavement outside the pharmacy with a long-handled broom, sweeping it this way and that.

Angie shrugged. 'Whatever you say, though I think you're over-reacting. There probably wasn't even a film in that CCTV camera.'

'Yes, but what if there was? Oh God, it's the police!'

Gilly clutched her arm so hard Angie yelped in pain. The local gendarme had pulled up outside the pharmacy and a uniformed officer was getting out of the car.

'Come on. We need to go,' she said.

'Yes, all right,' Angie conceded. 'We can go that way.' She pointed to the next street. It suddenly seemed sensible not to take unnecessary risks.

By the time they found the boutique, an hour or so later, Gilly had already bought several treats to take home, including pickled samphire -'Why would you?' - comfiture de vin, prunes stuffed with marzipan and a hideous-looking wicker basket in which to array her gourmet delights. She'd also bought postcards and a box of fruit-flavoured sweets to take into work with her. Nothing extortionate – but nothing stylish either.

Angie, however, liked to think she had more discerning taste. She stood in front of the shop window, positively drooling over the soft and beautifully crafted   leather bag.

'You can't afford that,' Gilly gasped, peering at the discreetly placed price tag.

'Hmm. It is a bit expensive.' Angie crouched down to get a better look. 'But it is lovely. Oh, I don't know, I do like it. Maybe I could splash out.'

Gilly stared at her in disbelief. 'It's a bag.'

'Yes, but...'

'A bag, not a car and you've got a perfectly decent one with you.'

This much was true, but designer labels didn't come cheap. Angie straightened up. 'Maybe if I just held it over my shoulder, you know?'

'No.'

If there was one thing Angie hated, it was someone telling her what she could or couldn't do. She liked the bag, she wanted the bag and she had just about made up her mind to go in and buy it and stuff the expense, when she was distracted by her phone ringing.

'What now?' she said, peering at the screen to see if it was Simon at long last. It wasn't. 'It's Dave,' she said, glancing up at her sister.

'Dave?' Gilly's cheeks turned pink. 'You mean, Dave the coach driver?'

'Yes.' She held the phone to her ear. 'Hello.'

'Ms Turner?'

'Yes.'

'Sorry to trouble you, but are you anywhere in the vicinity of the hotel?'

'Yes, well fairly close. Why?'

'I need you to come back. I'll meet you in reception.'

Angie raised her eyebrows at Gilly. 'Why?' she asked.

'Oh, it's probably nothing to worry about. I'll tell you when you get here.'

'He wants me to go back to the hotel,' she said, pocketing her phone and glancing up at her sister with a worried frown. Her thoughts were going into overdrive. Had there really been a family crisis? Was there something no one was telling her?

'Did he say why?'

'No.'

'Did he say me as well, or does he just want to see you?'

Angie gave her a withering glare. 'He didn't actually say. I presume he meant both of us.'

Gilly walked alongside her as they hurried down the town's main street. She was wearing sensible flat shoes, but Angie, as always, had plumped for something a little more stylish. Her toes were being pinched in her high-heeled sandals, but she managed to match her stride for stride.

'How did he have your mobile number?' Gilly asked.

'He had all our numbers, from yesterday, remember, when we went looking for Cyril.'

'Oh, yes of course, except he didn't have mine, because I was with him.' Gilly sounded relieved.

Angie shot her a questioning look but couldn't be bothered to say anything. She had bigger things to worry about than her sister being jealous because Dave had phoned her. What if someone had died, for goodness sake?

They reached the riverside footpath and were heading for the hotel when she spotted Carl sitting on a bench in front of the main entrance, smoking. He was on his own.

'Oh God,' she muttered. She really didn't want to talk to him now. But he had spotted her at almost the same time she had seen him. He stood up, smiling, and came strolling towards them. He wasn't wearing his leather jacket.

'Looks like someone's been hitting the shops,' he said, nodding his head in Gilly's direction. 'Buy anything nice?'

'Oh, souvenirs. Nothing special.' Gilly clutched the bags to her chest as if he might want to pinch them.

'I didn't see anything I fancied. Well, not in the shops, that is.' His gaze lingered on Angie for long enough to make her feel uncomfortable. At any other time, she would have been flattered to receive such attention, especially coming, as it did, from a younger man. But she was anxious to see what Dave wanted and flirting with Carl was the last thing on her mind.

'We need to get going,' she said. 'Sorry, Carl, but we're in a bit of a hurry.'

'Yes, we are,' Gilly agreed.

Carl didn't look like he was going to be put off so easily. He fell into step beside them and was practically rubbing shoulders with Angie as they mounted the steps to the hotel foyer.

'Glad to see you're looking so well,' he whispered. 'I didn't see you at breakfast and wondered if you had a hangover.'

'No, I was fine,' she lied. 'Just not very hungry.'

'That figures.' He tilted his head to one side and whispered, 'Fancy a hair of the dog later? You know, once you've taken your bags up to your room.'

'I'll see what Gilly wants to do,' she said. They all might need a drink after what Dave had to tell them. Something told her it was going to be bad news. Angie looked searchingly for him through the plate glass doors but couldn't see him.

'Great.' Carl rested his hand on the small of her back as they strode into the reception area. 'I'm sure you'll be able to persuade her,' he added, giving her a knowing wink.

Angie wasn't quite sure in what order things happened next. She had been distracted, looking for Dave. She certainly hadn't expected to see Simon. And he, it transpired, hadn't expected to see her arrive with another man in tow.

'Get your hands off my wife!' he bellowed, shoving Carl so hard he went staggering sideways across the room like a dancing marionette.

Gilly had screamed – Angie did remember that bit – as Carl bounced back like a prize fighter, fists raised.

165

'Steady, steady.' Dave had appeared in the midst of them, holding his hands out as if he was a referee. 'Everybody calm down.'

Angie was, for once, lost for words. She gaped at her, soon-to-be, ex-husband as if she had never seen him before.

'Carl, Mr Goodman, back off. This doesn't concern you,' Dave said. He was still standing between the two men, who were circling each other warily. Simon, overweight and flustered, was sweating profusely in his grey business suit and silk shirt and tie. His thinning scalp gleamed under the hotel lights. His brow was moist and his eyes glittered angrily.

Carl, having recovered his balance and his composure, was on the defensive and ready to attack. With his striking physique and muscular build, staff were laying odds on the possible outcomes. (Two of the waiters were later reprimanded by the hotel owner for visibly taking bets.) The receptionist was poised to ring for the local gendarmes.

A small crowd of weary pensioners, tired from a morning spent traipsing up to the chateau and around the town, had gathered in the foyer to watch the excitement. Word had spread like a Mexican wave round the bar. Even Geoffrey had appeared, sketch pad in hand, as if he was about to capture the action for posterity.

'Simon,' Angie said, aghast. 'What are you doing?'

'Looking for you,' he said, doing a couple of half-hearted jabs in Carl's direction.

Carl was ducking and weaving like a professional fighter and Dave was trying desperately to keep the two men apart.

'Back off, Carl,' he repeated.

'Why should I? He had a go at me.'

'He's her husband,' Dave groaned. 'Now can we all just calm down.'

'Husband?' Carl echoed, straightening up and staring at Angie. 'But I thought – oof!' The blow came to just below his ribs and caught him totally unprepared. Winded, he slumped to his knees.

'Yes, husband!' Simon said gleefully. Sweat was popping off his brow. He had started to mimic Carl's footwork and was hopping from toe to toe. It was making him pant heavily.

'Stop this right now!' Angie said, in the tone of voice that left no room for argument. 'I've never seen anything so ridiculous. Simon!'

Her husband stopped jogging on the spot and slumped against the bannisters of the polished oak staircase with apparent relief. Carl staggered to his feet and stood, clutching his side, with a pained expression on his face. Dave visibly breathed out and shook his head wearily.

'Gentlemen, I think there's been a bit of a misunderstanding here.'

'I'll say,' Carl muttered, glaring at Angie. 'One hell of a misunderstanding.'

Chapter Twenty-four

It was a wonder they hadn't been evicted from the hotel, Gilly thought. Such an embarrassing performance, and in full public view as well. She'd never seen anything like it. What on earth was Simon playing at – Rambo? And as for Carl – she allowed herself the satisfaction of a little smile – he'd certainly been taken down a peg or two. He was sitting at the foot of the stairs, clutching his side, with his grandmother tut-tutting over him and shaking her head wearily.

Dave was assuring the receptionist that she had no need to call the police, that everything was under control, whilst the group of interested sightseers had adjourned to the bar for lunchtime tipples.

Angie was consoling Simon – actually patting his sweating brow with a handkerchief donated by Edith.

'I always have one in my bag,' Edith said, 'for Cyril, you know. Oh, Cyril, no, not outside – this way, dear. We're going to the lounge bar now.'

Cyril was looking suitably bemused. 'Is the entertainment over?'

'Yes, dear, it's over.'

Gilly certainly hoped so. Carl was glaring at Simon with a particularly malevolent look on his face.

'Idiot,' he muttered, as he stood up and made his way slowly up the stairs, followed by an over-anxious Barbara.

'Do you need to see a doctor? I can get them to call one."

'No, I don't need to see a doctor.'

'Oh, but Carl. Carl, wait for me.'

Gilly glanced back at Angie. She seemed to have eyes only for Simon. In fact, she was fussing over him like a protective mother hen.

'What were you doing?' she was saying. 'Oh, darling, there was no need. You silly man.' She mopped his brow again. He looked exhausted.

Then again, he wasn't used to physical exertion. A leisurely round of golf didn't count for much. Gilly sincerely hoped he wasn't about to have a heart attack. She wondered if any of the hotel staff knew much about first aid.

'Right,' Dave said, coming back from placating the receptionist, who still looked in two minds as to whether she should be summoning assistance or not. 'What the hell was all that about?'

Angie was gazing up at Simon with adoring eyes and didn't appear to have heard. 'Oh, darling, you were so brave. You were ready to fight for me.'

'That's because I love you,' he gasped, still panting heavily. 'I don't want a divorce, Angie. I never wanted a divorce. I've always loved you.'

'Come on,' Dave said, gently pulling Gilly to one side. 'I think we should leave them to sort out their differences.'

'Oh but…' Gilly hesitated. 'Is he going to be all right?' She still thought Simon was a funny ruddy colour, and his breathing was laboured – all classic signs of trouble, according to her home doctor manual, which she virtually knew off by heart.

'He'll be fine,' Dave assured her. 'In fact, I think they both will. Come on.'

They didn't head for the lounge, much to Gilly's relief. She didn't want to face all those curious faces from the other passengers. That would be way too embarrassing. Instead, they headed outside and on to the riverside pathway.

It was well after mid-day and the clouds had parted to reveal blue skies. In the warm sunshine, with just a touch of a breeze, it was the perfect setting for a gentle walk along the riverbank.

'When did Simon turn up?' she asked.

'Not long before I called Angie,' Dave said.' He'd got an early morning flight to Tours and drove straight here in a hire car. Said something about a man having Angie's phone. I don't know. I can't remember,' he added. 'But he was in a right old state. What's the situation with them, anyway?'

'They're separated,' Gilly said. 'She got the decree nisi a couple of weeks ago. This holiday was to be a new start for her.'

'But?' he prompted. She had gone quiet.

Gilly stood at the water's edge, peering down at the swirling shallows. 'I think she still loves him. I think she was hurt by what he'd done.'

'Done?'

'He had an affair with his hairdresser.'

'Ah.' Dave nodded and then smiled. 'His hairdresser.'

It sounded funny the way he said it, but it really wasn't that funny. Despite herself, Gilly found herself smiling back at him. 'Simon doesn't have that much hair to play with, does he?'

'Nope.' Dave laughed. 'Exactly what I was thinking.'
They fell into step together as they continued their stroll over the bridge and into an adjacent park. The sun was warm on her face and Gilly wondered if she should take off her cardigan. She was starting to feel quite hot.

'What's the story with Carl, then?'

'Him, goodness, I wouldn't know where to start.'

Dave sat down on a bench and motioned her to join him. 'You can tell me,' he said, patting the seat. 'There's no hurry.'

'But it's your day off. Haven't you got things to do?'

'Possibly.' He grinned. 'But nothing that can't wait.' This,' he added, 'is much more interesting.'

Gilly found herself telling him everything – about the suspected drugs, and how frightened she had been; the news report and the missing leather jacket. 'Like the one you fished out of the river,' she reminded him. 'But Angie says it was all a misunderstanding. She says he's not like that. I think she was flattered he was showing her so much attention. But it does seem odd, when you think about it.' She paused in mid flow, suddenly aware that he was watching her intently, his lips curving into a thoughtful smile.

'That's some imagination you have there,' he said.

A warm flush crept up her neck and face. She fanned herself with her hand. 'That's what Angie says.' She made a show of removing her cardigan and folding it carefully onto her lap. 'Goodness, but it's getting hot, isn't it? I should have brought some sun cream. I might even have some.' She began fumbling through her handbag. It was more a distraction than anything else. She was achingly conscious of the fact that he was still watching her and it was making her feel flustered. He probably thought she was some sort of hysterical woman prone to flights of fancy and she didn't like to think of him imagining her like that.

'Do you think your sister will make it up with her husband?'

'I don't know,' she said, relieved at the change of subject. 'I hope so.'

'Really?'

'Yes.' She nodded. 'I like Simon. He's a good man.' She found the small tube of sun cream she had been searching for. It was a free sample that had come attached to the full-size one and was ideal for days out, or so it said on the label.

'Even though he had an affair.'

'He made a mistake.' She unscrewed the cap and squeezed a dollop of cream into the palm of her hand. 'I don't think he wanted to leave Angie. I think he was confused, and then she threw him out and it all went downhill from there.'

'Hell hath no fury.'

'Something like that.' She rubbed the cream into her arms and dabbed some on her cheeks and nose. 'Do you want some?'

Dave smiled. 'I'm fine, thanks. We could find a shadier spot, though, maybe through those trees.'

Gilly followed the line of his gaze. The copse looked cool and welcoming, with an avenue of beech and maple. It was tempting. Oh, but she couldn't. It wouldn't seem right. What would people think if they were seen together?

'Or we could go and get a cold drink.'

That sounded a more sensible option, Gilly thought. Besides which, she was rather thirsty. She had forgotten to bring a bottle of water with her.

He was looking at her with what seemed like an amused smile. Had he realised what she was thinking? The thought made her flush even more.

'I'd love a cold drink,' she said. 'Something with lots of ice in it.'

'My thoughts exactly.' He stood up and offered her a hand.

'I'm okay, thanks,' she said, wiping her fingers on a tissue. They were sticky with sun cream and moist with sweat. 'Oh dear, this stuff goes everywhere. What? Have I not rubbed it in properly?'

He was standing grinning at her, hands planted on each side of his waist. 'You look fine,' he said. The grin broadened. 'Come on, I know just the place.'

The terrace bar was set back from the river and had lots of cool and shady umbrellas to sit under. It was far enough away from the town centre to attract fewer visitors, but near enough not to be too isolated.

Gilly was glad they weren't on their own, glad of the distraction of small children throwing pebbles into the water. It gave her something to look at other than Dave. She sneaked a shy glance at him as he lifted his glass to his lips and took a long draught of cold beer. He was a nice man, she decided. Yes, that's what he was – a nice man, helpful, kind and intuitive. She took a mouthful of her drink. She had opted for lemonade, and now wished she had asked for something stronger, like a spritzer. She needed a bit of Dutch courage, if only to stop herself blushing every time he looked at her.

If only she could be more like Angie, she thought. Angie was never at a loss for words.

'So, what's your story?' he asked, setting his glass down on the wooden table and leaning back in his chair.

'My story?' she repeated.

'Yes. Why are you here with your sister and not your husband?

'Charles doesn't like going abroad,' she said. 'He's not too keen on Angie either.'

She took a quick gulp of her drink, then coughed and spluttered as the fizzy bubbles shot up her nose.

'And I take it he was less than pleased when you told him you were going away with your sister.'

'You could say that,' she said, 'but he thought Angie was paying, so that lessened the blow.'

'And did she?'

'What?'

'Pay for you.'

'No.'

'I see.' He gave her a long and considered stare, before glancing away.

A small boy was kneeling by the water's edge, trying to float a makeshift boat that his father had fashioned from a piece of paper. An older boy crouched beside him, making waves with the flat of his hand. The little boat bobbed and rocked in the ripples.

'Secrets and lies,' he said, shaking his head. 'That's how it all starts.' He took another mouthful of beer. 'I could make a boat like that.'

Gilly glanced back at the little boy. He was beaming with delight. His mother was kneeling beside him, camera posed in one hand, taking a picture.

'What do you mean?'

'It's easy. You take a bit of paper and fold it in half...'

'No, I mean, what you said. You said, "that's how it all starts". How what starts?'

'Oh, that.'

'Yes, that.' Gilly laid emphasis on the last word. 'Has Angie said something to you?'

'No.' He folded the menu in half, then turned down two of the corners, before flipping it over.

'I don't want a boat.'

'Course you do. Look how much fun that kid's having with his.'

Dave folded the paper again and held it up for her to admire.

'It's a hat, or a boat. You choose.'

'I'm not a child.'

'I had noticed.' He grinned knowingly and stood up. 'Come on, let's see if it floats.'

'Dave, wait.' She caught hold of his arm. 'I'm being serious.'

'So am I,' he said. 'I wasn't implying anything, Gilly, about you or your relationship with your husband. That's none of my business. It was just a stupid remark.' He leaned over and hauled her to her feet with one firm tug. 'This,' he brandished the paper boat at her, 'this is what's important now.'

172

His humour was infectious and she found herself smiling up at him. 'Are you crazy?'

'Possibly.' He performed a mock bow. 'Now if you would care to accompany me to the launching ceremony.' He offered her the formal use of his arm, and with a shy nod of her head, she took it.

'It'll sink, you know.'

'There is that possibility.'

'More like a certainty,' she predicted.

The family with the two young boys had wandered further along the river bank. Their boat was holding up well, despite various attempts to submerge it with small stones and gravel.

Gilly watched as first the father, and then the elder boy, took turns to pelt it, along with accompanying cannon and gunfire noises. The younger boy – he couldn't have been more than about three – was hanging on to his mother's hand and squealing with excitement.

'We should have champagne,' Gilly said.

'Technically, yes, we should.' Dave crouched down and set his boat onto the water – gently, very gently, as if it were a fledgling bird. He glanced up at her as she watched with eager anticipation. 'Having fun, Mrs Bennett?'

She smiled, nodding, 'Yes. Yes, I am.'

The boat tilted sideways almost immediately and started taking on water. The sail sank beneath the ripples, and the current carried the capsized vessel into the nearest patch of pond weed, where the folds of paper slowly unravelled.

'Think it was better as a hat,' Dave said, straightening up. 'But we could still have that champagne.'

'I wasn't serious,' Gilly said, laughing.

'No, but I was. Come on, I'll treat you,' he added. 'After all the drama you've been through on my coach trip, I'd say it was the least you deserve. We'll worry about potential drug dealers, murderers and adulterous brothers-in-law later.'

'You think I'm over-reacting, don't you?'

'Not at all. The world is a strange place.' He grinned. 'But you're safe with me.'

And as she followed him back to the terrace bar that was exactly how she felt.

Chapter Twenty-five

'I don't want to leave you here,' Simon complained, sipping a reviving gin and tonic in the lounge bar of the hotel. 'I'll get a room.'

'You'll do no such thing,' Angie said. 'Besides, they're fully booked with the coach party. And what would Gilly say? This is her holiday as well, you know.'

'Gilly wouldn't mind,' he muttered. 'She likes me.'

'No, Simon. You're not being fair.'

He sighed and dabbed at his brow with Cyril's handkerchief. He was still sweating profusely. Then again, his suit was pure wool and perhaps a tad too thick for the current temperature. Angie supposed he hadn't thought to bring something more casual with him.

'It's only for a few more days,' she added. 'We'll be home soon.'

'Couldn't I book us a room at another hotel – just the two of us?' he suggested.

'No.'

'All right, the three of us. Gilly can come too. I mean,' he glanced round the room that seemed to be full of elderly people and then back at Angie, 'you can't honestly tell me she'd be happier staying here with this crowd of geriatrics.'

'Actually, I think you'll find we both would. We're having a good time, if you hadn't realised. And some of these "geriatrics", as you call them, are quite fun.'

It was Simon's turn to look surprised. 'You don't like old people.'

'Yes, but most of this lot don't think they are old. There is a difference. I tell you what, if I have half their stamina by the time I reach my seventies I'll be ecstatic.'

Angie meant every word. This trip had been a real eye-opener for her, in more ways than one. Fun wasn't reserved for the young – that much was certain.

'If you say so,' he grumbled. 'But look, darling, I can't get a flight till tomorrow morning and besides,' he tilted his glass at her, 'I don't think I can drive.' He drained his glass quickly, as if to prove a point.

'Now you're just being childish,' Angie said.

'Desperate, more like.'

He looked deflated, like all the wind had gone out of his sails.

'I just want to be with you, darling. I've made so many mistakes. I know I messed up. I know I hurt you and I'll never forgive myself.' He shook his head wearily. 'What more can I say? I was an idiot.'

'Yes.' Angie covered his hand with her own. 'You were.' Her tone softened. 'But I wasn't the easiest person to live with. I must have driven you mad with all my mood swings.'

'I should have been more understanding,' he sighed, 'and I will be, I promise. We can go for counselling,' he added. 'We can talk things through.'

'You've never been much good at talking.'

'Only because you've never listened.'

Angie held her hands up to that one. Having spent years at the front of a classroom, she had perfected the art of talking over rabble-rousers, and instilling discipline at every opportunity. And perhaps it had left her open to being a bit of a dictator, but it had been a necessary part of her job. Not, she realised, her marriage.
'You're right,' she said, 'and I'm sorry. Maybe counselling would be a good idea.'

She finished her drink and decided she needed another one. They hadn't spoken like this for years, and she didn't want to stop now.

'Waiter?' He was beckoning the barman over. It was almost as if he could read her thoughts. 'Same again, please. Might as well,' he added, glancing back at her, 'seeing as how I'm not going anywhere tonight.'

'Simon, I don't see how you can stay here.'

'It's okay. I'll sleep in my car.'

'I don't know if that's a good idea. Not with your bad back.'

'Suggest something else, then?' he said, as he removed his jacket and draped it over the back of his chair.

'There's bound to be another hotel in town.'

'One would assume so.'

'Well then.'

'But I want to stay with you.'

Angie's heart gave a sudden thump against her rib cage. It was the way he said it. He wasn't just talking about the night ahead. After all this time, after all the months of heart-ache, bitterness, tears and regrets, he had finally put it into words. He wanted to stay with her. For months, she had longed for him to come back, but pride had got in the way. She'd ignored his texts, made derisory comments to the children (which had been completely wrong of her, but she hadn't been able to help herself) and pretended that she was happy being single and independent. But she'd been miserable as sin. Lonely, frustrated, desperate – three words to sum it all up. She'd spent a fortune on expensive clothes and treats for herself, lots of lunches out and spa breaks with the girls, everything she could think of to make herself feel better, but nothing had worked. It had all been an act. This was what she had been waiting for. This was what she wanted more than anything else in the whole world.

'I know, darling,' she said. 'I feel the same way, but it's just not practical. We need to think about Gilly,' she added. 'She's been going through a rough patch too and it wouldn't be fair to spoil her holiday. I can't ask her to move out just because you've turned up uninvited.'

'I'm going to have a word with reception,' he said, standing up.

'And ask them what, exactly?'

'If they've got a spare room. A single or a double. Anything would do.' He was gazing at her with such lust and longing that she suddenly felt twenty years younger and glamorous to boot.

'Simon. You've just had a fight with Carl in the middle of the hotel foyer. They're not going to offer you a room?'

He hesitated, then began to straighten his tie. 'I'm sure I can persuade them. I'll explain it was a misunderstanding.'

Angie wasn't convinced. She'd seen the way the staff had looked at him. 'Let's wait till Dave gets back,' she suggested, patting the chair. 'Come on, sit down. Don't do anything you might regret.'

'I've already done that,' he said, sitting down. 'I've made a mess of everything. Oh Christ,' he groaned, shaking his head. 'Angie, I don't know what to do.'

'Talk to me,' she said. She caught hold of his hand and held it firmly. 'Right now, Simon, that's all you need to do.'

Carl had had a brainwave. He liked to think of it as a 'eureka' moment – one of those thoughts that just seemed to pop up out of nowhere and yet seemed so obvious that he wondered why he hadn't thought of it sooner.

He was sitting in his grandmother's bedroom, whilst she fussed about looking for something to put on his bruises.

'I've got some pain-killing gel. I know I have. Anti-inflammatory,' she added, reading the label on the tube. 'I put it on me knees when me arthritis is paying up.'

'Give it here,' he muttered, not wanting to appear ungrateful, but anxious to get back to his own room and a bit of peace and privacy. As he took the tube from her, he knocked over a plastic container. The top had been loose and as it rolled over the dressing table, a cascade of white powder followed in its wake.

'Oh, Carl, that's my talcum powder,' Barbara gasped. 'Oh here, don't spill any more. That's all I've brought with me.'

'Talcum powder,' he echoed, dabbing a finger in it and sniffing dubiously. 'It doesn't smell of anything.'

'That's because it's unscented,' his gran said. 'I don't want to be smelling of cheap roses or violets, now do I? Not when I've got that posh perfume to wear.' (She'd indulged herself by buying a small but expensive bottle of eau de cologne in Paris and had taken to applying it liberally every day.)

Carl leaned back in his chair and pondered over the implications of what she was saying. Unscented talcum powder. It went hand in hand with Angie's comment about dodgy street traders and how you never knew what you were buying. That was it. Bloody hell, this could actually work.

He scooped a handful of the powder into the palm of his hand and stared at it, his mind working overtime. A few containers of this – he could seal it in plastic bags: it looked the business – and it wasn't his fault if it wasn't the real thing. How was he to know? He wasn't a user. He could plead ignorance, say he'd been duped by a rogue dealer or something, but at least he'd have something to show from his travels.

'Want me to rub it in for you?'

'What?' Carl glanced back at his grandmother who was hovering beside him with an anxious look on her face.

'The gel.'

'Oh that, no, thanks, I can do it.' He brushed the powder from his hands into the nearby waste paper bin. 'Sorry about that. I'll buy you some more.'

His grandmother leaned forwards to rescue the spilt container. 'That's all right, dear.' She held it upright and shook it slightly, before screwing on the plastic top. 'I've probably got enough to last me the rest of the holiday.'

'That's not the point,' he said. 'It's the least I can do.'
He very nearly kissed her at that moment. It was uncharacteristic, but man, did he feel like giving her one huge smacker. She might just have saved his life.

'I'm going to have a shower first, and then I'm going to go straight out and buy you some more talc.'

'There's really no need, Carl.'

'I know, but it'll make me feel better.'

'Oh, all right.' His gran beamed at him.' But make sure it's unscented.'

'Unscented,' he repeated, smiling thoughtfully. 'Right.'

It wasn't easy finding unscented talcum powder in a country famous for its perfume industry. Carl discovered this as he trawled the local boutique shops and department stores in the hunt for something distinctly less alluring. His lack of basic French didn't help him either. Most of the shop assistants, who had been willing and pleasant at first, became increasingly annoyed as he recoiled with every fresh tub they wafted under his nostrils. His requests for 'no scent' were met with hopeless shrugs of the shoulders and shaking of the head, and only in the final shop that he could find did an older woman appear to understand what he was after.

She made a rocking motion with her arms. 'You want it for baby, yes?'

'Sorry?'

'For baby?'

The penny dropped. 'Yes. Yes.' Carl breathed out a large sigh of relief. 'For the baby.'

'Follow me, please.'
So, there it was – loads of tubs of talcum powder, in amongst the nappies and wet- wipes and bottles of oil and baby lotion. Carl selected one and sniffed it warily. He couldn't smell anything.

The shop assistant was giving him a quizzical look as she made a show of tidying the nearby shelves. 'Is okay?'

'Yeah, thanks.' Carl picked up two containers, hesitated, then picked up another two. That ought to do it. As long as the powder was white and didn't smell, he was sorted. All he had to do now was find some clear plastic bags and he was in business. It was easy. He should have thought of it sooner. As he put the talc into the wire basket the assistant had given him and headed for the pay desk, he suddenly remembered the reason for his visit. He'd forgotten to get some for his grandmother. Oh well, another couple wouldn't hurt. It wasn't that expensive. He returned to the shelf and picked up another two containers.

As he did so, he became aware of a man loitering by the same counter. He was watching Carl, quite blatantly, it seemed.

Store detective, Carl thought. He'd met a few of them in his time.

'*Bonjour, monsieur.*' The man stepped closer. He had slicked-back dark hair and was wearing an expensive suit. Probably in his forties, though it was hard to tell.

Carl nodded. 'All right, mate.' He reached into his back pocket for his wallet.

'Ah, you are English.' The man stepped closer. He had a strong French accent. One gold tooth glinted amongst the white of his beaming smile.

'Yeah.'

'On holiday?'

'Yes.' Carl pulled out a handful of notes from his wallet and tilted his head in the direction of the check-out. 'Sorry, I need to pay for these.'

'But, of course.' The man rested his hand on Carl's arm. 'But then, maybe you come with me.'

'Why? Look, mate, I haven't done anything.' Carl yanked his arm free and took a step backwards.

'*Pardon, monsieur.* You misunderstand.' The man looked suitably apologetic. He gave a small shrug and tilted his head in the direction of Carl's basket. 'I think you are a man who likes leather, yes? Maybe black leather; maybe red?'

Carl gaped at him, appalled. Oh God, they had tracked him down. That CCTV footage in Paris, the image of him in his leather jacket. Oh shit. This creep wasn't a store detective at all. He was a plain-clothes police officer.

'Look, I can explain...'

'Please.' The man motioned him towards the till. 'Pay for your goods.'

Bloody hell. Carl slapped the notes down on the counter and could barely manage a smile as the check-out girl scanned his tubs of talc and placed them into a carrier bag. All he could think of was the man standing directly behind him. The man who was quite probably about to arrest him the moment he stepped onto the street. In fact, he was half expecting a squad car and armed officers waiting to greet him, or at least a couple of gendarmes with guns. They always carried guns here.

He snatched up the bag and headed for the door, his mind working overtime. They didn't have anything on him – no drugs, no connections, nothing but that grainy image on camera. It was a case of mistaken identity. He would have to bluff his way out of it and he'd need to be convincing. Otherwise he could see himself languishing in a French prison for years awaiting trial. He sucked in a deep breath and stepped out into the warm sunshine.

Outside, there was no one. Well, no one of any significance, just an old lady bent double with a shopping trolley, a young girl with a miniature poodle, a couple of youths loitering at the corner. Carl glanced back over his shoulder. If back-up hadn't arrived maybe he could make a run for it. He'd always been good as a sprinter, but no, he decided, this guy looked fit and muscular and he was too close for comfort.

'Please,' the man said, catching hold of Carl's arm again. 'Come with me.'

What was it with these French people? he thought. They were always wanting to grab hold of you. He jerked his arm free. 'Yeah, okay,' he muttered. He was half expecting to be clamped in handcuffs and was quite surprised when he wasn't. Maybe the man just wanted to ask him a few questions; an informal interview, nothing too heavy.

They walked abreast of each other up a narrow back street between two tall buildings. The stone-flagged pavement stank of urine. Around the corner and they reached another street, this time with three-storey houses, shuttered windows and parked cars.

Carl felt nervous and on edge.

'In here, please.'

The man pushed open a bright red door, fronted by tubs of scarlet and white geraniums.

'In here?' Carl said, puzzled. This didn't look right.

'*Mais, oui*'

Maybe it was a safe house; somewhere unofficial where they could interrogate him. It stood to reason if it was an undercover drugs operation. Shit! How had he got himself in this mess?

He followed the man through the door and found himself in a long and narrow hallway. A flight of stairs lay ahead of him. He could smell furniture polish and stale smoke. Voices, sounding mumbled and indistinct, came from somewhere upstairs.

Another man was coming down the stairs, a huge bulk of a man in a dark suit and a bald head. He gave a cursory nod at the pair of them. No questions – nothing spoken aloud – just that nod, and what looked like a knowing smile.

Carl felt his breathing quicken. He followed the first man into a small room, with a stone-tiled floor, a wooden table and chairs. Heavy net drapes masked the windows. The light came from a single bulb hanging from the ceiling in a lace-covered shade.

'Wait here, please.'

Carl nodded. This had to be the interview room. He dumped his bag of shopping on the scrubbed wooden table and the moment the man left the room, reached in his pocket for his tobacco. He rolled himself a cigarette and lit it, drawing in the smoke with a deep breath. Tough if they didn't like it. He needed something to calm him down. He paced the room.

Above the mantelpiece hung a large, gilded mirror. Two-way, probably. They usually were. He went over to the window and parted the drapes, but the windows were shuttered. That would be right. He sat down at the table to think. He needed to get his story straight. They couldn't pin anything on him. They didn't have anything. He just had to keep his wits about him.

'Okay.' The man returned, carrying a large holdall, which he placed on the floor.

Carl took a last drag and then stubbed it out before pocketing the dog-end in the pocket of his jeans.

'I think you will like this,' the man said.

Carl had the horrible suspicion that the man was about to produce his leather jacket from the holdall. He would deny it was his, of course, seeing as how it was the only bit of proof that would connect him to the murdered street trader in Paris.

He leaned back in his chair and folded his arms across his chest.

'Red PVC,' the man was saying, 'very good. Also black. You feel.'

The man was unpacking what looked like bondage outfits – lots of shiny plastic with chains and studs, and trousers, black leather trousers and crotch-less leather chaps.

Carl scraped back his chair and stood up. He was being shown a shiny black face mask that looked like something Anthony Hopkins had worn in *The Silence of the Lambs*.

'All very cheap. *Mais oui*, this is for you, I think.' The man held a leather singlet in front of him. 'Good for showing the muscles. You work out at gym, *non?*'

'Yeah.' Carl nodded. 'Yeah, the gym. Yeah, cool.' He sucked in a breath and tried to appear nonchalant, when inside, he had the almost uncontrollable urge to laugh. Fetish gear – that's what it was. This guy – unbelievably - was offering him fetish gear.

'Chains, I have chains, handcuffs, whips – you like whips?'

'No. Not for me.'

'Maybe this, so soft, so, how you say it, tactile?' The man was grinning as he laid a tight body suit in black PVC on the table. 'You need powder for this one.' He tilted his head in the direction of Carl's shopping bag. 'But it will slip on easy, like a second skin.' He ran his lips over his teeth as he spoke. He looked as if he was visualising the moment.

For Carl, the penny was starting to drop. Talcum powder; tight leather, skin hugging PVC; this wasn't a police station; far from it. In fact, it was the furthest you could possibly get one from one.

'You like?'

'Um.' Carl was lost for words. He'd been so sure he was about to interrogated on suspicion of murder, drugs dealing or whatever else they could pin on him. Never in a million years, had he pictured this scenario. He didn't know whether he felt relieved, or worried.

'For you a special price. Very cheap,' the man added. His gold tooth gleamed in the light from the overhead lamp. 'Maybe you want to try it on?'

He was giving him the same suggestive look the man in the toilets at the gay bar had given him.

'Nah,' He shook his head. He picked up the leather vest and pretended to examine it. 'You…er…you got anything my girlfriend might like?' He laid emphasis on the word girlfriend.

'But of course. Suspenders, stockings.' The man was delving into his bag.

'Yeah, that sort of thing.'

The distant thud, thud of music boomed from somewhere above them. Startled, Carl gazed up at the ceiling. He could hear shouting and laughter, footsteps running along the corridor. Suddenly the door banged open, and a woman – a semi-naked woman, in a topless red corset and not a lot else - half fell into the room.

'Pardon,' she said. She turned, laughing, and Carl was given a privileged view of her naked rear as she headed up the stairs. A man in black leather trousers and a crisp white shirt, unbuttoned at the neck, was leaning over the bannisters, dangling a bottle of champagne at her.

'They party,' his companion said and gave him an unsettling wink. 'All day, all night. Maybe you want to join them? We have very pretty girls. Lots of pretty girls.'

Carl couldn't believe it. He was in a brothel, and a kinky one at that. How had he ended up here? More to the point, how was he going to get out of it?

'Three hundred Euros.'

'Nah.' He shook his head. He wasn't averse to a bit of fantasy sex. He liked it when Debbie put on her nurse's uniform – now that turned him on – but Debbie wasn't here, and this weirdo was starting to annoy him.

He picked up the black bodysuit and smoothed it over the table, as if pondering the quality, fingered some frilly suspenders and examined some fishnets. He had to look interested, when, in reality, all he wanted to do was make a run for it.

By the half-open door stood the man that he now realised was a bouncer, all shaved head and dark glasses, with a chest measurement that had to be at least fifty inches under his dark jacket. He was watching Carl intently, arms held in front of him, twiddling his thumbs. Relaxed, but guarded.

Oh, shit, he thought. He didn't want any trouble. He picked up his bag of talcum powder. This hadn't been one of his better ideas.

'So, we have a deal, yes?'

'Yeah, yeah, cool,' Carl said, snatching up the bodysuit and stuffing it into his bag.

'And the stockings. Real lace. *Tres bon.*'

Carl wasn't sure Debbie would like them – black fishnets with scratchy elasticated tops - but it was worth it just to get out of there. He took out his wallet and counted out a handful of notes.

The man smiled, running his tongue over his lips like a lizard.

'*Merci beaucoup, monsieur.*'

'Yeah, whatever.'

Carl practically ran down the alleyway and out onto the main road, anxious to get away from the house before anyone saw him. He was tempted to chuck the whole carrier bag into the nearest waste-paper bin. What on earth was he going to do with a black plastic bodysuit? It was only the thought that he'd have to try and recoup his losses somehow, that stopped him from throwing it away. He'd have to try and sell it in on E-bay when he got back. He'd give Debbie the stockings and tell her they were proper French lace; not that she'd know any different, and it would save him from having to buy her anything else.

Jason might be suspicious about the powder, but he could plead ignorance in that respect. He didn't know what he was buying. Concealing it in baby powder tubs seemed like a good option to him, and the tubs had been sealed, which was even better.

Carl slowed to a walk. Yeah, that would work. He'd have his story all sorted before he got home. In the meantime, he'd stock up on tobacco and booze. He still had his credit card, and his gran would give him a loan if he asked her. At least that way he could be guaranteed a return for his investment.

Satisfied that he had covered all eventualities, Carl resolved to enjoy what was left of the holiday because, in his mind, and after the day he'd had, he bloody well deserved it.

***

Gilly was feeling a little bit light-headed and giggly. She wasn't used to drinking champagne – she wasn't really used to drinking at all, apart from the occasional glass of wine. This holiday had seen her consume more units in a week than she normally consumed in a year. She would have to go on a detox when she got home, she resolved, whilst nodding agreeably as the wine waiter topped up her glass.

In Dave's company, she felt like a different woman, a carefree, spirited, entertaining woman, who was capable of having fun, of taking risks, of doing, oh, all sorts.

'This isn't really me,' she said, as she sipped the glass of champagne.

'Maybe it should be.' Dave grinned. 'Anyway, you're on holiday and sampling the local produce. Where's the harm in that?'

'Well, if you put it like that,' she said, smiling. 'It is very nice.' She took another sip. 'I wonder what Angie and Simon are doing now. I can't believe he just turned up like that.'

'Do you want to go back to the hotel and find out?'

Gilly thought for a moment. She did, and then she didn't. She was enjoying spending time with Dave. Whatever her sister and her philandering husband were doing could probably wait.

'No,' she said. 'Not yet. I think I'll give them a bit longer to sort out their differences.'

'Good idea.'

His phone beeped as he was talking. He reached into his pocket and glanced at the screen.

Gilly took another sip of her champagne. As she lowered the glass, her attention was drawn to an elderly couple studying the menu at the entrance to the patio area. Oh, my goodness, it was the Braithwaites. They couldn't see her like this. What on earth would they think? She might be enjoying herself chatting to Dave, but she was also aware that she was a married woman, sitting drinking champagne with a man who wasn't her husband. It wasn't right and it could so

184

easily be construed as something very wrong. She snatched up her bag. 'Dave, I've got to go.'

'Hmm. What?' He looked up from his phone. 'Why?' He followed the line of her gaze. 'Oh, it's only the Braithwaites.' He raised his hand to give them a wave.

'Don't,' she said, panicking.

'Why?' he said, giving her a curious look as he lowered his hand.

'I don't want them to see me,' she said, hurriedly getting up from her seat. 'It might be awkward.'

'Why would it? Gilly, wait a minute.'

'Sorry.'

She flung her cardigan over one arm and backed rapidly away, putting some distance between them. Dave was staring after her with a somewhat bemused expression on his face, but she didn't care. From the corner of her eye she could see the elderly couple climbing the steps onto the terrace. A second later, and they would have seen her. She ducked into the interior of the restaurant and headed for the toilets. It was dark and gloomy after the brilliant sunshine outside, and she blinked like a bewildered owl as she made her way to the rear of the dining area. Her heart was thumping like mad, and she took her time waiting in the cubicle until she had calmed herself down. Then she washed her hands and applied a touch of lip gloss and a smattering of face powder. Her cheeks were looking quite pink. It was either the sun, the alcohol, or a combination of both. Either way, she was feeling a little bit light-headed. She fanned herself with a paper towel. Right, well, she couldn't hang about in here forever. It was time she made a move. She inhaled a deep breath. Sunglasses – where were her sunglasses? For a second she thought she might have left them on the table, but no, they were in her bag. She put them on and breathed in deeply, before forcing herself to walk outside again.

Dave was standing with his back to her pointing out something on a map Mr Braithwaite was showing him, whilst Mrs Braithwaite peered over his shoulder.

Gilly hurried down the steps and onto the riverside path, not daring to look back in case they spotted her. She felt flushed and excited in equal measures. Which was silly really – they hadn't been doing anything wrong. They'd only been talking. Oh yes, and drinking champagne. She smiled as she saw the sodden remnants of the paper boat, bobbing about in the shallows. He'd made that for her, she thought, hugging the memory to herself, just for her. Charles wouldn't have done anything remotely like that. He'd never have bought her champagne either. In fact, he could be an irritating bore when he wanted to be, which was, as she was beginning to realise, probably most of the time.

She felt a faint flicker of guilt that she hadn't phoned him in over twenty-four hours, but then realised that she didn't want to. He would only put a downer on her mood and there would be plenty of time for that when she got home. As it was, she couldn't wait to get back to the hotel to see Angie. She was dying to know what had happened between her sister and Simon (though she was a little bit concerned that his unannounced arrival might herald the end of their holiday together). She wasn't ready to go home just yet. In fact, the more she thought about it, she didn't want to go home at all.

Chapter Twenty-seven

'It's hardly what I would call "en-suite",' Simon grumbled, peering into the confines of the small windowless toilet cubicle.

'Well, it's certainly small, but Dave assures me it's functional,' Angie said. 'And besides, it's only for one night. I can't believe all the other hotels are booked up,' she added. 'How many did you try?'

'God knows. I gave up counting. There must be something going on that we're not aware of.'

'There's a music and light festival on in one of the chateaux – I think Gilly mentioned something about it but I wasn't really listening.' She undid the curtain ties on the windows and pulled them closed. 'There,' she said, stepping backwards to survey their surroundings. 'I think it looks quite cosy.'

The back seat of the coach had been piled with cushions and a blanket 'borrowed' from the top shelf of Angie's wardrobe.

'And there's hot water, tea and coffee on tap – oh, and Dave says there's a fridge at the front if you'd prefer a cold drink.'

'I'd prefer a bed,' Simon muttered, perching himself on the edge of the seat. 'I'll probably fall off this in the middle of the night and give myself a hernia or something.'

It had been arranged, after much persuasion on Angie's part (and desperation on his), that Simon would be allowed to spend the night in the coach on the hotel car park. It was better than a night in his car, admittedly, but apparently not quite what he had in mind.

'Are you sure I can't share your room?' he said. 'No one would know.'

'I think Gilly might notice,' Angie said. 'Anyway, you heard what Dave said - it's more than his job's worth to let you sneak into the hotel. In fact, he's probably taking a big risk letting you stay on his coach. He could get dismissed for this so you need to be quiet.'

'Well, I'm hardly likely to be raving the night away,' Simon said.

'Oh, I don't know.' Angie sat down on the seat beside him. 'Do you remember when we were students? When we went on that coach trip to Blackpool to see the illuminations?'

'Twenty-nine years ago,' Simon recalled.

'And we snuggled down under a blanket on the back seat.'

'It was pitch dark.'

'And freezing cold. The heater wasn't working, remember?'

'I remember.' Simon grinned.' We never did get to see the lights.'

Angie unfolded the blanket and laid it over their knees. 'We didn't miss them, though, did we?'

'Nope.' Simon reached for her hand and squeezed it. 'I can't believe it was so long ago and we've never been back. We should go there,' he added. 'When we get home. We'll make a point of it.'

'I don't think Blackpool holds the same thrill for me as it did when I was a penniless student.'

'Ah, but think of the memories.'

'I'm thinking of them,' Angie sighed, resting her head on his shoulder.

Simon turned and tilted her chin towards him with his fingers. 'Me too, darling,' he murmured, leaning forwards. 'Me too.'

***

Where was Dave? That's what Gilly wanted to know. She had expected him to be in the dining room with all the other guests, so it had come as some surprise to find he wasn't there. Still, it was his day off, she reminded herself. She couldn't blame him for wanting a bit of time to himself, especially as he had spent the early part of the evening sorting out the coach for Simon to sleep in. But it did mean she was having to share a table with Geoffrey and Barbara, who wouldn't have been her first choice of dining companions.

She picked at her asparagus spear with little enthusiasm. It was smothered in a thick and creamy sauce that was supposed to enhance the flavour, but she didn't like the rich and buttery taste. Geoffrey, however, was devouring his with relish.

'You can't beat a bit of fresh asparagus,' he said. 'Lightly steamed - that's the best way. It's so easy to overcook it.' He waved his fork in her direction. 'Don't you like it, Gilly?'

'Not really, no.'

'Mind if I...' He motioned at her plate.

'Be my guest,' she murmured, sliding it across the table towards him. Goodness, the man was an expert on cooking as well as architecture. Was there no end to his talents?

'I've never cooked asparagus,' Barbara said, dipping a chunk of bread into the creamy sauce. 'I don't think our Carl would like it. He's not one for fancy food.'

'Where is Carl?' Gilly asked, glancing across at her. She tried to suppress a shudder as she saw a dollop of sauce nestle on Geoffrey's chin and wondered if she should mention it to him before someone else did. She tapped discreetly at her own chin and tried to make eye contact with him, but he was too busy tucking into his extra portion of asparagus to notice.

'I dunno. He went shopping and I haven't seen him since,' Barbara said. 'He was going to buy me some talc.' She glanced up and her expression changed to one of disgust. Barbara apparently didn't do

188

discreet. The creamy sauce was glistening like snot on Geoffrey's chin. 'Here, you might want this,' she said, picking up her napkin. For one moment Gilly wondered if she was going to wipe his face for him. Or worse, moisten it with her tongue like her mother used to do when they were children. She prepared to cringe in her seat.

'You've dribbled a bit,' she said, thankfully just handing it to him.

'Oh dear, have I really?' Geoffrey took the napkin from her and gave Gilly an embarrassed smile as he mopped at his face. 'Sorry. Is that better?'

Gilly breathed out slowly and nodded. She wasn't going to mention the green sliver of asparagus wedged between his two front teeth. He'd notice it soon enough anyway.

'That was delicious,' he said, his dignity having been restored. 'Carl doesn't know what he's missing. And talking of missing...' His gaze swung back to Gilly. 'How's your sister? '

'She's fine.'

'That must have been quite a shock for her. Her husband turning up like that.'

'Yes. It was.'

'And she's with him now?'

'Yes.' Gilly knew Geoffrey was probing her for more information, but, quite frankly, it was none of his business. She patted her lips with her napkin and reached for the bottle of cold water that the waitress had left on the table for them. 'Barbara, do you want a glass?'

'Yes please, dear.'

'I wouldn't risk it,' Geoffrey said warningly. 'I expect it's tap water. I've asked for sparkling. Then you know what you're getting.'

'Oh.' Gilly hesitated. 'But I'm sure it will be all right. Dave said it's safe to drink the tap water here.'

'Well, that's up to him. I won't be taking any chances.'

As she poured Barbara a glass of water, she had a small and nagging doubt that Geoffrey might be right. One couldn't be too careful in foreign parts. Maybe she'd stick to the wine instead.
As she beckoned to the waiter, she caught a glimpse of Dave standing in the lobby talking into his mobile phone, and her stomach gave a sudden and unexpected lurch as he glanced across and smiled at her. She could feel the colour rushing to her cheeks.

'Yes, Madame?' The wine waiter hovered expectantly, conveniently blocking him from her view.

'Oh, um, a carafe of red wine, please.'

'Certainly.'

'A small one.' She was mindful of the champagne she had already drunk that afternoon. It wouldn't do to get too tiddly, she told herself. Then again, it might make dinner with Geoffrey and Barbara more bearable.

The main course, some sort of beef stew with tiny baby onions and a garlicky sauce, was actually quite tasty. Either that, or she was so hungry it wouldn't matter what she was eating. She wondered what Angie and Simon were having for dinner. Dave didn't like food to be taken on the coach. He had said that at the start of the trip. She glanced back to the lobby, but it was empty.

She was surprised at how disappointed she felt that he had gone without speaking to her. Then again, he was hardly going to come over and chat to her in the middle of the dining room. But she rather wished that he had.

'It was the last home of Leonardo Da Vinci,' Geoffrey was saying.

Distracted, she blinked back at him. He'd obviously been talking to her for some time. 'I'm sorry, what?'

'The Chateau du Clos-Luce.' He sighed. 'I told you. It's where we're going tomorrow.'

'Oh, right.' She took a gulp of her wine. 'Sorry, I misheard you.' She tried to force an interested expression onto her face. 'That'll be nice.'

'I've got a book about him upstairs, if you'd like borrow it.'

'Oh.' She looked to Barbara, hoping to draw her into the conversation, but Barbara had started to chat with Shirley at the table behind them. 'Maybe later,' she said.

Geoffrey looked delighted. 'Of course, you do realise that Leonardo...' He paused as her phone gave several loud bleeps.

'I'm sorry, that's mine,' she said, fumbling in her handbag. She stared in disbelief at the text message on the screen. It was from Dave.

'Do you need rescuing?' she read. She jerked her head up and glanced round. Was he watching her? She couldn't see him anywhere.

'Yes,' she texted back. Her cheeks felt scarlet as she stuffed the phone back in her bag.

Undeterred, Geoffrey was in full flow. 'He actually brought the Mona Lisa to Amboise in a leather bag tied to his mule.'

'Really? How fascinating,' she said. At any other time, it would have been. She loved finding out about the places they were visiting, but her phone kept bleeping, which was highly distracting. She tried to read the text without removing the phone from her handbag.

'Meet me outside,' it said. Outside? What, right outside? She peered at the steamed-up windows. Was Dave out there, staring in at them?

'Francois the First bought it, you see, and placed it in the Royal collection.'

'Bought what? Oh, you mean the Mona Lisa.' Gilly shook her head apologetically. 'Sorry, Geoffrey. I was listening to you, but I keep getting text messages and they're quite important. I hate to do this, but I'm going to have to excuse myself.'

He looked surprised.

'It's my husband,' she added, scraping back her chair. 'I promised to phone him and he's wondering why I haven't.'

Geoffrey nodded understandingly. 'That's okay. We can chat later.'

'Lovely.'

'And I'll loan you that book.'

'Book? Oh, yes. Great.'

Her heart was hammering fit to burst as she hurried into the foyer. She hated telling lies, even little and necessary white lies, but it was all she could think of and part of it was true. She had received a text message, just not from Charles. She stared down at her phone, wondering if she had read it properly without her glasses. The print always seemed so small on her phone, and she knew she should change the font, but she wasn't sure how.

'Meet me outside,' she read again. Yes, there was no mistaking it and it was from Dave. She had double checked just in case it was Angie wanting to get in touch with her.

The receptionist glanced up as she made her way across the carpeted floor. '*Bonsoir Madame.*'

'*Bonsoir.*'

As she went to push open the doors, she felt a tap on her arm.

'Going somewhere?' Dave said, and she spun round to find herself face to face with him.

'Well, yes...well, outside,' she blurted, flushing furiously.

'I didn't mean out on the street,' he laughed. 'I meant outside the dining room, as in lounge bar. We could have a coffee,' he suggested. 'Or dessert. You haven't sampled this evening's delicacy yet – a rather burnt cold custard, which is not for the faint-hearted.'

'You were watching me.'

'Only fleetingly,' he said. 'But, let's be honest, you were looking a bit bored.'

'And at what point did you decide I needed rescuing?'

Dave grinned. 'Let's just say, I came as soon as I was able. Now then, coffee, or have I tempted you to try the dessert?'

'I think I'll play safe and have a coffee.'

'Very wise,' he murmured, holding the door open for her. The lounge bar was virtually empty, with most of the residents still in the dining room. Maybe that was why he had suggested it, Gilly thought. They could spend a bit of time on their own and it wouldn't look out of place if people wandered in after dinner and found them having a coffee together.

'It was good of you to let Simon stay on the coach,' she told him, for want of something to say. She was feeling a little bit awkward, if she was honest with herself. She hovered beside Dave as he poured them two coffees from the cafetiere.

'I felt sorry for the poor bloke,' he said, picking up the cups and carrying them over to a table. 'He'd come a hell of a long way to see your sister. He must have been desperate.'

'Jealous, more like,' she said, following him to the table and sitting down opposite him. 'You saw how he reacted with Carl.'

'Well, whatever the reason, if they can sort things out by the morning, then there's no harm done. Personally,' he added, stirring a spoonful of sugar into his cup, 'I'd have stayed at home and waited for her to come back. It's only a couple more days and then she'll be home.'

'Two days can seem like a lifetime when you're unhappy.'

Dave stopped stirring and glanced over at her.

'Oh, I didn't mean...I mean,' she stammered, 'what I meant, was...'

'I know what you meant,' he said softly. 'You don't want to go home.'

Gilly gave a small nod.

'It's perfectly natural to feel that way.'

'It is?'

'Of course.' He grinned, and there was a kindly twinkle in his eye. 'You're having a wonderful holiday, so why would you want to go back to the humdrum and the day-to-day of normal life.'

What he was saying made sense, she supposed. She was enjoying herself, but she was enjoying the freedom of being on her own much more. Having this distance between herself and Charles had given her time to put things in perspective. Theirs was not a happy marriage. It was a marriage that had endured, rather than been embraced. She couldn't remember the last time Charles had asked for her opinion on anything. It had always been his word, his decision, his opinion, that counted. It wasn't an equal partnership, but she had put up with it. Why?

'Penny for them,' Dave said.

'What?'

'Your thoughts.' He smiled. 'You look miles away.'

'Sorry.' She picked up her cup and took a small sip of her coffee.

'I've been told I'm a good listener,' he added.

'Oh, it's just me being silly.' She replaced her cup on the saucer. It was too hot to drink. 'It's like you said. I've had a wonderful holiday and I don't want to go home. I've never done anything like this before and it's been amazing.'

'You've never been on a coach tour before?'

'Not since I was thirteen and with the Girl Guides.' She laughed. 'I always thought they were for old people.'

'Not necessarily,' Dave said. 'You'd be surprised how many youngsters we have on our tours.' He gave his coffee one last stir and then raised it to his lips. 'You'll need to come on another one. I can recommend a few places.'

'Thanks,' she said. 'I'd like that.'

He raised his eyes and stared thoughtfully across at her, one eyebrow quizzically raised. 'You're not happy at home, are you?'

'Not particularly, no,' she admitted. 'That's why this break has been so good for me.'

'In that case, maybe you need to change things.'

'That's easier said than done.'

'It doesn't have to be,' he said. He leaned back in his chair and considered her for a moment. 'Nothing is insurmountable, Gilly. You might think it is, but it isn't. You need to decide what's best for you.'

'Isn't that being selfish?'

'No, I don't think so.' He smiled. 'I'm sure your friends and family would prefer to see you happy, rather than miserable.'

'That's true.'

'There you go, then.'

Oh God, he was right. She knew it, deep down. She'd been muddling through her life for years, hoping that things would be different, but accepting her lot when it wasn't.

'I know you're scared, Gilly. Change is always difficult. That's why so many people get stuck in a rut year after year. It feels safer, easier.'

'Yes, it does.'

'But just imagine if you could change one thing and only one thing, what would it be?'

193

Gilly stared at him, her thoughts whirling. One thing. Goodness, how could she choose? There was so much she disliked about her life. She wanted to be smarter, more confident, more self-assured. She wanted to be that young woman, fresh from university, setting out on a career she loved, before life, love, marriage and kids got in her way. She wanted her self-esteem back. She wanted promotion at work as recognition of her efforts and loyalty, and inside, deep inside, she knew she didn't want Charles. They had grown worlds apart, yet a tiny part of her clung on, hoping things might get better. But they wouldn't. She knew they wouldn't.

'While you're thinking,' he said. 'I'll go get us a refill.'

'Not for me, thanks. I'm fine with this.' If she drank any more coffee she'd be awake all night, especially coffee as strong as this one.

'You don't mind if I get one.'

'No, go ahead.'

She watched him as he headed to the bar, at the casual, yet purposeful, way he strode across the room. He was such a lovely man. He was compassionate, intuitive, and thoughtful. He'd seen she was bored with Geoffrey and Barbara, and intervened. He'd taken pity on Angie and Simon and let them have his coach for the night. He'd provided her with hot tea and ginger on the ferry crossing from Dover. Whatever had happened on this trip, it was him who had been there to offer help and advice. Him – Dave Saunders. So, if she could change one thing, just the one, she'd change her husband for him, the kindest, most interesting man she had met in a very long time.

Startled at her own thoughts and guilty, lest he realise what she was thinking, she quickly dropped her gaze and began fiddling with one of the paper serviettes. He was talking to one of the passengers. She hoped he'd stay away long enough for the burning redness in her cheeks to subside, but not too long. She really wanted to talk to him again.

As she drained the last of her coffee from the cup, her phone rang. She answered it without looking at the screen, presuming it was Angie. It wasn't.

'Oh, so you've deigned to switch the damn thing on now?' Charles snapped, rudely awakening her from her moment of inward reflection. 'What's the point of having a bloody mobile if you never use it? I've a good mind to cancel the contract.'

'Good idea.'

'What?'

'Well, you might as well,' she sighed.

'What?'

'Charles, I can't talk now.'

'What do you mean, you can't talk now?'

'I'm sorry, I've got to go.'

'Gilly. Don't you dare hang up on me?'

But she did. It was simply a case of pressing a button. Call ended. And in case he thought he'd been cut off by accident, she chose to switch the whole thing off. There. She'd made her first change.

Dave hovered in front of the table, a questioning look on his face.

'Do you want a moment?'

'No.' She put the phone back in her handbag. 'I'm fine.'

Except that she wasn't. She was horrified at what she had just done. What on earth was the matter with her? It was Dave who was making her act all reckless and out of character. And it was stupid, because she knew this was just a brief interlude. That whatever she wished for would never happen, and that things would go back to normal once she got home.

To her horror, her eyes suddenly welled up with tears. She fumbled for a tissue and attempted to dab them away before he noticed.

'Gilly. What is it?' He sat opposite her, a look of genuine concern on his face.

'It's nothing, honestly.' She crumpled up the tissue and took in a steadying breath. 'I'm sorry. I think I need to go up to my room now.'

'No, wait.' He caught hold of her arm as she made to stand up. 'If I've said something to upset you...'

'You haven't.'

'Sure?'

She nodded.

All the while, he was staring at her, his gaze meeting hers with a long and searching look. 'Before you go,' he said. 'You haven't answered my question yet. What's the one thing you would change?' He tilted his head to one side as he looked at her. His expression was curious but concerned.

She gazed helplessly back at him. People were coming into the lounge bar. She could see the Braithwaites pouring themselves coffee from the cafetiere at the bar. Shirley and Linda were already seated by the window with what looked like a small nightcap of cognac. Geoffrey would be coming in next and he'd want to talk about his book on Leonardo Da Vinci. Whatever she wanted to say, or thought about saying to Dave, it was too late. The moment was lost. She shook her head. 'I couldn't decide.'

'That many?'

She nodded. Straightening up, she hooked her bag over her shoulder. 'I'll see you in the morning, Dave. Oh, and thanks for rescuing me.'

'All in the line of duty,' he said. 'Goodnight, Gilly.'

'Night.'

Her eyes were blurry with tears as she headed for the lift. What on earth was the matter with her? For one brief moment she'd wanted to stay with him, really wanted to stay with him, and she got the impression that maybe, just maybe, he wanted to stay with her too. Madness, utter madness. She dabbed at her eyes with the tissue and breathed in deeply as she stepped into the lift. She'd be glad when it was morning. Things always looked better after a good night's sleep. Except that tonight, she wasn't going to get much sleep at all.

Chapter Twenty-eight

Carl had bought himself a new leather jacket – one that was similar to the one he had chucked into the river, but not identical to the one shown on the grainy CCTV footage.

It had cost him a small fortune – or at least, it would do when he got his credit card bill - but he figured out that he needed a jacket and this one was near enough to the original to satisfy his grandmother's curiosity.

The shop assistant was folding it in layers of tissue paper and had produced a large cardboard carton in which to pack it.

'It's okay, I'm going to wear it,' he said.

'*Monsieur?*'

'Just remove the tags.' He pointed at the attached labels and made a scissor movement with his fingers.

'Ah, *oui.*' The girl nodded.

Carl glanced at his watch. It was after eight. Too late to get back to the hotel in time for dinner. Still, his gran would be fine. She'd made some friends on this trip, which was more than he could say for himself.

'Thanks.' He slipped his arms into the jacket and glanced at his reflection in the mirror. The motif was smaller across the shoulders and more discreet, which was good because it was of a leopard, not a dragon, but it looked similar enough to the one he had ditched. If his grandmother queried it he'd say she'd been mistaken, that it had been a big cat all along. Jason would say he was being paranoid and he'd hold his hands up to that one. What had started as a drunken comment on a boozy night out had turned into something much more sinister. Drug dealers, murders – he wanted none of it.

'*Merci, Monsieur.*'

Carl nodded and managed a half smile as he tucked his credit card back into his wallet. This holiday was costing him a bomb, what with talcum powder, unwanted bondage gear, and now a very expensive leather jacket. It was a good job they'd upped his credit limit. Still, it would all have to be paid off in the end. He had to make sure this trip earned him a profit, by whatever means it took.

The shops were still open as he wandered through the town. He bought a couple of bottles of whisky and some tobacco, which he intended to hide in his suitcase, then stopped off at a kebab shop because he realised he was starving. He hadn't eaten since breakfast. A couple of pints in a riverside bar topped off his evening so that, by the time he reached the hotel, he was feeling pleasantly mellow. He dumped his bags on the ground and decided to have one last cigarette in the car park, before going up to his room.

The flickering light from inside the coach caught his attention as he leaned back against the hotel wall. What on earth? He straightened up. He was feeling a bit unsteady on his feet, and his vision was blurred. He closed one eye, tried to focus, and then looked again. Yup, there was a light on in the coach. Whoa, so Driver Dave got lucky, did he? Carl flicked his ash on the ground. The curtains were closed. He could see condensation on the windows - and wait... He tilted his head to one side. He was sure he could hear voices. The lucky sod, he thought. It had to be Angie's sister. He'd been making a move on her ever since the ferry crossing. Nice. 'Course, if it had been him, he'd have preferred a hotel room, but there was no accounting for tastes. The back of a coach – classic. Carl grinned as he stubbed his cigarette out and tossed it into the drain.

He was still grinning when he reached his room and tossed his bags onto the bed. Dave Saunders – Mr Squeaky-clean coach driver. Who'd have thought it? No wonder the bloke wasn't married. He probably had a new woman every trip. 'Course, he'd have to like the more mature woman. There weren't that many young ones on the coach. But yeah, he could see the advantages. No commitment, no ties, just a bit of fun.

Carl was feeling decidedly envious, or frustrated, or maybe a bit of both. Either way, it wasn't going to do him any good thinking about it. He'd come here for a reason and, although things weren't panning out exactly as he had hoped, he had made some progress. He had one bottle of pills, spirits, tobacco and Baby powder, that he could hopefully pass off as something else. He'd get more cigarettes tomorrow and some spirits to stow in his gran's case. All was not lost. When Jason met him off the ferry at least he'd have something to show for his trouble. Okay, so he wasn't going to make his fortune, but it was a start.

He opened his holdall and took out the brown envelope containing the bottle of tablets he had bought from the street trader in Paris. (Poor sod, he reflected.) His grandmother had been carrying them round in her handbag, but he had asked for them back as a precaution. He didn't want her taking any of them by mistake. Not after he'd seen what they'd done to Angie. He thought they'd have smiley faces on them. That's what Jason had said. This lot looked like any other tablet, which was good. He held the bottle up to the light and peered closer at them. Yeah, that was good. He tucked them into the inner zipped pocket and chucked the brown envelope in the bin. It was better if they were plain. He'd feel uneasy carrying them if they didn't.

Maybe he'd put them in his gran's case, just to be on the safe side. They wouldn't check her things and even if they did, it would look harmless. What woman of her age didn't carry medication round with them?

The furtive tapping on his door startled him. He quickly shoved his purchases into the bag, zipped it shut and shoved it under the bed.

'Yes. What?'

'Oh, you are there.'

'What do you want, Gran?' he said, opening the door. His grandmother was beaming at him. Her cheeks were flushed.

'I just wanted to see if you were all right. You didn't come in to dinner.'

'Yeah, I'm sorry about that. I got held up.'

'Shopping?'

'Yes.'

'Oh.' She looked puzzled.

'But I managed to get you that talc you liked.' He didn't make any move to let her into the room.

'Oh, thanks, dear.' She nodded gratefully. 'There's a singer in the bar,' she added, waving her hand in the vague direction of the lift. 'If you're interested, that is. He's quite good. Shirley's there, only she's having trouble with her hearing aid.'

'Not really my scene, Gran,' Carl said.

'I know, but you could have a drink with me.'

It was the way she said it, not pleading, but plaintive. He sighed. She was right. He needed to spend more time with her, at least for appearances' sake. 'One drink,' he agreed. 'But you're buying.' He was almost out of ready cash. That last pint had cleaned him out. He only had coins left in his pocket.

Barbara beamed at him.

'You're such a good boy.'

'Tell me about it,' he muttered.

The singer was, to be fair, not bad at all. Either that, or Carl was more inebriated than he thought. The old folks seemed to love him, anyway. Geoffrey was humming along and swaying from side to side to 'Chanson d'amour'. Edith looked star-struck and told everyone he was the image of a young soldier she had met in Paris after the war and then surmised that maybe he was a son or grandson and she would go and ask him after he had finished singing. Cyril had fallen asleep in his chair. Or at least, Carl hoped he was asleep.

He peered closer as he raised his glass and took a long, slow draught of lager. Yes, Cyril was breathing, so that was good. It wouldn't do to upset Dave's little triste with news of a passenger's demise.

Although he expected it must happen from time to time – the odds were stacked in favour of it - judging by the average age of the group.

'I'm just going for a quick fag,' he told his gran, resting his hand on her shoulder. 'I won't be a minute.'

He resisted the urge to go into the car park. Being a voyeur had never been his style. Instead, he took a short stroll along the riverbank towards the stone-arched bridge. The air was fresh and helped clear his head. He was feeling pretty good, all things considered. As long as his mates back home didn't get to hear of him attending a pensioners' singsong, he'd be fine.

He turned back to the hotel. Dave Saunders was standing in the lobby, scrolling through messages on his mobile phone.

Carl approached him with a smile. 'All right, mate.'

'Yep.' He glanced up and pocketed the phone. 'You?'

'I'm good.' He paused, grinning.

Dave looked at him curiously. 'Can I help you with anything?'

'Nope.' He elbowed him good humouredly. 'Don't worry, I won't say anything.'

'About what?'

'You know.' He jerked his head towards the car park.

'Right.' Dave said.

He gave the impression that he didn't have a clue what Carl was talking about. It was an act, of course. All credit to the man. Nothing wrong with a bit of discretion.

'We've got an early start in the morning,' Dave told him. 'Breakfast is at seven and I need you all on the coach by eight. Is that going to be okay with you?'

'Yep, fine.'

'Good.'

There was nothing more to say. Carl gave him a knowing wink as he pushed open the door to the bar. His gran had linked arms with Shirley and Geoffrey and they were swaying in unison to an elderly Frenchman, playing a rousing tune on an accordion. It was all very jolly. Even Cyril was clapping his hands.

As Carl made his way to their table, he couldn't help wondering just how many of them would have hangovers in the morning.

Chapter Twenty-nine

Gilly went through the motions of taking off her make-up, brushing her hair and having a quick shower as if this was any ordinary night, on any ordinary day. But it wasn't. It was momentous. It was like everything she'd tried to ignore had suddenly become real. She didn't love her husband. She was bored with her marriage. Her job didn't inspire or excite her. Worse still, she had fallen for another man.

She stared glumly at her reflection as she sat in front of the dressing table mirror. Her hair was damp and plastered to her forehead; crow's feet gathered round her eyes and she had dark smudges of mascara, which she had attempted to remove with a bit of cotton wool and cleanser and failed miserably.

From down below, the rousing chant of music and singing was putting paid to all thoughts of an early night. No one could sleep through that racket.

She tugged a comb through her hair. What to do? What to do? It was like a mantra repeating itself over and over in her head. If she left Charles, where would she live? Could she manage to survive on her wages? Would she need to find another job? What would the children think?

She switched on the hairdryer and took her time blow-drying her hair. The constant drone helped to drown out her racing thoughts. It was still early, probably too early to attempt to sleep. Maybe she should go downstairs and join in the party. Although she wasn't sure if she was up to making small talk, not when she was feeling so distracted.

She picked up her mobile and switched it on again. As expected, there were several missed calls from her husband, and one voicemail that she deleted without listening to it. There was also a text from Dave. Her stomach gave a sudden and unexpected lurch. 'Don't forget the early start tomorrow,' she read. 'The coach leaves at eight.'

She sucked in a breath. It wasn't quite what she had expected. Hopes of a secret assignation, perhaps? Now, she felt disappointed, after the initial euphoria of seeing his name on the screen. He was only being professional and considerate, she realised, making sure his passengers knew what was going on. He'd probably sent the same message to all their phones – those that had them, of course.
Her fingers hovered over the screen. Should she text him back? Maybe a thank you, just so he knew she was thinking about him?

She was on the verge of replying, when she heard movement outside the bedroom door and the unmistakeable click of the lock, followed by the jiggling of the handle when the door wouldn't open.

'Gilly! Let me in. Hurry up. Oh God, she's put the double lock on.'

'Angie?' Gilly flew off the stool and rushed to the door. As she yanked it open both Angie and Simon virtually tumbled into the room.

'Quick, shut it,' Simon said.

She did as she was bid, before turning to face her sister, who was looking flushed and breathless. 'Angie,' she gasped. 'What's wrong? Why are you here? And why is he here?' she added, pointing a finger at Simon. He was sitting on the side of the bed, a pained expression on his face.

'It's his back,' Angie said, sitting beside him and running a soothing hand down his spine. 'You know the problems he has with it, and those coach seats were so uncomfortable.'

'And narrow,' Simon added.

'We couldn't sleep there, darling. I know we said we would, but it's only for one night.' She was levering Simon's shoes off as she spoke.

'What do you mean, it's only for one night? He can't stay here.'

'Why not?'

'Because, well, because,' Gilly spluttered, glancing at the two single beds. 'There's not enough room.'

'We can manage.'

'How?' Gilly sat down heavily on the small stool in front of the dressing table. 'There's no way the two of you can squeeze into one bed.'

'I'll sleep on the floor,' Simon said.

'No, you won't.' Angie patted his hand firmly. 'You've got to drive to the airport in the morning. You need a good night's sleep.'

'Oh, brilliant.' Gilly stood up and paced to the window. She peered through the net curtains, and pulled shut the sash window, which had been left ajar by the cleaner. 'So, you and I are sharing a bed, are we?'

'No, not necessarily,' Angie said. 'Not if you don't want to.' She glanced down at the wooden flooring. There was a thin rug in between the two single beds. 'I don't mind sleeping on the floor.'

'Good!' Gilly said.

Angie's face fell.

'Why don't we push the beds together and sleep across them?' Simon suggested. 'That might work.'

'Your feet would be hanging over the end.'

'That's a small price to pay. Anyway, I could move the chair across. It'll be fine.'

Gilly could hardly believe what she was hearing.

'It's not like it's a threesome, darling,' Angie told her, as if that made it sound acceptable, 'and Simon will sleep on the edge. I'll be in the middle.'

'Well that's all right, then,' Gilly snapped. She was about to say more, but the furtive tapping on the door had rendered her momentarily speechless. Who on earth? Her heart skipped a beat. It couldn't be Dave, could it? The knock came again, louder this time.

'Quick,' she hissed, 'hide in the bathroom.'

'We weren't seen,' Angie whispered, stumbling into the tiny cubicle, with Simon hurrying in her wake. 'I promise you, no one saw us come up here.'

'That's what you say,' Gilly muttered, adding 'Just a minute,' as she pulled the bathroom door shut. She tiptoed to the door. 'Who is it?'

'Only me.'

Well, that could be anyone. Her heart thumped heavily against her ribs. It didn't sound like Dave, and yet who else would come knocking on her door?

'I brought you that book.'

It was Geoffrey. Gilly didn't know whether she felt relieved or disappointed. She edged the door open a fraction. He was standing in the corridor wearing an open-necked shirt with a yellow cravat. Beige brown slacks and a pair of scruffy brown shoes completed his outfit.

'I thought you'd be downstairs for the entertainment,' he said, holding the well-leafed volume out towards her. 'Leonardo's life,' he added. 'I'm sure you'll find it fascinating.'

'Thank you. Actually, I was just getting changed.' She glanced over her shoulder, sure she could hear furtive giggles from the bathroom. 'I'll have a look at this later.'

'Excellent. I'll keep you a seat, shall I? The accordion player is very good.'

'Lovely.'

As she closed the door on him, the furtive giggles increased to a definite snigger.

'You really shouldn't encourage him,' Angie said, coming back into the bedroom and sitting on the bed. 'You know he's not your type.'

'Oh, and how would you know what my type is?' she snapped. 'You have no idea.' Flouncing across the room, she yanked open the wardrobe and snatched a dress off the hanger.

'Gilly?' Angie touched her gently on the arm. 'What is it? What's happened?' She motioned to Simon to stay in the bathroom as she spoke.

'Nothing. Everything. Oh, I don't know. It's all such a mess. I don't want to talk about it. In fact, I don't want to think about it.' She stepped into the dress and pulled it up as she spoke. 'So, I'm going to go downstairs to be entertained. I need something to take my mind off things, and in the meantime,' she stuffed her feet into a pair of heeled shoes and reached for her makeup bag, 'you two can sort this room out whichever way you want to do it, and hopefully,' she smeared a bright splash of lipstick on her lips and pouted, 'hopefully I'll have enough to drink that I'll crash out without caring where I sleep.'

Angie gaped at her. She looked appalled. 'Gilly, this isn't like you.'

'Maybe it's the new me,' she muttered, snatching up her bag. She knew she was acting out of character, knew that everyone expected her to be meek and agreeable and pleasant, but she was tired of being taken for granted.

'Oh, and before I forget, we've got an early start in the morning, so make sure you set the alarm.'

On that note, she marched out of the room, slamming the door behind her.

She was trembling as she stood waiting for the lift; half of her wondering what the heck she was playing at, and the other half shocked at how quickly her anger had flared up. Angie was right. It really wasn't like her, and now she knew the reason why. She'd been disappointed to see it was Geoffrey who had come looking for her. She'd hoped it would be Dave. Well, there you go, she thought. You don't always get what you want and she invariably didn't.

Stepping out of the lift into the reception area caused her a moment of panic. Did she really want to be doing this? Then she thought of Simon and Angie, and all three of them in a bed together trying to make small talk and pretending it wasn't embarrassing to be closeted in one room, especially with the way Simon was declaring undying love to her sister. And suddenly, alcohol and live music seemed the way forward.

Carl was propping up the bar as she made her way into the crowded lounge area, so it was inevitable that she would end up standing next to him in the queue for drinks. He gave her a peculiar sort of sideways leer. She didn't like the way he winked at her either.

'On your own?' he said.

'No.' She could see Geoffrey waving at her out of the corner of her eye. He had secured seats at the side of the small stage.

Carl followed the line of her gaze, then glanced back at her with a puzzled frown. 'Him?' He shook his head. 'Really?'

'I haven't a clue what you are on about,' Gilly said. 'Excuse me.' She beckoned to the barman. 'A carafe of red wine, please, to that table over there.'

It was a raucous evening. The coach passengers were joined by a few locals, and what had started as a night of singing became a night of dancing, with several of the group showing moves that would not have looked out of place in a dancing competition. Edith's foxtrot was memorable, and Roger Braithwaite and his wife made a credible attempt at the jive. It earned them a round of applause from the audience, anyway. Gilly declined Geoffrey's offer to join him on the floor, pleading sore feet from all the walking, so he took to it on his own, determined to show off his prowess at the twist. Barbara became his willing partner and the result was hilarious. All in all, it was a fun night and she really did enjoy herself.

'I haven't laughed so much in ages,' she told Barbara.

'Oh, that's good, lovey, cos you were looking a bit upset when you came in. Is your sister all right now?'

'She's fine.'

'Gone off with her husband, has she?'

'Yes.' Gilly nodded. 'She'll be back tomorrow.' She drained the dregs from her wine glass. The staff had put the main lights on and people were starting to make a move. Goodness, she thought, glancing at her watch, was that really the time? She reached for her shoes that she had kicked off under the table and slipped them on her feet. The stooping had made her a little bit light-headed, and she straightened up slowly.

'Do you need a hand?' Geoffrey said, offering her his arm.

She smiled weakly, trying not to shudder at the stained pool of sweat that was spreading down the underarms of his shirt, and shook her head. 'No, thanks, I'm fine.'

'I can walk you to your room.'

Don't be daft,' she said. That was the last thing she wanted. 'I'll see you tomorrow. Early start, remember?'

'I'll remember.'

Of course he would. Geoffrey was a stickler for punctuality. Gilly waited until she was in the lift before taking off her shoes again and clutching them in one hand. She really wasn't used to wearing high heels. Nor was she used to drinking quite so much wine. It had been a bit of a binge day and she was sure she'd feel the worse for it in the morning. But it had been a welcome and necessary distraction.

The lift doors opened with a ping and she stepped onto the landing. It was only when the doors closed behind her that she realised she wasn't on the right floor. She must have pressed the wrong button. She pressed for the lift again, but it had gone down to the lobby. Never mind. She would use the stairs.

The corridor seemed to stretch away in front of her and she had to place her hands on each side of the wall to keep herself steady. She giggled. Oh dear, she was really quite tipsy. She dropped her shoes. Her bag slid down to her elbow. As she stooped to pick them up and hoist her bag onto her shoulder at the same time, she crashed sideways into a door. Now how had that happened? She rubbed her aching arm.

At the same time, the door she had inadvertently banged into was flung open and there he was. The man she had been trying not to think about all night.

'Gilly? What the hell?'

She blinked up at him. He was wearing a T-shirt and boxer shorts. He looked nice, sort of crumpled and sleepy. Maybe he had been sleeping.

'I'm so sorry.' She flapped a hand in the vague direction of the lift. 'Wrong floor. I got off at the wrong floor.'

'Right. Well, give me a moment to put some trousers on and I'll take you to your room.'

She propped herself against the doorframe and tried not to watch him getting dressed. 'I could stay here,' she slurred. The room had two single beds. She could see that quite clearly. It seemed an obvious solution. She didn't want to go back to the room with Angie and Simon in it. Why should she, when she could stay here?

'What?' Dave had one leg in his jeans and was attempting to put his foot in the other leg, when she teetered past him and flopped onto one of the beds, the unmade bed. She was being practical and sensible.

'No, wait. Gilly, wait, you can't stay here.'

'Why can't I?' She yawned sleepily. 'I'm so tired and Simon snores really loud.'

'Simon?' Dave zipped up his jeans. 'What do you mean, Simon? Is he in your room?'

They both are.' She giggled. Her eyes were closing. She really couldn't keep them open much longer. 'And you're so lovely, Dave, so very... very lovely.'

'Gilly, get up.' He was holding her hands and trying to pull her upright.

'It'll be all right,' she murmured sleepily.

It won't.' He sounded desperate.

'Why won't it?'

'Because you're married, Gilly, and your husband wouldn't like it. You're also,' he added, shaking his head wearily, 'very, very drunk.' Those were the last words she heard, before she blacked out.

Chapter Thirty

The agenda for the day had been carefully planned to include a morning visit to Amboise, a bustling town on the south bank of the Loire, famed for its Chateau and for being Leonardo Da Vinci's final home, followed by an afternoon visit to a local winery in one of the many cave complexes.

It was the day Gilly had been looking forward to the most. She loved history and exploring old buildings, and the thought of visiting the manor house where Leonardo had spent the last three years of his life was so exciting. Her guide book said they would be able to see his bedroom and study, and that there were displays in the basement of many of his inventions, ranging from tanks to flying machines. There would also be opportunities to explore the gardens and have a snack in the adjoining tearoom and restaurant.

None of which, however, came to fruition. Gilly awoke to the worst hangover in her life, in a bed that wasn't hers and a room she didn't recognise. She lay back on the pillows staring up at the ceiling, waves of nausea making any movement minimal. Slowly, painfully, she turned her head to one side. The curtains were pale blue, sprigged with tiny yellow flowers. The window was open slightly, letting in a fresh breeze. On the dressing table – a pale beech one, totally unlike the one she remembered – she could see a folded note propped against the mirror. She raised herself up on her elbows. The bed beside her was empty. It looked as if it hadn't been slept in.

Oh God! Oh no! She flopped back on the pillow. What had she done? Oh, this was bad – very bad. Shreds of memory came back to her – memories that made her want to hide under the duvet and never come out. This was Dave's room. She was in his room, with only the vaguest recollection of how she had got there. She was dressed – fully dressed – well, that was something. She glanced at her watch, trying hard to focus on the small face. It was eleven thirty. Eleven thirty! She sat upright, then wished she hadn't. Why was she still here? Where was Dave? Gingerly, she pushed the duvet to one side and swung her legs to the floor.

Water – she needed water. She poured herself a glassful from the carafe on the bedside cabinet and drank it thirstily, savouring every mouthful. Then she shuffled over to the dressing table and picked up the note.

'Probably best you sleep things off. See you later, D'.
So, that was it. They'd gone without her. Gilly took another gulp of water. It was her own fault. She had no one to blame but herself.

Picking up her bag and shoes, she did what she should have done the night before and made her way to her own room. That too, was empty. Thankfully, the cleaners had been in and serviced the room, so she was able to curl up in bed without the risk of being disturbed by an overzealous housekeeper.

She took painkillers to ease her thumping headache, drank copious amounts of water and then dozed, on and off, for most of the afternoon.

It was Angie who woke her up when she barged into the room and slammed the door behind her – Angie in a temper, and with good reason, to be fair.

'Why didn't you switch your phone on?' she demanded. 'You could have been dead for all I knew. I've been texting you all day.'

'Didn't feel like speaking,' she mumbled, wincing as her sister flung open the curtains.

'Texting isn't speaking.'

'You know what I mean.'

'Yes, I do, but it didn't stop me being worried about you.'

'Sorry.' She rolled onto her back and stared up at the ceiling. She felt ghastly. No, worse than ghastly.

'I felt bad going without you, but Dave insisted you'd be okay. He said you'd be better off sleeping. He probably didn't want you puking on the coach,' Angie added, giving her a dubious look. 'What on earth got into you last night – apart from too much wine, obviously?'

Gilly groaned. 'I don't know.' She struggled to prop herself up on her elbows. Her head was thumping and she wondered if she should take some more painkillers. 'I think I made a bit of a fool of myself.'

'Nonsense – you just had too much to drink. We've all been there,' her sister reminded her.

'No, I mean,' she paused. 'I think I threw myself at Dave.'

'You did what?' Angie sounded incredulous.

'I threw myself at him. Quite literally, as it happened.'

'And?'

'And nothing.'

'Oh.' Angie gave her a sympathetic smile. 'Well, maybe he was being a gentleman – I mean, if you were a bit drunk, he might not have wanted to take advantage. He strikes me as a decent kind of bloke.'

'He wasn't interested. He really wasn't.' She groaned. 'Oh God, I've been such an idiot. I'll never be able to look him in the face again.'

'Nonsense.' Angie sat on the edge of the bed. 'He'll understand. I'm sure he will. You were a bit tipsy and you got carried away. It was out of character and he'll know that. There's no harm done.' She paused, then added, 'I guess that explains why he spent the night on the coach.'

'He slept on the coach?'

'Apparently so.'

'Oh.' Gilly sat up and rubbed her eyes. They felt gritty with sleep and makeup. 'Oh God, Angie, what have I done? I feel so humiliated.' She glanced up at her sister. 'Did he say anything else?'

'No – no.' She thought for a moment. 'Actually, he didn't say a lot, really. He was more annoyed that I had sneaked Simon into the hotel. He got his flight home okay,' she added, glancing at her watch. 'He must be nearly there by now.'

Well that was one problem solved. Having Simon around had been half the trouble. If he'd stayed on the coach none of this would have happened. But, oh dear, she did feel horribly embarrassed and ashamed of herself. How could she ever face Dave now? They would have to change seats, she decided. They'd move to the back of the coach – let someone else have the front seat. She couldn't possibly spend the rest of the trip sitting just behind him, catching him looking at her in the rear-view mirror. Except he hadn't been looking at her, had he? He'd been keeping an eye on his passengers. Looking out for all of them as he was paid to do. She, like a naïve idiot, had misread all the signals – totally and stupidly. Oh, what a fool she had been. Just because someone was nice to her didn't mean they fancied her. Except for Geoffrey, of course. He fancied her. The trouble was, she didn't fancy him.

With a groan, she stood up and headed for the bathroom to splash water on her face. How could she have got things so wrong? The cold water trickled down her neck and she patted it dry with the towel before blinking, teary-eyed at her reflection. Well, it was a lesson learned, that was for sure. She wouldn't make the same mistake again. On the other hand, it had given her food for thought.

'I'm glad you and Simon have made up,' she said, a few moments later. 'I presume the divorce is off?'

'It is for now,' Angie said, delving into her handbag for her phone that had just bleeped. 'Oh good, Simon's got home safely.' She glanced up. 'He's going to move his stuff back in while we're away – and talk to his solicitor, of course.'

'The children will be happy.'

'Yes.' Angie was in the middle of tapping out a text message. 'Yes, they will be.'

'I don't think I can go home.' Gilly said it quietly as if testing the words, getting used to the idea before she spoke it out loud.

'Hang on a tick – there, done it.' Angie had sent her text. She glanced up. 'What was that, darling?'

'I said, I don't think I can go home. Not now.'

'What? Why? You haven't done anything wrong.'

'But I wanted to.' She sat on the stool in front of the dressing table, staring at her reflection as if she was looking at a total stranger. She glanced back over her shoulder at her sister. 'I wanted to, Angie – very much.'

'Well, we all have our little fantasies.'

'This was different. I've never felt like this before.' She sighed and dragged her fingers through the tousled mess of her hair. 'If Dave had felt the same, I wouldn't have hesitated – I know I wouldn't – and that's not like me.'

'True,' Angie conceded.

'So, it made me think.' She reached for some cleansing wipes to remove the remnants of the previous night's makeup as she spoke. 'I realised that I don't love Charles. I don't think I've loved him for years. We've just gone through the motions of being married and I don't think either of us are happy. He makes me anxious and miserable and I've got used to feeling that way. But this holiday has changed everything – the way I feel, the way I act.' She rubbed some moisturising cream into her cheeks. 'I think, no, I know, I'm going to leave him.'

Angie looked stunned. She sat down heavily on the end of the bed. 'Gilly, darling, this is all a bit sudden.'

'Is it?' She sighed. 'I don't think so. For me, it can't come soon enough. I don't want to waste any more time and energy trying to prop up a tired marriage that should have ended years ago. You said it yourself. Charles is an arrogant bully.'

'Well, yes.'

'And I've been happier this week than I've been in ages.'

'Yes, but you're on holiday. That's what holidays are all about, relaxing, and enjoying yourself and getting away from the daily grind.'

'This is different. I really fancied Dave. He made me see that I could have a different life, if I chose it. That's what he said, that I should choose one thing to change my life.'

'Yes, but I don't think he meant you should ditch your husband.'

'Probably not.' She frowned, remembering his last words to her. He'd pushed her away because she was married. But what if she wasn't married? She lingered over the thought for a moment. What if... So many what ifs?

Angie was watching her with a troubled look on her face. 'I don't want you doing something you'll regret later.'

'I won't.' Gilly turned back to the mirror and started to brush the tangles out of her hair. Her only regret was that she hadn't done something about it sooner. For years she had lived in limbo. She could see that now. Never being truly happy, nor desperately unhappy either, just living each day much like any other day. But now she wanted more than that. She wanted to be happy. She wanted to enjoy life and live every moment. Was that too much to ask? 'I'm not going back to Charles,' she said. 'In fact, I may not go home at all.' She would have her own 'Shirley Valentine' moment, she thought. She had savings and assets that would tide her over until she got a job - maybe in a little French bistro, or in one of the galleries or museums in Paris. She would learn the language and rent an apartment. It would be an adventure, an opportunity, a last chance to be who she wanted to be.

'You can't just run away,' Angie said.

'Why not?'

'Because – well, just because. It wouldn't be right and you always like to do the right thing. You know you do.'

'Maybe that's where I've been going wrong all these years.'

'You haven't been going wrong.' Angie managed a weak smile. 'You did what was right at the time – for your family and for you. But this holiday has given you a taste of freedom and you've decided you rather like it.'

'Exactly.'

'But it's hard being on your own.'

How hard, Gilly wondered?

'It's all my fault,' Angie sighed. 'I talked you into this holiday.'

'For which I will be forever grateful. You ought to be pleased. You never liked Charles.'

'Yes, but I never expected you to leave him.'

Gilly shrugged. 'Neither did I.' If someone had told her, even a week ago, that she would be planning to leave her husband, she would have thought they were mad. But now it seemed obvious. It was the change she was looking for.

'So,' Angie said, 'what are you going to do?'

'I don't know.' She hadn't thought that far ahead. One step at a time and all that. 'Maybe I'll stay here. I could get a live-in job – a chambermaid or something like that.'

'In France?' Her sister sounded appalled. 'You can't speak French and you're frightened of drinking the water and eating foreign food. And what about your job? You'd have to give them notice. No, no, you can't stay here. You'll have to come home with me. If you're going to do this, darling, you need to do it properly. You need to plan your future, not rush into things without any thought of the consequences.'

Gilly considered this for a moment. 'You're probably right,' she said. As usual, the practicalities outweighed her romantic idea of just running away and starting a new life for herself. She would need to break the news to Charles – she owed him that much, and the children, of course. She would go home and she would make plans and she would give herself a future to look forward to; the future she felt she deserved.

But she would save those thoughts for another day. For the moment, she had another pressing and rather more embarrassing problem to attend to. The awkward task of facing Dave again.

Chapter Thirty-one

'Carl, I can't get my suitcase to close,' Barbara complained. 'Have you been putting some of your stuff in it?'

'Just some baccy and booze,' he said, omitting to mention the tubs of talcum powder that he had wrapped in plastic carrier bags and hidden under her bag of dirty washing. 'Here, let me do it.'

They had to have the cases packed and by their room doors by six in the morning, so Dave could load the coach while they were having an early breakfast.

Barbara had decided that she would have hers sorted before they went down to dinner on their final evening in the hotel. A fact that didn't please Carl, since he was expecting to pack things in the morning – or, in his case, just shove everything into his holdall. He liked to travel light.

He wrestled with the zip, while his gran tried to lean her weight on the bulging lid.

'Are you sure you're allowed to bring all this home?'

'Yes, if it's for personal use.'

His grandmother looked at him suspiciously. 'It won't get me into bother at customs, will it?'

'No, Gran.'

'Only I've seen those documentary programmes where they search people's cases.'

'They won't search your case,' he muttered, gritting his teeth. The zip strained at the seams. 'It'll be on the coach.'

'Right.' She didn't sound convinced.

He gave one last tug and the zip closed. 'You're not going to want anything out of this in the morning, are you?' he said.

She shook her head. 'No, I'll put me nightie and stuff in my overnight bag.'

'Right. Well, I might as well take it back to my room. Then I can pop them both out at six and you can stay in bed a bit longer.'

'Oh, you're such a good boy.' Gran beamed. 'I'll just do my hair and then we'll go down for dinner, shall we?'

'Yeah – meet me in the lobby. I'm going for a fag first.'

The suitcase weighed a ton, even for someone like Carl who was used to lifting weights at the gym. Mind you, four bottles of spirits didn't weigh light, and he had another couple in his holdall. He'd managed to hide most of the talcum powder, apart from one tub, which he would take in his bag. The inner pocket of the suitcase held ten packs of tobacco and he'd get a couple of cartons of fags in his bag.

It was up to Jason how he got rid of the powder – he would just plead ignorance. Say it was bought in good faith and hidden in baby powder containers.

He dumped the case on the floor of his room. He might rearrange things later, when they'd had dinner, maybe try and hide another bottle of spirits in there. In the meantime, he was anxious to get downstairs to grab a beer and a fag. A morning spent trawling round some old manor house wasn't his cup of tea, though he'd been intrigued by some of the inventions in the gallery at the rear. The visit to the wine cellars had been much more to his liking. The tunnels had been hewn out of the limestone and went on for miles, all stacked floor to ceiling with thousands of bottles of wine. It had been quite a trek, but they got free wine at the end of it and a chance to buy a few bottles at discounted prices, which Dave had promised to load onto the coach for them. All in all, a good trip.

He'd been surprised to see Angie on her own though. What was it with those sisters? First, it had been Gilly on her own, and now it was Angie. Had they fallen out? More to the point, had Gilly fallen out with Dave? He'd been conspicuous by his absence at the entertainment the previous night and he'd been sure it was because he was with Gilly on the back seat of the coach. Now he wasn't so sure, since she'd been hanging out with that twit Geoffrey later on. Women! He'd never understand them.

He made his way downstairs and outside the hotel, deciding to sit on the bench overlooking the river, but Angie had beaten him to it. She was busy texting on her phone as he wandered up to her and sat down.

'I take it your husband isn't here,' he said,' only I don't want to run the risk of getting thumped again.'

'Yes, he's gone,' she said, smiling. She pocketed the phone. 'I suppose I owe you an apology.'

'Nah – doesn't matter.' Carl lit a cigarette and inhaled deeply. 'So,' he said, 'home tomorrow.'

'Yes.'

'Been a good week though,' he added. 'Eventful, if not different.'

Angie nodded. 'Your grans enjoyed it, hasn't she?'

'Yeah, she's had a ball. I suppose I have in a way.' He glanced sideways at her and grinned. 'It had its moments. Could have been better, but...'

'It wasn't to be. Anyway, I was far too old for you.'
Carl raised an eyebrow at her. 'I've always liked more mature women.'

'Oh, shut up.' Angie smiled. 'You'll have me blushing next.'

215

'Well, at least your sister made the most of her time away.'

Angie gave him a hard look. 'What do you mean?'

'Her and Dave. Oh, come on,' he added, 'you must have known.'

'No.' She was shaking her head vehemently at him. 'You've got that wrong.'

'I don't think so,' he said. 'I'm telling you, last night, when you'd gone off with your husband, they were on the coach together, with the curtains drawn.'

'No. They weren't.' Angie shook her head again. Her cheeks had gone pink. 'And I don't think you should say things like that. Gilly's married.'

'Yeah, well so are you, though it would have been nice if you'd told me that in the first place.' He laughed. 'Might have saved me getting a black eye and bruised ribs.'

'Don't exaggerate,' Angie said.

'Just saying it how it is.'

'Whatever.' She stood up and gave a small shudder. The breeze was freshening up after the warmth of the day and it was starting to get quite chilly. 'I'm going in for dinner.'

'With your sister?'

'Yes.' Her eyes narrowed slightly. 'Why?'

'Just wondered.' He gave a small shrug. 'I thought she was maybe sick or something. I missed her on the trip today.'

'I'll be sure to tell her that.' Angie smiled. It was obvious she wasn't going to say any more. 'See you later Carl.'

He took a last puff of his cigarette and tossed it into the river. So, Angie was denying it and Dave would no doubt keep quiet. It probably wasn't good for customer relations if the driver was found to be shagging one of the passengers on the back seat of his coach. But he knew what he had seen, and there had definitely been someone on the coach that night.

He watched with idle curiosity as Geoffrey came ambling along the towpath towards him, carrying his sketch pad and a backpack. Still wearing those silly sandals with socks halfway up his calves – some blokes had no idea. 'All right?' he said, giving him a nod.

'Yes, thank you. Oh, er, by the way,' Geoffrey hesitated for a moment. 'I, er, couldn't help noticing you'd thrown your cigarette end into the water. It's probably not a good idea to do that.'

'You what?' Carl said.

'It's not good for the environment: pollution, that sort of thing.'

Carl tried to suppress a laugh as he glanced at the fast-flowing river, and at the assortment of flotsam and jetsam bobbing about in the ripples: empty plastic bottles, bits of paper, a couple of cans.

'Right,' he said.

'And, of course, there's the problem with the wildlife – swans and ducks, and even the fish. This river, apparently, is one of the few....'

'Yes, okay, I get the message,' Carl said, standing up and brushing the remnants of ash from his dark jeans. He didn't want to have to listen to another of the man's local history lessons. He'd heard enough of them on the coach. Two hours of him prattling on about Leonardo Da Vinci's house, when most of the passengers were asleep, and those that weren't were pretending to be. 'I won't do it again,' he said, and since they were going home in the morning, and would have precious little time to admire the flowing waters of the River Cher, he was being sincere. 'Sorry.'

I hope you don't mind me mentioning it.'

'Not at all,' Carl lied.

'Only I don't like to cause offence.'

'None taken.'

Now go up to your room and leave me alone, you annoying little man, he thought. Aloud he said, 'Well, better catch up with my gran. She'll be waiting to go into dinner.'

'Ah yes – the last supper,' Geoffrey said, hoisting his backpack over one shoulder. 'Well, I won't keep you.'

Carl found his grandmother in the lobby, scribbling the last of her postcards.

'Just want to get these in the post,' she said, glancing up at him. 'There's a box in reception.'

'What's the bloody point?' Carl said. 'You'll be home tomorrow. You might as well hand them out and save the postage.'

Barbara scowled at him. 'People like getting postcards from foreign places.'

'I don't.'

'And I've done one for your Aunt Jenny. Do you want to hear what I've written?'

'No.'

Barbara continued to read it out regardless. 'Weather has been lovely and we have been to lots of castles and places of interest. The hotel is very nice and Carl has been spoiling me. There.' She moistened a stamp and pressed it firmly in place. 'Pop those in the box, will you, dear. Me knees are playing up a bit. Must have been all that walking. I'll just sit here till you're ready.'

'More like the dancing last night,' Carl said wryly

'Ooh yes, I'd forgotten about that.'

It wasn't something he would forget in a hurry – the sight of his gran and Geoffrey doing their own version of the twist. He strolled over to the reception desk and handed the girl the postcards.

'*Merci.*'

The newspaper was lying on the counter. The girl had obviously been reading it and left it to take the cards from him. Even upside down, he could make out the photograph of the Paris bistro. He coughed and cleared his throat.

'May I....er...borrow this – just for a moment.'

'But, of course.' The girl waved it away with a sweep of her hand.

'Thanks.'

He sat on a chair in the foyer, trying to make out the gist of the story, but he couldn't speak French, let alone read it. It was a national newspaper, so it had to be important.

'*Un homme a ete arrete hier a Paris, soupconne du meurtre de Yusef Roussillom dans une prise de medicaments.*'

What the hell did that mean?

He glanced back as the lift doors opened. It was Geoffrey and he was on his own. Carl was relieved to see he had ditched the sketchpad and rucksack; his only concession to getting ready for dinner, it seemed. In for a penny, in for a pound. 'Hey, Geoffrey,' he said, waving him over. 'Can you help me with something?' He pointed at the newspaper. 'I need to see what this says, and I don't understand French. Can you translate it for me?'

'I'm afraid I don't read French.'

This, from the man who professed to know everything. Carl frowned. He was so sure Geoffrey would be the man to ask.

'But you could always Google it,' he added.

'What?'

'On your phone. Google it – French to English, and it'll translate it for you.'

'It will?'

'Indeed it will. I use it all the time when I'm travelling.' He leaned forwards. 'What is it, anyway?'

'Nothing. Well, actually, it's racing.' Carl decided that it was probably best if Geoffrey didn't see what he was looking at. He might start asking awkward questions. 'I like a gamble.'

'I suspected you were a bit of a chancer,' he replied. There was something scathing in the tone of his voice.

'Yeah, well, sometimes it's worth it,' Carl said. 'Thanks, by the way. I'll give it a go.'

He waited until Geffrey had ambled into the dining room, before hastily tapping the unfamiliar text into his phone as instructed, and there it was, as if by magic.

'*A man was arrested in Paris yesterday on suspicion of murdering Yusef Roussillon in a drugs related shooting,*' he read. He exhaled deeply. Thank God for that.

He deleted the text, pocketed his phone, and folded up the newspaper. It meant the police wouldn't be looking for him now. He was in the clear. It was annoying that he'd had to ditch his leather jacket, but it had been the right thing to do at the time. He could relax now.

'Carl! Cooee! Shall we go in?' called his gran in her normal unassuming manner from halfway across the lobby. 'We want to get a good table.'

'Why not?' he said, strolling to join her. 'You go first. I'll follow.'

He didn't notice the police car that had pulled up outside the hotel, nor the officer who climbed out and strode into reception. As he sat down opposite his gran's two new friends, Shirley and Linda, who had saved them a place, he managed an amiable smile. He could keep up the pretence for one more night. In less than twenty-four hours they'd all be back home, returned to their boring suburban lives, as if nothing had happened.

Or at least, that was Carl's take on the matter. For others, it was slightly different.

Chapter Thirty-two

'I don't think I can face Dave,' Gilly said, peering mournfully at her pallid reflection in the mirror. 'I feel so embarrassed.'

'Oh, nonsense,' Angie said, picking up her handbag and giving it to her. 'Come on, we're off down to dinner and you're going to stop your worrying. He'll be fine about it. I promise you.'

'But what must he think of me?'

'Quite frankly, I don't think it matters. After tomorrow you're never going to see him again, so what's the problem?'

Blunt, but true. Gilly could always rely on her sister to state the facts, obvious though they were. But it didn't make things any easier. She felt mortified at the way she had behaved, the way she had misinterpreted Dave's genuine desire to be helpful to mean something more.

The only consolation was that at least it had given her the push she needed to make changes in her life; changes that were well overdue. She would move in with her sister on her return home. Angie had told her she could stay as long as she liked, but she suspected that she was just being polite, especially as Simon had only just moved back in. So, she would look for somewhere to rent, probably, and then she'd think about changing her job, either pushing for the promotion she thought she was owed or looking around for something that interested and excited her. The future was all about change. The present was something to be dealt with first.

Gilly hooked the bag over her shoulder and stood up.

'Ready?' Angie asked.

She nodded.

The wait for the lift was interminable. Gilly could feel her heart thudding heavily against her ribcage. She wasn't sure if the nausea she felt was due to her hangover, or to nerves. Either way, she wasn't sure if she could stomach dinner.

'It'll be fine,' Angie assured her. 'Just treat it as a joke. Have a laugh about it, and then forget it ever happened.'

They were joined in the lift by the Braithwaites, who were most anxious to know how Gilly was, seeing as how she had missed one of the most memorable outings of the whole holiday.

'You would have loved Amboise,' Roger told her. 'It was beautiful, wasn't it, dear?'

'Oh yes, beautiful, and you know, we nearly lost Cyril again, in the caves. He does have a habit of wandering off, doesn't he? But the guide was very good, found him behind some of the barrels, so we didn't waste too much time looking for him.'

'Gilly had a migraine,' Angie explained. 'We thought it best if she stayed in bed, but she's fine now. Aren't you?' she added, giving her a warning look.

Gilly nodded.

'Oh, but it leaves you so washed out,' Mrs Braithwaite sympathised. 'I used to get them a lot when I was younger. That explains why you look so pale, dear.'

Nothing to do with blind terror, then, Gilly thought.

She was terrified she was going to bump into Dave the moment they got out of the lift, but fortunately, the way was clear. As they took their seats in the dining room, she caught a glimpse of him in the foyer. He was flicking through the pages of a newspaper. He wasn't with anyone. Maybe she should just man up and talk to him now, while he was on his own. Yes, she would. She swallowed nervously. She could. She pushed her chair back and stood up.

'Gilly, where are you going?' Angie said.

'To put things right,' she replied, tilting her head to one side, 'before I lose my nerve.'

Angie followed the line of her gaze.   'Ah, I see.'

Gilly wasn't sure what she was going to say to him. 'Sorry' seemed the most appropriate word. She would apologise for her behaviour and do as Angie suggested and try to make light of it.

He looked up as she approached, and for a brief moment she was sure she detected a flicker of alarm on his face. He folded up the newspaper and laid it to one side. 'Gilly,' he said, standing up. 'How are you?'

She blushed. 'Mortified, embarrassed, ashamed – what more can I say?' She sucked in a deep breath as she stood in front of him.' Dave, I am so sorry about last night. Honestly, I don't know what I was thinking. Well, I wasn't thinking, was I? Oh God, I'm so sorry.'

'Hey, hey,' he said soothingly. 'It's okay.'

'It's not okay. I can't believe I behaved so badly. Me, of all people.'

'You had a lot on your mind.'

'I was drunk.'

'Just a bit,' he said, his eyes twinkling.

'I never drink – not when I'm at home, anyway.' She sighed. 'And now you're laughing at me.'

'Well, it was quite funny, when you think about it.'

'I'd rather not.' She stared glumly at her feet. 'I just wanted to apologise.' She glanced up, aware that he was still watching her. He had such a kind and caring expression on his face. She wished he wouldn't look at her like that. Her stomach was doing ridiculous somersaults. If only she didn't find him so attractive. 'I, um, I'm sorry you had to sleep on the coach last night. It can't have been very comfortable for you.'

'It wasn't. But don't say sorry again,' he added, holding his hand up. His eyes were still laughing at her. 'There's only so many apologies I can take.'

'Sorry,' she said, without thinking.

This time he laughed out loud and Gilly felt her cheeks burn. 'I meant to say thank you,' she said meekly. 'For looking after me. You are a gentleman and I appreciate that, very much.'

This time it was Dave's turn to look embarrassed. 'Yeah, well, sometimes I wish I wasn't. My loss, not yours.' He gave her a thoughtful smile. Gilly wondered if he was regretting his decision to turn her away as much as she was.

'Go and enjoy your dinner,' he said, tilting his head in the direction of the restaurant. 'Make the most of your last night in France. You'll be home this time tomorrow.'

'Yes, I suppose so.' It was what she was dreading the most. 'It's been a lovely week,' she said, 'for so many reasons. I'll never forget it.' Nor you, she thought, half turning to walk away. That was when she saw the police car. It was parked right outside the front entrance. A uniformed officer was mounting the steps to the foyer.

Gilly thought she was going to be sick. Her stomach muscles clenched like fists. Oh my God! They must have seen the footage from the pharmacy. They were looking for them. She jerked her head round, searching for Angie. Her sister was deep in conversation with the Braithwaites, over by the entrance to the dining room. She was oblivious to what was going on.

'Gilly?' Dave had got to his feet. 'Are you all right?'

'Huh? Oh. What?' She was panicking.

'You're shaking all over.'

'Too much wine last night.' She clamped a hand over her mouth. 'Sorry, Dave.' She managed to reach the ladies toilets on the ground floor, where she stood hunched over a basin, sucking in deep mouthfuls of air. She couldn't throw up. She wouldn't throw up. She'd be fine. She just had to calm down. Deep breaths. That was it – in for four, hold, and out for eight. In for four, hold, and out for eight. She'd read somewhere that it would calm her instantly. It didn't. Oh my God, what was she going to do?

She splashed some cold water on her face and patted it with a paper towel. Her frightened reflection stared back at her from the mirror. She looked like a rabbit caught in the headlights; all wide-eyed and frozen. She heard the door opening and darted into the nearest cubicle, locking it firmly behind her.

'Gilly? Are you in here?'

Angie – oh thank God! She slid the bolt open. 'The police are here.'

'Yes, I know. I've spoken to them.'

'You've what?'

Angie was leaning towards the mirror, applying a fresh coat of lipstick. 'I've spoken to them,' she repeated, pouting at her reflection, then glancing back at her with a resigned smile. 'Quite a nice young man, actually. Spoke perfect English. Honestly, I don't know what you're getting so worked up about.'

'But... but they must have seen the footage.'

'Yes, and they were asking Dave if they could check everyone's passports. That's when I went over and said, was it about the tablets we'd found in the street and put through the pharmacy letterbox?'

'You did what?'

'Well, honesty is the best policy, and I didn't want Carl knowing what we'd done, which he would do if they started asking everyone questions. Apparently,' she added, dabbing her cheeks with a bit of blusher. 'They were ecstasy tablets. Highly illegal, of course. No wonder they made me feel so euphoric.'

'Angie!'

'What? Look, it's all sorted, darling. There's nothing to worry about.'

Gilly wasn't so sure. 'Did he believe you?'

'Of course, he believed me. Why wouldn't he?' She grinned. 'I can be very convincing when I need to be. The officer said I'd done the right thing, and then he left. Now stop looking so paranoid. It's the last night and we're going to enjoy ourselves. Come on, let's go to dinner.'

They had a table by the window, overlooking the fast-flowing waters of the river.

Gilly was glad of the distraction; glad she could sit with her back to everyone and enjoy the tranquil view; the pretty pots of flowers, the stone bridge, the passing traffic trundling along the road. She had lots to think about; the rest of her life, for starters.

***

'Have a trial separation,' Angie suggested. 'Don't burn all your bridges in one go. You might change your mind.'

'I won't.' Gilly folded her tops and T-shirts and laid them in her suitcase, one on top of the other. 'It's taken me too long to get this far.'

Angie was tossing her clothes in any old way, and stuffing worn items inside her shoes to help them keep their shape. 'What time do we have to put these outside the door?'

'Six o' clock.'

'Blimey – that's early.'

'I know, but it's a long drive to Calais from here, and we're supposed to be getting the ferry late afternoon.'

'Don't remind me.' Angie pulled a face. 'You've still got some of those sea-sickness tablets left, haven't you? Only I don't want a repeat of last time.'

'Neither do I.' Gilly waved the packet of tablets under her sister's nose. 'I'll keep them in my handbag. We can both have one if the sea looks choppy.'

'I'm having one whatever. I don't want to feel nauseous when I see Simon. He says he'll pick us up from Dover, so we don't have to go all the way to the interchange.'

'Oh good.' Gilly folded her last remaining dress and patted it down on the top of her neatly packed clothes. 'That'll save us a bit of time.'

'I haven't said anything to him about... well, you know.'

'Good. I don't want him ringing Charles – not till I've had a chance to speak to him.'

'You're still not answering his calls, then?'

'No.' She shook her head. 'I don't want to talk to him.'

Angie stuffed her fold-up slippers and a slinky wrap down the side pocket of her suitcase. 'There,' she added. 'I'm done. Fancy a last drink at the bar?'

Gilly gave her a withering look. 'If I ever drink again, it will be too soon.' She closed her case and zipped it shut. 'No, I'm going to have an early night, if you don't mind. But you go. You can give that book back to Geoffrey at the same time.' The volume about Leonardo Da Vinci's life and times lay untouched on the dressing table. She hadn't had a chance to read it, and she didn't see the point in looking at it now.

'He'll be disappointed,' Angie said, picking up the book and leafing through the pages. 'You know how he likes talking to you.'

'Tough.'

'But it's the last night - the very last night of our holiday.' Her voice was wheedling and inevitably persuasive. 'We might never do this again.'

'Oh, all right,' she sighed. 'If you insist.'

Angie's phone rang as they were waiting for the lift. She answered it and raised her eyebrows at her sister as she did so.

'It's Charles,' she said, handing over her mobile. 'And he wants to speak to you.'

Gilly couldn't take the call in the corridor. She didn't know what she was going to say to him, but she didn't want anyone else overhearing, so she headed back to the bedroom.

As it transpired, she didn't have to say much at all. He was in an apopletic rage.

'Five times you've ignored me.'

'Charles, I didn't have any battery in my...'

'Five times. So, then I have to ring your bloody sister, and half the time that goes to voicemail. I've left you messages. I've sent you texts. What do I get? Nothing. Not one thing. What's wrong with you, woman?'

'Well, I've been...'

'And then you'll be expecting me to pick you up.'

'I'll get a taxi.'

'And I've no idea what time you're getting back. This isn't good enough, Gilly. I don't know how many times I have to tell you....'

She cut him off. She couldn't bear to hear him ranting and raving for one more second. Or ever again, come to that. She glanced up at Angie, who was waiting by the door, a sympathetic half-smile on her face.

'Let's go,' she said, handing her back her phone. 'Let's make the most of it.'

It seemed as if the majority of the coach passengers were in the hotel bar, enjoying their final evening together. Cyril was dozing in a seat in the corner, but Edith was looking flushed and animated as she conversed with Linda and had obviously had more than her standard small glass of white wine. Barbara was with Shirley and the Braithwaites, and Gloria was in conversation with Carl at the bar.

'He said he liked mature women,' Angie said, smirking. 'Do you think I should rescue him?'

'I'd rather you didn't,' Gilly said, sipping a glass of iced tonic water. Her head was thumping and she couldn't decide if it was the noise in the bar, the tail end of her hangover, or the million jumbled thoughts that were crowding her mind. She couldn't believe Charles had rung Angie's mobile. And the way he had shouted at her had been unbelievable. He certainly knew how to sour the mood. Well it only served to reinforce her decision to leave him. She didn't have to put up with that sort of treatment; not from him, not from anyone. She would be her own woman; strong, independent, scared initially, of course, but determined. Or at least, she hoped she'd be.

The tonic water hit the right spot. It was cold and refreshing and she was happy to have another. She didn't need the gin that Angie was enjoying. In fact, she might never touch alcohol again. She'd had enough killer hangovers to last a lifetime, and the shame and humiliation that had accompanied them. It was far better to keep a clear head. Particularly with the plans she had in mind.

She stayed in the bar for another hour or so, even managing to sing along when the accordian player encouraged everyone to join in. It was good therapy, but it didn't last. She was tired, and the constant chatter and noise was starting to get to her.

'I'm just going to finish this and then I'm going to bed,' she told Angie. 'Why don't you join the others and let me have an early night?'

'Oh.' Angie looked disappointed. 'Well, if you're sure?'

'I'm sure. Go on, have that last drink with Carl. You know you want to, and I think he's probably had enough of Gloria by now.'

'All right.' She smiled. 'I'll have one more g and t, and then I'll follow you up. I won't be long.'

Gilly made her way out of the bar and across the foyer to the lift. As she stood waiting, the doors opened with a ping and she came face to face with Dave.

'Oh.' She sidestepped just as he did the same. It was an awkward moment.

'Sorry.'

'No, go on.' He held the doors open for her with his foot.

'Aren't you getting out?'

He smiled. 'Changed my mind.'

Gilly felt her heart do a quick double thud against her chest. She stepped into the lift beside him and swallowed nervously as the doors closed, closeting them in together. She could almost feel the heat exuding from him. The hairs on the back of her neck were tingling at the sheer proximity of him and she wondered if he could feel it too.

'Packed your case?'

'Yes.' She nodded, staring dumbly at her feet. She felt tongue-tied and awkward.

'Gilly, I wanted to...'

'Dave...' They both spoke together, then stopped. She glanced up at him. He was watching her expectantly. 'You first,' she said.

His eyes narrowed slightly. Then he pulled her into his arms and kissed her, long and hard, before releasing her with a rueful frown. 'Sorry. I can't always be a gentleman and I've been wanting to do that all week.'

'Me too,' she said quietly.

The lift doors opened. They had reached her floor. She glanced at him shyly. 'I ought to go.'

'I know.' He sighed and shook his head. 'In a minute.' He pressed the button and the lift doors closed on them. Grinning, he drew her into his arms and kissed her again. This time there was no awkwardness and no surprise. It seemed like the most natural thing in the world to be doing.

Gilly felt weak with longing for this man – this gorgeous, lovely hunk of a man.

The lift doors pinged open. They were on the top floor.

Dave rested his arm round her waist as he pressed the down button.

'We could go to my room,' she said. Her cheeks were flushing but she didn't care. She was beyond caring. She didn't want this moment to end.

Nor, it seemed, did he.

'My room's closer,' he said, 'and we won't be disturbed.'

'Good point.'

His fingers clasped hers as they waited for the lift to descend. Gilly's heart was racing. She was going to do this. She really was, and to hell with the consequences. This was her moment, her time, and she wanted nothing more than to lie it his arms, to be held by him and loved by him. It might only be for one night, but it was a start. It wasn't over. Nothing was over and everything was changing. She could feel it in every inch of her being. This night was the beginning of the rest of her life.

Chapter Thirty-three

A hurried breakfast was followed by an early departure from the charming little town of Montrichard for the coach party's long haul to the port of Calais.

Gilly had been awake long before her alarm had gone off. All she could think about was those few short hours she had spent with Dave, the warmth in his eyes, the firm touch of his hands, the way he had held her and kissed her and more. Her cheeks burned. She'd never been with another man apart from Charles, but she couldn't remember ever feeling so loved and so special. Dave made her feel like that. Him; this man sitting on the coach in front of her that she barely knew yet felt like she'd known forever. It had been one momentous and unforgettable evening and one she would never forget. No matter what happened in the future, their time together had been precious. It had meant something to her. It had meant everything to her.

'God, I wish I hadn't stayed up so late,' Angie groaned. 'I'm exhausted. Must have been after three before I crawled into bed. You were out for the count.'

'Was I? Well, I was pretty tired.'

'I don't see why. You'd been in bed most of the day.'

Gilly smiled. And most of the evening too, though she wasn't going to tell her sister that. 'You can sleep on the coach,' she said. 'It's not as if there's anything else to do. The scenery is pretty boring from the motorway.'

They had a long day of travelling ahead of them. Five hundred kilometres across France, with a promised visit to a hypermarket before they boarded the ferry at Calais.

Angie, like most of the passengers, dozed on and off as the coach traversed France.

Gilly slept for a couple of hours and woke to find Dave watching her in his mirror. She smiled and he smiled back. She wondered what he was thinking. Wondered if he felt anything for her, or if it had just been about the sex? Maybe this was this what he did; seduce lonely women and make them feel important. Well, if he did, he was good at it, she thought. She felt radiant and glowing and positively vibrant.

When they stopped for a break she wanted to stay behind and talk to him, but he had been commandeered by some of the other passengers, so she had to make do with following Angie into the cafeteria instead.

'All I want,' her sister muttered, 'is a decent cup of tea. They don't boil the water properly here, and who has hot milk with tea?'

'The French, presumably,' Gilly said. 'Why don't you have a coffee? It might perk you up a bit.'

'Think I'll stick to water. I feel dehydrated.'

Gilly stirred a spoonful of sugar into her black coffee. She didn't normally sweeten it, but it was rather strong.

Dave was standing in the queue and she couldn't help but watch him; every movement; every smile and tilt of his head as he spoke to the girl behind the counter; his soft chuckle as he nodded and picked up his tray, and then he was turning and coming straight towards them.

Gilly gulped back a mouthful of hot coffee and spluttered into a serviette, her eyes watering. 'Sorry,' she choked, gasping, as Angie watched her with a look of alarm on her face. 'That went down the wrong way.'

'Ladies.' Dave set his tray down on their table. 'May I?'

Gilly nodded, feeling her cheeks redden. It was so hard to act normally, when all she wanted to do was hug him. He had changed her life. Things would never be the same again. Her whole perspective had changed, and even if nothing else happened between them, she had that to thank him for.

'You must get fed up with all the driving,' Angie said, and took a swig from her bottle of water. 'I know I would.'

He shrugged. 'You get used to it.'

'Well, rather you than me. I'm just going to pop to the loo,' she added, picking up her bag. 'Won't be a tick.'

'Convenient,' Dave said quietly, lowering his head towards Gilly. 'I've been wanting to get you on your own.'

'Me too,' she said. 'About last night....'

He grinned, and she felt his hand reaching for hers, under the table. He squeezed it gently, firmly, his fingers stroking hers. 'No regrets?'

'God, no.'

'Me neither.'

'I haven't told Angie.'

'Then don't. Well, not yet, anyway.' He gave her a wink. 'All in good time.'

She nodded. 'I can't believe this is the last day.'

'Or the first. Depends how you want to look at it.' He released her hand and leaned back in his chair as Angie came hurrying back to the table, her designer bag slung over one shoulder.

The first day – yes, it could be, Gilly thought, it really could be – and that's exactly how she would think of it.

By the time they reached Calais, the blue skies had been replaced by a dull, leaden grey, and a misty drizzle had started to fall. The visit to the hypermarket took less than half an hour, but it gave Angie a chance to stock up on gin, and Gilly to buy an expensive bottle of champagne.

'Oh yes, and what are you celebrating?' Angie asked her. 'Me and Simon getting back together, or you and Charles splitting up?'

'Both, probably,' she said. 'I don't know. Maybe the future and all it holds?'

'I'll drink to that.'

'Right, folks,' Dave said, switching on the microphone. 'We'll be going through Border control shortly, so if you can all have your passports ready. Shouldn't take too long. They normally send a couple of officers on board to check them.'

He had pulled the coach into a holding area, joining the queue of other coaches waiting to be cleared and waved through to the ferry. As he sat at the wheel, the engine idling, Gilly caught him watching her in the mirror again. She smiled. He really was a gorgeous man; her new man.

'Passport,' Angie said, jolting Gilly from her thoughts, and pointing at the uniformed officers assembling on the forecourt. 'You need to get it out to show them.'

Gilly peered out of the window, her heart sinking.' They're sending dogs on board,' she said, 'Sniffer dogs.'

'So?' Angie didn't seem in the least bit perturbed. 'They won't find anything.'

'I know, but...' She couldn't help remembering the incident with Carl and the ecstasy tablets. What if he had managed to get hold of something else while they had been in France? What if he really was a drug dealer?

'Passport,' Angie repeated, poking Gilly's bag. 'Come on, hurry up.'

Gilly's heart had sunk further. One of the officers was talking to Dave as he opened up the coach luggage locker. Several of the passengers were craning their necks to see what was going on, including Carl, who had risen from his seat and was peering down at the open hatch.

Dave climbed back on the coach. 'Just a spot check, folks, nothing to worry about. Shouldn't take long.'

Another of the officers – a woman this time, had boarded the coach and was making her way down the aisle, glancing right and left

230

at the offered passports. She wasn't really looking at them, Gilly decided. It was just an automatic gesture on her part. It was the dogs that were causing the problem. One of them, a pretty-looking black field spaniel, was barking excessively. It had run up and down the aisle, and was now lying halfway under Edith's seat. Cyril was patting it on the top of it's head.

The officer was talking into her radio – rather furtively, by the look of things.

Two more Border Agency officers were approaching the coach.

'What's going on?' Gilly whispered.

'I think the dog's found something.'

'Like what?'

Angie leaned down on the pretext of adjusting the strap on her sandal, and that's when she saw it – a miniscule amount of white powder on the floor by Cyril's feet – the sort of powder that could quite easily have originated from a crushed tablet. Oh shit! She straightened up. She hadn't managed to pick them all up when Gilly had dropped the bottle of pills. Oh double shit!

Her horrified expression told Gilly all she needed to know.

'Such a nice doggy,' Cyril was saying. 'Nice doggy.'

Everyone on the coach was talking at once. The spaniel was led away, much to Cyril's dismay, and was now running around happily on the tarmac with a yellow tennis ball in it's mouth.

Dave climbed back on board and switched on the microphone. He looked genuinely concerned.

'Right, folks. We've been asked to go to the shed on your right whilst they search the coach. If you'd like to make your way there, hand luggage only, please.'

'Will we be late getting home then,' someone called from the back – Linda, Gilly thought. 'Only my son was going to meet me in Thurrock.'

'Can't say for sure,' Dave said. 'They'll be as quick as they can.'

The passengers filed dutifully off the coach. It was a short walk across the tarmac to the grey Portakabin that was their destination.

As they lined up outside, Gilly was surprised to see the dogs working themselves up into a bit of a frenzy as they sniffed the passengers at the front of the queue.

'That's Cyril,' Angie said.' He can't be carrying anything illegal.'

'He's on medication,' Edith was saying, as the pair of them were escorted towards a separate waiting area by a uniformed officer. 'Do you want to see his tablets?'

'And Geoffrey – oh my God!' Gilly choked. 'They're frisking him.'

231

'He doesn't look bothered.' Angie said, reaching for her glasses. 'In fact, if you ask me, I think he's enjoying the extra attention.'

Gilly had to concede that Geoffrey was indeed smiling, as the officer gave him the quick once-over, running his hands up and down his chest, down the sleeves of his rain jacket, and finally down his pleated beige walking shorts.

'They must have trodden that tablet all down the aisle,' Angie said. 'It'll be on everyone's shoes.'

'So why isn't it on ours?' Gilly whispered. The dogs had ignored the pair of them and were now barking at Shirley.

' Maybe because it was behind us?' Angie suggested. 'It was by Cyril's foot.'

'Oh God, what have we done?'

'Nothing. Now just remember that.' Angie gripped her arm so tightly she could feel her nails digging into her skin. 'We have done nothing wrong. This is all down to Carl and his dodgy dealing. But he'll get his come-uppance. Don't you worry.'

'What do you mean?'

Angie smiled. 'Wait and see.'

The passengers whom the dogs had ignored were shown into a small office with a handful of plastic chairs and a coffee machine.

Carl, who had been chain smoking like a trooper, was the first to take advantage of the facilities, making himself a cup of strong black coffee. Angie preferred to take a swig of gin from the litre bottle in her bag.

Gilly was watching the proceedings through the grimy window. The others in the small and rather select little group had chosen to wait on the tarmac, to escape the stuffy claustrophobia of the waiting room. 'Oh blimey, I think they're arresting Linda. She's gesticulating a lot and shaking her fist at them.'

'She probably can't hear what they're saying,' Angie said.

'Oh, it's all right. Dave's gone to intervene. I think he's explaining things to her. She looks like she's calmed down a bit.'

'Yes, and maybe you could explain something to me,' Angie said, turning to give Carl one of her sternest school teacher gazes.

'Like what?'

'Well, call it coincidence, but it strikes me as distinctly odd that over half the coach party, including dear, demented Cyril and his wife, have been stopped by the Border Agency on suspicion of carrying illegal substances. Now, as far as I'm aware, you were the only one who actually had anything to hide.'

'Yeah, but that was an innocent mistake.'

'Oh, do me a favour, she said, her voice lowering, ' I think you still have something to hide.'

He glanced sideways at her.

'Or at least,' she added, 'your grandmother has.'

The silence was all the more audible after Carl's sudden intake of breath. Gilly looked from her sister, to Carl and back to her sister again. 'What's going on?' she said. 'What do you know that I don't?'

Angie smiled. 'Are you going to tell her, or am I?'

'What?' Carl looked suddenly alarmed. 'I don't know what you're talking about. Tell her what?'

'Oh, just the small matter of those tablets you hid in your grandmother's case in the hope that she'd get them through customs for you.'

Gilly gave him a scornful look. 'You gave your grandmother the tablets. Oh Carl, how could you?' She was trying hard not to smile.

'Look, it's not what you think. I'm not a drug dealer,' Carl protested. The muscles in his left cheek were starting to twitch. 'Honest to God, Angie.'

'Oh, shut up, Carl. I knew you were up to something when you took your gran's case last night. I had a feeling you were hiding something in it. And if you've any sense, you'll be grateful that I managed to swap it back before Customs went through her luggage.'

'You did what?' His voice had risen dramatically.

Gilly shushed him with a panicked wave of her hand. The others were still gathered outside and she didn't think this conversation should be overheard.

'I swapped it,' she repeated. 'I put the tablets back in your bag, Carl. I took the opportunity when Dave was loading the luggage locker. It's all right, he didn't see me do it.'

'Yes, but – but that means....'

'That they're in your bag. Yes, it does.' Angie smirked.' And I think that's what those officers are checking right now. Can you see, Gilly? They have got the bags out, haven't they?'

'Yes, I think so.' Gilly had her nose pressed almost to the glass. 'They've emptied out everything. The dogs are having a good sniff round.'

Carl looked as if he was going to have some sort of seizure.

'Of course, it's a good job we left the ecstasy tablets – you know, the ones you bought in Paris – at the pharmacy in Montrichard, otherwise you'd be in real trouble now,' Angie said.

'What?' Carl spun back from the window.

Angie gave him a condescending smile. 'Let's face it, you're really not cut out for this smuggling lark, are you, Carl? Mind you, I think they've found something else in your bag and it seems to be causing them a great deal of hilarity. Oh dear. What have you been buying?'

There, on the ground, lay several containers of talcum powder. One of the officers was smirking as he unravelled the shiny black PVC body suit, and then held it up for all to see. He was modelling it, turning this way and that, and grinning broadly.

'Interesting choice of attire,' Angie observed.

'Isn't that for, um, some sort of fetish?' Gilly said. She turned to stare at Carl. He didn't look the sort. Was he gay, she wondered? Or did he just have masochistic tendencies?

'For fuck's sake! Carl slumped down onto the plastic seat.

'Of course, it might take some explaining – talcum powder in your holdall – if it is talcum powder,' she added. 'But then again, with all that shiny tight black PVC...'

'Of course it's bloody talcum powder.' He hung his head in his hands and groaned, 'I'm never going to live this down, am I?'

'Probably not.' Angie smiled. 'By the way, was that tobacco for your own personal use? You really need to think about cutting down, Carl.'

Carl groaned again as he saw them sorting out the packs of tobacco, piling them up, one on top of the other. 'Do you know how much I'm out of pocket? Christ! I'm up to my neck in debt and this was the way I was going to get it sorted. How am I going to do that if they confiscate everything I've bought.'

Try working hard like the rest of us,' she replied. 'Now then, what's happening with the others?'

The pensioners had been shepherded back towards the coach. Dave was looking exasperated. A couple of women, including Linda, looked tearful. Cyril was wandering towards another coach parked at the rear of theirs, and his wife was hurrying after him, calling, 'This way, darling – no, it's this coach – Cyril, this coach!' The dogs were still milling round, wagging their tails and looking very excited. The Border Agency officers just looked perplexed.

'They're letting us through,' Dave said, coming to the door and poking his head around. 'They haven't found anything else, and they've done a thorough search. I'm not sure what to make of it all.' He gave Carl a hard and suspicious look as he spoke.

'So can we go to the ferry now?' Angie said.

'Yes, we can.'

'What about my tobacco?' muttered Carl.

'It's back in your holdall with the…er…fetish gear,' Dave said, smirking. 'I think they thought you might need a cigarette or two, considering your lifestyle choice.'

'That bloody outfit isn't for me.'

'Course it isn't.'

Carl was still scowling as they all piled back onto the coach. The amused glances from the officers on the tarmac was obviously getting to him. He looked as if he was tempted to give them a two-finger salute, but Dave's warning glare stopped him.

'I didn't know you liked fancy dress,' Barbara was saying.

'I do not like fancy dress. Just sit down, Gran, and stop fussing.'

Gilly sat by the window, staring out through the misty drizzle as the coach lumbered slowly through the bulkhead doors of the ferry and down into the bowels of the ship. She was feeling happy – inexplicably and gloriously happy. In the short space of a few days her life had changed forever. She wasn't going back. She knew that now. She was heading towards a new and exciting future and yes, there'd be problems and difficult decisions to make, but nothing worth having ever came easy.

'Hand me the new brochure,' she said, pointing a finger at the travel guide Dave had left in the magazine rack on the back of every seat.

Why?' Angie said. 'What are you planning?'

'Nothing yet,' she replied, flicking through the colourful pages, 'but there's no harm in looking, is there?'

Chapter Thirty four

One year later

The coach interchange was heaving with crowds of passengers, some sitting patiently flicking through the pages of a newspaper, others drinking coffee and tea from paper cups, some standing on the foyer, watching the coaches sweeping into the parking bays to be unloaded.

'I thought you said this was going to be a romantic weekend in Paris,' Simon grumbled. 'It's like being in a cattle market.'

'Means to an end,' Angie said, peering into her compact mirror and dabbing her face with powder. 'They'll be calling us to our coach soon, so if you need the loo you'd better go now.' She flipped her compact shut and glanced around. 'I can't see Gilly anywhere, can you?'

'No, but if she's in the gents, I'll let you know.'

Angie pulled a face at him. The coach trip had been her idea. Well, her sister's really. Gilly had said the reunion weekends were a way of meeting up with fellow passengers from previous trips, and that it might be nice if they could all get away together. Angie wasn't so sure, but she was anxious to see her sister again. It had been months since they had last met up.

'Cooee! Yoohoo! Angie!' Barbara's unmistakeable shriek carried halfway across the crowded waiting room. The older woman was bustling toweards her carrying a large plastic shopping bag. She was wearing a crimson raincoat, with matching red headscarf and red shoes.

She looked like the pensioner's version of Dorothy in *The of Wizard of Oz*, Angie thought, trying to suppress a smile.

'I thought that was you. I told Carl, "That's Angie over there". He's with Debbie,' she added, plonking herself down in the seat that Simon had newly vacated. 'They got married, you know.'

'Good. I'm glad.' Angie followed the line of her gaze and saw Carl standing by the revolving doors, attempting to roll a cigarette. A woman with blonde hair, drawn up in a tight pony tail was standing beside him. He glanced up and gave Angie a brief nod. She smiled. He looked exactly the same – close shaven, rugged, attractive.

'Course, I'm paying for this weekend,' Barbara said. 'It's my treat. Ever since me numbers came up. I've been using the same ones for years – every week.'

Angie looked back at her. 'You won the lottery?'

'Yes, I did. Not a fortune, mind,' she added. 'Not like those multi-millionaire winners, but enough to keep us comfortable and splash out on a few things. So when I saw this weekend advertised, I thought we should go for it. Be nice to see Shirley and Linda again, and you and your sister of course.' She stared round the crowded waiting area. 'Where is she, anyway?'

'I haven't seen her yet.'

'Oh.'

'But she'll be here.'

'That'll be nice for you. Oh look, there's Geoffrey. You'll excuse me, dear, I must have a word with him. I've packed me dancing shoes.'

'Who the hell was that?' Simon said, resuming his place on the hard plastic chair beside her.

'Carl's grandmother,' Angie said. 'And before you ask, yes, he is here. He's over there.' She pointed.

'Well that's one more person to avoid.'

'Oh I don't know.' Angie patted his hand fondly. 'I'm sure he's forgiven you for thumping him. He's married now.'

'Good.'

The tannoy crackled and emitted a loud, high-pitched squeal. 'Will all passengers for…Sorry.' The squeal continued as the operator adjusted the sound levels.

'That might be for us,' Angie whispered. 'Oh dear, and I still haven't seen Gilly. Maybe I should text her?'

'Will all passengers for the Paris weekend please make their way to Bay Seven. That's Bay Seven for the Paris weekend reunion tour.'

'Are you sure she said she was coming?'

'Yes. This was her idea.' Angie hitched her leather bag over one shoulder and stood up. 'She might be in the ladies. You know what she's like.'

'She's not,' Simon said, nudging her arm. 'She's over there. Good grief. What on earth is she wearing? That's not normal holiday attire.'

Angie turned and stared, her eyes widening in disbelief. Gilly was striding purposefully towards them, a beaming smile on her face and she was wearing – a uniform? Angie's mouth opened into a silent oh. Blue navy skirt and smart white blouse with a gold badge, tailored jacket, smart court shoes – she looked like an air hostess.

'Travel courier, actually,' she said, laughing delightedly as she hugged her sister and brother-in-law in turns. 'It's my job.'

'Your what?' Angie choked.

'I didn't tell you before. I wanted it to be a surprise.'

237

'I don't believe it,' Simon spluttered.

Gilly did a little twirl in front of them. 'And I shall be accompanying you on your trip this weekend and giving you a guided tour of the highlights of Paris.'

Angie was speechless – delighted, but speechless. Her sister looked so different – so self-assured and happy.

'Along with Dave, of course – our driver.'

'What? What? You mean, you and him…all this time…Why didn't you tell me?' Angie groaned. 'When you said you were moving away for a new job, I thought it was with the library. You said it was a transfer and that you needed to get away.'

'Which I did.'

'Yes, but you never said…'

Gilly was smiling at her. 'I needed to find my own way,' she said. 'You had your own problems to resolve as a couple. You didn't need mine as well. Besides, it was easier to do it this way – my decisions and my mistakes.'

'Yes, but you and Dave. I mean, you could have told me that much at least.'

'I needed to know if it was right, first.'

'And was it?'

'What do you think?' She gave her a shy smile.

'Darling, I think you look blooming marvellous,' Angie said, giving her a big hug. 'I'm just in shock, that's all.'

The tannoy crackled once more. 'This is the last call for passengers going to Paris. Bay Seven for the reunion trip to Paris, please.'

Gilly stepped to one side and adopted a more formal pose. 'Now then, if you'd like to follow me, please.' She gave Angie a warm and knowing smile as the passengers began to head for the parking bay. 'Your coach and your driver are waiting.'

Other novels by the same author include

Green Wellies and Wax Jackets ISBN 1898030995 (Braiswick)

Muddy Boots ISBN 9780955700835 (Braiswick)

A Love Betrayed (pen name Morag Lewis) ISBN 0709038860 (Robert Hale Ltd)

Printed in Great Britain
by Amazon